The Civil War Novels: 4

The Civil War Novels: 4

The Shades of the Wilderness
A Story of
Lee's Great Stand

•

The Tree of Appomattox
A Story of the
Civil War's Close

Joseph A. Altsheler

LEONAUR

The Civil War Novels: 4
The Shades of the Wilderness & The Tree of Appomattox
by Joseph A. Altsheler

FIRST EDITION

Leonaur is an imprint of Oakpast Ltd

Material original to this edition and this editorial selection
copyright © 2009 Oakpast Ltd

ISBN: 978-1-84677-614-4 (hardcover)
ISBN: 978-1-84677-613-7 (softcover)

http://www.leonaur.com

Publisher's Note

The views expressed in this book are not necessarily
those of the publisher.

Contents

THE CIVIL WAR NOVELS

She Shades of
the Wilderness

A Story of
Lee's Great Stand

Characters in the Civil War Novels

PRINCIPAL CHARACTERS

Harry Kenton	a lad who fights on the Southern side
Dick Mason	cousin of Harry Kenton, who fights on the Northern side
Colonel George Kenton	father of Harry Kenton
Mrs Mason	mother of Dick Mason
Juliana	Mrs Mason's devoted coloured servant
Colonel Arthur Winchester	Dick Mason's regimental commander
Colonel Leonidas Talbot	commander of the Invincibles, a Southern regiment
Lieutenant Colonel Hector St Hilaire	second in command of the Invincibles
Alan Hertford	a Northern cavalry leader
Philip Sherburne	a Southern cavalry leader
William J Shepard	a Northern spy
Daniel Whitley	a Northern sergeant and veteran of the plains
George Warner	a Vermont youth who loves mathematics
Frank Pennington	a Nebraska youth, friend of dick mason
Arthur St Clair	a native of Charleston, friend of Harry Kenton
Tom Langdon	friend of Harry Kenton
George Dalton	friend of Harry Kenton
Bill Skelly	mountaineer and guerrilla
Tom Slade	a guerrilla chief
Sam Jarvis	the singing mountaineer

Ike Simmons	Jarvis' nephew
Aunt "Suse"	a centenarian and prophetess
Bill Petty	a mountaineer and guide
Julien de Langeais	a musician and soldier from Louisiana
John Carrington	famous Northern artillery officer
Dr Russell	principal of the Pendleton School
Arthur Travers	a lawyer
James Bertrand	a messenger from the South
John Newcomb	a Pennsylvania colonel
John Markham	a Northern officer
John Watson	a Northern contractor
William Curtis	a Southern merchant and blockade runner
Mrs Curtis	wife of William Curtis
Henrietta Garden	a seamstress in Richmond
Dick Jones	a North Carolina mountaineer
Victor Woodville	a young Mississippi officer
John Woodville	father of Victor Woodville
Charles Woodville	uncle of Victor Woodville
Colonel Bedford	a Northern officer
Charles Gordon	a Southern staff officer
John Lanham	an editor
Judge Kendrick	a lawyer
Mr Culver	a state senator
Mr Bracken	a tobacco grower
Arthur Whitridge	a state senator

HISTORICAL CHARACTERS

Abraham Lincoln	President of the United States
Jefferson Davis	President of the Southern Confederacy
Judah P Benjamin	member of the Confederate cabinet
U S Grant	Northern commander
Robert B Lee	Southern commander
Stonewall Jackson	Southern general
Philip H Sheridan	Northern general
George H Thomas	"the Rock of Chickamauga"

Albert Sidney Johnston	Southern general
A P Hill	Southern general
W S Hancock	Northern general
George B Mc Clellan	Northern general
Ambrose B Burnside	Northern general
Turner Ashby	Southern cavalry leader
J E B Stuart	Southern cavalry leader
Joseph Hooker	Northern general
Richard S Ewell	Southern general
Jubal Early	Southern general
William S Rosecrans	Northern general
Simon Bolivar Buckner	Southern general
Leonidas Polk	Southern general and bishop
Braxton Bragg	Southern general
Nathan Bedford Forrest	Southern cavalry leader
John Morgan	Southern cavalry leader
George J Meade	Northern general
Don Carlos Buell	Northern general
W T Sherman	Northern general
James Longstreet	Southern general
P G T Beauregard	Southern general
William L Yancey	Alabama orator
James A Garfield	Northern general, afterwards President of the United States

. . . . and many others

IMPORTANT BATTLES DESCRIBED IN THE CIVIL WAR SERIES

Bull Run	Kernstown	Cross Keys
Winchester	Port Republic	The Seven Days
Mill Spring	Fort Donelson	Shiloh
Perryville	Stone River	The Second Manassas
Antietam	Fredericksburg	Chancellorsville
Gettysburg	Champion Hill	Vicksburg
Chickamauga	Missionary Ridge	The Wilderness
Spottsylvania	Cold Harbor	Fisher's Hill
Cedar Creek	Appomattox	

Foreword

The Shades of the Wilderness is the seventh volume of the Civil War Series, of which the predecessors have been *The Guns of Bull Run, The Guns of Shiloh, The Scouts of Stonewall, The Sword of Antietam, The Star of Gettysburg* and *The Rock of Chickamauga.* The romance in this story reverts to the Southern side and deals with the fortunes of Harry Kenton and his friends. It takes them on the retreat from Gettysburg, gives the hero a short period of social life in Richmond, describes the great battles of the Wilderness and Spottsylvania, and ends with the deadlock in the trenches before Petersburg.

CHAPTER 1

The Southern Retreat

A train of wagons and men wound slowly over the hills in the darkness and rain toward the South. In the wagons lay fourteen or fifteen thousand wounded soldiers, but they made little noise, as the wheels sank suddenly in the mud or bumped over stones. Although the vast majority of them were young, boys or not much more, they had learned to be masters of themselves, and they suffered in silence, save when some one, lost in fever, uttered a groan.

But the chief sound was a blended note made by the turning of wheels, and the hoofs of horses sinking in the soft earth. The officers gave but few orders, and the cavalrymen who rode on either flank looked solicitously into the wagons now and then to see how their wounded friends fared, though they seldom spoke. The darkness they did not mind, because they were used to it, and the rain and the coolness were a relief, after three days of the fiercest battle the American continent had ever known, fought in the hottest days that the troops could recall.

Thus Lee's army drew its long length from the fatal field of Gettysburg, although his valiant brigades did not know that the clump of trees upon Cemetery Hill had marked the high tide of the Confederacy. All that memorable 4th of July, following the close of the battle they had lain, facing Meade and challenging him to come on, confident that while the invasion of the North was over they could beat back once more the invasion of the South.

They had no word of complaint against their great commander, Lee. The faith in him, which was so high, remained unbroken, as it was destined to remain so to the last. But men began to whisper to one another, and say if only Jackson had been there. They mourned anew that terrible evening in the Wilderness when Lee had lost his mighty lieutenant, his striking arm, the invincible Stonewall. If the man in the old slouch hat had only been with Lee on Seminary Ridge it would now be the army of Meade retreating farther into the North, and they would be pursuing. That belief was destined to sink deep in the soul of the South, and remain there long after the Confederacy was but a name.

The same thought was often in the mind of Harry Kenton, as he rode near the rear of the column, whence he had been sent by Lee to observe and then to report. It was far after midnight now, and the last of the Southern army could not leave Seminary Ridge before morning. But Harry could detect no sign of pursuit. Now and then, a distant gun boomed, and the thunder muttered on the horizon, as if in answer. But there was nothing to indicate that the Army of the Potomac was moving from Gettysburg in pursuit, although the President in Washington, his heart filled with bitterness, was vainly asking why his army would not reap the fruits of a victory won so hardly. Fifty thousand men had fallen on the hills and in the valleys about Gettysburg, and it seemed, for the time, that nothing would come of such a slaughter. But the Northern army had suffered immense losses, and Lee and his men were ready to fight again if attacked. Perhaps it was wiser to remain content upon the field with their sanguinary success. At least, Meade and his generals thought so.

Harry, toward morning came upon St. Clair and Langdon riding together. Both had been wounded slightly, but their hurts had not kept them from the saddle, and they were in cheerful mood.

"You've been further back than we, Harry," said St. Clair. "Is Meade hot upon our track? We hear the throb of a cannon now and then."

"It doesn't mean anything. Meade hasn't moved. While we didn't win we struck the Yankees such a mighty blow that they'll have to rest, and breathe a while before they follow."

"And I guess we need a little resting and breathing ourselves," said Langdon frankly. "There were times when I thought the whole world had just turned itself into a volcano of fire."

"But we'll come back again," said St. Clair. "We'll make these Pennsylvania Dutchmen take notice of us a second time."

"That's the right spirit," said Langdon. "Arthur had nearly all of his fine uniform shot off him, but he's managed to fasten the pieces together, and ride on, just as if it were brand new."

But Harry was silent. The prescient spirit of his famous great grandfather, Henry Ware, had descended upon his valiant great grandson. Hope had not gone from him, but it did not enter his mind that they should invade Pennsylvania again.

"I'm glad to leave Gettysburg," he said. "More good men of ours have fallen there than anywhere else."

"That's true," said St. Clair, "but Marse Bob will win for us, anyhow. You don't think any of these Union generals here in the East can whip our Lee, do you?"

"Of course not!" said Happy Tom. "Besides, Lee has me to help him."

"How are Colonel Talbot and Lieutenant-Colonel St. Hilaire?" asked Harry.

"Sound asleep, both of 'em," replied St. Clair. "And it's a strange thing, too. They were sitting in a wagon, having resumed that game of chess which they began in the Valley of Virginia, but they were so exhausted that both fell sound asleep while playing. They are sitting upright, as they sleep, and Lieutenant-Colonel St. Hilaire's thumb and forefinger rest upon a white pawn that he intended to move."

"I hope they won't be jarred out of their rest and that they'll sleep on," said Harry. "Nobody deserves it more."

He waved a hand to his friends and continued his ride toward the rear. The column passed slowly on in silence. Now and then gusts of rain lashed across his face, but he liked the feeling. It was a fillip to his blood, and his nerves began to recover from the tremendous strain and excitement of the last four days.

Obeying his orders he rode almost directly back toward the field of Gettysburg from which the Southern forces were still marching. A friendly voice from a little wood hailed him, and he recognized it at once as that of Sherburne, who sat his horse alone among the trees.

"Come here, Harry," he said.

"Glad to find you alive, Sherburne. Where's your troop?"

"What's left of it is on ahead. I'll join the men in a few minutes. But look back there!"

Harry from the knoll, which was higher than he had thought, gazed upon a vast and dusky panorama. Once more the field of Gettysburg swam before him, not now in fire and smoke, but in vapours and misty rain. When he shut his eyes he saw again the great armies charging on the slopes, the blazing fire from hundreds of cannon and a hundred thousand rifles. There, too, went Pickett's brigades, devoted to death but never flinching. A sob burst from his throat, and he opened his eyes again.

"You feel about it as I do," said Sherburne. "We'll never come back into the North."

"It isn't merely a feeling within me, I know it."

"So do I, but we can still hold Virginia."

"I think so, too. Come, we'd better turn. There goes the field of Gettysburg. The rain and mist have blotted it out."

The panorama, the most terrible upon which Harry had ever looked, vanished in the darkness. The two rode slowly from the knoll and into the road.

"It will be daylight in an hour," said Sherburne, "and by that time the last of our men will be gone."

"And I must hasten to our commander-in-chief," said Harry.

"How is he?" asked Sherburne. "Does he seem downcast?"

"No, he holds his head as high as ever, and cheers the men. They say that Pickett's charge was a glorious mistake, but he takes all the blame for it, if there is any. He doesn't criticize any of his generals."

"Only a man of the greatest moral grandeur could act like that. It's because of such things that our people, boys, officers and all, will follow him to the death."

"Good-by, Sherburne," said Harry. "Hope I'll see you again soon."

He urged his horse into a faster gait, anxious to overtake Lee and report that all was well with the rear guard. He noticed once more, and with the greatest care that long line of the wounded and the un-wounded, winding sixteen miles across the hills from Gettysburg to Chambersburg, and his mind was full of grave thoughts. More than two years in the very thick of the greatest war, then known, were sufficient to make a boy a man, at least in intellect and responsibility.

Harry saw very clearly, as he rode beside the retreating but valiant army that had failed in its great attempt, that their role would be the defensive. For a little while he was sunk in deep depression. Then invincible youth conquered anew, and hope sprang up again. The night was at the darkest, but dawn was not far away. Fugitive gusts of wind drenched him once more, but he did not mind it, nor did he pay any attention to the occasional growl of a distant gun. He was strong in the belief that Meade would not pursue—at least not yet. A general who had just lost nearly one-third of his own army was not in much condition to follow his enemy.

He urged his horse to increased speed, and pressed on toward the head of the column. The rain ceased and cool puffs of wind came out of the east. Then the blackness there turned to grey, which soon deepened into silver. Through the silver veil shot a bolt of red fire, and the sun came over the hills.

Although the green world had been touched with brown by the hot sun of July it looked fresh and beautiful to Harry. The brown in the morning sunlight was a rosy red, and the winds of dawn were charged with life. His horse, too, felt the change and it was easy now to force him into a gallop toward a fire on a low hill, which Harry felt sure had been built to cook breakfast for their great commander.

As he approached he saw Lee and his generals standing before the blaze, some eating, and others drinking. An orderly, near by, held the commander's famous horse, Traveller, and two or three horses belonging to the other generals were trying to find a little grass between the stony outcrops of the hills. Harry felt an overwhelming curiosity, but he kept it in restraint, dismounting at a little distance, and approaching on foot.

He could not observe much change in the general's appearance. His handsome grey suit was as neat as ever, and the three stars, the only marks of his rank that he wore, shone untarnished upon his collar. The dignified and cheerful manner that marked him before Gettysburg marked him also afterward. To Harry, so young and so thoroughly charged with the emotions of his time and section, he was a figure to be approached with veneration.

He saw the stalwart and bearded Longstreet and other generals whom he knew, among them the brilliant Stuart in his brilliant plumage, but rather quiet and subdued in manner now, since he had not come to Gettysburg as soon as he was needed. Harry hung back a little, fearing lest he might be regarded as thrusting himself into a company so much his superior in rank, but Lee saw him and beckoned to him.

"I sent you back toward Gettysburg to report on our withdrawal, Lieutenant Kenton," he said.

"Yes, sir. I returned all the way to the field. The last of our troops should be leaving there just about now. The Northern army had made no preparation for immediate pursuit."

"Your report agrees with all the others that I have received. How long have you been without sleep?"

"I don't know, sir," he said at last. "I can't remember. Maybe it has been two or three days."

Stuart, who held a cup of coffee in his hand, laughed. "The times have been such that there are generals as well as lieutenants," he said, "who can't remember when they've slept."

"You're exhausted, my lad," said Lee gravely and kindly, "and there's nothing more you can do for us just now. Take some breakfast with us, and then you must sleep in one of the wagons. An orderly will look after your horse."

Lee handed him a cup of coffee with his own hand, and Harry, thanking him, withdrew to the outer fringe of the little group, where he took his breakfast, amazed to find how hungry he was, although he had not thought of food before. Then without a word, as he saw that the generals were engrossed in a conference, he withdrew.

"You'll find Lieutenant Dalton of the staff in the covered wagon over there," said the orderly who had taken his horse. "The general sent him to it more'n two hours ago."

"Then I'll be inside it in less than two minutes," said Harry.

But with rest in sight he collapsed suddenly. His head fell forward of its own weight. His feet became lead. Everything swam before his eyes. He felt that he must sleep or die. But he managed to drag himself to the wagon and climbed inside. Dalton lay in the centre of it so sound asleep that he was like one dead. Harry rolled him to one side, making room for himself, and lay down beside him. Then his eyes closed, and he, too, slept so soundly that he also looked like one dead.

He was awakened by Dalton pulling at him. The young Virginian was sitting up and looking at Harry with curiosity. He clapped his hands when the Kentuckian opened his eyes.

"Now I know that you're not dead," he said. "When I woke up and found you lying beside me I thought they had just put your body in here for safekeeping. As that's not the case, kindly explain to me and at once what you're doing in my wagon."

"I'm waking up just at present, but for an hour or two before that I was sleeping."

"Hour or two? Hour or two? Hear him! An orderly who I know is no liar told me that you got in here just after dawn. Now kindly lift that canvas flap, look out and tell me what you see."

Harry did as he was told, and was amazed. The same rolling land-scape still met his eyes, and the sun was just about as high in the sky as it was when he had climbed into the wagon. But it was in the west now instead of the east.

"See and know, young man!" said Dalton, paternally. "The entire day has elapsed and here you have lain in ignorant slumber, careless of everything, reckless of what might happen to the army. For twelve hours General Lee has been without your advice, and how, lacking it, he has got this far, Heaven alone knows."

"It seems that he's pulled through, and, since I'm now awake, you can hurry to him and tell him I'm ready to furnish the right plans to stop the forthcoming Yankee invasion."

"They'll keep another day, but we've certainly had a good sleep, Harry."

"Yes, a provision or ammunition wagon isn't a bad place for a worn-out soldier. I remember I slept in another such as this in the Valley of Virginia, when we were with Jackson."

He stopped suddenly and choked. He could not mention the name of Jackson, until long afterward, without something rising in his throat.

The driver obscured a good deal of the front view, but he suddenly turned a rubicund and smiling face upon them.

"Waked up, hev ye?" he exclaimed. "Wa'al it's about time. I've looked back from time to time an' I wuzn't at all shore whether you two gen'rals wuz alive or dead. Sometimes when the wagon slanted a lot you would roll over each other, but it didn't seem to make no diffunce. Pow'ful good sleepers you are."

"Yes," said Harry. "We're two of the original Seven Sleepers."

"I don't doubt that you are two, but they wuz more'n seven."

"How do you know?"

"'Cause at least seven thousand in this train have been sleepin' as hard as you wuz. I guess you mean the 'rig'nal Seventy Thousand Sleepers."

Harry's spirits had returned after his long sleep. He was a lad again. The weight of Gettysburg no longer rested upon him. The Army of Northern Virginia had merely made a single failure. It would strike again and again, as hard as ever.

"It's true that we've been slumbering," he said, "but we're as wide awake now as ever, Mr. Driver."

"My name ain't Driver," said the man.

"Then what is it?"

"Jones, Dick Jones, which I hold to be a right proper name."

"Not romantic, but short, simple and satisfying."

"I reckon so. Leastways, I've never wanted to change it. I'm from No'th Calliny, an' I've been followin' Bobby Lee a pow'ful long distance from home. Fine country up here in Pennsylvany, but I'd ruther be back in them No'th Calliny mountains. You two young gen'rals may think it's an easy an' safe job drivin' a wagon loaded with ammunition. But s'pose you have to drive it right under fire, as you most often have to do, an' then if a shell or somethin' like it hits your wagon the whole thing goes off kerplunk, an' whar are you?"

"It's a sudden an' easy death," said Dalton, philosophically.

"Too sudden an' too easy. I don't mind tellin' you that seein' men killed an' wounded is a spo't that's beginnin' to pall on me. Reckon I've had enough of it to last me for the next thousand years. I've forgot, if I ever knowed, what this war wuz started about. Say, young

21

fellers, I've got a wife back thar, a high-steppin', fine-lookin' gal not more'n twenty years old—I'm just twenty-five myself, an' we've got a year-old baby the cutest that wuz ever born. Now, when I wuz lookin' at that charge of Pickett's men, an' the whole world wuz blazin' with fire, an' all the skies wuz rainin' steel and lead, an' whar grass growed before, nothin' but bayonets wuz growin' then, do you know what I seed sometimes?"

"What was it?" asked Harry.

"Fur a secon' all that hell of fire an' smoke an' killin' would float away, an' I seed our mountain, with the cove, an' the trees, an' the green grass growin' in it, an' the branch, with the water so clear you could see your face in it, runnin' down the centre, an' thar at the head of the cove my cabin, not much uv a buildin' to look at, no towerin' mansion, but just a stout two-room log cabin that the snows an' hails of winter can't break into, an' in the door wuz standin' Mary with the hair flyin' about her face, an' her eyes shinin', with the little feller in her arms, lookin' at me 'way off as I come walkin' fast down the cove toward 'em, returnin' from the big war."

There was a moment's silence, and Dalton said gruffly to hide his feelings:

"Dick Jones, by the time this war is over, and you go walking down the cove toward your home, a man with moustache and side whiskers will come forward to meet you, and he'll be that son of yours."

But Dick Jones cheerfully shook his head.

"The war ain't goin' to last that long," he said confidently, "an' I ain't goin' to git killed. What I saw will come true, 'cause I feel it so strong."

"There ought to be a general law forbidding a man with a young wife and baby to go to a war," said Harry.

"But they ain't no sich law," said Dick Jones, in his optimistic tone, "an' so we needn't worry 'bout it. But if you two gen'rals should happen along through the mountains uv western No'th Calliny after the war I'd like fur you to come to my cabin, an' see Mary an' the baby an' me. Our cove is named Jones' Cove, after my father, an' the branch that runs through it runs into Jones' Creek, an' Jones' Creek runs into the Yadkin River an' our county is Yadkin. Oh, you could find it plumb easy, if two sich great gen'rals as you wuzn't ashamed to eat sweet per-taters an' ham an' turkey an' co'n pone with a wagon driver like me."

Harry saw, despite his playful method of calling them generals, that he was thoroughly in earnest, and he was more moved than he would have been willing to confess.

"Too proud!" he said. "Why, we'd be glad!"

"Mebbe your road will lead that way," said Jones. "An' ef you do, jest remember that the skillet's on the fire, an' the latch string is hangin' outside the do'."

The allusion to the mountains made Harry's mind travel far back, over an almost interminable space of time now, it seemed, when he was yet a novice in war, to the home of Sam Jarvis, deep in the Kentucky mountains, and the old, old woman who had said to him as he left: "You will come again, and you will be thin and pale, and in rags, and you will fall at the door. I see you coming with these two eyes of mine."

A little shiver passed over him. He knew that no one could penetrate the future, but he shivered nevertheless, and he found himself saying mechanically:

"It's likely that I'll return through the mountains, and if so I'll look you up at that home in the cove on the brook that runs into Jones' Creek."

"That bein' settled," said Jones, "what do you gen'rals reckon to do jest now, after havin' finished your big sleep?"

"Your wagon is about to lose the first two passengers it has ever carried," replied Harry. "Orderlies have our horses somewhere. We belong on the staff of General Lee."

"An' you see him an' hear him talk every day? Some people are pow'ful lucky. I guess you'll say a lot about it when you're old men."

"We're going to say a lot about it while we're young men. Good-by, Mr. Jones. We've been in some good hotels, but we never slept better in any of them than we have in this moving one of yours."

"Good-by, you're always welcome to it. I think Marse Bob is on ahead."

The two left the wagon and took to a path beside the road, which was muddy and rutted deeply by innumerable hoofs and wheels. But grass and foliage were now dry after the heavy rains that followed the Battle of Gettysburg, and the sun was shining in late splendour. The army, taking the lack of pursuit and attack as proof that the enemy had suffered as much as they, if not more, was in good spirits, and many of the men sang their marching songs. A band ahead of them suddenly began to play mellow music, *Partant Pour La Syrie*, and other old French songs. The airs became gay, festive, uplifting to the soul, and they tickled the feet of the young men.

"The Cajun band!" exclaimed Harry. "It never occurred to me that they weren't all dead, and here they are, playing us into happiness!"

"And the Invincibles, or what's left of them, won't be far away," said Dalton.

23

They walked on a little more briskly and beside them the vast length of the unsuccessful army still trailed its slow way back into the South. The sun was setting in uncommon magnificence, clothing everything in a shower of gold, through which the lilting notes of the music came to Harry and Dalton's ears. Presently the two saw them, the short, dark men from far Louisiana, not so many as they had been, but playing with all the fervour of old, putting their Latin souls into their music.

"And there are the Invincibles just ahead of them!" exclaimed Dalton. "The two colonels have left the wagon and are riding with their men. See, how erect they sit."

"I do see them, and they're a good sight to see," said Harry. "I hope they'll live to finish that chess game."

"And fifty years afterward, too."

A shout of joy burst from the road, and a tall young man, slender, dark and handsome, rushed out, and, seizing the hands of first one and then the other, shook them eagerly, his dark eyes glittering with happy surprise.

"Kenton! Dalton!" he exclaimed. "Both alive! Both well!"

It was young Julien de Langeais, the kinsman of Lieutenant-Colonel Hector St. Hilaire, and he too was unhurt. The lads returned his grasp warmly. They could not have kept from liking him had they tried, and they certainly did not wish to try.

"You don't know how it rejoices me to see you," said Julien, speaking very fast. "I was sad! very sad! Some of my best friends have perished back there in those inhospitable Pennsylvania hills, and while the band was playing it made me think of the homes they will never see any more! Don't think I'm effusive and that I show grief too much, but my heart has been very heavy! Alas, for the brave lads!"

"Come, come, de Langeais," said Harry, putting his hand on his shoulder. "You've no need to apologize for sorrow. God knows we all have enough of it, but a lot of us are still alive and here's an army ready to fight again, whenever the enemy says the word."

"True! True!" exclaimed de Langeais, changing at once from shadow to sunshine. "And when we're back in Virginia we'll turn our faces once more to our foe!"

He took a step or two on the grass in time to the music which was now that of a dance, and the brilliant beams of the setting sun showed a face without a care. Invincible youth and the invincible gayety of the part of the South that was French were supreme again. Dalton, looking at him, shook his Presbyterian head. Yet his eyes expressed admiration.

"I know your feelings," said Harry to the Virginian.

"Well, what are they?"

"You don't approve of de Langeais' lightness, which in your stern code you would call levity, and yet you envy him possession of it. You don't think it's right to be joyous, without a care, and yet you know it would be mighty pleasant. You criticize de Langeais a little, but you feel it would be a gorgeous thing to have that joyous spirit of his."

Dalton laughed.

"You're pretty near the truth," he said. "I haven't known de Langeais so very long, but if he were to get killed I'd feel that I had lost a younger brother."

"So would I."

Two immaculate youths, riding excellent horses, approached them, and favoured them with a long and supercilious stare.

"Can the large fair person be Lieutenant Kenton of the staff of the commander-in-chief?" asked St. Clair.

"It can be and it is, although we did not think to see him again so soon," replied Happy Tom Langdon, "and the other—I do not allude to de Langeais—is that spruce and devout young man, Lieutenant George Dalton, also of the staff of the commander-in-chief."

"Why do we find them in such humble plight, walking on weary feet in a path beside the road?"

"For the most excellent reason in the world, Arthur."

"And what may that reason be, Tom?"

"Because at last they have come down to their proper station in life, just as surely as water finds its level."

"But we'll not treat them too sternly. We must remember that they also serve who walk and wait."

But St. Clair and Langdon, their chaff over, gave them happy greeting, and told them that the two colonels would be rejoiced to see them again, if they could spare a few minutes before rejoining their commander.

"And here is an orderly with both your horses," said St. Clair, "so, under the circumstances, we'll sink our pride and let you ride with us."

De Langeais, with a cheerful farewell until the next day, returned to his command, and Harry and Dalton, mounting, were in a few minutes beside the Invincibles. Colonel Leonidas Talbot and Lieutenant-Colonel Hector St. Hilaire turned their horses from the road into the path and saluted them with warmth.

"We caught a glimpse of you just after our departure, Harry," said Colonel Talbot, "but we did not know what had happened since. There is always a certain amount of risk attending the removal of a great army."

25

"I am glad, Leonidas, that you used the word 'removal' to describe our operations after our great victory at Gettysburg," said Lieutenant-Colonel St. Hilaire. "I have been feeling about for the right word or phrase myself, but you have found it first."

"Do you think it was a victory, sir?" asked Harry.

"Undoubtedly. We have won several vast and brilliant triumphs, but this is the greatest of them all. We have gone far into the enemy's country, where we have struck him a terrible blow, and now, of our own choice—understand it is of our own choice—we withdraw and challenge him to come and repeat on our own soil our exploit if he can. It is like a skilled and daring prize fighter who leaps back and laughingly bids his foe come on. Am I not right, Leonidas?"

"Neither Aristotle nor Plato was ever more right, Hector, old friend. Usually there is more to a grave affair than appears upon the surface. We could have gone on, after the battle, to Philadelphia, had we chosen, but it was not alone a question of military might that General Lee had to decide. He was bound to give weight to some very subtle considerations. You boys remember your Roman history, do you not?"

"Fragments of it, sir," replied Harry.

"Then you will recall that Hannibal, a fine general, to be named worthily with our great Lee so far as military movements are concerned, after famous victories over greatly superior numbers of Romans, went into camp at Capua, crowded with beauty, wine and games, and the soldiers became enervated. Their fibre was weakened and their bodies softened. They were quicker to heed the call to a banquet than the call to arms."

"Unless it was the arms of beauty, Leonidas."

"Well spoken, Hector. The correction is most important, and I accept it. But to take up again the main thread of my discourse. General Lee undoubtedly had the example of the Carthaginian army and Capua in mind when he left Gettysburg and returned toward the South. Philadelphia is a great city, far larger and richer than any in our section. It is filled with magnificent houses, beautiful women, luxury of every description, ease and softness. Our brave lads, crowned with mighty exploits and arriving there as conquerors, would have been received with immense admiration, although we are official enemies. And the head of youth is easily turned. The Army of Northern Virginia, emerging from Philadelphia, to achieve the conquest of New York and Boston would not be the army that it is to-day. It would lack some of that fire and dash, some of the extraordinary courage and tenacity which have enabled it to surpass the deeds of the veterans of Hannibal and Napoleon."

"But, sir, I've heard that the people of Philadelphia are mostly Quakers, very sober in dress and manner."

"Harry, my lad, when you've lived as long as I have you will know that a merry heart may beat beneath a plain brown dress, and that an ugly hood cannot wholly hide a sweet and saucy face. The girls—God bless 'em—have been the same in all lands since the world began, and will continue so to the end. While this war is on you boys cannot go a-courting, either in the North or South. Am I not right, Hector, old friend?"

"Right, as always, Leonidas. I perceive, though, that the sun is about to set; not a new thing, I admit, but we must not delay our young friends, when the general perhaps needs them."

"Well spoken again, Hector. You are an unfailing fount of wisdom. Good night, my brave lads. Not many of the Invincibles are left, but every one of them is a true friend of you both."

As they rode across the darkening fields Harry and Dalton knew that the colonel spoke the truth about the Invincibles.

"I like a faith such as theirs," said Dalton.

"Yes, it can often turn defeat into real victory."

They quickly found the general's headquarters, and as usual, whenever the weather permitted, he had made arrangements to sleep in the open air, his blankets spread upon soft boughs. Harry and Dalton, having slept all day, would be on night duty, and after supper they sat at a little distance, awaiting orders.

Coolness had come with the dark. A good moon and swarms of bright stars rode in the heavens, turning the skies to misty silver, and softening the scars of the army, which now lay encamped over a great space. Lee was talking with Stuart, who evidently had just arrived from a swift ride, as an orderly near by was holding his horse, covered with foam. The famous cavalryman was clothed in his gorgeous best. His hat was heavy with gold braid, and the broad sash about his waist was heavy with gold, also. Dandy he was, but brilliant cavalryman and great soldier too! Both friend and foe had said so.

Harry, sitting on the grass, with his back against a tree, watched the two generals as they talked long and earnestly. Now and then Stuart nervously switched the tops of his own high riding boots with the little whip that he carried, but the face of Lee, revealed clearly in the near twilight, remained grave and impassive.

After a long while Stuart mounted and rode away, and Sherburne, who had been sitting among the trees on the far side of the fire, came over and joined Harry and Dalton. He too was very grave.

"Do you know what has happened?" he said in a low tone to the two lads.

"Yes, there was a big battle at Gettysburg, and as we failed to win it we're now retreating," replied Harry.

"That's true as far as it goes, but it's not all. We've heard—and the news is correct beyond a doubt—that Grant has taken Vicksburg and Pemberton's army with it."

"Good God, Sherburne, it can't be so!"

"It shouldn't be so, but it is! Oh, why did Pemberton let himself be trapped in such a way! A whole army of ours lost and our greatest fortress in the West taken! Why, the Yankee men-of-war can steam up the Mississippi untouched, all the way from the Gulf to Minnesota."

Harry and Dalton were appalled, and, for a little while, were silent.

"I knew that man Grant would do something terrible to us," Harry said at last. "I've heard from my people in Kentucky what sort of a general he is. My father was at Shiloh, where we had a great victory on, but Grant wouldn't admit it, and held on, until another Union army came up and turned our victory into defeat. My cousin, Dick Mason, has been with Grant a lot, and I used to get a letter from him now and then, even if he is in the Yankee army. He says that when Grant takes hold of a thing he never lets go, and that he'll win the war for his side."

"Your cousin may be right about Grant's hanging on," said Dalton with sudden angry emphasis, "but neither he nor anybody else will win this war for the Yankees. We've lost Vicksburg, and an army with it, and we've retreated from Gettysburg, with enough men fallen there to make another army, but they'll never break through the iron front of Lee and his veterans."

"Hope you're right," said Sherburne, "but I'm off now. I'm in the saddle all night with my troop. We've got to watch the Yankee cavalry. Custer and Pleasanton and the rest of them have learned to ride in a way that won't let Jeb Stuart himself do any nodding."

He cantered off and the lads sat under the trees, ready for possible orders. They saw the fire die. They heard the murmur of the camp sink. Lee lay down on his bed of boughs, other generals withdrew to similar beds or to tents, and the two boys still sat under the trees, waiting and watching, and never knowing at what moment they would be needed.

CHAPTER 2

The Northern Spy

But the night remained very quiet. Harry and Dalton, growing tired of sitting, walked about the camp, and looked again to their horses, which, saddled and bridled, were nevertheless allowed to nip the grass as best they could at the end of their lariats. The last embers of the fire went out, but the moon and stars remained bright, and they saw dimly the sleeping forms of Lee and his generals. Harry, who had seen nothing strange in Meade's lack of pursuit, now wondered at it. Surely when the news of Vicksburg came the exultant Army of the Potomac would follow, and try to deliver a crushing blow.

It was revealed to him as he stood silent in the moonlight that a gulf had suddenly yawned before the South. The slash of Grant's sword in the West had been terrible, and the wound that it made could not be cured easily. And the Army of Northern Virginia had not only failed in its supreme attempt, but a great river now flowed between it and Virginia. If the Northern leaders, gathering courage anew, should hurl their masses upon Lee's retreating force, neither skill nor courage might avail to save them. He suddenly beheld the situation in all its desperation; he shivered from head to foot.

Dalton saw the muscles of Harry's face quivering, and he noticed a pallor that came for an instant.

"I understand," he said. "I had thought of it already. If a Northern general like Lee or Stonewall Jackson were behind us we might never get back across the Potomac. It's somewhat the same position that we were in after Antietam."

"But we've no Stonewall Jackson now to help us."

Again that lump rose in Harry's throat. The vision of the sober figure on Little Sorrel, leading his brigades to victory, came before him, but it was a vision only.

"It's strange that we've not come in contact with their scouts or cavalry," he said. "In that fight with Pleasanton we saw what horsemen they've become, and a force of some kind must be hanging on our rear."

"If it's there, Sherburne and his troop will find it."

"I think I can detect signs of the enemy now," said Harry, putting his glasses to his eyes. "See that hill far behind us. Can't you catch the gleam of lights on it?"

"I think I can," replied Dalton, also using glasses. "Four lights are there, and they are winking, doubtless to lights on another hill too far away for us to see."

"It shows that the enemy at least is watching, and that while we may retreat unattacked it will not be unobserved. Hark! do you hear that, George? It's rifle shots, isn't it?"

"Yes, and a lot of 'em, but they're a long distance away. I don't think we could hear 'em at all if it were not night time."

"But it means something! There they go again! I believe it's a heavy skirmish and it's in the direction in which Sherburne rode."

"The general's up. It's likely that one of us will be sent to see what it's all about."

General Lee and his whole staff had risen and were listening attentively. The faint sound of many shots still came, and then a sharper, more penetrating crash, as if light field guns were at work. The commander beckoned to Harry.

"Ride toward it," he said briefly, "and return with a report as soon as you can."

Harry touched his cap, sprang upon his horse and galloped away. He knew that other messengers would be dispatched also, but, as he had been sent first, he wished to arrive first. He found a path among the trees along which he could make good speed, and, keeping his mind fixed on the firing, he sped forward.

Thousands of soldiers lay asleep in the woods and fields on either side of him, but the thud of the horse's hoofs awakened few of them. Nor did the firing disturb them. They had fought a great battle three days long, and then after a tense day of waiting under arms, they had marched hard. What to them was the noise made by an affair of outposts, when they had heard so long the firing of a hundred and fifty thousand rifles and three or four hundred big guns? Not one in a hundred stood up to see.

The country grew rougher, and Harry was compelled to draw his horse down to a walk. But the firing, a half-mile or more ahead, maintained its volume, and as he approached through thick underbrush, being able to find no other way, he dismounted and led his horse. Presently he saw beads of flame appearing among the bushes, seen a moment, then gone like a firefly, and as he went further he heard voices. He had no doubt that it was the Southern pickets in the undergrowth, and, calling softly, he received confirmatory replies.

A rifleman, a tall, slender fellow in ragged butternut, appeared beside him, and, recognizing Harry's near-grey uniform as that of an officer, said:

"They're dismounted cavalry on the other side of a creek that runs along over there among the bushes. I don't think they mean any real attack. They expect to sting us a little an' find out what we're about."

"Seems likely to me too. They aren't strong enough, of course, for an attempt at rushing us. What troops are in here in the woods on our side?"

"Captain Sherburne's cavalry, sir. They're a bit to our right, an' they're dismounted too. You'll find the captain himself on a little knoll about a hundred yards away."

"Thanks," said Harry, and leading his horse he reached the knoll, to find the rifleman's statement correct. Sherburne was kneeling behind some bushes, trying with the aid of glasses and moonlight to pick out the enemy.

"That you, Harry?" he said, glancing back.

"Yes, Captain. The general has sent me to see what you and the rest of you noisy fellows are doing."

"Shooting across a creek at an enemy who first shot at us. It's only under provocation that we've roused the general and his staff from sleep. Use your glasses and see what you can make out in those bushes on the other side! Keep down, Harry! For Heaven's sake keep down! That bullet didn't miss you more than three inches. You wouldn't be much loss to the army, of course, but you're my personal friend."

"Thanks for your advice. I intend to stay so far down that I'll lie almost flat."

He meant to keep his word, too. The warning had been a stern one. Evidently the sharpshooters who lay in the thickets on the Union side of the creek were of the first quality.

"There's considerable moonlight," whispered Sherburne, "and you mustn't expose an inch of your face. I take it that we have Custer's cavalry over there, mixed with a lot of scouts and skirmishers from the Northwest, Michigan and Wisconsin, most likely. They're the boys who can use the rifles in the woods. Had to do it before they came here, and they're a bad lot to go up against."

"It's a pretty heavy fire for a mere scouting party. If they want to discover our location they can do it without wasting so much powder and lead."

"I think it's more than a scout. They must have discovered long since just where we are. I imagine they mean to shake our nerve by constant buzzing and stinging. I fancy that Meade and his generals after deciding not to pursue us have changed their minds, perhaps under pressure from Washington, and mean to cut us off if they can."

"A little late."

"But not too late. We're still in the enemy's country. The whole population is dead against us, and we can't make a move that isn't known within an hour to the Union leaders. I tell you, Harry, that if we didn't have a Lee to lead I'd be afraid that we'd never get out of Pennsylvania."

"But we have a Lee and the question is settled. What a volley that was! Didn't you feel the twigs and leaves falling on your face?"

"Yes, it went directly over our heads. It's a good thing we're lying so close. Perhaps they intend to force a passage of the creek and stampede at least a portion of our camp."

"And you're here to prevent it."

"I am. They can't cross that creek in face of our fire. We're good night-hawks. Every boy in the South knows the night and the woods, and here in the bush we're something like Indians."

"I'm the descendant of a famous Indian fighter myself," said Harry. And there, surrounded by deep gloom and danger, the spirit of his mighty ancestor, the great Henry Ware, descended upon him once more. An orderly had taken their horses to the rear, where they would be out of range of the bullets, and, as they crouched low in the bushes, Sherburne looked curiously at him.

Harry's face as he turned from the soldier to the Indian fighter of old had changed. To Sherburne's fascinated gaze the eyes seemed amazingly vivid and bright, like those of one who has learned to see in the dark. The complexion was redder—Henry Ware had always burned red instead of brown—like that of one who sleeps oftener in the open air than in a house. His whole look was dominant, compelling and fierce, as he leaned on his elbows and studied the opposing thickets through his glasses.

The glasses even did not destroy the illusion. To Sherburne, who had learned Harry's family history, the great Henry Ware was alive, and in the flesh before him. He felt with all the certainty of truth that the Union skirmishers in the thicket could not escape the keen eyes that sought them out.

"I can see at least twenty men creeping about among the bushes, and seeking chances for shots," whispered Harry.

"I knew that you would see them."

It was Harry's turn to give a look of curiosity.

"What do you mean, Captain?" he asked.

"I knew that you had good eyes and I believed that with the aid of the glasses you would be able to trace figures, despite the shelter of the bushes. Study the undergrowth again, will you, Harry, and tell me what more you can see there?"

"I don't need to study it. I can tell at one look that they're gathering a force. Maybe they mean to rush the creek at a shallow place."

"Is that force moving in any direction?"

"Yes, it's going down the creek."

"Then we'll go down the creek with it. We mustn't be lacking in hospitality."

Sherburne drew a whistle from his pocket and blew a low call upon it. Scores of shadowy figures rose from the undergrowth, and followed his lead down the stream. Harry was still able to see that the force on the other side was increasing largely in numbers, but Sherburne reminded him that his duties, as far as the coming skirmish was concerned, were over.

"General Lee didn't send you here to get killed," he said. "He wants you instead to report how many of us get killed. You know that while the general is a kind man he can be stern, too, and you're not to take the risk. The orderly is behind that hill with your horse and mine."

Harry, with a sigh, fell back toward the hill. But he did not yet go behind it, where the orderly stood. Instead he lay down among the trees on the slope, where he could watch what was going forward, and once more his face turned to the likeness of the great Indian fighter.

He saw Sherburne's dismounted troop and others, perhaps five hundred in all, moving slowly among the bushes parallel with the stream, and he saw a force which he surmised to be of about equal size, creeping along in the undergrowth on the other side. He followed both bodies with his glasses. With long looking everything became clearer and clearer. The moonlight had to him almost the brilliancy of day.

His eyes followed the Union force, until it came to a point where the creek ran shallow over pebbles. Then the Union leader raised his sword, uttered a cry of command, and the whole force dashed at the ford. The cry met its response in an order from Sherburne, and the thickets flamed with the Southern rifles.

The advantage was wholly with the South, standing on the defence in dark undergrowth, and the Union troop, despite its desperate attempts at the ford, was beaten back with great loss.

Harry waited until the result was sure, and then he walked slowly over the hill toward the point, where the orderly was waiting with the horses. The man, who knew him, handed him the reins of his mount, saying at the same time:

"I've a note for you, sir."

"For me?"

"Yes, sir. It was handed to me about fifteen minutes ago by a large man in our uniform, whom I didn't know."

"Probably a dispatch that I'm to carry to General Lee."

"No, sir. It's addressed to you."

The note was written in pencil on a piece of coarse grey paper, folded several times, but with a face large enough to show Harry's name upon it. He wondered, but said nothing to the sentinel, and did not look at the note again, until he had ridden some distance.

He stopped in a little glade where the moonlight fell clearly. He still heard scattered firing behind him, but he knew that the skirmish was in reality over, and he concluded that no further attempt by Union detachments to advance would be made in the face of such vigilance. He could report to General Lee that the rear of his army was safe. So he would delay and look at the letter that had come to him out of the mysterious darkness. The superscription was in a large, bold hand, and read:

Lieutenant Harry Kenton
Staff of General Robert E. Lee
C. S. A., Commander-in-Chief
Army of Northern Virginia

He felt instinctively that something uncommon was coming, and, as most people do when they are puzzled at the appearance of a letter, he looked at it some seconds before opening it. Then he read:

Mr. Kenton:
I have warned you twice before, once when Jefferson Davis was inaugurated at Montgomery, and once again in Virginia. I told you that the South could never win. I told you that she might achieve brilliant victories, and she may achieve them even yet, but they will avail her nothing. Victories permit her to maintain her position for the time being, but they do not enable her to advance. A single defeat causes her to lose ground that she can never regain.

34

I tell you this as a warning. Although your enemy, I have seen you more than once and talked with you. I like you and would save your life if I could. I would induce you, if I could, to leave the army and return to your home, but that I know to be impossible. So, I merely tell you that you are fighting for a cause now lost. Perhaps it is pride on my part to remind you that my early predictions have come true, and perhaps it is a wish that the thought I may plant in your mind will spread to others. You have lost at Gettysburg a hope and an offensive that you can never regain, and Grant at Vicksburg has given a death blow to the Western half of the Confederacy.

As for you, I wish you well.

William J. Shepard

Harry stared in amazement at this extraordinary communication, and read it over two or three times. He was not surprised that Shepard should be near, and that he should have been inside the Confederate lines, but that he should leave a letter, and such a letter, for him was uncanny. His first feeling, wonder, was succeeded by anger. Did Shepard really think that he could influence him in such a way, that he could plant in his mind a thought that would spread to others of his age and rank and weaken the cause for which he fought? It was a singular idea, but Shepard was a singular man.

But perhaps pride in recalling the prediction that he had made long ago was Shepard's stronger motive, and Harry took fire at that also. The Confederacy was not beaten. A single defeat—no, it was not a defeat, merely a failure to win—was not mortal, and as for the West, the Confederacy would gather itself together there and overwhelm Grant!

Then came a new emotion, a kind of gratitude to Shepard. The man was really a friend, and would do him a service, if it could be done, without injuring his own cause! He could not feel any doubt of it, else the spy would not have taken the risk to send him such a letter. He read it for the last time, then tore it into little pieces which he entrusted to the winds.

The firing behind him had died completely, and there was no sound but the rustle of dry leaves in the light wind, nothing to tell that there had been sharp fighting along the creek, and that men lay dead in the forest. The moon and the stars clothed everything in a whitish light, that seemed surcharged with a powerful essence, and this essence was danger.

The spirit of the great forest ranger descended upon him once more, and he read the omens, all of which were sinister. He foresaw terrible campaigns, mighty battles in the forest, and a roll of the dead so long that it seemed to stretch away into infinity.

Then he shook himself violently, cast off the spell, and rode rapidly back with his report. Lee had risen and was standing under a tree. He was fully dressed and his uniform was trim and unwrinkled. Harry thought anew as he rode up, what a magnificent figure he was. He was the only great man he ever saw who really looked his greatness. Nothing could stir that calm. Nothing could break down that loftiness of manner. Harry was destined to feel then, as he felt many times afterward, that without him the South had never a chance. And the choking came in his throat again, as he thought of him who was gone, of him who had been the right arm of victory, the hammer of Thor.

But he hid all these feelings as he quickly dismounted and saluted the commander-in-chief.

"What have you seen, Lieutenant Kenton?" asked Lee.

"A considerable detachment of the enemy tried to force the passage of the creek in our right rear. They were met by Captain Sherburne's troop dismounted, and three companies of infantry, and were driven back after a sharp fight."

"Very good. Captain Sherburne is an alert officer."

He turned away, and Harry, giving his horse to an orderly, again resumed his old position under a tree, out of hearing of the generals, but in sight. Dalton was not there, but he knew that skirmishing had occurred in other directions, and doubtless the Virginian had been sent on an errand like his own.

He had a sense of rest and realization as he leaned back against the tree. But it was mental tension, not physical, for which relief came, and Shepard, much more than the battle at the creek, was in his thoughts.

The strong personality of the spy and his seeming omniscience oppressed him again. Apparently he was able to go anywhere, and nothing could be hidden from him. He might be somewhere in the circling shadows at that very moment, watching Lee and his lieutenants. His pulses leaped. Shepard had achieved an extraordinary influence over him, and he was prepared to believe the impossible.

He stood up and stared into the bushes, but sentinels stood there, and no human being could pass their ring unseen. Presently Dalton came, made a brief report to General Lee and joined his comrade. Harry was glad of his arrival. The presence of a comrade brought him back to earth and earth's realities. The sinister shadows that oppressed him melted away and he saw only the ordinary darkness of a summer night.

The two sat side by side. Dalton perhaps drew as much strength as Harry from the comradeship, and they watched other messengers arrive with dispatches, some of whom rolled themselves in their blankets at once, and went to sleep, although three, who had evidently slept in the day, joined Harry and Dalton in their vigil.

Harry saw that the commander-in-chief was holding a council at that hour, nearer morning than midnight. A general kicked some of the pieces of burned wood together and fanned them into a light flame, enough to take away the slight chill that was coming with the morning. The men stood around it, and talked a long time, although it seemed to Harry that Lee said least. Nevertheless his tall figure dominated them all. Now and then Harry saw his face in the starshine, and it bore its habitual grave and impassive look.

The youth did not hear a word that was said, but his imaginative power enabled him to put himself in the place of the commander-in-chief. He knew that no man, however great his courage, could fail to appreciate his position in the heart of a hostile country, with a lost field behind him, and with superior numbers hovering somewhere in his rear or on his flank. He realized then to the full the critical nature of their position and what a mighty task Lee had to save the army.

One of his young comrades whispered to him that the Potomac, the barrier between North and South, was rising, flooded by heavy rains in both mountains and lowlands, and that a body of Northern cavalry had already destroyed a pontoon bridge built by the South across it. They might be hemmed in, with their backs to an unfordable river, and an enemy two or three times as numerous in front.

"Don't you worry," whispered Dalton, with sublime confidence. "The general will take us to Virginia."

Harry projected his imagination once more. He sought to put himself in the place of Lee, receiving all the reports and studying them, trying to measure space that could not be measured, and to weigh a total that could not be weighed. Greatness and responsibility were compelled to pay thrice over for themselves, and he was glad that he was only a young lieutenant, the chief business of whom was to fetch and carry orders.

Shafts of sunlight were piercing the eastern foliage when the council broke up, and shortly after daylight the Southern army was again on the march, with Northern cavalry and riflemen hanging on its flanks and rear. Harry was permitted to rejoin, for a while, his friends of the Invincibles and he found Colonel Leonidas Talbot and Lieutenant-Colonel Hector St. Hilaire riding very erect, a fine colour in their faces.

"You come from headquarters, Harry, and therefore you are omniscient," said Colonel Talbot. "We heard firing in the night. What did it mean?"

"Only skirmishers, Colonel. I think they wanted to annoy us, but they paid the price."

"Inevitably. Our general is as dangerous in retreat as in advance. I fancy that General Meade will not bring up his lagging forces until we near the Potomac."

"They say it's rising, sir, and that it will be very hard to cross."

"That creates a difficulty but not an impossibility. Ordinary men yield to difficulties, men like our commander-in-chief are overcome only by impossibilities. But the further we go, Harry, the more reconciled I grow to our withdrawal. I have seen scarcely a friendly face among the population. I would not have us thrust ourselves upon people who do not like us. It would go very hard with our kindly Southern nature to have to rule by force over people who are in fact our brethren. Defensive wars are the just wars, and perhaps it will be really better for us to retire to Virginia and protect its sacred soil from the tread of the invader. Eh, Hector?"

"Right, as usual, Leonidas. The reasons for our retirement are most excellent. We have already spoken of the fact that Philadelphia might prove a Capua for our young troops, and now we are relieved from the chance of appearing as oppressors. It can never be said of us by the people of Pennsylvania that we were tyrants. It's an invidious task to rule over the unwilling, even when one rules with justice and wisdom. It's strange, perhaps, Leonidas, but it's a universal truth, that people would rather be ruled by themselves in a second rate manner than by the foreigner in a first rate manner. Now, the government of our states is attacked by Northern critics, but such as it is, it is ours and it's our first choice. Do we bore you, Harry?"

"Not at all, sir. I never listen to either you or Colonel Talbot without learning something."

The two colonels bowed politely.

"I have wished for some time to speak to you about a certain matter, Hector," said Colonel Talbot.

"What is it, Leonidas?"

"During the height of that tremendous artillery fire from Little Round Top I was at a spot where I could see the artillerymen very well whenever the smoke lifted. Several times, I noticed an officer directing the fire of the guns, and I don't think I could have been mistaken in his identity."

"No, Leonidas, you were not. I too observed him, and we could not possibly be mistaken. It was John Carrington, of course."

"Dear old John Carrington, who was with us at West Point, the greatest artilleryman in the world. And he was facing us, when the fortunes of the South were turning on a hair. If any other man had been there, directing those guns, we might have taken Cemetery Hill."

"That's true, Leonidas, but it was not possible for any other man to be in such a place at such a time. Granting that such a crisis should arise and that it should arise at Gettysburg you and I would have known long before that John would be there with the guns to stop us. Why, we saw that quality in him all the years we were with him at West Point. The world has never seen and never will see another such artilleryman as John Carrington."

"Good old John. I hope he wasn't killed."

"And I hope so too, from the bottom of my heart. But we'll know before many days."

"How will you find out?" asked Harry curiously.

Both colonels laughed genially.

"Because he will send us signs, unmistakable signs," replied Colonel Talbot.

"I don't understand, sir."

"His signs will be shells, shrapnel and solid shot. We may not have a battle this week or next week, but a big one is bound to come some time or other and then if any section of the Northern artillery shows uncommon deadliness and precision we'll know that Carrington is there. Why, we can recognize his presence as readily as the deer scents the hunter. We'll have many notes to compare with him when the war is over."

Harry sincerely hoped that the three would meet in friendship around some festive table, and he was moved by the affection and admiration the two colonels held for Carrington. Doubtless the great artilleryman's feelings toward them were the same.

They went into camp once more that night in a pleasant rolling country of high hills, rich valleys, scattered forests, and swift streams of clear water. Harry liked this Northern land, which was yet not so far from the South. It was not more beautiful than his own Kentucky, but it was much trimmer and neater than the states toward the Gulf. He saw all about him the evidences of free labour, the proof that man worked more readily, and with better results, when success or failure were all his own.

He was too young to spend much time in concentrated thinking, but as he looked upon the neat Pennsylvania houses and farms and the cultivated fields he felt the curse of black slavery in the South, but he felt also that it was for the South itself to abolish it, and not for the armed hand of the outsider, an outsider to whom its removal meant no financial loss and dislocation.

Despite himself his mind dwelt upon these things longer than before. He disliked slavery, his father disliked it, and nearly all their friends and relatives, and here they were fighting for it, as one of the two great reasons of the Civil War. He felt anew how strangely things come about, and that even the wisest cannot always choose their own courses as they wish them.

A fire, chiefly for cooking purposes, had been built for the general and his staff in a cove surrounded by trees. A small cold spring gushed from the side of a hill, flowed down the centre of the cove, and then made its way through the trees into the wider world beyond. It was a fine little spring, and before the general came, the younger members of the staff knelt and drank deeply at it. It brought thoughts of home to all these young rovers of the woods, who had drunk a thousand times before at just such springs as this.

Soon Lee and his generals sat there on the stones or on the moss. Longstreet, Stuart, Pickett, Alexander, Ewell, Early, Hill and many others, some suffering from wounds, were with their commander, while the young officers who were to fetch and carry sat on the fringe in the woods, or stretched themselves on the turf.

Harry was in the group, but except in extreme emergency he would not be on duty that night, as he had already been twenty-four hours in the saddle. Nevertheless he was not yet sleepy, and lying on his blanket, he watched the leaders confer, as they had conferred every other night since the Battle of Gettysburg. He was aware, too, that the air was heavy with suspense and anxiety. He breathed it in at every breath. Cruel doubt was not shown by words or actions, but it was an atmosphere which one could not mistake.

Word had been brought in the afternoon by hard riders of Stuart that the Potomac was still rising. It could not be forded and the active Northern cavalry was in between, keeping advanced parties of the Southern army from laying pontoons. Every day made the situation more desperate, and it could not be hidden from the soldiers, who, nevertheless, marched cheerfully on, in the sublime faith that Lee would carry them through.

Harry knew that if the Army of the Potomac was not active in pursuit its cavalrymen and skirmishers were. As on the night before, he heard the faint report of shots, and he knew that rough work was going forward along the doubtful line, where the fringes of the two armies almost met. But hardened so much was he that he fell asleep while the generals were still in anxious council, and the fitful firing continued in the distant dark.

CHAPTER 3

The Flooded River

Harry and Dalton were aroused before daylight by Colonel Peyton of Lee's staff, with instructions to mount at once, and join a strong detachment, ready to go ahead and clear a way. Sherburne's troop would lead. The Invincibles, for whom mounts had been obtained, would follow. There were fragments of other regiments, the whole force amounting to about fifteen hundred men, under the command of Sherburne, who had been raised the preceding afternoon to the rank of Colonel, and whose skill and valour were so well known that such veterans as Colonel Talbot and Lieutenant Colonel St. Hilaire were glad to serve under him. Harry and Dalton would represent the commander-in-chief, and would return whenever Colonel Sherburne thought fit to report to him.

Harry was glad to go. While he had his periods of intense thought, and his character was serious, he was like his great ancestor, essentially a creature of action. His blood flowed more swiftly with the beat of his horse's hoofs, and his spirits rose as the free air of the fields and forests rushed past him. Moreover he was extremely anxious to see what lay ahead. If barriers were there he wanted to look upon them. If the Union cavalry were trying to keep them from laying bridges across the Potomac he wanted to help drive them away.

Harry and Dalton had a right as aides and messengers of Lee to ride with Sherburne, but before they joined him they rode among the Invincibles, who were in great feather, because they too, for the time being, rode, and toiled in neither dust nor mud.

"Colonel Sherburne may think a good deal of his own immediate troop," said St. Clair to Harry, "but if the men of the Invincibles could achieve so much on foot they'll truly deserve their name on horseback. Where is this enemy of ours? Lead us to him."

"You'll find him soon enough," said Harry. "You South Carolina talkers have learned many times that the Yankees will fight."

"Yes, Harry, I admit it freely. But you must admit on your part that the South Carolinians will fight as well as talk, although at present most of the South Carolinians in this regiment are Virginians."

"But not our colonel and lieutenant-colonel," said Happy Tom. "Real old South Carolina still leads."

"May they always lead!" said Harry heartily, looking at the two grey figures.

"Tell Colonel Sherburne," said Happy Tom, who was in splendid spirits, "that we congratulate him on his promotion and are ready to obey him without question."

"All right. He'll be glad to know that he has your approval."

"He might have the approval of worse men. I feel surging within me the talents of a great general, but I'm too young to get 'em recognized."

"You'll have to wait until the sections are not fighting each other, but are united against a common foe. But meanwhile I'll tell Colonel Sherburne that if he gets into a tight pinch not to lose heart as you are here."

Saluting Colonel Talbot and Lieutenant-Colonel St. Hilaire, Harry and Dalton rode to the head of the column, where Sherburne led. They ate their breakfast on horseback, and went swiftly down a valley in the general direction of the Potomac. The dawn had broadened into full morning, clear and bright, save for a small cloud that hung low in the southwest, which Sherburne noticed with a frown.

"That's a little cloud and it looks innocent," he said to Harry, "but I don't like it."

"Why not?"

"Because in the ten minutes that I've been watching it I've been able to notice growth. I'm weather-wise and we may have more rain. More rain means a higher Potomac. A higher Potomac means more difficulty in crossing it. More difficulty in crossing it means more danger of our destruction, and our destruction would mean the end of the Confederacy."

He spoke with deadly earnestness as he continued to look at the tiny dusky spot on the western sky. Harry had a feeling of awe. Again he realized that such mighty issues could turn upon a single hair. The increase or decrease of that black splotch might mean the death or life of the Confederacy. As he rode he watched it.

His heart sank slowly. The little baby cloud, looking so harmless,

43

was growing. He said to himself in anger that it was not, but he knew that it was. Black at the centre, it radiated in every direction until it became pale grey at the edges, and by and by, as it still spread, it gave to the southwest an aspect that was distinctly sinister.

Sherburne shook his head and the gravity of his face increased. As the cloud grew alarm grew with it in his mind.

"Maybe it will pass," said Harry hopefully.

"I don't think so. It's not moving away. It just hangs there and grows and grows. You're a woodsman, Harry, and you ought to feel it. Don't you think the atmosphere has changed?"

"I didn't have the courage to say so until you asked me, but it's damper. If I were posing as a prophet I should say that we're going to have rain."

"And so should I. Usually at this period of the year in our country we want rain, but now we dread it like a pestilence. At any other time the Potomac could rise or fall, whenever it pleased, for all I cared, but now it's life and death."

"Our doubts are decided and we've lost. Look, sir the whole southwest is dark now!"

"And here come the first drops!"

Sherburne sent hurried orders among the men to keep their ammunition and weapons dry, and then they bent their heads to the storm which would beat almost directly in their faces. Soon it came without much preliminary thunder and lightning. The morning that had been warm turned cold and the rain poured hard upon them. Most of the horsemen were wet through in a short time, and they shivered in their sodden uniforms, but it was a condition to which they were used, and they thought little of themselves but nearly all the while of the Potomac.

Few words were spoken. The only sounds were the driving of the rain and the thud of many hoofs in the mud. Harry often saw misty figures among the trees on the hills, and he knew that they were watched by hostile eyes as the Northern armies in Virginia, were always watched with the same hostility. It was impossible for Lee's men to make any secret march. The population, intensely loyal to the Union, promptly carried news of it to Meade or his generals.

Twice he pointed out the watchers to Sherburne who merely shrugged his shoulders.

"I might send out men and cut off a few of them," he said, "but for what good? Hundreds more would be left and we'd merely be burdened with useless prisoners. Here's a creek ahead, Harry, and look how muddy and foamy it is! It's probably raining harder higher up in the hills than it is here, and all these creeks and brooks go to swell the Potomac."

The swift water rose beyond their stirrups and there was a vast splashing as fifteen hundred men rode through the creek. It was a land of many streams, and a few miles farther on they crossed another, equally swollen and swift.

They had hoped that the rain, like the sudden violence of a summer shower, would pass soon, but the skies remained a solid grey and it settled into a steady solemn pour, cold and threatening, and promising to continue all day long. They could see that every stream they crossed was far above its normal mark, and the last hope that they might find the Potomac low enough for fording disappeared.

The watchers on the hills were still there, despite the rain, but they did no sharpshooting. Nor did the Southern force do damage to anybody or anything, as it passed. Near noon Sherburne resolved to build a fire in a cove protected by cliffs and heavy timber, and give his men warm food lest they become dispirited.

It was a task to set the wet wood, but the men of his command, used to forest life, soon mastered it. Then they threw on boughs and whole tree trunks, until a great bonfire blazed and roared merrily, thrusting out innumerable tongues of red and friendly flame.

"Is there anything more beautiful than a fine fire at such a time?" said St. Clair to Harry. "As it blazes and eats into the wood it crackles and those crackling sounds are words."

"What do the words say?"

"They say, 'Come here and stand before me. So long as you respect me and don't come too close I'll do you nothing but good. I'll warm you and I'll dry you. I'll drive the wet from your skin and your clothes, and I'll chase the cold out of your body and bones. I'll take hold of your depressed and sunken heart and lift it up again. Where you saw only grey and black I'll make you see gold and red. I'll warm and cook your food for you, giving you fresh life and strength. With my crackling coals and my leaping flames I'll change your world of despair into a world of hope.'"

"Hear! Hear!" said Happy Tom. "Arthur has turned from a sodden soldier into a giddy poet! Is any more poetry left in the barrel, Arthur?"

"Plenty, but I won't turn on the tap again to-day. I've translated for you. I've shown you where beauty and happiness lie, and you must do the rest for yourself."

They crowded about the huge fire which ran the entire length of the cove, and watched the cooks who had brought their supplies on horseback. Great quantities of coffee were made, and they had bacon and hard biscuits.

Although the rain still reached them in the cove they forgot it as they ate the good food—any food was good to them—and drank cup after cup of hot coffee. Youthful spirits rose once more. It wasn't such a bad day after all! It had rained many times before and people still lived. Also, the Potomac had risen many times before, but it always fell again. They were riding to clear the way for Lee's invincible army which could go wherever it wanted to go.

"Men on horseback looking at us!" hailed Happy Tom. "About fifty on a low hill on our right. Look like Yankee cavalrymen. Wonder what they take us for anyway!"

Harry, St. Clair, Langdon and Dalton walked to the edge of the cove, every one holding a cup of hot coffee in his hand. Sherburne was already there and with his glasses was examining the strange group, as well as he could through the sweeping rain.

"A scouting party undoubtedly," he said, "but weather has made their uniforms and ours look just about alike. It's equally certain though that they're Yankees. No troop of ours so small would be found here."

Harry was also watching them through glasses, and he took particular note of one stalwart figure mounted upon a powerful horse. The distance was too great to recognize the face, but he knew the swing of the broad shoulders. It was Shepard and once more he had the uneasy feeling winch the man always inspired in him. He appeared and reappeared with such facility, and he was so absolutely trackless that he had begun to appear to him as omniscient. Of course the man knew all about Sherburne's advance and could readily surmise its purpose.

"They're an impudent lot to sit there staring at us in that supercilious manner," said Colonel Talbot. "Shall I take the Invincibles, sir, and teach them a lesson?"

Sherburne smiled and shook his head.

"No, Colonel," he said, "although I thank you for the offer. They'd melt away before you and we'd merely waste our energies. Let them look as much as they please, and now that the boys have eaten their bread and bacon and drunk their coffee, and are giants again, we'll ride on toward the Potomac."

"Do we reach it to-day, sir?" asked Colonel Talbot.

"Not before to-morrow afternoon, even if we should not be interrupted. This is the enemy's country and we may run at any time into a force as large as our own if not larger."

"Thank you for the information, Colonel Sherburne. My ignorance of geography may appear astonishing to you, although we had to study it very hard at West Point. But I admit my weakness and I add, as perhaps some excuse, that I have lately devoted very little attention to the Northern states. It did not seem worth my time to spend much study on the rivers, and creeks and mountains of what is to be a foreign country—although I may never be able to think of John Carrington and many other of my old friends in the army as the foreigners they're sure to become. Has the thought ever occurred to you, Colonel, that by our victories we're making a tremendous lot of foreigners in America?"

"It has, Colonel Talbot, but I can't say that the thought has ever been a particularly happy one."

"It's the Yankees who are being made into foreigners," said Lieutenant-Colonel St. Hilaire. "The gallant Southern people, of course, remain what they are."

"They're going," said Harry. "They've seen enough of us."

The distant troop disappeared over the crest of the hill. Harry had noticed that Shepard led the way as if he were the ruling spirit, but he did not consider it necessary to say anything to the others about him. The trumpet blew and Sherburne's force, mounting, rode away from the cove. Harry cast one regretful glance back at the splendid fire which still glowed there, and then resigned himself to the cold and rain.

They did not stop again until far in the night. The rain ceased, but the whole earth was sodden and the trees on the low ridge, on which Sherburne camped, dripped with water. Spies might be all around them, but for the sake of physical comfort and the courage that he knew would come with it, he ordered another big fire built. Vigilant riflemen took turns in beating up the forests and fields for possible enemies, but the young officers once more enjoyed the luxury of the fire. Their clothing was dried thoroughly, and their tough and sinewy frames recovered all their strength and elasticity.

"To enjoy being dry it is well to have been wet," said Dalton sententiously.

"That's just like you, you old Presbyterian," said Happy Tom. "I suppose you'll argue next that you can't enjoy Heaven unless you've first burned in the other place for a thousand years."

"There may be something in that," said Dalton gravely, "although the test, of course, would be an extremely severe one."

"I know which way you're headed, George."

"Then tell me, because I don't know myself."

"As soon as this war is over you'll enter the ministry, and no sin will get by you, not even those nice little ones that all of us like to forgive."

"Maybe you're right, Happy, and if I do go into the ministry I shall at once begin long and earnest preparation for the task which would necessarily be the most difficult of my life."

"And may I make so bold as to inquire what it is, George?"

"Your conversion, Happy."

Langdon grinned.

"But why do you want to convert me, George? I'm perfectly happy as I am."

"For your own well being, Tom. Your happiness is nothing to me, but I want to make you good."

Both laughed the easy laugh of youth, but Harry looked long at Dalton. He thought that he detected in him much of the spirit of Stonewall Jackson, and that here was one who had in him the makings of a great minister. The thought lingered with him.

St. Clair was carefully smoothing out his uniform and brushing from it the least particle of mud. His first preoccupation always asserted itself at the earliest opportunity, and in a very short time he was the neatest looking man in the entire force. Harry, although he often jested with him about it, secretly admired this characteristic of St. Clair's.

"You boys sleep while you can," said Sherburne, "because we can't afford to linger in this region. Our safety lies in rapid marching, giving the enemy no chance to gather a large force and trap us. Make the best of your time because we're up and away an hour after midnight."

The young officers were asleep within ten minutes, but the vigilant riflemen patrolled the country in a wide circuit about them. Sherburne himself, although worn by hard riding, slept but little. Anxiety kept his eyes open. He knew that his task to find a passage for the army across the swollen Potomac was of the utmost importance and he meant to achieve it. He understood to the full the dangerous position in which the chief army of the Confederacy stood. His own force might be attacked at any moment by overwhelming numbers and be cut off and destroyed or captured, but he also knew the quality of the men he led, and he believed they were equal to any task.

As he sat by the fire thinking sombrely, a figure in the brush no great distance away was watching him. Shepard, the spy, in the darkness had passed with ease between the sentinels, using the skill of an Indian in stalking or approaching, and now, lying well hidden, almost flat upon his stomach, he surveyed the camp. He looked at Sherburne, sitting on a log and brooding, and he made out Harry's figure wrapped in a blanket and lying with his feet to the fire.

Shepard's mind was powerfully affected. An intense patriot, something remote and solitary in his nature had caused him to undertake this most dangerous of all trades, to which he brought an intellectual power and comprehension that few spies possess. As Harry had discovered long since, he was a most uncommon man.

Now Shepard as he gazed at this little group felt no hatred for them or their men. He had devoted his life to the task of keeping the Union intact. His work must be carried out in obscure ways. He could never hope for material reward, and if he perished it would be in some out-of-the-way corner, perhaps at the end of a rope, a man known to so few that there would be none to forget him. And yet his patriotism was so great and of such a fine quality that he viewed his enemies around the fire as his brethren. He felt confident that the armies of the North would bring them back into the Union, and when that occurred they must come as Americans on an equal footing with other Americans. They could not be in the Union and not of it.

But Shepard's feeling for his official enemies would not keep him from acting against them with all the skill, courage and daring that he possessed in such supreme measure. He knew that it was Sherburne's task to open a way for the Army of Northern Virginia to the Potomac and to find a ford, or, in cooperation with some other force, to build a bridge. It was for him to defeat the plan if he could.

While the rain all the day before had brought gloom to the hearts of Sherburne and his men it had filled his with joy, as he thought of the innumerable brooks and creeks that were pouring their swollen waters into the Potomac, already swollen too. He meant now to follow Sherburne's force, see what plan it would attempt, what point, perhaps, it would select for the bridge, and then bring the Union brigades in haste to defeat it.

It is said that men often feel when they are watched, although the watcher is invisible, but it was not so in Sherburne's case. He did not in the least suspect the presence of Shepard or of any foe, and the spy, after he had seen all he wished, withdrew, with the same stealth that had marked his coming.

An hour after midnight all were awakened and they rode away. The next day they reached the Potomac near Williamsport, where their pontoon bridge had been destroyed, and looked upon the wide stream of the Potomac, far too deep for fording.

"If General Lee is attacked on the banks of this river by greatly superior forces," said Sherburne, "he'll have no time to build bridges. If we didn't happen to be victorious our forces would have to scatter into the mountains, where they could be hunted down, man by man."

"But such a thing as that is unthinkable, sir," said Harry. "We may not win always, but here in the East we never lose. Remember Antietam and the river at our back."

"Right you are, Harry," said Sherburne more cheerfully. "The general will get us out of this, and here is where we must cross. The river may run down enough in two or three days to permit of fording. God grant that it will!"

"And so say I!" repeated Harry with emphasis.

"I mean to hold this place for our army," continued Sherburne.

"A reserved seat, so to speak."

"Yes, that's it. We must keep the country cleared until our main force comes up. It shouldn't be difficult. I haven't heard of any considerable body of Union troops between us and the river."

They made camp rapidly in a strong position, built their fires for cooking, set their horses to grazing and awaited what would come. It was a dry, clear night, and Harry, who had no duties, save to ride with a message at the vital moment, looked at once for his friends, the Invincibles.

St. Clair met him and held up a warning hand, while Happy touched his lip with his finger. Before the double injunction of silence and caution, Harry whispered:

"What's happened?"

"A tragedy," replied St. Clair.

"And a victory, too," said Happy Tom.

"I don't understand," said Harry.

"Then look and you will," said St. Clair.

He pointed to a small clear space in which Colonel Leonidas Talbot and Lieutenant-Colonel Hector St. Hilaire sat on their blankets facing each other with an empty cracker box between them, upon which their chess men were spread. The firelight plainly revealed a look of dismay upon the face of Colonel Talbot, and with equal plainness a triumphant expression upon that of Lieutenant-Colonel St. Hilaire.

"Colonel Talbot has lost his remaining knight," whispered St. Clair. "I don't know how it came about, but when the event occurred we heard them both utter a cry. Listen!"

"I fail even yet, Hector, to see just how it occurred." said Colonel Talbot.

"But it has occurred, Leonidas, and that's the main thing. A general in battle does not always know how he is whipped, but the whipping hurts just as much."

"You should not show too much elation over your triumph, Hector. Remember that he laughs best who laughs last."

"I take my laugh whenever I can, Leonidas, because no one knows who is going to laugh last. It may be that he who laughs in the present will also laugh at the end. What do you mean by that move, Leonidas?"

"That to you is a mystery, Hector. It's like one of Stonewall Jackson's flanking marches, and in due time the secret will be revealed with terrible results."

"Pshaw, Leonidas, you can't frighten a veteran like me. That for your move, and here's mine in reply."

The two grey heads bent lower over the board as the colonels made move after move. The youths standing in the shadow of the trees watched until the second time that night the two uttered a simultaneous cry. But they were very different in quality. Now Colonel Talbot's expressed victory and Lieutenant-Colonel St. Hilaire's consternation.

"Your bishop, Hector!" exclaimed Colonel Talbot. "Pious and able gentleman as he is, an honour to his cloth, he is nevertheless my captive."

"I admit that it was most unexpected, Leonidas. You have matched my victory with one of yours. It was indeed most skilful and I don't yet see what led to it."

"Did I not warn you a little while ago that you couldn't frighten me? I prepared a trap for you, and thus I rise from defeat to victory."

"At any rate we are about even on the evening's work, Leonidas, and we have made more progress than for the whole six months preceding. It seems likely now that we can finish our game soon."

A sudden crash of rifle fire toward the east and from a point not distant told them no. They rose to their feet, but they put the chessmen away very deliberately, while the young officers hastened to their posts. The fire continued and spread about them in a half circle, accompanied now and then by the deeper note of a light field gun. Sherburne made his dispositions rapidly. All the men remained on foot, but a certain number were told off to hold the horses in the centre of the camp.

"We're attacked by a large force," said Sherburne, "Our scouts gave us warning in time. Evidently they wish to drive us away from here because this will be the ford in case the river falls in time."

51

"Then you look for a sharp fight?"

"Without question. And remember that you're to avoid all risk if you can. It's not your business to get shot here, but it is your business, and your highly important business, to ride back to General Lee with the news of what's happening. In order to do that it's necessary for you to remain alive."

"I obey orders," said Harry reluctantly.

"Of course you do. Keep back with the men who are holding the horses. That fire is growing fast! I'm glad we were able to find a camp so defensible as this hill."

He hurried away to watch his lines and Harry remained at his station near the horses, where Dalton was compelled by the same responsibility to stay with him. It was the first time that Harry had been forced to remain a mere spectator of a battle raging around him, and while not one who sought danger for danger's sake, it was hard work to control himself and remain quiet and unmoved.

"I suspect they're trying to cut us off completely from our own army," he said to Dalton.

"Seems likely to me, too," said Dalton. "Wipe us out here, and hold the river for themselves. Our scouts assured us that there was no large force of the enemy in this region. It must have been gathered in great haste."

"In whatever way it was gathered, it's here, that's sure."

There was a good moon now, and, using his glasses, Harry saw many details of the battle. The attack was being pressed with great vigour and courage. He saw in a valley numerous bodies of cavalry, firing their carbines, and he saw two batteries, of eight light guns each, move forward for a better range. Soon their shells were exploding near the hill on which Harry stood, and the fire of the rifles, unbroken now, grew rapidly in volume.

But the men under Sherburne, youthful though most of them might be, were veterans. They knew every trick of war, and columns of infantry swept forward to meet the attack, preceded by the skirmishers, who took heavy toll of the foe.

"If they'd been able to make it a surprise they might have rushed us," said Harry.

"Nobody catches Sherburne sleeping," said Dalton.

"That's true, and because they can't they won't be able to overcome him here. Now there go our rifles! Listen to that crash. I fancy that about a thousand were fired together, and they weren't fired for nothing."

"No," said Dalton, "but the Yankees don't give way. You can see by their line of fire that they're still coming. Look there! A powerful body of horse is charging!"

It was unusual to see cavalry attack at night, and the spectacle was remarkable, as the moonlight fell on the raised sabres. But the defiant rebel yell, long and fierce, rose from the thicket, and, as the rifles crashed, the entire front of the charging column was burned away, as if by a stroke of lightning. But after a moment of hesitation they came on, only to ride deeper into a rifle fire which emptied saddles so fast that they were at last compelled to turn and gallop away.

"Brave men," said Harry. "A gallant charge, but it had to meet too many Southern rifles, aimed by men who know how to shoot."

"But their infantry are advancing through that wood," said Dalton. "Hear them cheering above the rifle fire!"

The Northern shout rang through the forest, and the rebel yell, again full of defiance, replied. The cavalry had been driven off, but the infantry and artillery were far from beaten. The sixteen guns of the two batteries were massed on a hill and they began to sweep the Southern lines with a storm of shells and shrapnel. The forest and the dark were no protection, because the guns searched every point of the Southern line with their fire. Sherburne's men were forced to give ground, before cannon served with such deadly effect.

"What will the colonel do?" asked Dalton. "The big guns give the Yankees the advantage."

"He'll go straight to the heart of the trouble," said Harry. "He'll attack the guns themselves."

He did not know actually in what manner Sherburne would proceed, but he was quite sure that such would be his course. The wary Southern leader instantly detailed a swarm of his best riflemen to creep through the woods toward the cannon. In a few minutes the gunners themselves were under the fire of hidden marksmen who shot surpassingly well. The gunners, the cannoneers, the spongers, the rammers and the ammunition passers were cut down with deadly certainty.

The captain of the guns, knowing that the terrible rifle fire was coming from the thickets, deluged the woods and bushes with shells and shrapnel, but the riflemen lay close, hugging the ground, and although a few were killed and more wounded, the vast majority crept closer and closer, shooting straight and true in the moonlight. The fire from the batteries became scattered and wild. Their crews were cut down so fast that not enough men were left to work the guns, and their commander reluctantly gave the order to withdraw to a less exposed position.

"Rifles triumphant over artillery," said Harry, who studied everything through his glasses; "but of course the dusk helped the riflemen."

"That's true," said Dalton, "but it takes good men like Sherburne to use the favouring chances. Now our boys are charging!"

The tremendous rebel yell swelled through the forest, and the Southern infantry rushed to the attack. Harry saw that the charge was successful, and his ears told him so too. The firing moved further and further away, and soon declined in volume.

"They've been beaten off," said Harry.

"At least for the time," said Dalton, "but I've an idea they'll hang on our front and may attack again in a day or so."

"How then are you and I to get through and tell General Lee that this is the place to bridge the Potomac, if it's to be bridged at all?"

Dalton shook his head.

"I don't know," he replied, "and I won't think about it until Colonel Sherburne gives his orders."

The sounds of battle died in the distant woods. The last shot, whether from cannon or rifle, was fired, and the Southern troops returned to their positions, which they began to fortify strongly. Sherburne appeared presently, his uniform cut by bullets in two or three places, but his body untouched. He drew Harry and Dalton aside, where their words could not be heard by anybody else.

"You two," he said, "were to report to General Lee when I thought fit. Well, the time has come; Harry, you go first, and, at a suitable moment, George will follow. We have news of surpassing importance. We took a number of prisoners in that battle and we were also lucky enough to rescue several of our men who had been held as captives. We've learned from them that General Meade, after making up his mind to pursue, followed straight behind us for a while, but he has now turned and gone southward in the direction of Frederick. He will cross South Mountain, advance toward Sharpsburg, and attempt to smash us here, with our backs to this swollen river. Why, some of the Federal leaders consider the Army of Northern Virginia as good as destroyed already!"

He spoke with angry emphasis.

"But it isn't," said Harry.

"No, it isn't. Doubtless General Lee will learn from scouts of his own of General Meade's flanking movement, but we mustn't take the chance. Moreover, we must tell him that this is the place for our army to cross. If the river runs down in two or three days we'll have a ford here."

"I'm ready to go at any moment," said Harry. "Night helping me, I may be able to ride through the lines of our enemies out there."

"No, Harry, you must not go that way. They're so vigilant that you would not have any possible chance. Nor can you ride. You must leave your horse behind."

"What way then must I go, sir?"

"By the river. We have gathered up a few small boats, used at the crossing here. You can row, can't you?"

"Fairly well, sir."

"'Twill do, because you're not to stay in the boat long. I want you to drop down the stream until you're well beyond the Federal lines. Then leave the boat and strike out across the country for General Lee. You know the way. You can buy or seize a horse, and you must not fail."

"I will not fail," said Harry confidently.

"You'll succeed if anybody will, and now you must be off. Your pistols are loaded, Harry? You may have to use them."

They did not delay a minute, going down the shelving shore to the Potomac, where a man held a small boat against the bank.

"Get in, Harry," said Sherburne "You'd better drop down three or four miles, at least. Good-by and good luck."

He shook hands with his colonel and Dalton, took the oars and pulled far out into the stream.

CHAPTER 4

A Herald to Lee

When he swept out upon the sullen bosom of the Potomac, Harry looked back only once. He saw two dim figures going up the bank, and, at its crest, a line of lights that showed the presence of the Southern force. There was no sound of firing, and he judged that the enemy had withdrawn to a distance of two or three miles.

The night had turned darker since the battle ceased, and not many stars were out. Clouds indicated that flurries of rain might come, but he did not view them now with apprehension. Darkness and rain would help a herald to Lee. The current was strong, and he did not have to pull hard, but, observing presently that the far shore was fringed with bushes, he sent the boat into their shadow.

He did not anticipate any danger from the southern shore, but the old inherited caution of the forest runners was strong within him. Under the hanging bushes he was well hidden, but, in some places, the flood in the river had turned the current back upon itself, and he was compelled to pull with vigour on the oars.

The clouds that had threatened did not develop much, and while the forests were dark, the surface of the river showed clearly in the faint moonlight. Any object upon it could be seen from either bank, and Harry was glad that he had sought the shelter of the overhanging bushes. He realized now that in this region, which was really the theatre of war, many scouts and skirmishers must be about.

The bank above him was rather high and quite steep, for which he was glad, as it afforded protection. A half mile farther down he came to the mouth of a creek coming in from the South, and just as he passed it he heard voices on the bank. He held his boat among the bushes on the cliff and listened. Several men were talking, but he judged them to be farmers, not soldiers. Yet they talked of the battle that night, and Harry surmised that they were looking at the lights in the Southern camp which might yet be visible from the high point on which they stood. He could not gather from their words whether they were Northern or Southern sympathizers, but it did not matter, as he had no intention of speaking to them, hoping only that they would go away in a few minutes and let him continue his journey unseen.

His hope speedily came to pass. He heard their voices sinking in the distance, and leaving the shelter of the bushes he pulled down the stream once more. Then he found that he had deceived himself about the clouds. If they had retired, they had merely recoiled, to use the French phrase, in order to gather again with greater force.

During his short stay among the bushes at the foot of the cliff the whole heavens had blackened and the air was surcharged with the heavy damp and density that betoken a coming storm. The lightning blazed across the river thrice, and he heard a mutter which was not that of cannon. Then came rain and a rushing wind and the surface of the river was troubled grievously. It rose up in waves like those of a lake, and Harry's boat rocked and tumbled so badly that in a few minutes it was half-full of water.

Fearing he might sink, carrying with him his great message, he pulled again, but fiercely now, for the southern bank and the shelter of the bushes, which, fortunately for him, grew here in the water's edge. He shoved his boat with all his might among them, as their tops snapped and crackled in the hurricane. But he knew he was safe there, and he continued to push until it reached the edge of the land.

The river would be swollen by another storm, but for the present it did not bother him greatly. He was more immediately concerned with his wish to get back to Lee as soon as possible, and he was grateful for that dense clump of bushes, growing in the very water's edge, because the wind was blowing like a hurricane and the waves were chasing one another on the Potomac, like the billows on a lake. He was a fair oarsman, but it would have taken greater skill than his to have kept his boat afloat in the tempestuous river.

The bushes formed an absolute protection. His boat swayed with them, which saved it from being damaged, and the overhanging lee of the cliff kept most of the rain from him. He also wrapped about his body the pair of blankets that he always carried, and he sat there not only in safety, but with a certain physical pleasure.

Once more amid surroundings with the like of which Henry Ware had been so familiar, the soul of his great ancestor seemed to have descended upon him. Most young officers, no matter how brave or how skilled in war, would have been awed and alarmed. He had no comrades at his elbow. There was no light, no friendly sound to encourage him, he was as truly alone, so far as his present situation was concerned, as any pioneer had ever been in the heart of the wilderness. But for him there was pleasure at that moment in being alone. He did not quiver when the thunder rolled and crashed above his head, and the lightning blazed in one Titanic sword slash after another across the surface of the river. Rather, the wilderness and majesty of the scene appealed to him. Leaning well back in his boat with his blankets closely wrapped about him, he watched it, and his soul rose with the storm.

Harry knew from its sudden violence that the rain would soon pass, and if the waves abated a little he would certainly take his boat into the river and try his fortunes again. Yet a precious hour was lost, and nothing could replace it. The thunder ceased by and by and there was only dim lightning on the far horizon. The waves began to abate, and, taking off his blankets, he pushed his boat once more into the stream.

It rocked prodigiously and shipped water, but by strenuous effort he kept it afloat, and as the wind sank still further he decided that he would seek the northern shore and disembark as soon as possible. It would be easier to steal through the thickets than to navigate what amounted to a wild sea. But the banks were yet too high and steep for a landing, and he continued to row, keeping now near the middle of the stream.

Wind and rain were dying fast, and he heard a sound behind uncommonly like the distant swish of oars. It sent an unpleasant thrill through him, because he wished to be alone on the river at that particular time, but his eyes, tracing a course through all the dusk and gloom, rested upon another boat, about two hundred yards away, containing a single occupant.

A farmer or a riverman, Harry thought, but to his great astonishment the man suddenly raised himself up a little and shouted to him in a tremendous voice to halt. Harry had not the least idea of stopping for anybody. He bent to his oars and rowed swiftly on. Again came that shout to halt, and it seemed more insolent to him than before. He put a few more ounces of strength into his arms and shoulders and increased his speed.

The pursuer, suddenly drawing in his oars, raised a rifle from the bottom of his boat, and fired point blank at the fugitive. The bullet whistled so near Harry that he felt his ear burn, and at first thought he was hit. He would have been glad to fire back, but his pistols could not

58

carry like his enemy's rifle, and there was nothing to do but flee. Once again he sought to draw a few more ounces of energy from his body. But the man behind him was a much greater oarsman than he and gained rapidly. The stranger, shouting another command to halt, to which no attention was paid, fired a second time, and the bullet went through the side of Harry's boat, barely scraping his knee as it passed.

His rage became intense. He had been shot at many times in battle, and many times he had fired his pistols into the opposing masses, but here upon this river a man sought his life, as the savages of old sought the hunter. Another glance showed him that pursuer had closed up half the distance between them, and, snatching one of the pistols from his belt, he fired. He knew that he had missed, as he saw the water spurt up beside the boat, but he thought that his bullet and the probability of more might delay the pursuit. Nevertheless the man came on as boldly and as fast as ever. If he fired a third time he could scarcely miss at such short range.

It seemed to Harry the gift of Heaven, that a whole pack of clouds should drift above them at that moment, deepening the obscurity and making the pursuing boat, although it was so near, a shapeless form in the mist. He could not see the features of the man, but he was able to discern his large and powerful figure, and he noticed the rhythmic manner in which his arms and shoulders worked at the oars. Obviously he had no chance to escape him by flight, and drawing his second pistol he fired. The bullet struck the boat but did no damage. The man came on faster than ever. Harry took a desperate resolution, and, whirling his boat about, he rowed it straight at his pursuer, who was now almost level with him. He intended to ram and take his chances. His movement was so quick and unexpected that it succeeded. The bow of his boat, helped perhaps by a wave, struck the other with such violence that both were shattered and sank instantly.

Harry went down with his craft, but in a few seconds came up again, his mouth and eyes full of muddy water. He was a splendid swimmer, and his eyes clearing in a moment he looked toward the northern shore, seeking an easy place for landing. They encountered ten feet away a large sun-browned face and two burning eyes.

"Shepard!" Harry gasped.

"And so it was you, Lieutenant Kenton. Perhaps if I had known it was you I wouldn't have fired upon you."

"Don't let that deter you. We're enemies."

"I merely said 'perhaps!' I like you, but that wouldn't keep me from stopping you by any method I could from reaching Lee."

"I'm sure it wouldn't. I like you, too, Mr. Shepard, but we're enemies here in this river, deadly enemies, and I mean to beat you off."

"One may mean to do a thing and yet not do it. I'm the larger and the more powerful. Besides, I'm toughened by superior age. You'd better surrender, Mr. Kenton. I don't want to do you any bodily harm."

"I admit that you're larger and stronger, but on land only. I'm the better swimmer. We're both floating now, but if you'll make a comparison, Mr. Shepard, you'll find that I'm doing it with the greatest ease. Take my advice, and swim to the southern bank of the river while I go to the northern. I say it in all good faith."

"I've no doubt of that, but the young are likely to over-estimate their powers. I'm a good swimmer, and you can't escape me."

"The important point is not whether I can escape you, but whether you can escape me. Since you have lost your boat and your rifle and we're in such a treacherous and unstable element as water, I occupy the superior position. The young may indeed over-estimate their powers, but in swimming at least I'm a competent critic. For instance, you're holding your shoulders too high, and you kick too much. You're splashing water, a useless waste of energy. Now observe me. The surface of this river is rough. Little waves are yet running upon it, but I float as easily as a fish, come up to see by the moon what time it is. It is not egotism on my part, merely a recognition of the facts, but I warn you, Mr. Shepard, to swim to the other shore and let me alone."

The two were not ten feet apart, and, despite the lightness of their talk, their eyes burned with eagerness and intensity. Harry knew that Shepard would not dream of turning back. Yet in the water he awaited the result with a confidence that he would not have felt on land.

"It's your move, Mr. Shepard," he said.

The intensity of Shepard's gaze increased, and Harry never took his eyes from those of his enemy. He intended like a prize fighter to read there what the man's next effort would be.

"I don't see that it's my move," said Shepard, as he floated calmly.

"You're following me for the purpose of capturing me."

"To capture you, or delay you. Meanwhile, it seems to me that I'm delaying you very successfully. I can't see that you're making much progress towards Lee."

"That depends upon which way this river is flowing. You note that we float gently with the stream."

"It's a poor argument. The Potomac flows directly by Washington, and if we were to float on we'd float into the heart of great Northern fortresses instead of Lee's camp."

"That's true as far as it goes, but it doesn't go far enough. I'm leaving the river soon. You can have it all then."

"Thanks, but I think I'll go with you, Lieutenant Kenton."

"Then come to the bottom!" exclaimed Harry, as he dived forward like a flash, seized Shepard by the ankles and headed for the bottom of the river with him. The water gurgled in his eyes and ears and nose, but he held on for many seconds, despite the man's desperate struggles. Then he was forced to let go and rise.

As his head shot above the stream he saw another shooting up in the same manner about fifteen feet away. Both were choked and gasping, but Harry managed to say:

"I didn't intend for you to come up so soon."

"I suppose not, but perhaps you didn't pause to think that when you rose I'd rise with you."

"Yes, that's true. It seems to me that matters grow complicated. Can't you persuade yourself, Mr. Shepard, to go and leave me alone? I really have no use for you here."

"I'd like to oblige you, Lieutenant Kenton, but I intend to see that you don't reach General Lee."

"Still harping upon that? It seems to me that you're a stupidly stubborn man. Don't you know that I'm going anyhow?"

Harry had never ceased to watch his eyes, and he saw there the signal of a coming movement. Shepard dived suddenly for him, intending to repeat his own trick, but the youth was like a fish in the water, and he darted to the right. The man came up grasping nothing. Harry laughed. The chagrin of Shepard compelled his amusement, although he liked the man.

"I wish you'd go away, Mr. Shepard," he said. "On land you could, perhaps, overpower me, but in the water I think I'm your master. All through my boyhood I devoted a great deal of my time to swimming. Dr. Russell of the Pendleton Academy—but you never knew him— used to say that if I would swim less and study more I could make greater pretensions to scholarship."

Shepard, swimming rather easily, regarded him thoughtfully.

"While we talk to each other in this more or less polite manner, Mr. Kenton," he said, "we must not forget that we're in deadly earnest. I mean to take you, and our scouts mean to take every other messenger who goes out from Colonel Sherburne's camp. You know, and I know, that if the Army of Northern Virginia does not reach in a few days that camp, where there is a ford in ordinary weather, it will be driven up against the Potomac and we can accumulate such great forces against it that it cannot possibly escape. Even at Sherburne's place its escape is more than doubtful, if it has to linger long."

"Yes, I know these things quite well, Mr. Shepard. I know also, as you do, that General Meade's army is not in direct pursuit, and, that in a flanking movement, he is advancing across South Mountain and toward Sharpsburg. It is a march well calculated and extremely dangerous to General Lee, if he does not hear of it in time. But he will hear of it soon enough. A comrade of mine, George Dalton, will tell him. Others from Colonel Sherburne's camp will tell him, and I mean to tell him too. I hope to be the first to do so."

Harry never deceived himself for a moment. He knew that although Shepard liked him, he would go to the uttermost to stop him, and as for himself, while he had a friendly feeling for the spy, he meant to use every weapon he could against him. Realizing that he could not linger much longer, as the chill of the water was already entering his body, he swam closer to Shepard, still staring directly into his eyes. How thankful he was now for those innumerable swimmings in the little river that ran near Pendleton! Everything learned well justifies itself some day.

Although there was but little moonlight they were so close together that they could see the eyes of each other clearly, and Harry detected a trace of uneasiness in those of Shepard. A good swimmer, the water nevertheless was not his element, and although a man of great physique and extraordinary powers, he longed for the solid earth under his feet.

Harry drew himself together as if he were going to dive, but instead of doing so suddenly raised himself in the water and shot forth his clenched tight fist with all his might. Shepard was taken completely by surprise and he sank back under the water, leaving a blood stain on its surface. Harry watched anxiously, but Shepard came up again in a moment or two, gasping and swimming wildly. The point of his jaw was presented fairly and Harry struck again as hard as he could in the water. Shepard with a choked cry went under and Harry, diving forward, seized his body, bringing it to the surface.

Shepard was senseless, but getting an arm under his shoulders Harry was able to swim with him to the northern shore, although it took nearly all his strength. Then he dragged him out upon the bank, and sank down, panting, beside him.

The great Civil War in America, the greatest of all wars until nearly all the nations of Europe joined in a common slaughter, was a humane war compared with other wars approaching it in magnitude. It did not occur to Harry to let Shepard drown, nor did he leave him senseless on the bank. As soon as his own strength returned he dragged him into a half-sitting position, and rubbed the palms of his hands. The spy opened his eyes.

"Good-by, Mr. Shepard," said Harry. "I'm bound to leave before you recover fully because then I wouldn't be your match. I'm sorry I had to hit you so hard, but there was nothing else to do."

"I don't blame you. It was man against man."

"The water was in my favour. I'm bound to admit that on land you'd have won."

"At any rate I thank you for dragging me out of the river."

"You'd have done as much for me."

"So I would, but our personal debts of gratitude can't be allowed to interfere with our military duty."

"I know it. Therefore I take a running start. Good-by."

"We'll meet again."

"But not on this side of the Potomac. It may happen when the Army of Northern Virginia and the Army of the Potomac go into battle on the other side of the river."

Harry darted into the forest, and ran for a half-hour. He meant to put as much distance as possible between Shepard and himself before the latter's full strength returned. He knew that Shepard would follow, if he could, but it was not possible to trail one who had a long start through dark and wet woods.

He came through the forest and into a meadow surrounded by a rail fence, on which he sat until his breath came back again. He had forgotten all about his wet uniform, but the run was really beneficial to him as it sent the blood leaping through his veins and warmed his body.

"So far have I come," said Harry, "but the omens promise a hard march."

He had his course fixed very clearly, and a veteran now in experience, he could guide himself easily by the moon and stars. The clouds were clearing away and a warm wind promised him dry clothing, soon. Long afterward he thought it a strange coincidence that his cousin, Dick Mason, in the far South should have been engaged upon an errand very similar in nature, but different in incident.

He crossed the meadow, entered an orchard and then came to a narrow road. The presence of the orchard indicated the proximity of a farmhouse, and it occurred to Harry that he might buy a horse there. The farmer was likely to be hostile, but risks must be taken. He drew his pistols. He knew that neither could be fired after the thorough wetting in the river, but the farmer would not know that. He saw the house presently, a comfortable two-story frame building, standing among fine shade trees. Without hesitation he knocked heavily on the door with the butt of a pistol.

He was so anxious to hasten that his blows would have aroused the best sleeper who ever slept, and the door was quickly opened by an elderly man, not yet fully awake.

"I want to buy a horse."

"Buy a horse? At this time of the night?"

He was about to slam the door, but Harry put his foot over the sill and the muzzle of his pistol within six inches of the man's nose.

"I want to buy a horse," he repeated, "and you want to sell one to me. I think you realize that fact, don't you?"

"Yes, I do," replied the man, looking down the muzzle of the big horse pistol.

"Come outside and close the door behind you. I know you haven't on many clothes, but the night's warm, and you need fresh air."

The man with the muzzle of the pistol still near his nose, obeyed. But as he looked at the weapon he also had a comprehensive view of the one who held it.

"Wet ain't you?" he said.

"Do you think it necessary to put it in the form of a question?"

"I don't like to say, unless I'm shore."

"Where do you keep your horses?"

"In the barn here to the left. What kind of a horse did you think you'd keer fur most, stranger?"

"The biggest, the strongest and fastest you've got"

"I thought mebbe you'd want one with wings, you 'pear to be in such a pow'ful hurry. I wish you wouldn't keep that pistol so near to my nose. 'Sides, you've gethered so much mud an' water 'bout you that you ain't so very purty to look at!"

"It's your own mud and water. I didn't bring it into this country with me."

"Which means that you don't belong in these parts. I reckon lookin' at you that you wuz one o' them rebels that went to Gettysburg and then come back ag'in."

"Exactly right, Mr. Farmer. I'm an officer in General Lee's army."

"Then I wuz right 'bout you needin' a horse with wings. An' I guess all the men in your army need horses with wings. Don't be in such a tarnal hurry. You're goin' to stay right up here with us, boarders, so to speak, till the war is over."

Harry laughed.

"Kind of you," he said, "but here is the stable and do you open the stall doors one by one, and let me see the horses. At the first sign of any trick I pull the trigger."

"Well, as I don't like violence I'll show you the horses. Here's the grey mare, five years old, swift but can't last long. This is old Rube, nigh onto ten, mighty strong, but as balky as a Johnny Reb hisself. Don't want him! No? Then I think that's about all."

"No it's not! You open that last stall door at once!"

The farmer made a wry face, and threw back the door with a slam. Harry still covering the man with the pistol that couldn't go off, saw a splendid bay horse about four years old.

"Holding out on me, were you?" he said. "Did you think a Confederate officer could be fooled in that manner?"

"I reckon I oughtn't to have thought so. I've always heard that the rebels had mighty good eyes for Yankee horseflesh."

"I'll let that pass, because maybe it's true. Now, saddle and bridle him quicker than ever before in your life."

The farmer did so, and Harry took care to see that the girth was secure.

"At how much did you value this horse?" he asked.

"I did put him down at two hundred dollars, but I reckon he's worth nothin' to me now."

"Here's your money. When General Lee goes through the enemy's country he pays for what he takes."

He thrust a roll of good United States bills into the astonished man's hand, and sprang upon the horse. Then he turned from the stable and rode swiftly up the road, but not so swiftly that he did not hear a bullet singing past his ears. A backward glance showed him an elderly farmer in his night clothes standing on his porch and reloading his rifle.

"Well, I can't blame you, I suppose," said Harry. "You can guess pretty well what I am, and it's your business to stop me."

But he rode fast enough to be far beyond the range of a second bullet, and maintained a good pace for a long time, through hilly and wooded country. His uniform dried upon him, and his hardy form felt no ill result from the struggle in the river. The horse was strong and spirited, and Harry knew that he could carry him without weariness to Lee. He looked upon his mission as already accomplished, but his ambition to reach the commander-in-chief first was yet strong.

He rode throughout the rest of the night and dawn and the pangs of hunger came together. But he decided that he would not turn from his path to seek food. He would go on straight for Lee and let hunger have its way. He had a splendid horse under him and he was faring quite as well as he had a right to expect. He thought of Shepard, and felt pity for him. The man had only striven to do his duty, and while he had used force he had been very courteous and polite about it. Harry was bound to acknowledge that his had been a very chivalrous enemy and only his superiority in swimming had enabled him to win over Shepard. He was glad that he had saved him and had left him on the bank, so to speak, to dry.

Then Shepard faded away with the mists and vapours that were retreating before a brilliant dawn. The country was high, rolling, and the foliage, although much browned by the July sun, which was unusually hot that year, was still dense. Most of the hills were heavy with forest, but all the valleys between were fertile and well cultivated. With the dew of the morning fresh upon it the whole region was refreshing and soothing to the eye with a look of peace, where in reality there was no peace. Many thin columns of smoke lying blue against the silver sky told where farmhouses stood, and hunger suddenly seized upon Harry again.

Hunger is natural to youth, and his severe exertions all through the night had greatly increased it. It became both a pain and a weakness. His shoulders drooped with fatigue, and he felt that he must have food or faint by the way.

He was ashamed of his physical weakness, but he knew that unless he found food his faintness would increase, and hunger alone would stop him, where so able a man as Shepard could not. His uniform, faded anyhow, was so permeated with the dried mud of the river that it would take a keen eye to tell whether it was Federal or Confederate, and he need not disclose his identity in this region, which was so strongly for the Union. He made up his mind quickly and rode for the nearest farmhouse.

Harry knew that he was inviting risks. His pistols were still useless but they would be handy for threats, and he should be able to take care of himself at a farmhouse.

The house that he had chosen was only a few hundred yards away, its white walls visible among trees, and the clatter of his horse's hoofs brought a man from a barn in the rear. Harry noted him keenly. He was youngish, stalwart and the look out of his blue eyes was fearless. He came forward slowly, examining his visitor, and his manner was not altogether hospitable. Harry decided that he had to deal with a difficult customer but he had no idea of turning back.

"Good morning," he said politely.

"Good morning."

"I wish some breakfast and I will pay. I've ridden all night in our service."

"You've so much dried mud on you that you look as if you'd been passin' through a river."

"Correct. That's exactly what happened."

"But there's none on your horse."

"He didn't pass with me. I'm willing to answer any reasonable number of questions, but, as I told you before, I ride on an important service. I must have breakfast at once, and I'll pay."

"Whose service? Ours or Reb's?"

"A military messenger can't answer the chance questions of those by the roadside. I tell you I want breakfast at once."

"Fine horse you ride, stranger. How long have you had him?"

"All this year."

"Funny. When I saw him last week he belonged to Jim Kendall down by the Potomac, an' livin' on this very road, too."

"It isn't half as funny as you think. Hands up! Now call to your wife as loud as you can to bring me coffee and food at the gate! I know they're ready in the kitchen. I can smell 'em here. Out with it, call as fast as and as loud as you can, or off goes the top of your head!"

Although a horse pistol held in a firm hand was thrust under his nose, the man's blue eyes glared hate and defiance, and his mouth did not open. Harry, in his excitement and anger, forgot that the charge in his weapon was ruined and hence it was no acting with him when his own eyes blazed down at the other and he fairly shouted:

"I give you until I can count ten to call your wife! One! two! three! four! five! six! seven! eight! nine!—"

"Sophy! Sophy!" cried the farmer, who saw death flaming in the eyes that looked into his, "Come! Come a-runnin'!"

A good looking young woman threw open a door and ran, frightened, toward the gate, where she saw her husband under the pistol muzzle of a wild and savage looking man on horseback.

"Sophy," said the farmer, "bring this infernal rebel a cup of coffee and a plate of bread and meat. If it weren't for his pistol I'd drag him off his horse and carry him to General Meade, but he's got the drop on me!"

"And Sophy," said Harry, who was growing cooler, "you make it a big tin cup of coffee and you see that the plate is piled high with meat and bread. Now don't you make one mistake. Don't you come back with any weapon in your hand in place of food, and don't you fire on me from the house with the family rifle. You're young and you're good looking, and, doubtless the widow of our friend here with the upraised hands, wouldn't have to wait long for another husband just as good as he is."

The woman paled a little, and Harry knew that some thought of the family rifle had been in her mind. The husband's glare became ferocious.

"You can take your hands down," said Harry. "I've no wish to torture you, and I'm satisfied now that you're not armed."

The man dropped his arms and the woman hurried to the kitchen. Harry did not watch her, but kept his eyes continually upon the man, who he knew would take advantage of his first careless moment, and spring for him like a tiger. A pistol that he couldn't fire wouldn't be of much use to him then.

But the woman returned with a big tin cup of smoking coffee and a plate piled high with bread and bacon and beefsteak. It was a welcome sight. The aspect of the whole world became brighter at once, and the pulse of hope beat high. But happiness did not make him relax caution.

"Stand back about ten feet more," he said to the man, "I don't like your looks."

"What's the matter with my looks?"

"It's not exactly your looks I mean, though they're scarcely worthy of the lady, your wife, but it's rather your attitude or position which reminds me of a lion or a tiger about to spring upon something it hates."

The man, with a savage growl, withdrew a little.

"I'd like to put a bullet through you," he said.

"I've no doubt of it, your eyes show it, but before I take a polite leave of you I want to tell you that I did not steal this horse from your friend, Jim Kendall. I paid for it at his own valuation."

"Confederate money that won't be worth a dollar a bale before long."

"Oh, no, bills that were made and stamped at Washington, and I pay for this breakfast in silver."

He dropped it into the hand of the woman, as he took the huge cup of coffee from her. Then he drank deep and long, and again and again, draining the last drop of the brown liquid.

"I hope it's burnt the lining out of your throat," said the man savagely.

"It was warm, but I like it that way. It was good indeed, and I'm sorry, Madame, that you have such a violent and ill-tempered husband. Maybe your next will be a much better man."

"John is neither violent nor ill-tempered. He's never said a harsh word to me since we were married. But he hates the rebels dreadfully."

"That's too bad. I don't hate him and I'm glad you can give him a good character. A man's own wife knows best. Now, I'm going to eat this breakfast as I ride on. You'll find the plate on the fence a quarter of a mile ahead."

He bowed to both, and still keeping a wary eye on the man, thrust his pistol into his belt, and as his horse moved forward at a swift and easy gait he began to eat with a ravenous appetite.

A backward glance showed husband and wife still gazing at him. But it was only for a moment. They ran into the house and a little further on Harry looked back again. They had reappeared and he almost expected to hear again the whistle of a rifle shot, fired from a window. But the distance was much too great, and he devoted renewed attention to the demands of hunger.

When he had finished his breakfast he put the plate upon the fence as he had promised, and, looking back for the last time, he saw an American flag wave to and fro on the roof of the house. He felt a thrill of alarm. It must be a signal concerning him and it could be made only to his enemies. Speaking sharply to his horse, he urged him into a gallop.

CHAPTER 5

The Dangerous Road

The road led in the general direction of Lee's army and Harry knew that if he followed it long enough he was bound to reach his commander, but the two words "long enough" might defeat everything. Undoubtedly a Federal force was near, or the farmer and his wife would not be signalling from the roof of their house.

A plucky couple they were and he gave them all credit, but he was aware that while he had secured breakfast from them they had put the wolves upon his trail. There were high hills on both the right and left of the road, and, as he galloped along he examined them through his glasses for flags answering the signal on the house. But he saw nothing and the thickness of the forest indicated that even if the signals were made there it was not likely he could see them.

Now he wisely restrained the speed of his horse, so full of strength and spirit that it seemed willing to run on forever, and brought him down to a walk. He had an idea that he would soon be pursued, and then a fresh horse would be worth a dozen tired ones.

The road continued to run between high, forested hills, splendid for ambush, and Harry saw what a danger it was not to have knowledge of the country. He understood how the Union forces in the South were so often at a loss on ground that was strange to them.

The road now curved a little to the left, and a few hundred yards ahead another from the east merged with it. Along this road the forest was thinner, and upon it, but some distance away, he saw bobbing heads in caps, twenty, perhaps, in number. He knew at once that they were the enemy, called by the signal, and leaning forward he spoke in the ear of his good horse.

"You and I haven't known each other long," he said, "but we're good friends. I paid honest and sufficient money for you, when I could have ridden away on you without paying a cent. I know you have a powerful frame and that your speed is great. I really believe you're the fastest runner in all this part of the state. Now, prove it!"

The horse stretched out his neck, and the road flew behind him, his body working like a mighty machine perfectly attuned, even to its minutest part. Harry's words had met a true response. He heard a cry on the cross road, and the bobbing heads came forward much faster. Either they had seen him or they had heard the swift beat of his horse's hoofs. Loud shouts arose, but he saw the uniforms of the men, and he knew that they belonged to the Northern army.

He went past the junction of the roads, as if he were flying, but he was not a bit too soon, as he heard the crack of rifles, and bullets struck in the earth behind him. He knew that they would follow, hang on persistently, but he had supreme confidence in the speed and strength of his horse, and youth rode triumphant. It was youth more than anything else that made him raise himself a little in his saddle, look back to his pursuers and fling to them a long, taunting cry, just as Henry Ware more than once had taunted his Indian pursuers before disappearing in a flight that their swiftest warriors could not match.

But the little band of Union troopers clung to the chase. They too had good horses, and they knew that the man before them was a Southern messenger, and in those hot July days of 1863 all military messages carried on the roads north of the Potomac were important. The fate of an army or a nation might turn upon any one of them, and the lieutenant who led the little Union troop was aware of it. He was a man of intelligence and a consuming desire to overtake the lone horseman lay hold of him. He knew, as well as any general, that since Gettysburg the fate of the South was verily trembling in the balance, and the slightest weight somewhere might decide the scales. So he resolved to hang on through everything and the chances were in his favour. It was his own country. The Federal troops were everywhere, and any moment he might have aid in cutting off the fugitive.

When Harry eased his horse's flight he saw the troop, very distant but still pursuing, and he read the mind of the Union leader. He was saving his mounts, trailing merely, in the hope that Harry would exhaust his own horse, after which he and his men would come on at great speed.

Harry looked down at his horse and saw that he was heaving with his great effort. He knew that he had made a mistake in driving him so hard at first, and with the courage of which only a young veteran would have been capable he brought the animal almost to a walk, and resolutely kept him there, while the enemy gained. When they were almost within rifle shot he increased his speed again, but he did not seek for the present to increase his gain.

As long as their bullets could not reach him his horse should merely go stride for stride with theirs, and when the last stretch was reached, he would send forward the brave animal at his utmost speed. His were the true racing tactics drawn from his native state. He had no doubt of his ability to leave his pursuers far behind when the time came, but his true danger was from interference. He too knew that many Union cavalry troops were abroad, and he watched on either flank for them as he rode on. At the crest of every little hill he swept the whole country, but as yet he saw nothing but peaceful farmhouses.

The day was clear and bright, not so warm as its predecessors, and he calculated by the sun that he was going straight toward Lee. He knew that a great army always marched slowly, and he was able to reckon with accuracy just how far the Army of Northern Virginia had come since Gettysburg. He should reach it in the morning, with full information about the Potomac, and the best place for a crossing.

He arrived at the crest of a hill higher than the others, and saw the Union troop, about a quarter of a mile behind, stop beside a clump of tall trees. Their action surprised Harry, who had thought they would never quit as long as they could find his trail. To his further surprise he saw one of the men dismount and begin to climb the tallest of the trees. Then he brought his glasses into play.

He saw the climber go up, up, until he had reached the last bough that would support him. Then he drew some thing from his pocket which he unrolled and began to wave rapidly. It was a flag and through his powerful glasses Harry clearly saw the Stars and Stripes. It was evident that they were signalling, but when one signals one usually signals to somebody. His breath shortened for a moment. He believed that the man in the tree was talking with his flag about the fugitive. Where was the one to whom he was talking?

He looked to both left and right, searching the fields and the forests, and saw nothing. Then, as he was sweeping his glasses again in a half curve he caught a glimpse of something straight ahead that made the great pulse in his throat beat hard. About a mile in front of him another man in a tree was waving a flag and beneath the tree were horsemen.

Harry knew now that the two flags were talking about the Confederate messenger between. The one behind said: "Look out! He's young, riding a bay horse and he's coming directly toward you," to which the one in front replied, "We're waiting. He can't escape us. There are fields with high fences on either side of the road and if he manages to break through the fence he's an easy capture in the soft and muddy ground there."

Harry thought hard and fast, while the two flags talked so contemptuously about him. The fields were unquestionably deep with mud from the heavy rains, but he must try them. It was lucky that he had seen the flags while both forces were out of rifle shot. He decided for the western side, sprang from his horse and threw down a few rails. In a half minute he was back on his horse, leaped him over the fence, and struck across the field.

It had been lately ploughed and the going was uncommonly heavy. It would be just as heavy however for his pursuers, and his luck in seeing their signals would put him out of range before they reached the field. But it was a wide field and his horse's feet sank so deep in the mud that he dismounted and led him. When he was two-thirds of the way across a shout told him that the two forces had met, and had discovered the ruse of the fugitive. It did not take much intelligence to understand what he had done, because he was yet in plain sight, and a few of the cavalrymen took pot shots at him, their bullets falling far short. Harry in his excited condition laughed at these attempts. Almost anything was a triumph now. He shook his fist at them and regretted that he could not send back a defiant shot.

The cavalrymen conferred a little. Then a part pursued across the field, and two detachments rode along its side, one to the north and the other to the south. Harry understood. If the mud held him back sufficiently they might pass around the field and catch him on the other side. He continued to lead his horse, encouraging him with words of entreaty and praise.

"Come on!" he cried. "You won't let a little mud bother you. You wouldn't let yourself be overtaken by a lot of half-bred horses not fit to associate with you?"

The brave animal responded nobly, and what had been the far edge of the field was rapidly coming nearer. Beyond it lay woods. But the flanking movement threatened. The two detachments were passing around the field on firm ground, and Harry knew that he and his good horse must hasten. He talked to him continually, boasting about him, and together they reached the fence, which he threw down in all haste. Then he led his weary horse out of the mud, sprang upon his back and galloped into the bushes.

He knew that the horses passing around the field on firm ground would be fresh, and that he must find temporary hiding, at least as soon as he could. He was in deep thickets now and he galloped on, careless how the bushes scratched him and tore his uniform. The Union cavalry would surely follow, but he wanted a little breathing time for his horse, and in eight or ten minutes he stopped in the dense undergrowth. The horse panted so hard that any one near would have heard him, but there was no other sound in the thicket. The rest was valuable for both. Harry was able to concentrate his mind and consider, while the panting of the horse gradually ceased, and he breathed with regularity. The young lieutenant patted him on the nose and whispered to him consolingly.

"Good, old boy," he said, "you've brought me safely so far. I knew that I could trust you."

Then he stood quite still, with his hand stroking the horse's nose to keep him silent. He had heard the first sounds of search. To his right was the distant beat of hoofs and men's voices. Evidently they were going to make a thorough search for him, and he decided to resume his flight, even at the risk of being heard.

He led the horse again, because the forest was so dense that one could scarcely ride in it, and he thought, for a while, that he had thrown off the pursuit, but the voices came again, and now on his left. They had never relaxed the hunt for an instant. They had a good leader, and Harry admitted that in his place he would have done the same.

The country grew rougher, being so steep and hilly that it was not easy of cultivation, and hence remained clothed in dense forest and undergrowth. Twice more Harry heard the sound of pursuing voices and hoofs, and then the noise of running water came to his ears. Twenty yards farther and he came to a creek flowing between high banks, on which the forest grew so densely that the sun was scarcely able to reach the water below.

The creek at first seemed to be a bar to his advance, but thinking it over he led his horse carefully down into the stream, mounted him and rode with the current, which was not more than a foot deep. Fortunately the creek had a soft bottom and there was no ringing of hoofs on stones.

He went slowly, lest the water splash too much, and kept a wary watch on the banks above, which were growing higher. He did not know where the creek led, but it offered both a road and concealment, and it seemed that Providence had put it there for his especial help.

He rode in the bed of the stream fully an hour, and then emerged from the hills into a level and comparatively bare country. It was a region utterly unknown to him, but with his splendid idea of direction and the sun to guide him he knew his straight course to Lee. The country before him seemed to be given up wholly to grass, as he noticed neither corn nor wheat. He saw several farm hands, but decided to keep away from them. That was no country for the practice of horsemanship by a lone Confederate soldier, nor did he like to be the fox in a fox hunt.

Yet the fox he was. He chose a narrow road leading between cedars, and when he had advanced upon it a few hundred yards he heard the sound of a trumpet behind him, and at the edge of the woods that he had left. He saw horsemen in blue emerging and he had no doubt that they were the same men whom he had eluded in the thickets.

"Their pursuit of me is getting to be a habit," he said to himself with the most intense annoyance. "It's a good thing, my brave horse, that you've had a long rest."

He shook up the reins and began to gallop. He heard a faint shout in the distance and saw the troopers in pursuit. But he did not fear them now. Numerous fences would prevent them from flanking him, and he saw that the road led on, straight and level. He shook the reins again and the horse lengthened his stride.

He felt so exultant that he laughed. It would be easy enough now to distance this Union troop. Then the laugh died suddenly on his lips. A bullet whistled so near his face that it almost took away his breath. An elderly farmer standing in his own door had fired it, and Harry snatched one of the pistols from his own belt, remembering then with rage that it could not be fired. He shouted to his horse and made him run faster.

A bullet struck the pommel of his saddle and glanced off. A boy in an orchard had fired it. A load of bird-shot, a handful it seemed to Harry, flew about his ears. A bent old man who ought to have been sitting on a porch in a rocking chair had discharged it from the edge of a wood. A squirrel hunter on a hill took a pot shot at him and missed.

Harry was furious with anger. Decidedly this was no place for a visitor from the South. He did not detect the faintest sign of hospitality. Men and women alike seemed to dislike him. A powerful virago hurled a stone at his head, which would have struck him senseless had it not missed, and a farmer standing by a fence had a shotgun cocked and ready to be fired as he passed, but Harry, snatching one of the useless pistols from his belt, hurled it at him with all his might. It struck the man a glancing blow on the head, felling him as if he had been shot, and then Harry, thinking quickly, acted with equal quickness.

He reined in his horse with such suddenness that he nearly shot from the saddle. Then he leaped down, seized the shotgun from under the hands of the fallen man, sprang on his horse and was away again, sending back a cry of defiance.

Harry had never before in his life been so furious. To be hunted thus by a whole countryside, as if he were a mad dog, was intolerable. It was not only a threat to one's life, it was also an insult to one's dignity to be treated as an animal. Although he was armed now the insult continued. The call of the trumpet sounded almost without ceasing, and the Union troopers uttered many shouts as do those who chase the fox, although Harry knew that their cries were intended to rouse the farmers who might head him off.

The chase grew hotter, but he felt better with the shotgun. It was a fine double-barrelled weapon of the latest make, and he hoped that it was loaded with buckshot. He was a sharpshooter, and he could give a good account of any one who came too near.

Yet with the trumpet shrilling continually behind him the huntsmen gathered fast on either flank. It was yet the day when nearly every house in America, outside a town, contained a rifle, and bullets fired from a distance began to patter around Harry and his horse. The riflemen were too far away to be reached with the shotgun, and it seemed inevitable to him that in time a bullet would strike him. He was truly the fox, and he knew that nothing could save him but forest.

It was in his favour that the country was so broken and wooded so heavily, and fixing his eyes on trees a half-mile ahead he raced for them. If none of this yelling pack dragged him down he felt sure that he might escape again in the forest. The trees swiftly came nearer, but the shots on either flank increased. More than ever he felt like the fox with the hounds all about him, and just one slender chance to reach the burrow ahead.

He felt his horse shake and knew that he had been hit. Yet the brave animal ran on as well as ever, despite the triumphant shout behind, which showed that he must be leaving a trail of blood. But the woods, thick and inviting, were near, and he believed that he would reach them. The horse shook again, much more violently than before, and then fell to his knees. Harry leaped off, still clutching the shotgun, just as the brave animal fell over on his side and began to breathe out his life.

He heard again that shout of triumph, but he was one who never gave up. He had alighted easily on his feet. The trees were not more than fifteen yards away and he disappeared among them as bullets clipped bark and twigs about him.

He breathed a deep sigh of thankfulness when he entered the forest. It was so dense, and there was so much undergrowth that the horsemen could not follow him there. If they came on foot, and spread out, as they must, to hunt him, he had the double-barrelled shotgun and it was a deadly weapon. The fox had suddenly become the panther, alert, powerful, armed with claws that killed.

Harry went deep into the thickets before he sat down. He had no doubt that they would follow him, but at present he was out of their sight and hearing. He felt a mixture of elation and sadness, elation over his temporary escape, and sadness over the loss of his gallant horse. But one could not dwell long on regrets at such a time, and, advancing a little farther, he sat down among the densest bushes that he could find with the shotgun across his knees.

Now Harry saw that the horse had really done all that it was possible for him to do. He had brought him to the wood, and within he would have been a drawback. A man on foot could conceal himself far more easily. Everything favoured him There were bushes and vines everywhere and he could be hidden like a deer in its covert.

He looked up at the sun shining through the tops of the trees and saw that he had kept to his true course. His flight had taken him directly toward Lee at a much faster pace than he would have come otherwise. The enemy had driven him on his errand at double speed. He felt that he could spare a little time now, while he waited to see what the pursuit would do.

His feeling of exultation was now unalloyed. Deep in the forest with his foes looking for him in vain, the spirit of Henry Ware was once more strong within him. He was the reincarnation of the great hunter. He lay so still, clasping the shotgun, that the little creatures of the woods were deceived. A squirrel ran up the trunk of an oak six feet away, and stood fearlessly in a fork with his bushy tail curved over his back. A small grey bird perched on a bough just over Harry's head and poured out a volume of song. Farther away sounded the *tap tap* of a woodpecker on the bark of a dead tree.

Harry, although he did not move, was watching and listening with intense concentration, but his ears now would be his surest signals. He could not see deep in the thickets, but he could hear any movement in the underbrush a hundred yards away. So far there was nothing but the hopping of a rabbit. The bird over his head sang on. There was no wind among the branches, not even the flutter of leaves to distract his attention from anything that might come on the ground.

He rejoiced in this period of rest, of the nerves, rather than purely physical. He had been keyed so high that now he relaxed entirely, and soon lay perfectly flat, but with the shotgun still clasped in his arms. He had a soft couch. Under him were the dead leaves of last year, and over him was the pleasant gloom of thick foliage, already turning brown. The bird sang on. His clear and beautiful note came from a point directly over his head, but Harry could not see his tiny body among the leaves. He became, for a little while, more interested in trying to see him than in hearing his pursuers.

It was annoying that such a volume of sound should come from a body that could be hidden by a leaf. If a man could shout in proportion to his own size he might be heard eight to ten miles away. It was an interesting speculation and he pursued it. While he was pursuing it his mind relaxed more and more and travelled farther and farther away from his flight and hiding. Then his heavy eyelids pulled down, and, while his pursuers yet searched the thickets for him, he slept.

But his other self, which men had thought of as far back as Socrates, kept guard. When he had slept an hour a tiny voice in his ear, no louder than the ticking of a watch, told him to awake, that danger was near. He obeyed the call, sleep was lifted from him and he opened his eyes. But with inherited caution he did not move. He still lay flat in his covert, trusting to his ears, and did not make a leaf move about him.

His ears told him that leaves were rustling not very far away, not more than a hundred feet. His power of hearing was great, and the forest seemed to make it uncommonly sensitive and delicate.

He knew that the rustling of the leaves was made by a man walking. By and by he heard his footfalls, and he knew that he wore heavy boots, or his feet would not have crushed down in such a decisive manner. He was looking for something, too, because the footfalls did not go straight on, but veered about.

Harry was well aware that it was a Union soldier, and that he was the object of his search. He was a clumsy man, not used to forests, because Harry heard him stumble twice, when his feet caught on vines. Nor was any comrade near, or he would have called to him for the sake of companionship. Harry judged that he was originally a mill hand, and he did not feel the least alarm about him, laughing a little at his clumsiness and awkwardness, as he trod heavily among the bushes, tripped again on the vines, and came so near falling that he could hear the rifle rattle when it struck a tree. He did not have the slightest fear of the man, and at last, raising his head, he took a look.

All his surmises were justified. He saw a great hulking youth of heavy and dull countenance, carrying a rifle awkwardly, his place obviously around some town and not in the depths of a forest, looking for a wary enemy, who knew more of the wilderness than he could ever learn in all his life. Harry saw that he was perspiring freely and that he looked more like the hunted than the hunter. His eyes expressed bewilderment. He was obviously lonely and apprehensive, not because he was a coward, but because the situation was so strange to him.

Besides his rifle he carried a large knapsack, so much distended that Harry knew it to be full of food. It was this that decided him. A soldier, like an army, must travel on his stomach, and he wanted that knapsack. Moreover he meant to get it. He levelled his shotgun and called in a low tone, but a tone so sharp that it could be heard distinctly by the one to whom it was addressed:

"Throw up your hands at once!"

The man threw them up so abruptly that the rifle fell from his shoulder into the bushes, and he turned around, staring face toward the point from which the command had come. Harry saw at once that he was of foreign birth, probably. The features inclined to the Slav type, although Slavs were not then common in this country, even in the mill towns of the North.

"Are you an American?" asked Harry, standing up.

"All but two years of my life."

"The first two years then, as I see you speak good English. What's your name?"

"Michael Stanislav."

"Do you think that anybody named Michael Stanislav has the right to interfere in the quarrel of the Northern and Southern states? Don't the Stanislavs have trouble enough in the country where the Stanislavs grow?"

The big youth stared at him without understanding.

"Do you know who I am?" asked Harry, severely.

"The running rebel that we all look for."

"Rebels don't run. Besides, there are no rebels. Anyway I'm not the man you're looking for. My name is Robin Hood."

"Robin Hood?"

"Yes, Robin Hood! Didn't you ever hear of him?"

"Never."

"Then you have the honour of hearing of him and meeting him at the same time. As I said, my name is Robin Hood and my trade is that of a benevolent robber. I lie around in the greenwood, and I don't work. I've a lot of followers, Friar Tuck and others, but they're away for a while. They're as much opposed to work as I am. That's why they're my followers. We're the friends of the poor, because they have nothing we want, and we're the enemies of the rich because they have a lot we do want and that we often take. Still, we couldn't get along very well, if there were no rich for us to rob. It's like taking sugar water from a maple tree. We won't take too much, because it would kill the tree and we want to take its sugar water again, and many times. Do you understand?"

"Yes," replied the big youth, but Harry knew he didn't. Harry meanwhile was listening keenly to all that was passing in the forest, and he was sure that no other soldier had wandered near. It was perhaps partly a feeling of loneliness on his own part that caused him to linger in his talk with Michael Stanislav.

"Michael," he continued, "you appreciate our respective positions, don't you?"

"Ah!" said Michael, in a puzzled voice.

"I've explained carefully to you that I'm Robin Hood, and you at the present moment represent the rich."

"I am not rich. Before I turn soldier I work in a mill at Bridgeport."

"That's all very well, but you can't get out of it by referring to your past. Just now you are a proxy of the rich, and it's my duty to rob you."

The mouth of the big fellow expanded into a wide grin.

"You won't rob me," he said. "I have not a cent."

"But I'm going to rob you just the same. Don't you dare to drop a hand toward the pistols in your belt. If you do I'll blow your head off. I'm covering you with a double-barrelled shotgun. Each barrel contains about twenty buckshot, and at close range their blast would be so terrific that you'd make an awful looking corpse."

"I hold up my hands a long time. Don't want to be any kind of a corpse."

"That's the good boy. Steady now. Don't move a muscle. I'm going to rob you. It's a brief and painless operation, much easier than pulling a tooth."

He deftly removed the two pistols and the accompanying ammunition from the man's belt, placing them in his own. His belt of cartridges he put on the ground beside the fallen rifle, and then as he felt a glow of triumph he passed the well-filled knapsack from the stalwart shoulders of the other to his own shoulders, equally stalwart.

"Is everything in it first class, Michael?" he demanded with much severity.

"The best. Our army feeds well."

"It's a good thing for you that it's so. Robin Hood is never satisfied with anything second class, and he's likely to be offended if you offer it to him. On the whole, Michael, I think I like you and I'm glad you came this way. But do you care for good advice?"

"Yes, sir."

"That's right. Say 'sir' to me. It pleases my robber's heart. Then, my advice to you is never again to go into the woods alone. All the forest looks alike to those who don't know it, and you're lost in a minute. Besides, it's filled with strange and terrible creatures, Robin Hood—that's me, though I have some redeeming qualities—the Erymanthean boar, the Hydra-headed monster, Medusa of the snaky locks, Cyclops, Polyphemus with one awful eye, the deceitful Sirens, the Old Man of the Mountain, Wodin and Osiris, and, last and most terrible of all, the Baron Munchausen."

A flicker of fear appeared in the eyes of the captive.

"But I'll see that none of these monsters hurt you," said Harry consolingly. "The open is directly behind you, about a mile. Right about! Wheel! Well done! Now, you won't see me again, but you'll hear me giving commands. Forward, march! Quit stumbling! No true forester ever does! Nor is it necessary for you to run into more than three trees! Keep going! No, don't curve! Go straight ahead, and re-member that if you look back I shoot!"

Michael walked swiftly enough. He deemed that on the whole he had fared well. The great brigand, Robin Hood, had spared his life and he had lost nothing. The army would replace his weapons and am-munition and he was glad enough to escape from that terrible forest, even if he were driven out of it.

Harry watched him until he was out of sight, and then picking up the rifle and belt of cartridges he fled on soundless feet deeper into the forest. Two or three hundred yards away he stopped and heard a great shouting. Michael, no longer covered by a gun, had realized that something untoward had happened to him, and he was calling to his comrades. Harry did not know whether Michael would still call the man who had held him up, Robin Hood, nor did he care. He had secured an excellent rifle which would be much more useful to him than a shotgun, and his course still led straight toward the point where he should find Lee's army on the march. He felt that he ought to throw away the shotgun, as two weapons were heavy, but he could not make up his mind to do so.

A hundred yards farther and he heard replies to Michael's shouts, and then several shots, undoubtedly fired by the Union troops them-selves, as signals of alarm. He laughed to himself. Could such men as these overtake one who was born to the woods, the great grandson of Henry Ware, the most gifted of the borderers, who in the woods had not only a sixth sense, but a seventh as well? And his great grandson had inherited many of his qualities.

Harry, in the forest, felt only contempt for these youths of Central Europe who could not tell one point of the compass from another. He guided his own course by the sun, and continued at a good pace until he could hear shouts and shots no longer. Then in the dense woods, where the shadows made a twilight, he came to a tiny stream flowing from under a rock. He knelt and drank of the cool water, and then he opened Michael's knapsack. It was truly well filled, and he ate with deep content. Then he drank again and rested by the side of the pool.

As he reflected over his journey Harry concluded that Providence had watched over him so far, but there was much yet to do before he reached Lee. Providence had a strange way of watching over a man for a while, and then letting him go. He would neglect no precaution. The forest would not continue forever and then he must take his chances in the open.

Still burning with the desire to be the first to reach Lee, he put the rifle and the shotgun on either shoulder, and set off at as rapid a pace as the thickets would permit. But he soon stopped because a sound almost like that of a wind, but not a wind, came to his ears. There was a breeze blowing directly toward him, but he paid no attention to it, because to him most breezes were pleasant and friendly. But the other sound had in it a quality that was distinctly sinister like the hissing of a snake.

Harry paused in wonder and alarm. All his instincts warned him that a new danger was at hand. The breath of the wind suddenly grew hot, and sparks carried by it blew past him. He knew, in an instant, that the forest was on fire behind him and that tinder dry, it would burn fast and furious. Changing from a walk to a run, he sped forward as swiftly as he could, while the flames suddenly sprang high, waved and leaped forward in chase.

CHAPTER 6

Tests of Courage

Harry did not know how the woods had been set on fire, and he never knew. He did not credit it to the intent of Michael and his comrades, but he thought it likely that some of these men, ignorant of the forest, had built a campfire. His first thought was of himself, and his second was regret that so fine a stretch of timber should be burned over for nothing.

But he knew that he must hurry. Nor could he choose his way. He must get out of that forest even if he ran directly into the middle of a Union brigade. The wind was bringing the fire fast. It leaped from one tree to another, despite the recent rains, gathering volume and power as it came. Sparks flew in showers, and fragments of burned twigs rained down. Twice Harry's face was scorched lightly and he had a fear that one of the blazing twigs would set his hair on fire. He made another effort, and ran a little faster, knowing full well that his life was at stake.

The fire was like a huge beast, and it reached out threatening red claws to catch him. He was like primeval man, fleeing from one of the vast monsters, now happily gone from the earth. He was conscious soon that another not far from him was running in the same way, a man in a faded blue uniform who had dropped his rifle in the rapidity of his flight.

Harry kept one eye on him but the stranger did not see him until they were nearly out of the wood. Then Harry, with a clear purpose in view, veered toward him. He saw that they would escape from the fire. Open fields showed not far ahead, and while the sparks were numerous and sometimes scorched, the roaring red monster behind them would soon be at the end of his race. He could not follow them into the open fields.

When the two emerged from the forest Harry was not more than fifteen feet from the stranger, who evidently took him for a friend and who was glad to have a comrade at such a time. They raced across fields in which the wheat had been cut, and then sank down four or five hundred yards from the fire, which was crackling and roaring in the woods with great violence, and sending up leaping flames.

"I was glad enough to get out of that. Do you think the rebels set it on fire?"

"I don't think so, but I was as pleased as you to escape from it, Mr. Haskell."

"Why, how did you know my name?" exclaimed the man in wonder.

"Why should I forget you? I've seen you often enough. Your name is John Haskell and you belong to the Fifth Pennsylvania."

"That's right, but I don't seem to recall you."

"It takes a lot of us some time to clear up our minds wholly after such a battle as Gettysburg. In some ways I've been in a sort of confused state myself. I dare say you've seen me often enough."

"That's likely."

"Pity you had your horse shot under you, Mr. Haskell. A man who is carrying important messages at a time like this can't do very well without his horse."

"How did you know I'd lost my horse?"

"Oh, I'm a mind reader. I can tell you a lot now. You carry your dispatch in the left-hand pocket of your waistcoat, just over your heart. And it hasn't been long, either, since you lost your horse, perhaps not more than an hour."

Haskell stared at him, but Harry's face was innocent. Nevertheless he had read Haskell's name and regiment on his canteen, cut there with his own knife. It was a mere guess that he was a dispatch bearer, but he had located the dispatch, because at the mention of the word "message" the man's hand had involuntarily gone to his left breast to see if the dispatch were still there. Boots with little dirt on them indicated that he had been riding.

"A mind reader!" said Haskell, with suspicion. "What business has a mind reader in this war?"

"He could be of enormous value. If he were a real mind reader he could tell his general exactly what the opposing general intended to do. I'm employed at a gigantic salary for that particular purpose."

"I guess you're trying to be funny. Why do you carry both a rifle and a shotgun?"

"In order to hit the target with one, if the other misses. I always use the rifle first, because if the bullet doesn't get home the shotgun, spreading its charge over a much wider area, is likely to do something."

"Now I know you're trying to be funny. As I'm going about my business as fast as I can, I'll leave you here."

"I like you so well that I can't bear to see you go. Don't move. My rifle covers your heart exactly and you are not more than ten feet away. I shall have no possible need of the shotgun. Keep your hands away from your belt. You're in a dangerous position, Mr. Haskell."

"I believe you're an infernal rebel."

"Take out the objectionable adjective 'infernal' and you're right. Keep those hands still, I tell you."

"What do you want?"

"Your dispatches! Oh, I must have 'em. Unbutton your coat and waistcoat and hand 'em to me at once. I hate to take human life, but war demands a terrible service, and I mean what I say!"

His voice rang with determination. The man slowly unbuttoned his waistcoat and took out a folded dispatch.

"Put it on the ground in front of you. That's right, and don't you reach for it again. Now, lay your canteen beside it!"

"What in thunder do you want with my canteen? It's empty!"

"I can fill it again. This is a well watered country. That's right; put it beside the dispatch. Now you walk about one hundred yards to the right with your back to me. If you look around at all I fire, and I'm a good marksman. Stand there ten minutes, and then you can move on! That's right! Now march!"

The man walked away slowly and when he had gone about half the distance Harry, picking up the dispatch, took flight again across the fields. Climbing a fence, he looked back and saw the figure of John Haskell, standing motionless on a hill. He knew that the man was not likely to remain in that position more than half the allotted time. It was certain that he would soon turn, despite the risk, but Harry was already beyond his reach.

He leaped from the fence, crossed another field and entered a wood. There he paused among the trees and saw Haskell returning. But when he had come a little distance, he shook his head doubtfully, and then walked toward the north.

"A counsel of wisdom," chuckled Harry, who was going in quite another direction. "I think I'll read my dispatch now."

He opened it and blessed his luck. It was from Meade to Pleasanton, directing him to cut in with all the cavalry he could gather on the enemy's flank. The Potomac was in great flood and the Army of Northern Virginia could not possibly cross. If it were harried to the utmost by the Union cavalry the task of destroying it would be much easier.

"So it would," said Harry to himself. "But Pleasanton won't get this dispatch. Providence has not deserted me yet; and it's true that fortune favours the brave. I'm John Haskell of the Fifth Pennsylvania and I can prove it."

He had put the canteen over his shoulder and the name upon it was a powerful witness in his favour. The dispatch itself was another, and his faded uniform told nothing.

Harry had passed through so much that a reckless spirit was growing upon him, and he had succeeded in so much that he believed he would continue to succeed. Regretfully he threw the shotgun away, as it would not appear natural for a messenger to carry it and a rifle too.

He went forward boldly now, and, when an hour later he saw a detachment of Union cavalry in a road, he took no measures to avoid them. Instead he went directly toward the horsemen and hailed them in a loud voice. They stopped and their leader, a captain, looked inquiringly at Harry, who was approaching rapidly.

Harry held up both hands as a sign that he was a friend, and called in a loud voice:

"I want a horse! And at once, if you please, sir!"

He had noticed that three led horses with empty saddles, probably the result of a brush with the enemy, and he meant to be astride one of them within a few minutes.

"You're a cool one," said the captain. "You come walking across the field, and without a word of explanation you say you want a horse. Don't you want a carriage too?"

"I don't need it. But I must have a horse, Captain. I ride with a message and it must be of great importance because I was told to go with it at all speed and risk my life for it. I've risked my life already. My horse was shot by a band of rebels, but luckily it was in the woods and I escaped on foot."

As he spoke he craftily moved the canteen around until the inscription showed clearly in the bright sunlight. The quick eyes of the captain caught it at once.

"You do belong to the Fifth Pennsylvania," he said. "Well, you're a long way from your regiment. It's back of that low mountain over there, a full forty miles from here, I should say."

Harry felt a throb of relief. It was his only fear that these men themselves should belong to the Fifth Pennsylvania, a long chance, but if it should happen to go against him, fatal to all his plans.

"I don't want to join my regiment," he said. "I'm looking for General Pleasanton."

"General Pleasanton! What can you happen to want with him?"

Harry gave the officer a wary and suspicious look, and then his eyes brightened as if he were satisfied.

"I told you I was riding with a message," he said, "and that message is for General Pleasanton. It's from General Meade himself and it's no harm for me to show it to so good a patriot as you."

"No, I think not," said the captain, flattered by the proof of respect and confidence.

Harry took the letter from his pocket. It had been sealed at first, but the warmth of the original bearer's body with a little help from Harry later had caused it to come open.

"Look at that," said Harry proudly as he took out the paper.

The captain read it, and was mightily impressed. He was, as Harry had surmised, a thoroughly staunch supporter of the Union. He would not only furnish this valiant messenger with a good horse, but he would help him otherwise on his way.

"Dexter," he called to an orderly, "bring the sorrel mare. She was ridden by a good man, Mr. Haskell, but he met a sharpshooter's bullet. Jump up."

Harry sprang into the saddle, and, astride such a fine piece of horseflesh, he foresaw a speedy arrival in the camp of General Lee.

"I'll not only mount you," said the captain, "but we'll see you on the way. General Pleasanton is on Lee's left flank and, as our course is in that direction, we'll ride with you, and protect you from stray rebel sharpshooters."

Harry could have shouted aloud in anger and disappointment. While the captain trusted him fully, he would not be much more than a prisoner, nevertheless.

"Thank you very much, Captain," he said, "but you needn't trouble yourself about me. Perhaps I'd better go on ahead. One rides faster alone."

"Don't be afraid that we'll hold you back," said the captain, smiling. "We're one of the hardest riding detachments in General Pleasanton's whole cavalry corps, and we won't delay you a second. On the contrary, we know the road so well that we'll save you wandering about and losing time."

Harry did not dare to say more. And so Providence, which had been watching over him so well, had decided now to leave him and watch over the other fellow. But he had at least one consolation. Pleasanton was on Lee's flank and their ride did not turn him from the line of his true objective. Every beat of his horse's hoofs would bring him nearer to Lee. Invincible youth was invincibly in the saddle again, and he said confidently to the captain:

"Let's start."

"All right. You keep by my side, Haskell. You appear to be brave and intelligent and I want to ask you questions."

The tone, though well meant, was patronizing, but Harry did not resent it.

"This troop is made up of Massachusetts men, and I'm from Massachusetts too," continued the captain. "My name is Lester, and I had just graduated from Harvard when the war began."

"Good stock up there in Massachusetts," said Harry boldly, "but I've one objection to you."

"What's that?"

"Everything wonderful in our history was done by you. No chance was left for anybody else."

"Well, not everything, but almost everything. Good old Massachusetts! As Webster said, 'There she stands!'"

"It was mostly New York and Pennsylvania that stood at Gettysburg."

"Yes, you did very well there."

"Don't you think, Captain, that a nation or a state is often lucky in its possession of writers?"

"I don't catch your drift exactly."

"I'll make an illustration. I've often wondered what were the Persian accounts of Marathon and Thermopylae, of Salamis and Plataea. Now most of our history has been written by Massachusetts men."

"And you insinuate that they have glorified my state unduly?"

"The expression is a trifle severe. Let's say that they have dwelled rather long upon the achievements of Massachusetts and not so long upon those of New York and Pennsylvania."

"Then let New York and Pennsylvania go get great writers. No state can be truly great without them. There's another detachment of ours just ahead, but we'll talk to them only a minute or two."

The second detachment reported that Pleasanton, with a heavy cavalry force, was about six miles farther west and that there was a fair road all the way. They should overtake him in an hour.

Harry's heart beat hard. Unless something happened within that hour he would never reach Lee, and his brain began to work with extraordinary activity. Plans passed in review before it as rapidly as pictures on a film, but all were rejected. He was in despair. They were trotting rapidly down a smooth road. A quarter of an hour passed and then a half-hour. A low bare hill appeared immediately on their right, and Harry saw beyond it the tops of trees.

"Captain Lester," he said, "suppose that you and I ride to the crest of the hill. You have strong glasses, so have I, and we may see something worth while. The men will ride on, but we can easily overtake them."

"Not a bad idea, Haskell," said the captain, still in that slightly patronizing tone. "I judge by your speech that you're a well educated man, and you appear to think."

They rode quickly to the summit, and Lester, putting his glasses to his eyes, gazed westward over a vast expanse of cultivated country. But Harry looking immediately down the slope, saw the forest that he wished.

Lester swept the glasses in a wide circle, looking for Union troops. His own troop was about a hundred yards ahead and the hoofbeats were growing fainter. Then Harry's courage almost failed him, but necessity was instant and cruel. Still he modified the blow, nor did he use any weapon, save one that nature had given him.

"Look out!" he cried, and as Lester turned in astonishment he struck him on the point of the jaw. Even as his fist flashed forward he held back a little and his full strength was not in the blow.

Nevertheless it was sufficient to strike Lester senseless, and he slid from his horse. Harry caught him by the shoulder and eased him in his fall. Then he lay stretched on his back in the grass like one asleep, with his horse staring at him. Harry knew that he would revive in a minute or two, and with a "Farewell, Captain Lester," he galloped down the slope and into the covering woods.

He knew that Lester's men, finding that they did not follow, would quickly come back, and he raced his horse among the trees as fast as he dared. A couple of miles between him and the hill and he felt safe, at least so far as the troop of Captain Lester was concerned. Fortune seemed to have made him a favourite again, but he knew that dangers were still as thick around him as leaves in Vallombrosa.

He tied his horse, climbed a tree, and used his glasses. Two miles to the west the bright sun flashed on long lines of mounted men, obviously the horsemen of Pleasanton. How was he to get through that cavalry screen and reach Lee? He did not see a way, but he knew that to find, one must seek. His desire to get through, intense as it always had been, was now doubled. He not only carried the news to Lee about the possible ford, but he also bore Meade's dispatch to Pleasanton, directing a movement which, if successful, must be most dangerous to the Army of Northern Virginia.

He descended the tree and waited a while in the forest. He found a spring at which he drank, and he filled the canteen. It was a precious canteen with the name of John Haskell engraved upon it, and he meant that it should carry him through all dangers into his camp. But he did not mean to use it yet. If he rode into Pleasanton's ranks they would merely take his letter to the general, and that would be the failure of his real mission.

Night was now not far distant, and, concluding that he had a much better chance to run the gantlet under its cover, he still waited in the wood until the twilight came.

Wrapped in a coil of dangers he was ready to risk anything. Quickness, resource and boldness, of which the last had been most valuable, had brought him so far, and, encouraged by success, he rode forward full of confidence.

On his right was a small house standing among the usual shade trees, and, approaching it without hesitation, he spoke to a man who stood in the yard.

"Which way is General Pleasanton?" he asked.

The man hesitated.

"I belong to the Fifth Pennsylvania," said Harry, pointing to the name on the canteen, still visible in the twilight. The man's eyes brightened and he replied:

"Down there," pointing toward the southwest.

"I've a message for him and I don't want to run into any of the rebel raiders."

"Then you keep away from there," he said, pointing due west.

"What's the trouble in that direction?"

"Jim Hurley was here about an hour ago. The whole country is terribly excited about these big armies marching over it, and he said that our cavalry was riding on fast. A lot of it was ahead of the rebel army, but straight there in the west some of the rebel horsemen had spread out on their own flank. If you went that way in the night you'd be sure to run right into a nest of 'em."

"So the Johnnies are west of us, your friend Hurley said. Tell me again what particular point I have to watch in order to keep away from them."

"Almost as straight west as you can make it. A valley running east and west cuts in there and it's full of the rebels. It's the only place all along here where they are."

"And consequently the only place for me to avoid. Thanks. Your information may save me from capture. Good night."

"Good night and good luck."

Harry rode toward the southwest until a dip in the valley hid him from possible view of the man at the house. Then he turned and rode due west, determined to reach as soon as possible those "rebel raiders" in the valley, but fully aware that he must yet use every resource of skill, courage and patience.

The twilight turned into night, clear, dry and bright. Unless it was raining in the mountains the flood in the Potomac could not be increasing. Here, at last, the conditions were all that he wished. The captured haversack still contained plenty of food, and, as he rode, he ate. He had learned long ago that food was as necessary as weapons to a soldier, and that one should eat when one could. Moreover, he was always hungry.

He kept among trees wherever possible, and, as the night grew, and the stars came out in the dusky blue, he enjoyed the peace. Even though he searched with his glasses he could not see soldiers anywhere, although he knew they were in the hollows and the forests. A pleasant breeze blew, and an owl, reckless of armies, sent forth its lonesome hoot.

But he kept his horse's head straight for the narrow valley where the "rebel raiders" rode. He met presently a small detachment of Connecticut men, but the sight of his canteen and letter was sufficient for them. Again he rode southwest, merely to turn due west once more, after he had passed from their sight, and near the head of the valley he encountered two men in blue on horseback watching. They were alert, well-built fellows and examined Harry closely, a process to which long usage had reconciled him.

"I hear that the rebels are down in that valley, comrade," he said.

"So they are," replied the elder and larger of the men. "We've got to ask you who you are and which way you're going."

"John Haskell, Fifth Pennsylvania, with dispatches from General Meade to General Pleasanton. They're tremendously important, too, and I've got to be in a hurry."

"More haste less speed. You know the old saying. In a time like this it's sometimes better for a man to know where he's going than it is to get there, 'cause he may arrive at the wrong place."

"Good logic, comrade, but I must hurry just the same. Which is my best way to find General Pleasanton?"

"Southwest. But I'm bound to tell you a few things first."

"All right. What are they?"

"You and I must be kinsfolk."

"How do you make that out?"

"Because my name is William Haskell, and I belong to the Fifth Pennsylvania, the same regiment that you do."

"Is that so? It's strange that we haven't met before. But funny things happen in war."

"So they do. Awfully funny. Now my brother's name is John Haskell, and you happen to be carrying his canteen, but you've changed looks a lot in the last few days, Brother John."

Haskell's voice had been growing more menacing, and Harry, with native quickness, was ready to act. When he saw the man's pistol flash from his belt he went over the side of his horse and the bullet whistled where his body had been. His own rifle cracked in reply, but Haskell's horse, not he, took the bullet, and, screaming with pain and fright, ran into the woods as the rider slipped from his back.

Harry, realizing that his peril was imminent and deadly, fired one of his pistols at the second man, who fell from his horse, too badly wounded in the shoulder to take any further part in the fight.

But Harry found in Haskell an opponent worthy of all his skill and courage. The Union soldier threw himself upon the ground and fired at Harry's horse, which instantly jerked the bridle from his hand and fled as the other had done. Harry dropped flat in the grass and leaves and listened, his heart thumping.

But luck had favoured him again. He lay in a slight depression and any bullet fired at him would be sure to go over him unless he raised his head. He could not see his enemies, but he could depend upon his wonderful power of hearing, inherited and cultivated, which gave him an advantage over his opponents. He heard the wounded man groan ever so lightly, and then the other whisper to him, "Are you much hurt, Bill?" The reply came in a moment: "My right shoulder is put out for the time, and I can't help you now." Presently he heard the slight sound of the other crawling toward him. Evidently this Haskell was a fearless fellow, bound to get him, and he called from the shadow in which he lay.

"You'd better stop, Haskell! I've got the best pair of ears in all this region, and I hear you coming! Crawl another step and you meet a bullet! But I want to tell you first that your interesting brother John is all right. I didn't kill him. I merely robbed him."

"Robbed him of what?"

"Oh, of several things."

"What things?"

"They don't concern you, Haskell. These are matters somewhat above you."

"They are, are they? Well, maybe they are, but I'm going to see that you don't get away with the proceeds of your robbery."

Harry didn't like his tone. It was fierce and resolute, and he realized once more that he had a man of quality before him. If Haskell had behaved properly he would have withdrawn with his wounded comrade. But then he was an obstinate Yankee.

He raised up ever so little and glanced across the intervening space, seeing the muzzle of a rifle not many yards away. There could be no doubt that Haskell was watchful and would continue watching. He drew his head back again and said:

"Let's call it a draw. You go back to your army, Mr. Haskell, and I'll go back to mine."

"Couldn't think of it. As a matter of fact, I'm with my army now; that is, I'm in its lines, while you can't reach yours. All I've got to do is to hold you here, and in the course of time some of our people will come along and take you."

"Do you think I'm worth so much trouble?"

"In a way it's a sort of personal affair with me. You admit having robbed my brother, and I feel that I must avenge him. He has been acting as a dispatch rider, and I can make a pretty shrewd guess about what you took from him. So I think I'll stay here."

Harry blamed himself bitterly for his careless and unfortunate expressions. He did not fear the result of a duel with this man, being the master of woodcraft that he was, but he was losing time, valuable time, time more precious than gold and diamonds, time heavy with the fate of armies and a nation. He grew furiously angry at everything, and angriest at Haskell.

"Mr. Haskell," he called, "I'm getting tired of your society, and I make you a polite request to go away."

"Oh, no, you're not tired. You merely think you are, and I couldn't consider conceding to your request. It's for your good more than mine. My society is elevating to any Johnny Reb."

"Then I warn you that I may have to hurt you."

"How about getting hurt yourself?"

Harry was silent. His acute ears brought him the sound of Haskell moving a little in his own particular hollow. The lonesome owl hooted twice more, but there was no sound to betoken the approach of Union troops in the forest. The duel of weapons and wits would have to be fought out alone by Haskell and himself.

He went over everything again and again and he concluded that he must rely upon his superior keenness of ear. He could hear Haskell, but Haskell could not hear him, and there was Providence once more taking him into favour. Summer clouds began to drift before the moon, and many of the stars were veiled. It was possible that Haskell's eyes also were not as keen as his own.

When the darkness increased, he began to crawl from the little shallow. Despite extreme precautions he made a slight noise. A pistol flashed and a bullet passed over him. It made his muscles quiver, but he called in a calm voice:

"Why did you do such a foolish thing as that? You wasted a perfectly good bullet."

"Weren't you trying to escape? I thought I heard a movement in the grass."

"Wasn't thinking of such a thing. I'm just waiting here to see what you'll do. Why don't you come on and attack?"

"I'm satisfied with things as they are. I'll hold you until morning and then our men will be sure to come and pick you up."

"Maybe it will be our men who will come and pick you up."

"Oh, no; they're too busy leaving Gettysburg behind 'em."

Harry nevertheless had succeeded in leaving the shallow and was now lying on its farther bank. Then he resumed the task of crawling forward on his face, and without making any noise, one of the most difficult feats that a human being is ever called upon to do.

At the end of a dozen feet, he paused both to rest and to listen. His acute ears told him that Haskell had not moved from his own place, and his eyes showed him that the darkness was increasing. Those wonderful, kindly clouds were thickening before the moon, and the stars in troops were going out of sight.

But he did not relax his caution. He knew that he could not afford to make any sound that would arouse the suspicions of Haskell, and it was a quarter of an hour before he felt himself absolutely safe. Then he passed around a big tree and arose behind its trunk, appreciating what a tremendous luxury it was to be a man and to stand upon one's own feet.

He had triumphed again! The stars surely were with him. They might play little tricks upon him now and then to tantalize him, but in the more important matters they were on his side. He stretched himself again and again to relieve the terrible stiffness caused by such long and painful crawling, and then, unable to resist an exultant impulse, he called loudly:

"Good-by, Haskell!"

There was a startled exclamation and a bullet fired at random cut the leaves twenty yards away. Harry, making no reply, fled swiftly through the forest toward the valley where the rebel raiders rode.

CHAPTER 7

In the Wagon

He ran at first, reckless of impediments, and there was a sound of crashing as he sped through the bushes. He was not in the least afraid of Haskell. He had his rifle and pistols and in the woods he was infinitely the superior. He did not even believe that Haskell would pursue, but he wanted to get far beyond any possible Federal sentinels as soon as possible.

After a flight of a few hundred yards he slackened speed, and began to go silently. The old instincts and skill of the forester returned to him. He knew that he was safe from immediate pursuit and now he would approach his own lines carefully. He was grateful for the chance or series of chances that always took him toward Lee. It seemed now that his enemies had merely succeeded in driving him at an increased pace in the way he wanted to go.

He was descending a slope, thickly clothed with undergrowth. A few hundred yards farther his knees suddenly crumpled under him and he sank down, seized at the same time with a fit of nervous trembling. He had passed through so many ordeals that strong and seasoned as he was and high though his spirits, the collapse came all at once. He knew what was the matter and, quietly stretching himself out, he lay still that the spell might pass.

The lonesome owl, probably the same one that he had heard earlier, began to hoot, and now it was near by. Harry thought he could make out its dim figure on a branch and he was sure that the red eyes, closed by day, were watching him, doubtless with a certain contempt at his weakness.

"Old man, if you had been chased by the fowler as often as I have," were the words behind his teeth, addressed to the dim and fluffy figure, "you wouldn't be sitting up there so calm and cocky. Your tired head would sink down between your legs, your feathers would be wet with perspiration and you'd be so tired you'd hardly be able to hang on to the tree."

Came again the lonesome hoot of the owl, spreading like a sinister omen through the forest. It made Harry angry, and, raising himself up a little, he shook his fist again at the figure on the branch, now growing clearer in outline.

"'Bird or devil?'" he quoted.

The owl hooted once more, the strange ominous cry carrying far in the silence of the night.

"Devil it is," said Harry, "and quoth your evil majesty 'never more.' I won't be scared by a big owl playing the part of the raven. It's not 'nevermore' with me. I've many a good day ahead and don't you dare tell me I haven't."

Came the solemn and changeless hoot of the owl in reply.

Harry's exertions and excitement had brought too much blood to his head and he was seeing red. He raised himself upon his elbows and stared at the owl which stared back from red rimmed eyes, cold, emotionless, implacable. He had been terribly shaken, and now a superstitious fright overcame him. The raven and the albatross were in his mind and he murmured under his breath passages from their ominous poems. The scholar had his raven, the mariner had his albatross and now he alone in the forest had his owl, to his mind the most terrible bird of the three.

Came again that solemn and warning cry, the most depressing of all in the wilderness, while the changeless and sinister eyes stared steadily at him. Then Harry remembered that he had a rifle, and he sat up. He would slay this winged monster. There was light enough for him to draw a bead, and he was too good a marksman to miss.

He dropped the muzzle of the rifle in a sudden access of fear as he remembered the albatross. A shiver ran through every nerve and muscle, and so heavily was he oppressed that he felt as if he had just escaped committing murder. He rubbed his hand across his damp forehead and the act brought him out of that dim world in which he had been living for the last ten or fifteen minutes.

"Bird of whatever omen you may be, I'll not shoot you. That's certain," he said, "but I'll leave you to your melancholy predictions just as soon as I can."

He stood up somewhat unsteadily, and renewed the descent of the slope. Near its foot he came to a brook and bathing his face plentifully in the cool water he felt wonderfully refreshed. All his strength was flowing back swiftly.

Then he entered the valley, pressing straight toward the west, and soon heard the tread of horses. He knew that they must be the cavalry of his own army, but he withdrew into the bushes until he was assured. A dozen men riding slowly and warily came into view, and though the moonlight was wan he recognized them at once. When they were opposite him he stepped from his ambush and said:

"A happy night to you, Colonel Talbot."

Colonel Leonidas Talbot was a brave man, but seldom in his life had he been so shaken.

"Good God, Hector!" he cried. "It's Harry Kenton's ghost!"

Lieutenant-Colonel Hector St. Hilaire turned pale.

"I don't believe in ghosts, Leonidas," he said, "but this one certainly looks like that of Harry Kenton."

"Colonel Talbot," called Harry, "I'm not a ghost. I'm the real Harry Kenton, hunting for our army."

"Pale but substantial," said St. Clair, who rode just behind the two colonels. "He's our old Harry himself, and I'd know him anywhere."

"No ghost at all and the Yankee bullets can't make him one," said Happy Tom.

A weakness seized Harry and a blackness came before his eyes. When he recovered St. Clair was holding him up, and Colonel Talbot was trying to pour strong waters down his throat.

"How long have I been this way?" he asked anxiously.

"About sixty seconds," replied Colonel Talbot, "but what difference does it make?"

"Because I'm in a big hurry to get to General Lee! Oh! Colonel! Colonel! You must speed me on my way! I've got a message from Colonel Sherburne to General Lee that means everything, and on the road I captured another from General Meade to General Pleasanton. Put me on a horse, won't you, and gallop me to the commander-in-chief!"

"Are you strong enough to ride alone?"

"I'm strong enough to do anything now."

"Then up with you! Here, on Carter's horse! Carter can ride behind Hubbell! St. Clair, you and Langdon ride on either side of him! You should reach the commander-in-chief in three-quarters of an hour, Harry!"

"And there is no Yankee cavalry in between?"

"No, they're thick on the slopes above us! You knew that, but here you're inside our own lines. Judging by your looks you've had quite a time, Harry. Now hurry on with him, boys!"

"So I have had, Colonel, but the appearance of you, Lieutenant-Colonel St. Hilaire and the boys was like a light from Heaven. Good-by!"

"Good-by!" the two colonels called back, but their voices were already dying in the distance as Harry and his comrades were now riding rapidly down the valley, knee to knee, because St. Clair and Langdon meant to keep very close to him. They saw that he was a little unsteady, and that his eyes were unnaturally bright. They knew, too, that if he said he had great news for General Lee he told the truth, and they meant that he should get there with it in the least time possible.

The valley opened out before them, broadening considerably as they advanced. The night was far gone, there was not much moonlight, but their eyes had grown used to the dark, and they could see well. They passed sentinels and small detachments of cavalry, to whom St. Clair and Langdon gave the quick password. They saw fields of wheat stubble and pastures and crossed two brooks. The curiosity of Langdon and St. Clair was overwhelming but they restrained it for a long time. They could tell by his appearance that he had passed through unimaginable hardships, but they were loath to ask questions.

An owl on their right hooted, and both of them saw Harry shiver.

"What makes an owl's cry disturb you so, Harry?" asked Langdon.

"Because one of them tried to put the hoodoo on me as they say down in your country, Happy. I was lying back there in the forest on the hill and the biggest and reddest-eyed owl that was ever born sat on a bough over head, and kept telling me that I was finished, right at the end of my rope. But he was a liar, because here I am, with you fellows on either side of me, inside our lines and riding to the camp of the commander-in-chief."

"I think you're a bit shaky, Harry," said St. Clair, "and I don't wonder at it. If I had been through all I think you've been through I'd tumble off that horse into the road and die."

"Has any messenger come from Colonel Sherburne at the river to General Lee?"

"Not that I've heard of. No, I'm sure that none's come," replied St. Clair.

"Then I'll get to him first. Don't think, Arthur, it's just a foolish ambition of mine to lead, but the sooner some one reaches the general the better."

"We'll see that you're first old man," said Langdon. "It's not more than a half-hour now."

But Harry reeled in his saddle. The singular weakness that he had felt a while back returned, and the road grew dark before him. With a mighty effort he steadied himself in the saddle and St. Clair heard him say in a fierce undertone: "I will go through with it!" St. Clair looked across at Langdon and the signalling look of Happy Tom replied. They drew in just a little closer. Now and then they talked to him sharply and briskly, rousing him again and again from the lethargy into which he was fast sinking.

"Look! In the woods over there, Harry!" exclaimed St. Clair. "See the men stretched asleep on the grass! They're the survivors of Pickett's brigades that charged at Gettysburg."

"And I was there!" said Harry. "I saw the greatest charge ever made in the history of the world!"

He reeled a little toward St. Clair, who caught him by the shoulder and straightened him in the saddle.

"Of course you had a pleasant, easy ride from the Potomac," said Happy Tom, "but I don't understand how as good a horseman as you lost your horse. I suppose he ran away while you were picking berries by the roadside."

"Me pick berries by the roadside, while I'm on such a mission!" exclaimed Harry indignantly, rousing himself up until his eyes flashed, which was just what Happy wished. "I didn't see any berries! Besides I didn't start on a horse. I left in a boat."

"A boat? Now, Harry, I know you've turned romancer. I guess your mystic troubles with the owl—if you really saw an owl—have been a sort of spur to your fancy."

"Do you mean to say, Tom Langdon, that I didn't see an owl and talk with him? I tell you I did, and his conversation was a lot more intelligent than yours, even if it was unpleasant."

"Of course it was," said St. Clair. "Happy's chief joy in life is talking. You know how he chatters away, Harry. He hates to sleep, because then he loses good time that he might use in talk. I'll wager you anything against anything, Harry, that when the Angel Gabriel blows his horn Happy will rise out of his grave, shaking his shroud and furious with anger. He'll hold up the whole resurrection while he argues with Gabriel that he blew his horn either too late or too early, or that it was a mighty poor sort of a horn anyhow."

"I may do all that, Harry," said Happy, "but Arthur is sure to be the one who will raise the trouble about the shroud. You know how finicky he is about his clothes. He'll find fault with the quality of his shroud, and he'll say that it's cut either too short or too long. Then he'll insist, while all the billions wait, on draping the shroud in the finest Greek or Roman toga style, before he marches up to his place on the golden cloud and receives his harp."

Harry laughed.

"That'll be old Arthur, sure," he said. Then his head drooped again. Fatigue was overpowering him. St. Clair and Langdon put a hand on either shoulder and held him erect, but Harry was so far sunk in lethargy that he was not conscious of their grasp. Men looked curiously at the three young officers riding rapidly forward, the one in the centre apparently held on his horse by the other two.

St. Clair took prompt measures.

"Harry Kenton!" he called sharply.

"Here!"

"Do you know what they do with a sentinel caught asleep?"

"They shoot him!"

"What of a messenger, bearing great news who has ridden two or three days and nights through a thousand dangers, and then becomes unconscious in his saddle within five hundred yards of his journey's end?"

"The stake wouldn't be too good for him," replied Harry as with a mighty effort he shook himself, both body and mind. Once more his eyes cleared and once more he sat erect in his saddle without help.

"I won't fail, Arthur," he said. "Show the way."

"There's a big tree by the roadside almost straight ahead," said St. Clair. "General Lee is asleep under that, but he'll be as wide awake as any man can be a half-minute after you arrive."

They sprang from their horses, St. Clair spoke quickly with a watching officer who went at once to awaken Lee. Harry dimly saw the form of the general who was sleeping on a blanket, spread over small boughs. Near him a man in brilliant uniform was walking softly back and forth, and now and then impatiently striking the tops of his high yellow-topped boots with a little riding whip. Harry knew at once that it was Stuart, but the cavalry leader had not yet noticed him.

Harry saw the officer bend over the commander-in-chief, who rose in an instant to his feet. He was fully dressed and he showed grey in the dusky light, but he seemed as ever calm and grave. Harry felt instantly the same swell of courage that the presence of Jackson had always brought to him. It was Lee, the indomitable, the man of genius, who could not be beaten. He heard him say to the officer who had awakened him, "Bring him immediately!" and he stepped forward, strengthening himself anew and filled with pride that he should be the first to arrive, as he felt that he certainly now was.

"Lieutenant Kenton!" said Lee.

"Yes, sir," said Harry, lifting his cap.

"You were sent with Colonel Sherburne to see about the fords of the Potomac."

"I was, sir."

"And he has sent you back with the report?"

"He has, sir. He did not give me any written report for fear that I might be captured. He did me the honour to say that my verbal message would be believed."

"It will. I know you, as I do the other members of my staff. Proceed."

"The Potomac is in great flood, sir, and the bridge is destroyed. It can't be crossed until it runs down to its normal depth."

Harry saw other generals of high rank drawing near. One he recognized as Longstreet. They were all silent and eager.

"Colonel Sherburne ordered me to say to you, sir," continued Harry, "that the best fords would be between Williamsport and Hagerstown when the river ran down."

"When did you leave him?"

"Nearly two days ago, sir."

"You have made good speed through a country swarming with our enemy. You are entitled to rest."

"It's not all, sir?"

"What else?"

"On my way I captured a messenger with a letter from General Meade to General Pleasanton. I have the message, sir."

He brought forth the paper from his blouse and extended it to General Lee, who took it eagerly. Some one held up a torch and he read it aloud to his generals.

"And so Meade means to trap me," he said, "by coming down on our flank!"

"Since the river is unfordable he'll have plenty of time to attack us there," said Longstreet.

"But will he dare to attack?" said Stuart defiantly. "He was able to hold his own in defence at Gettysburg, but it's another thing to take the offensive. We hear that General Meade is cautious and that he makes many complaints to his government. A complainer is not the kind of man who can destroy the Army of Northern Virginia."

"Sometimes it's well to be cautious, General," said Lee.

Then he turned to Harry and said:

"Again I commend you."

Harry saluted proudly, and then fell unconscious at the feet of General Lee.

When the young staff officer awoke, he was lying in a wagon which was moving slowly, with many jolts over a very rough road. It was perhaps one of these jolts that awoke him, because his eyes still felt very heavy with sleep. His position was comfortable as he lay on a heap of blankets, and the sides of the wagon looked familiar. Moreover the broad back of the driver was not that of a stranger. Moving his head into a higher place on the blankets he called.

"Hey you, Dick Jones, where are you taking me?"

Jones turned his rubicund and kindly face.

"Don't it beat all how things come about?" he said. "This wagon wasn't built for passengers, but I have you once and then I have you twice, sleepin' like a prince on them blankets. I guess if the road wasn't so rough you'd have slept all the way to Virginia. But I'm proud to have you as a passenger. They say you've been coverin' yourself with glory. I don't know about that, but I never before saw a man who was so all fired tuckered out."

"Where did you find me?"

"I didn't exactly find you myself. They say you saluted General Lee so deep and so strong that you just fell down at his feet an' didn't move, as if you intended to stay there forever. But four of your friends brought you to my wagon feet foremost, with orders from General Lee if I didn't treat you right that I'd get a thousand lashes, be tarred an' feathered, an' hung an' shot an' burned, an' then be buried alive. For all of which there was no need, as I'm your friend and would treat you right anyway."

"I know you would," laughed Harry. "You can't afford to lose your best passenger. How long have I been sleeping in this rough train of yours?"

"Since about three o'clock in the morning."

"And what time might it be now."

"Well it might be ten o'clock in the morning or it might be noon, but it ain't either."

"Well, then, what time is it?"

"It's about six o'clock in the afternoon, Mr. Kenton, and I judge that you've slept nigh on to fifteen hours, which is mighty good for a man who was as tired as you was."

"And what has the army been doing while I slept?"

"Oh, it's been marchin' an' marchin' an' marchin'. Can't you hear the wagons an' the cannons clinkin' an' clankin'? An' the hoofs of the horses beatin' in the road? An the feet of forty or fifty thousand men comin' down ker-plunk! ker-plunk! an' all them thousands talkin' off an' on? Yes, we're still marchin', Mr. Kenton, but we're retreatin' with all our teeth showin' an' our claws out, sharpened specially. Most of the boys don't care if Meade would attack us. They'd be glad of the chance to get even for Gettysburg."

There was a beat of hoofs and St. Clair rode up by the side of the wagon.

"All right again, Harry?" he said cheerfully. "I'm mighty glad of it. Other messengers have got through from Sherburne, confirming what you said, but you were the first to arrive and the army already was on the march because of the news you brought. Dalton arrived about noon, dead beat. Happy is coming with a horse for you, and you can rejoin the staff now."

"Before I leave I'll have to thank Mr. Jones once more," said Harry. "He runs the best passenger service that I know."

"Welcome to it any time, either you or your friend," said Jones, saluting with his whip.

CHAPTER 8

The Crossing

Harry left the wagon at midnight and overtook the staff, an orderly providing him with a good horse. Dalton, who had also been sleeping in a wagon, came an hour or two later, and the two, as became modest young officers, rode in the rear of the group that surrounded General Lee.

Although the darkness had come fully, the Army of Northern Virginia had not yet stopped. The infantry flanked by cavalry, and, having no fear of the enemy, marched steadily on. Harry closely observed General Lee, and although he was well into his fifties he could discern no weakness, either physical or mental, in the man who had directed the fortunes of the South in the terrific and unsuccessful three days at Gettysburg and who had now led his army for nearly a week in a retreat, threatened, at any moment, with an attack by a veteran force superior in numbers. All the other generals looked worn and weary, but he alone sat erect, his hair and beard trimmed neatly, his grave eye showing no sign of apprehension.

He seemed once more to Harry—youth is a hero-worshiper—omniscient and omnipotent. The invasion of the North had failed, and there had been a terrible loss of good men, officers and soldiers, but, with Lee standing on the defensive at the head of the Army of Northern Virginia, in Virginia, the South would be invincible. He had always won there, and he always would win there.

Harry sighed, nevertheless. He had two heroes, but one of them was gone. He thought again if only Stonewall Jackson had been at Gettysburg. Lee's terrible striking arm would have smitten with the hammer of Thor. He would have pushed home the attack on the first day, when the Union vanguard was defeated and demoralized. He would have crushed the enemy on the second day, leaving no need for that fatal and terrific charge of Pickett on the third day.

"You reached the general first," said Dalton, "but I tried my best to beat you."

"But I started first, George, old fellow. That gave me the advantage over you."

"It's fine of you to say it. The army has quickened its pace since we came. A part of it, at least, ought to arrive at the river to-morrow, though their cavalry are skirmishing continually on our flanks. Don't you hear the rifles?"

Harry heard them far away to right and left, like the faint buzzing of wasps, but he had heard the same sound so much that it made no impression upon him.

"Let 'em buzz," he said. "They're too distant to reach any of us, and the Army of Northern Virginia is passing on."

Those were precious hours. Harry knew much, but he did not divine the full depths of the suspense, suffered by the people beyond the veil that clothed the two armies. Lincoln had been continually urging Meade to pursue and destroy his opponent, and Meade, knowing how formidable Lee was, and how it had been a matter of touch and go at Gettysburg, pursued, but not with all the ardour of one sure of triumph. Yet the man at the White House hoped continually for victory, and the Southern people feared that his hopes would come true.

It became sure the next day that they would reach the Potomac before Meade could attack them in flank, but the scouts brought word that the Potomac was still a deep and swollen river, impossible to be crossed unless they could rebuild the bridges.

Finally the whole army came against the Potomac and it seemed to Harry that its yellow flood had not diminished one particle since he left. But Lee acted with energy. Men were set to work at once building a new bridge near Falling Waters, parts of the ruined pontoon bridges were recovered, and new boats were built in haste. But while the workmen toiled the army went into strong positions along the river between Williamsport and Hagerstown.

Harry found himself with all of his friends again, and he was proud of the army's defiant attitude. Meade and the Army of the Potomac were not far away, it was said, but the youthful veterans of the South were entirely willing to fight again. The older men, however, knew their danger. The disproportion of forces would be much greater than at Gettysburg, and even if they fought a successful defensive action with their back to the river the Army of the Potomac could bide its time and await reinforcements. The North would pour forth its numbers without stint.

Harry rode to Sherburne with a message of congratulation from General Lee, who told him that he had selected the possible crossing well, and that he had shown great skill and valour in holding it until the army came up. Sherburne's flush of pride showed under his deep tan.

"I did my best," he said to Harry, who knew the contents of the letter, "and that's all any of us can do."

"But General Lee has a way of inspiring us to do our best."

"It's so, and it's one of the reasons why he's such a great general. Watch those bridge builders work, Harry! They're certainly putting their souls and strength into it."

"And they have need to do so. The scouts say that the Army of the Potomac will be before us to-morrow. Don't you think the river has fallen somewhat, Colonel?"

"A little but look at those clouds over there, Harry. As surely as we sit here it's going to rain. The rivers were low that we might cross them on our march into the North, just smoothing our way to Gettysburg, and now that Gettysburg has happened they're high so we can't get back to the South. It looks as if luck were against us."

"But luck has a habit of changing."

Harry rode back to headquarters, whence he was sent with another dispatch, to Colonel Talbot, whom he found posted well in advance with the Invincibles.

"This note," said the colonel, "bids us to watch thoroughly. General Meade and his army are expected on our front in the morning, and there must be no chance for a surprise in the night, say a dash by their cavalry which would cut up our rear guard or vanguard—upon my soul I don't know which to call it. Harry, as you can see by the note itself, you're to remain with us until about midnight, and then make a full report of all that you and I and the rest of us may have observed upon this portion of the front or rear, whichever it may be. Meanwhile we share with you our humble rations."

Harry was pleased. He was always glad when chance or purpose brought him again into the company of the Invincibles. St. Clair and Langdon were his oldest comrades of the war, and they were like brothers to him. His affection for the two colonels was genuine and deep. If the two lads were like brothers to him, the colonels were like uncles.

"Is the Northern vanguard anywhere near?" asked Harry.

"Skirmishing is going on only four or five miles away," replied Colonel Leonidas Talbot. "It is likely that the sharp shooters will be picking off one another all through the night, but it will not disturb us. That is a great curse of war. It hardens one so for the time being. I'm a soldier, and I've been one all my life, and I suppose soldiers are necessary, but I can't get over this feeling. Isn't it the same way with you, Hector?"

"Exactly the same, Leonidas," replied Lieutenant-Colonel Hector St. Hilaire. "You and I fought together in Mexico, Leonidas, then on the plains, and now in this gigantic struggle, but under whatever guise and, wherever it may be, I find its visage always hideous. I don't think we soldiers are to blame. We don't make the wars although we have to fight 'em."

"Increasing years, Hector, have not dimmed those perceptive faculties of yours, which I may justly call brilliant."

"Thanks, Leonidas, you and I have always had a proper conception of the worth of each other."

"If you will pardon me for speaking, sir," said St. Clair, "there is one man I'd like to find, when this war is over."

"'What is the appearance of this man, Arthur?" asked Colonel Talbot.

"I don't know exactly how he looks, sir, though I've heard of him often, and I shall certainly know him when I meet him. You understand, sir, that, while I've not seen him, he has very remarkable characteristics of manner."

"And what may those be, Arthur? Are they so salient that you would recognize them at once?"

"Certainly, sir. He has an uncommonly loud voice, which he uses nearly all the time and without restraint. Words fairly pour from his tongue. Facts he scorns. He soars aloft on the wings of fancy. Many people who have listened to him have felt persuaded by his talk, but he is perhaps not so popular now."

"An extraordinary person, Arthur. But why are you so anxious to find him?"

"Because I wish, sir, to lay upon him the hands of violence. I would thrash him and beat him until he yelled for mercy, and then I would thrash him and beat him again. I should want the original pair of seven-leagued boots, not that I might make such fast time, but that I might kick him at a single kick from one county to another, and back, and then over and over past counting. I'd duck him in a river until he gasped for breath, I'd drag him naked through a briar patch, and then I'd tar and feather him, and ride him on a rail."

"Heavens, Arthur! I didn't dream that your nature contained so much cruelty! Who is this person over whose torture you would gloat like a red Indian?"

"It is the man who first said that one Southerner could whip five Yankees."

"Arthur," said Colonel Talbot, "your anger is just and becomes you. When the war is over, if we all are spared we'll form a group and hunt this fellow until we find him. And then, please God, if the gallows of Haman is still in existence, we'll hang him on it with promptness and dispatch. I believe in the due and orderly process of the law, but in this case lynching is not only justifiable, but it's an honour to the country."

"Well spoken, Leonidas! Well spoken!" said Lieutenant-Colonel Hector St. Hilaire. "I'm glad that Arthur mentioned the matter, and we'll bear it in mind. You can count upon me."

"And here is coffee," said Happy Tom. "I made this myself, the camp cook liking me and giving me a chance. I'd really be a wonderful cook if I had the proper training, and I may come to it, if we lose the war. Still, the chance even then is slight, because my father, when red war showed its edge over the horizon, put all his money in the best British securities. So we could do no more than lose the plantation."

"Happy," said Colonel Talbot, gravely rebuking, "I am surprised at your father. I thought he was a patriot."

"He is, sir, but he's a financier first, and I may be thankful for it some day. I'll venture the prediction right now that if we lose this war not a single Confederate bill will be in the possession of Thomas Langdon, Sr. Others may have bales of it, worth less per pound than cotton, but not your humble servant's father, who, I sometimes think, has lots more sense than your humble servant's father's son."

Colonel Leonidas Talbot shook his head slowly.

"Finance is a mystery to me," he said. "In the dear old South that I have always known, the law, the army and the church were and are considered the high callings. To speak in fine, rounded periods was considered the great gift. In my young days, Harry, I went with my father by stage coach to your own State, Kentucky, to hear that sublime orator, the great Henry Clay."

"What was he speaking about, sir?" asked Harry.

"I don't remember. That's not important. But surely he was the noblest orator God ever created in His likeness. His words flowing like music and to be heard by everybody, even those farthest from the speaker, made my pulse beat hard, and the blood leap in my veins. I was heart and soul for his cause, whatever it was, and, yet I fear me, though I do not wish to hurt your feelings, Harry, that the state to which he was such ornament, has not gone for the South with the whole spirit that she should have shown. She has not even seceded. I fear sometimes that you Kentuckians are not altogether Southern. You border upon the North, and stretching as you do a long distance from east to west and a comparatively short distance from north to south, you thus face three Northern States across the Ohio—Ohio, Indiana and Illinois, and the pull of three against one is strong. You see your position, don't you? Three Yankee states facing you from the north and only one Southern state, Tennessee, lying across your whole southern border, that is three against one. I fear that these odds have had their effect, because if Kentucky had sent all of her troops to the South, instead of two-thirds of them to the North, the war would have been won by us ere this."

"I admit it," said Harry regretfully. "My own cousin, who was more like a brother to me, is fighting on the other side. Kentucky troops on the Union side have kept us from winning great victories, and many of the Union generals are Kentuckians. I grieve over it, sir, as much as you do."

"But you and your people should not take too much blame to yourselves, Harry," said Lieutenant-Colonel Hector St. Hilaire, who had a very soft heart. "Think of the many influences to which you were exposed daily. Think of those three Yankee states sitting there on the other side of the Ohio—Ohio, Indiana and Illinois—and staring at you so long and so steadily that, in a way, they exerted a certain hypnotic force upon you. No, my boy, don't feel badly about it, because the fault, in a way, is not so much yours as it is that of your neighbours."

"At any rate," said Happy Tom, with his customary boldness and frankness, "we're bound to admit that the Yankees beat us at making money."

"Which may be more to our credit than theirs," said Colonel Talbot, with dignity. "I have found it more conducive to integrity and a lofty mind to serve as an officer at a modest salary in the army rather than to gain riches in trade."

"But somebody has to pay the army, sir."

"Thomas, I regret to tell you that inquiry can be pushed to the point of vulgarity. I have been content with things as they were, and so should you be. Ah, there are our brave boys singing that noble battle song of the South! Listen how it swells! It shows a spirit unconquerable!"

Along the great battle front swelled the mighty chorus:

"Come brothers! Rally for the right!

"The bravest of the brave

"Sends forth her ringing battle cry

"Beside the Atlantic wave!

"She leads the way in honour's path;

"Come brothers, near and far,
"Come rally round the bonnie blue flag
"That bears a single star."

"A fine song! A fine song most truly," said Colonel Talbot. "It heartens one gloriously!"

But Harry, usually so quick to respond, strangely enough felt depression. He felt suddenly in all its truth that they had not only failed in their invasion, but the escape of the army was yet a matter of great doubt. The mood was only momentary, however, and he joined with all his heart as the mighty chorus rolled out another verse:

"Now Georgia marches to the front
"And beside her come
"Her sisters by the Mexique sea
"With pealing trump and drum,
"Till answering back from hill and glen
"The rallying cry afar,
"A nation hoists the bonnie blue flag
"That bears a single star!"

They sang it all through, and over again, and then, after a little silence, came the notes of a trumpet from a far-distant point. It was played by powerful lungs and the wind was blowing their way but they heard it distinctly. It was a quaint syncopated tune, but not one of the Invincibles had any doubt that it came from some daring detachment of the Union Army. The notes with their odd lilt seemed to swell through the forest, but it was strange to both of the colonels.

"Do any of you know it?" asked Colonel Talbot.

All shook their heads except Harry.

"What is it, Harry?" asked Talbot.

"It's a famous poem, sir, the music of which has not often been heard, but I can translate from music into words the verse that has just been played:

"In their ragged regimentals
"Stood the old Continentals
"Yielding not,
"When the grenadiers were lunging
"And like hail fell the plunging
"Cannon shot;
"When the files of the isles
"From the smoky night encampment
"Bore the banner of the rampant Unicorn
"And *grummer, grummer*,

111

"Rolled the roll of the drummer,
"Through the morn!"

The bugler played on. It was the same tune, curious, syncopated and piercing the night shrilly. Whole brigades of the South stood in silence to listen.

"What do you think is its meaning?" asked Lieutenant-Colonel St. Hilaire.

"It's in answer to our song and at the same time a reproach," replied Harry, who had jumped at once to the right conclusion. "The bugler intends to remind us that the old Continentals who stood so well were from both North and South, and perhaps he means, too, that we should stand together again instead of fighting each other."

"Then let the North give up at once," snapped Colonel Talbot.

"But in the trumpeter's opinion that means we should be apart forever."

"Then let him play on to ears that will not heed."

But the bugler was riding away. The music came faintly, and then died in one last sighing note. It left Harry grave and troubled, and he began to ask himself new questions. If the South succeeded in forcing a separation, what then? But the talk of his comrades drove the thought from his mind. Colonel Talbot sent St. Clair, Langdon and a small party of horsemen forward to see what the close approach of the daring bugler meant. Harry went with them.

Scouts in the brushwood quickly told them that a troop of Union cavalry had appeared in a meadow some distance ahead of them, and that it was one of their number who had played the song on the bugle. Should they stalk the detachment and open fire? St. Clair, who was in command, shook his head.

"It would mean nothing now," he said, and rode on with his men, knowing that the watchful Southern sharpshooters were on their flanks. It was night now, and a bright moon was coming out, enabling them to use their glasses with effect.

"There they are!" exclaimed Harry, pointing to the strip of forest on the far side of the opening, "and there is the bugler, too."

He was studying the party intently. The brilliant moonlight, and the strength of his glasses made everything sharp and clear and his gaze concentrated upon the bugler. He knew that man, his powerful chest and shoulders, and the well-shaped head on its strong neck. Nor did he deny to himself that he had a feeling of gladness when he recognized him.

"It's none other," he said aloud.

"None other what?" asked St. Clair.

"Our warning bugler was Shepard, the Union spy. I can make him out clearly on his horse with his bugle in his hand. You'll remember my telling you how I had that fight with him in the river."

"And perhaps it would have been better for us all if you had finished him off then."

"I couldn't have done it, Arthur, nor could you, if you had been in my place."

"No, I suppose not, but these Yankees are coming up pretty close. It's sure proof that Meade's whole army will be here in the morning, and the bridge won't be built."

"It may be built, but, if Meade chooses a battle, a battle there will be. Heavy forces must be very near. You can see them now signalling to one another from hill to hill."

"So I do, and this is as far as we ought to go. A hundred yards or two farther and we'll be in the territory of the enemy's sharpshooters instead of our own."

They remained for a while among some bushes, and secured positive knowledge that the bulk of the Army of the Potomac was drawing near. Toward midnight Harry returned to his commander-in-chief and found him awake and in consultation with his generals, under some trees near the Potomac. Longstreet, Rhodes, Pickett, Early, Anderson, Pender and a dozen others were there, all of them scarred and tanned by battle, and most of them bearing wounds.

Harry stood back, hesitating to invade this circle, even when he came with dispatches, but the commander-in-chief, catching sight of him, beckoned. Then, taking off his cap, he walked forward and presented a note from Colonel Talbot. It was brief, stating that the enemy was near, and Lee read it aloud to his council.

"And what were your own observations, Lieutenant Kenton?" asked the commander-in-chief.

"As well as I could judge, sir, the enemy will appear on our whole front soon after daybreak."

"And will be in great enough force to defeat us."

"Not while you lead us, sir."

"A courtier! truly a courtier!" exclaimed Stuart, smoothing the great feather of his gorgeous hat, which lay upon his knee.

Harry blushed.

"It may have had that look," he said, "but I meant my words."

"Don't tease the lad," said the crippled Ewell. "I knew him well on Jackson's staff, and he was one of our bravest and best."

"A jest only," said Stuart. "Don't I know him as well as you, Ewell? The first time I saw him he was riding alone among many dangers to bring relief to a beleaguered force of ours."

"And you furnished that relief, sir," said Harry.

"Well, so I did, but it was my luck, not merit."

"Be assured that you have no better friend than General Stuart," said General Lee, smiling. "You have done your duty well, Lieutenant Kenton, and as these have been arduous days for you you may withdraw, and join your young comrades of the staff."

Harry saluted and retired. Before he was out of ear shot the generals resumed their eager talk, but they knew, even as Harry himself, that there was but one thing to do, stand with their backs to the river and fight, if Meade chose to offer battle.

He slept heavily, and when he awoke the next day Dalton, who was up before him, informed him that the Northern army was at hand. Snatching breakfast, he and Dalton, riding close behind the commander-in-chief, advanced a little distance and standing upon a knoll surveyed the thrilling spectacle before them. Far along the front stretched the Army of the Potomac, horse, foot and guns, come up with its enemy again. Harry was sure that Meade was there, and with him Hancock and Buford and Warren and all the other valiant leaders whom they had met at Gettysburg. It was nine days since the close of the great battle, and doubtless the North had poured forward many reinforcements, while the South had none to send.

Harry appreciated the full danger of their situation, with the larger army in front of them, and the deep and swollen torrent of the Potomac behind them. But he did not believe that Meade would attack. Lee had lost at Gettysburg, but in losing he had inflicted such losses upon his opponent, that most generals would hesitate to force another battle. The one who would not have hesitated was consolidating his great triumph at Vicksburg. Harry often thought afterward what would have happened had Grant faced Lee that day on the wrong side of the Potomac.

His opinion that Meade would not attack came from a feeling that might have been called atmospheric, an atmosphere created by the lack of initiative on the Union side, no clouds of skirmishers, no attacks of cavalry, very little rifle firing of any kind, merely generals and soldiers looking at one another. Harry saw, too, that his own opinion was that of his superior officer. Watching the commander-in-chief intently he saw a trace of satisfaction in the blue eyes. Presently all of them rode back.

Thus that day passed and then another wore on. Harry and Dalton had little to do. The whole Army of Northern Virginia was in position, defiant, challenging even, and the Army of the Potomac made no movement forward. Harry watched the strange spectacle with an excitement that he did not allow to appear on his face. It was like many of those periods in the great battles in which he had taken a part, when the combat died, though the lull was merely the omen of a struggle, soon to come more frightful than ever.

But here the struggle did not come. The hours of the afternoon fell peacefully away, and the general and soldiers still looked at one another.

"They're working on the bridge like mad," said Dalton, who had been away with a message, "and it will surely be ready in the morning. Besides, the Potomac is falling fast. You can already see the muddy lines that it's leaving on its banks."

"And Meade's chance is slipping, slipping away!" said Harry exultingly. "In three hours it will be sunset. They can't attack in the night and to-morrow we'll be gone. Meade has delayed like McClellan at Antietam, and, doubtless as McClellan did, he thinks our army much larger than it really is."

"It's so," said Dalton. "We're to be delivered, and we're to be delivered without a battle, a battle that we could ill afford, even if we won it."

Both were in a state of intense anxiety and they looked many times at the sun and their watches. Then they searched the hostile army with their glasses. But nothing of moment was stirring there. Lower and lower sank the sun, and a great thrill ran through the Army of Northern Virginia. In both armies the soldiers were intelligent men—not mere creatures of drill—who thought for themselves, and while those in the Army of Northern Virginia were ready, even eager to fight if it were pushed upon them, they knew the great danger of their position. Now the word ran along the whole line that if they fought at all it would be on their side of the river.

Harry and Dalton did not sleep that night. They could not have done so had the chance been offered. They like others rode all through the darkness carrying messages to the different commands, insuring exact cooperation. As the hours of the night passed the aspect of everything grew better. The river had fallen so fast that it would be fordable before morning. But after midnight the clouds gathered, thunder crashed, lightning played and the violent rain of a summer storm enveloped them again. Harry viewed it at first with dismay, and then he found consolation. The darkness and the storm would cover their retreat, as it had covered the retreat of their enemy, Hooker, after Chancellorsville.

Harry and Dalton rode close behind Lee, who sat erect on his white horse, supervising the first movement of troops over the new and shaking bridge. Harry noted with amazement that despite his enormous exertions, physical and mental, and an intense anxiety, continuous for many days, he did not yet show signs of fatigue. Word had come that a part of the army was already fording the river, near Williamsport, but this bridge near Falling Waters was the most important point. General Lee and his staff sat there on their horses a long time, while the rain beat unheeded upon them.

Few scenes are engraved more vividly upon the mind of Harry Kenton than those dusky hours before the dawn, the flashes of lightning, the almost incessant rumble of thunder, the turbid and yellow river across which stretched the bridge, a mere black thread in the darkness, swaying and dipping and rising and creaking as horse and foot, and batteries and ammunition wagons passed upon it.

There were torches, but they flared and smoked in the rain and cast a light so weak and fitful that Harry could not see the farther shore. The Army of Northern Virginia marched out upon a shaking bridge and disappeared in the black gulf beyond. Only the lack of an alarm coming back showed that it was reaching the farther shore.

"Dawn will soon be here," said Dalton.

"So it will," said Harry, "and most of the troops are across. Ah, there go the Invincibles! Look how they ride!"

Colonel Leonidas Talbot and Lieutenant-Colonel Hector St. Hilaire at the head of their scanty band were just passing. They took off their hats, and swept a low bow to the great chief who sat silently on his white horse within a few yards of them. Then, side by side, they rode upon the shaking bridge, followed by Langdon, St. Clair and their brave comrades, and disappeared, where the bridge disappeared, in the rain and mist.

"Brave men!" murmured Lee.

Harry, always watching his commander-in-chief, saw now for the first time signs of fatigue and nervousness. The tremendous strain was wearing him down. But while the rain still poured and ran in streams from his grey hair and grey beard, the rear guard of the Army of Northern Virginia passed upon the bridge, and Stuart, all his plumes bedraggled, rode up to his chief, a smoking cup of coffee in his hand.

"Drink this, General, won't you?" he said.

He seized it, drank all of the coffee eagerly, and then handing back the cup, said:

"I never before in my life drank anything that refreshed me so much."

Then he, with his staff, Stuart and some other generals rode over the bridge, disappearing in their turn into the darkness and mist that had swallowed up the others, but emerging, as the others had done, into the safety of the Southern shore.

Meade and his generals had held a council the night before but nearly all the officers advised against attack. This night he made up his mind to move against Lee anyhow, and was ready at dawn, only to find the whole Southern army gone.

CHAPTER 9

In Society

Harry, when the dawn had fully come, was sent farther away toward the ford to see if the remainder of the troops had passed, and, when he returned with the welcome news, the rain had ceased to fall. The army was rapidly drying itself in the brilliant sunshine, and marched leisurely on. He felt an immense relief. He knew that a great crisis had been passed, and, if the Northern armies ever reached Richmond, it would be a long and sanguinary road. Meade might get across and attack, but his advantage was gone.

The same spirit of relief pervaded the ranks, and the men sang their battle songs. There had been some fighting at one or two of the fords, but it did not amount to much, and no enemy hung on their rear. But no stop was made by the staff until noon, when a fire was made and food was cooked. Then Harry was notified that he and Dalton were to start that night with dispatches for Richmond. They were to ride through dangerous country, until they reached a point on the railroad, wholly within the Southern lines, when they would take a train for the Confederate capital.

They were glad to go. They felt sure that no great battles would be fought while they were gone. Neither army seemed to be in a mood for further fighting just yet, and they longed for a sight of the little city that was the heart of the Confederacy. They were tired of the rifle and march, of cannon and battles. They wished to be a while where civilized life went on, to hear the bells of churches and to see the faces of women.

It seemed to them both that they had lived almost all their lives in war. Even Jeb Stuart's ball, stopped by the opening guns of a great battle, was far, far away, and to Harry, it was at least a century since he had closed his Tacitus in the Pendleton Academy, and put it away in his desk. That old Roman had written something of battles, but they were no such struggles as Chancellorsville and Gettysburg had been. The legions, he admitted in his youthful pride, could fight well, but they never could have beaten Yank or Reb.

He and Dalton slept through the afternoon and directly after dark, well equipped and well-armed, they made their start into the South. But in going they did not neglect to pass the camp of the Invincibles who were now in the apex of the army farthest south. They had found an unusually comfortable place on a grassy plot beside a fine, cool spring, and most of them were lying down. But Colonel Talbot and Lieutenant-Colonel Hector St. Hilaire sat on empty kegs, with a board on an empty box between them. The great game which ran along with the war had been renewed. St. Clair and Langdon sat on the grass beside them, watching the contest.

The two colonels looked up at the sound of hoofs and paused a moment.

"I'm getting his king into a close corner, Harry," said Colonel Talbot, "and he'll need a lot of time for thinking. Where are you two going, or perhaps I shouldn't ask you such a question?"

"There's no secret about it," replied Harry. "We're going to Richmond with dispatches."

"He was incorrect in saying that he was getting my king into a close corner, as I'll presently show him," said Lieutenant-Colonel St. Hilaire; "but you boys are lucky. I suppose you'll stay a while in the capital. You'll sleep in white beds, you'll eat at tables, with tablecloths on 'em. You'll hear the soft voices of the women and girls of the South, God bless 'em!"

"And if you went on to Charleston you'd find just as fine women there," said Colonel Leonidas Talbot.

He sighed and a shade of sadness crossed his face. Harry heard and saw and understood. He remembered a night long, long ago in that heat of rebellion, when he had looked down from the window of his room, and, in the dark, had seen two figures, a man and a woman, upon a piazza, Colonel Talbot and Madame Delaunay, talking softly together. He had felt then that he was touching almost unconsciously upon the thread of an old romance. A thread slender and delicate, but yet strong enough in its very tenderness and delicacy to hold them both. The perfume of the flowers and of the old romance that night in the town so far away came back. He was moved, and when his eyes met Colonel Talbot's some kind of an understanding passed between them.

"The good are never rewarded," said Happy Tom.

"How so?" asked Harry.

"Because the proof of it sits on his horse here before us. Why should a man like George Dalton be sent to Richmond? A sour Puritan who does not know how to enjoy a dance or anything else, who looks upon the beautiful face of a girl as a sin and an abomination, who thinks to be ugly is to be good, who is by temperament and education unfit to enjoy anything, while Thomas Langdon, who by the same measurements is fit to enjoy everything, is left here to hold back the Army of the Potomac. It's undoubtedly a tribute to my valour, but I don't like it."

"Thomas," said Colonel Leonidas Talbot, gravely, "you're entirely too severe with our worthy young friend, Dalton. The bubbles of pleasure always lie beneath austere and solemn exteriors like his, seeking to break a way to the surface. The longer the process is delayed the more numerous the bubbles are and the greater they expand. If scandalous reports concerning a certain young man in Richmond should reach us here in the North, relating his unparalleled exploits in the giddier circles of our gay capital, I should know without the telling that it was our prim young George Dalton."

"You never spoke truer words, Leonidas," said Lieutenant-Colonel Hector St. Hilaire. "A little judicious gallantry in youth is good for any one. It keeps the temperature from going too high. I recall now the case of Auguste Champigny, who owned an estate in Louisiana, near the Louisiana estate of the St. Hilaires, and the estates of those cousins of mine whom I visited, as I told you once.

"But pardon me. I digress, and to digress is to grow old, so I will not digress, but remain young, in heart at least. I go back now. I was speaking of Auguste Champigny, who in youth thought only of making money and of making his plantation, already great, many times greater. The blood in his veins was old at twenty-two. He did not love the vices that the world calls such. But yet there were times, I knew, when he would have longed to go with the young, because youth cannot be crushed wholly at twenty-two. There was no escape of the spirits, no wholesome blood-letting, so to speak, and that which was within him became corrupt. He acquired riches and more riches, and land and more land, and at fifty he went to New Orleans, and sought the places where pleasures abound. But his true blossoming time had passed. The blood in his veins now became poison. He did the things that twenty should do, and left undone the things that fifty should do. Ah! Harry, one of the saddest things in life is the dissipated boy of fifty! He should have come with us when the first blood of youth was upon him. He could have found time then for play as well as work. He could have rowed with us in the slender boats on the river and bay-ous with Mimi and Rosalie and Marianne and all those other bright and happy ones. He could have danced, too. It was no strain, we never danced longer than two days and two nights without stopping, and the festivals, the gay fete days, not more than one a week! But it was not Auguste's way. A man when he should have been a boy, and then, alas! a boy when he should have been a man!"

"You speak true words, Hector," said Colonel Leonidas Talbot, "though at times you seem to me to be rather sentimental. Youth is youth and it has the pleasures of youth. It is not fitting that a man should be a boy, but middle-age has pleasures of its own and they are more solid, perhaps more satisfying than those of youth. I can't conceive of twenty getting the pleasure out of the noble game of chess that we do. The most brilliant of your young French Creole dancers never felt the thrill that I feel when the last move is made and I beat you."

"Then if you expect to experience that thrill, Leonidas, continue the pursuit of my king, from which you expect so much, and see what will happen to you."

Colonel Talbot looked keenly at the board, and alarm appeared on his face. He made a rapid retreat with one of his pieces, and Harry and Dalton, knowing that it was time for them to go, reached down from their saddles, shook hands with both, then with St. Clair and Happy Tom, and were soon beyond the bounds of the camp.

They rode on for many hours in silence. They were in a friendly land now, but they knew that it was well to be careful, as Federal scouts and cavalry nevertheless might be encountered at any moment. Two or three times they turned aside from the road to let detachments of horsemen pass. They could not tell in the dark and from their hiding places to which army they belonged, and they were not willing to take the delay necessary to find out. They merely let them ride by and resumed their own place on the road.

Harry told Dalton many more details of his perilous journey from the river to the camp of the commander-in-chief, and he spoke particularly of Shepard.

"Although he's a spy," he said, "I feel that the word scarcely fits him, he's so much greater than the ordinary spy. That man is worth more than a brigade of veterans to the North. He's as brave as a lion, and his craft and cunning are almost superhuman."

He did not tell that he might easily have put Shepard forever out of the way, but that his heart had failed him. Yet he did not feel remorse nor any sense of treachery to his cause. He would do the same were the same chance to come again. But it seemed to him now that a duel had begun between Shepard and himself. They had been drifting into it, either through chance or fate, for a long time. He knew that he had a most formidable antagonist, but he felt a certain elation in matching himself against one so strong.

They rode all night and the next day across the strip of Maryland into Virginia and once more were among their own people, their undoubted own. They were now entering the Valley of Virginia where the great Jackson had leaped into fame, and both Harry and Dalton felt their hearts warm at the greetings they received. Both armies had marched over the valley again and again. It was torn and scarred by battle, and it was destined to be torn and scarred many times more, but its loyalty to the South stood every test. This too was the region in which many of the great Virginia leaders were born, and it rejoiced in the valour of its sons.

Food and refreshment were offered everywhere to the two young horsemen, and the women and the old men—not many young men were left—wanted to hear of Gettysburg. They would not accept it as a defeat. It was merely a delay, they said. General Lee would march North once more next year. Harry knew in his heart that the South would never invade again, that the war would be for her henceforth a purely defensive one, but he said nothing. He could not discourage people who were so sanguine.

Every foot of the way now brought back memories of Jackson. He saw many familiar places, fields of battle, sites of camps, lines of advance or retreat, and his heart grew sad within him, because one whom he admired so much, and for whom he had such a strong affection, was gone forever, gone when he was needed most. He saw again with all the vividness of reality that terrible night at Chancellorsville, when the wounded Jackson lay in the road, his young officers covering his body with their own to protect him from the shells.

When they reached the strip of railroad entering Richmond they left their horses to be sent later, and each took a full seat in the short train, where he could loosen his belt, and stretch his limbs. It was a crude coach, by the standards of to-day, but it was a luxury then. Harry and Dalton enjoyed it, after so much riding horseback, and watched the pleasant landscape, brown now from the July sun, flow past.

Their coach did not contain many passengers, several wounded officers going to Richmond on furlough, some countrymen, carrying provisions to the capital for sale, and a small, thin, elderly woman in a black dress, to whom Harry assigned the part of an old maid. He noticed that her features were fine and she had the appearance of one who had suffered. When they reached Richmond and their passes were examined, he hastened to carry her bag for her and to help her off the train. She thanked him with a smile that made her almost handsome, and quickly disappeared in the streets of the city.

"A nice looking old maid," he said to Dalton.

"How do you know she's an old maid?"

"I don't know. I suppose it's a certain primness of manner."

"You can't judge by appearances. Like as not she's been married thirty years, and it's possible that she may have a family of at least twelve children."

"At any rate, we'll never know. But it's good, George, to be here in Richmond again. It's actually a luxury to see streets and shop windows, and people in civilian clothing, going about their business."

"Looks the same way to me, Harry, but we can't delay. We must be off to the President, with the dispatches from the Army of Northern Virginia."

But they did not hurry greatly. They were young and it had been a long time since they had been in a city of forty thousand inhabitants, where the shop windows were brilliant to them and nobody on the streets was shooting at anybody else. It was late July, the great heats were gone for the time at least, and they were brisk and elated. They paused a little while in Capitol Square, and looked at the Bell Tower, rising like a spire, from the crest of which alarms were rung, then at the fine structure of St. Paul's Church. They intended to go into the State House now used as the Confederate Capitol, but that must wait until they reported to President Davis.

They arrived at the modest building called the White House of the Confederacy, and, after a short wait in the anteroom, they were received by the President. They saw a tall, rather spare man, dressed in a suit of home-knit grey. He received them without either warmth or coldness. Harry, although it was not the first time he had seen him, looked at him with intense curiosity. Davis, like Lincoln, was born in his own State, Kentucky, but like most other Kentuckians, he did not feel any enthusiasm over the President of the Confederacy. There was no magnetism. He felt the presence of intellect, but there was no inspiration in that arid presence.

A man of Oriental features was sitting near with a great bunch of papers in his hand. Mr. Davis did not introduce Harry and Dalton to him, and he remained silent while the President was asking questions of the messengers. But Harry watched him when he had a chance, interested strongly in that shrewd, able, Eastern face, the descendant of an immemorial and intellectual race, the man who while Secretary of State was trying also to help carry the tremendous burden of Confederate finance. What was he thinking, as Harry and Dalton answered the President's questions about the Army of Northern Virginia?

"You say that you left immediately after our army crossed the Potomac?" asked the President.

"Yes, sir," replied Harry. "General Meade could have attacked, but he remained nearly two days on our front without attempting to do so."

A thin grey smile flitted over the face of the President of the Confederacy.

"General Meade was not beaten at Gettysburg, but I fancy he remembered it well enough."

Harry glanced at Benjamin, but his Oriental face was inscrutable. The lad wondered what was lurking at the back of that strong brain. He was shrewd enough himself to know that it was not always the generals on the battlefield who best understood the condition of a state at war, and often the man who held the purse was the one who measured it best of all. But Benjamin never said a word, nor did the expression of his face change a particle.

"The Army of Northern Virginia is safe," said the President, "and it will be able to repel all invasion of Virginia. General Lee gives especial mention of both of you in his letters, and you are not to return to him at once. You are to remain here a while on furlough, and if you will go to General Winder he will assign you to quarters."

Both Harry and Dalton were delighted, and, although thanks were really due to General Lee, they thanked the President, who smiled dryly. Then they saluted and withdrew, the President and the Secretary of State going at once into earnest consultation over the papers Mr. Benjamin had brought.

Harry felt that he had left an atmosphere of depression and said so, when they were outside in the bright sunshine.

"If you were trying to carry as much as Mr. Davis is carrying you'd be depressed too," said Dalton.

"Maybe so, but let's forget it. We've got nothing to do for a few days but enjoy ourselves. General Winder is to give us quarters, but we're not to be under his command. What say you to a little trip through the capitol?"

"Good enough."

Congress had adjourned for the day, but they went through the building, admiring particularly the Houdon Washington, and then strolled again through the streets, which were so interesting and novel to them. Richmond was never gayer and brighter. They were sure that the hated Yankees could never come. For more than two years the Army of Northern Virginia had been an insuperable bar to their advance, and it would continue so.

Harry suddenly lifted his cap as some one passed swiftly, and Dalton glancing backward saw a small vanishing figure.

"Who was it?" he asked.

"The thin little old maid in black whom we saw on the train. She may have nodded to me when I bowed, but it was such a little nod that I'm not certain."

"I rather like your being polite to an insignificant old maid, Harry. I'd expect you, as a matter of course, to be polite to a young and pretty girl, over polite probably."

"That'll do, George Dalton. I like you best when you're preaching least. Come, let's go into the hotel and hear what they're talking about."

After the custom of the times a large crowd was gathered in the spacious lobby of Richmond's chief hotel. Among them were the local celebrities in other things than war, Daniel, Bagby, Pegram, Randolph, and a half-dozen more, musicians, artists, poets, orators and wits. People were quite democratic, and Harry and Dalton were free to draw their chairs near the edge of the group and listen. Pegram, the humorist, gave them a glance of approval, when he noticed their uniforms, the deep tan of their faces, their honest eyes and their compact, strong figures.

Harry soon learned that a large number of English and French newspapers had been brought by a blockade runner to Wilmington, North Carolina, and had just reached the capital, the news of which these men were discussing with eagerness.

"We learn that the sympathies of both the French and English governments are still with us," said Randolph.

"But these papers were all printed before the news of Vicksburg and Gettysburg had crossed the Atlantic," said Daniel.

"England is for us," said Pegram, "only because she likes us little and the North less. The French Imperialists, too, hate republics, and are in for anything that will damage them. When we beat off the North, until she's had enough, and set up our own free and independent republic, we'll have both England and France annoying us, and demanding favours, because they were for us in the war. Sympathy is something, but it doesn't win any battles."

"A nation has no real friend except itself," said Bagby. "Whatever the South gets she'll have to get with her own good right arm."

"I can predict the first great measure to be put through by the Southern Government after the war."

"What will it be?"

"The abolition of slavery."

"Why, that's one of the things we're fighting to maintain!"

"Exactly so. You're willing to throw away a thing of your own accord, when you're not willing to throw it away because another orders you to do so. Wars are due chiefly to our misunderstanding of human nature."

Then Pegram turned suddenly to Harry. "You're from the field?" he said. "From the Army of Northern Virginia?"

"Yes," replied Harry. "My name is Kenton and I'm a lieutenant on the staff of General Lee. My friend is George Dalton, also of the commander-in-chief's staff."

"Are you from Kentucky?" asked Daniel curiously.

"Yes, from a little town called Pendleton."

"Then I fancy that I've met a relative of yours. I returned recently from a small town in North Georgia, the name of which I may not give, owing to military reasons, necessary at the present time, and I met while I was there a splendid tall man of middle years, Colonel George Kenton of Kentucky."

"That's my father!" said Harry eagerly. "How was he?"

"I thought he must be your father. The resemblance, you know. I should say that if all men were as healthy as he looked there would be no doctors in the world. He has a fine regiment and he'll be in the battle that's breeding down there. Grant has taken Vicksburg, as we all know, but a powerful army of ours is left in that region. It has to be dealt with before we lose the West."

"And it will fight like the Army of Northern Virginia," said Harry. "I know the men of the West. The Yankees win there most of the time, because we have our great generals in the East and they have theirs in the West."

"I've had that thought myself," said Bagby. "We've had men of genius to lead us in the East, but we don't seem to produce them in the West. People are always quoting Napoleon's saying that men are nothing, a man is everything, which I never believed before, but which I'm beginning to believe now."

Then the talk veered away from battle and back to social, literary and artistic affairs, to all of which Harry and Dalton listened eagerly. Both had minds that responded to the more delicate things of life, and they were glad to hear something besides war discussed. It was hard for them to think that everything was going on as usual in Europe, that new books and operas and songs were being written, and that men and women were going about their daily affairs in peace. Yet both were destined to live to see the case reversed, the people of the States setting the world an example in moderation and restraint, while the governments of Europe were deluging that continent with blood.

"If this war should result in our defeat," said Bagby, "we won't get a fair trial before the world for two or three generations, and maybe never."

"Why?" asked Dalton.

"Because we're not a writing people. Oh, yes, there's Poe, I know, the nation's greatest literary genius, but even Europe honoured him before the South did. We've devoted our industry and talents to politics, oratory and war. We don't write books, and we don't have any newspapers that amount to much. Why, as sure as I'm sitting here, the moment this war is over New England and New York and Pennsylvania, particularly New England, will begin to pour out books, telling how the wicked Southerners brought on the war, what a cruel and low people we are, the way in which we taught our boys, when they were strong enough, how to beat slaves to death, and the whole world will believe them. Maybe the next generation of Southerners will believe them too."

"Why?" asked Harry.

"Why? Why? Because we don't have any writers, and won't have any for a long time! The writer has not been honoured among us. Any fellow with a roaring voice who can get up on the stump and tell his audience that they're the bravest and best and smartest people on earth is the man for them. You know that old story of Andy Jackson. Somebody taunted him with being an uneducated man, so at the close of his next speech he thundered out: *E pluribus unum! Multum in parvo! Sic semper tyrannis!* So it was all over. Old Andy to that audience, and all the others that heard of it, was the greatest Latin scholar in the world."

"But that may apply to the North, too," objected Harry.

"So it would. Nevertheless they'll write this war, and they'll get their side of it fastened on the world before our people begin to write."

"But if we win we won't care," said Randolph. "Success speaks for itself. You can squirm and twist all you please, and make all the excuses for it that you can think up, but there stands success glaring contemptuously at you. You're like a little boy shooting arrows at the Sphinx."

Thus the conversation ran on. Both Harry and Dalton were glad to be in the company of these men, and to feel that there was something in the world besides war. All the multifarious interests of peace and civilization suddenly came crowding back upon them. Harry remembered Pendleton with its rolling hills, green fields, and clear streams, and Dalton remembered his own home, much like it, in the Valley of Virginia, not so far away.

"Do you remain long in Richmond?" asked Randolph.

"A week at least," replied Harry.

"Then you ought to see a little of social life. Mrs. John Curtis, a leading hostess, gives a reception and a dance to-morrow night. I can easily procure invitations for both of you, and I know that she would be glad to have two young officers freshly arrived from our glorious Army of Northern Virginia."

"But our clothes!" said Dalton. "We have only a change of uniform apiece, and they're not fresh by any means."

All the men laughed.

"You don't think that Richmond is indulging in gorgeous apparel do you?" said Daniel. "We never manufactured much ourselves, and since all the rest of the world is cut off from us where are the clothes to come from even for the women? Brush up your uniforms all you can and you'll be more than welcome. Two gallant young officers from the Army of Northern Virginia! Why, you'll be two Othellos, though white, of course."

Harry glanced at Dalton, and Dalton glanced at Harry. Each saw that the other wanted to go, and Daniel, watching them, smiled.

"I see that you'll come," he said, "and so it's settled. Have you quarters yet?"

"Not yet," replied Harry, "but we'll see about it this afternoon."

"I'll have the invitations sent to you here at this hotel. All of us will be there, and we'll see that you two meet everybody."

Both thanked him profusely. They were about to go, thinking it time to report to General Winder, when Harry noticed a thin woman in a black dress, carrying a large basket, and just leaving the hotel desk. He caught a glimpse of her face and he knew that it was the old maid of the train. Then something else was impressed upon his mind, something which he had not noticed at their first meeting, but which came to him at their second. He had seen a face like hers before, but the resemblance was so faint and fleeting that he could not place it, strive as he would. But he was sure that it was there.

"Who is that woman?" he asked.

Daniel shook his head and so did Randolph, but Bagby spoke up.

"Her name is Henrietta Carden," he said, "and she's a seamstress.

I've seen her coming to the hotel often before, bringing new clothes to the women guests, or taking away old ones to be repaired. I believe that the ladies account her most skilful. It's likely that she'll be at the Curtis house, in a surgical capacity, to-morrow night, as a quick repairer of damaged garments, those fine linen and silk and lace affairs that we don't know anything about. Mrs. Curtis relies greatly upon her and I ought to tell you, young gentlemen, that Mr. Curtis is a most successful blockade runner, though he takes no personal risk himself. The Curtis house is perhaps the most sumptuous in Richmond. You'll see no signs of poverty there, though, as I told you, officers in old and faded clothes are welcome."

Harry saw Henrietta Carden carrying the large basket of clothes, go out at a side door, and he felt as if a black shadow like a menace had passed across the floor. But it was only for an instant. He dismissed it promptly, as one of those thoughts that come out of nothing, like idle puffs of summer air. He and Dalton bade a brief farewell to their new friends and left for the headquarters of General Winder. An elderly and childless couple named Lanham had volunteered to take two officers in their house near Capitol Square, and there Harry and Dalton were sent.

They could not have found a better place. Mr. and Mrs. Lanham were quiet people, who gave them an excellent room and a fine supper. Mrs. Lanham showed a motherly solicitude, and when she heard that they were going to the Curtis ball on the following night she demanded that their spare and best uniforms be turned over to her.

"I can make them look fresh," she insisted, "and your appearance must be the finest possible. No, don't refuse again. It's a pleasure to me to do it. When I look at you two, so young and strong and so honest in manner and speech, I wish that I had sons too, and then again I'm glad I have not."

"Why not, Mrs. Lanham?" asked Harry.

"Because I'd be in deadly fear lest I lose them. They'd go to the war—I couldn't help it—and they'd surely be killed."

"We won't grieve over losing what we've never had," smiled Mr. Lanham. "That's morbid."

Harry and Dalton did their best to answer all the questions of their hosts, who they knew would take no pay. The interest of both Mr. and Mrs. Lanham was increased when they found that their young guests were on the staff of General Lee and before that had been on the staff of the great Stonewall Jackson. These two names were mighty in the South, untouched by any kind of malice or envy, and with legends to cluster around them as the years passed.

"And you really saw Stonewall Jackson every day!" said Mrs. Lanham. "You rode with him, talked with him, and went into battle with him?"

"I was in all his campaigns, Mrs. Lanham," replied Harry, modestly, but not without pride. "I was with him in every battle, even to the last, Chancellorsville. I was one of those who sheltered him from the shells, when he was shot by our own men. Alas! what an awful mistake. I—"

He stopped suddenly. He had choked with emotion, and the tears came into his eyes. Mrs. Lanham saw, and, understanding, she quickly changed the subject to Lee. They talked a while after supper, called dinner now, and then they went up to their room on the second floor.

It was a handsome room, containing good furniture, including two single beds. Their baggage had preceded them and everything was in order. Two large windows, open to admit the fresh air, looked out over Richmond. On a table stood a pitcher of ice water and glasses.

"Our lot has certainly been cast in a pleasant place," said Dalton, taking a chair by one of the windows.

"You're right," said Harry, sitting in the chair by the other window. "The Lanhams are fine people, and it's a good house. This is luxury, isn't it, George, old man?"

"The real article. We seem to be having luck all around. And we're going to a big ball to-morrow night, too. Who'd have thought such a thing possible a week ago?"

"And we've made friends who'll see that we're not neglected."

"It's an absolute fact that we've become the favourite children of fortune."

"No earthly doubt of it."

Then ensued a silence, broken at length by a scraping sound as each moved his chair a little nearer to the window.

"Close, George," said Harry at length.

"Yes, a bit hard to breathe."

"When fellows get used to a thing it's hard to change."

"Fine room, though, and those are splendid beds."

"Great on a winter night."

"You've noticed how the commander-in-chief himself seldom sleeps under a tent, but takes his blankets to the open?"

"Wonder how an Indian who has roamed the forest all his life feels when he's shut up between four walls for the first time."

"Fancy it's like a prison cell to him."

"Think so too. But the Lanhams are fine people and they're doing their best for us."

"Do you think they'd be offended if I were to take my blankets, and sleep on the grass in the back yard?"

"Of course they would. You mustn't think of such a thing. After this war is over you've got to emerge slowly from barbarism. Do you remember whether at supper we cut our food with our knives and lifted it to our mouths with forks, or just tore and lifted with our fingers?"

"We used knife and fork, each in its proper place. I happened to think of it and watched myself. You, I suppose, did it through the force of an ancient habit, recalled by civilized surroundings."

"I'm glad you remember about it. Now I'm going to bed, and maybe I'll sleep. I suppose there's no hope of seeing the stars through the roof."

"None on earth! But my bed is fine and soft. We'd be all right if we could only lift the roof off the house. I'd like to hear the wind rubbing the boughs together."

"Stop it! You make me homesick! We've got no right to be pining for blankets and the open, when these good people are doing so much for us!"

Each stretched himself upon his bed, and closed his eyes. They had not been jesting altogether. So long a life in the open made summer skies at night welcome, and roofs and walls almost took from them the power of breathing.

But the feeling wore away after a while and amid pleasurable thoughts of the coming ball both fell asleep.

CHAPTER 10

The Missing Paper

Harry and Dalton did not awake until late the next morning and they found they had not suffered at all from sleeping between four walls and under a roof. Their lungs were full of fresh air, and youth with all its joyous irresponsibility had come back. Harry sprang out of bed.

"Up! up! old boy!" Harry cried to Dalton. "Don't you hear the bugles calling? not to battle but to pleasure! There is no enemy in our front! We don't have to cross a river with an overwhelming army pressing down upon us! We don't have to ride before the dawn on a scout which may lead us into a thicket full of hostile riflemen. We're in a city, boy, and our business now is beauty and pleasure!"

"Harry," said Dalton, "you ought to go far."

"Why, George? What induces you to assume the role of a prophet concerning me?"

"Because you're so full of life. You're so keen about everything. You must have a heart and lungs of extra steam power."

"But I notice you don't say anything about brain power. Maybe you think it's the quiet, rather silent fellows like yourself, George, who have an excess of that."

"None of your irony. Am I not looking forward to this ball as much as you are? I was a boy when I entered the war, Harry, but two years of fighting day and night age one terribly. I feel as if I could patronize any woman under twenty-five, and treat her as quite a simple young thing."

"Try it, George, and see what happens to you."

"Oh, no! I merely said I felt that way. I've too much sense to put it into action."

"Do you know, George, that when this war is over it will be really time for us to be thinking about girls. We'll be quite old enough. They say that many of the Yankee maidens in Philadelphia and New York are fine for looks. I wonder if they'll cast a favouring eye on young Southern officers as our conquering armies go marching down their streets!"

"It's too remote. Don't think about it, Harry. Richmond will do us for the present."

"But you can let a fellow project his mind into the future."

"Not so far that we'll be marching as conquerors through Philadelphia and New York. Let's deal with realities."

"I've always thought there was something of the Yankee about you, George, not in political principles—I never question your devotion to the cause—but in calculating, weighing everything and deciding in favour of the one that weighs an ounce the most."

"Are you about through dressing? You've taken a minute longer than the regular time."

There was a knock at the door, and, when Dalton opened it a few inches, a black head announced through the crack that breakfast was ready.

"See what a disgrace you're bringing upon us," said Dalton. "Delaying everything. Mrs. Lanham will say that we're two impostors, that such malingerers cannot possibly belong to the Army of Northern Virginia."

"Lead on," said Harry. "I'm ready, and I'm hungry as every soldier in the Southern army always is."

They had a warm greeting from their hospitable hosts, followed by an abundant breakfast. Then at Mrs. Lanham's earnest solicitation they turned over their dress uniforms to her to be repaired and pressed. Then they went out into the streets again, and spent the whole day rambling about, enjoying everything with the keen and intense delight that can come only to the young, and after long abstinence. Richmond was not depressed. Far from it. There had been a wonderful transformation since those dark days when the army of McClellan was near enough to see the spires of its churches. The flood of battle had rolled far away since then, and it had never come back. It could never come back. It was true that the Army of Northern Virginia had failed at Gettysburg, but it was returning to the South unassailed, and was ready to repeat its former splendid achievements. Harry went to the post office, and found there, to his great surprise and delight, a letter from his father, written three or four days after Vicksburg.

My dear son:
The news has just come to us that the Army of Northern Virginia, while performing prodigies of valour, has failed to carry

all the Northern positions at Gettysburg. Only complete success could warrant a further advance. I assume therefore that General Lee is retreating and I assume also that you, Harry, my beloved son, are alive, that you came unharmed out of that terrible battle. It does not seem possible to me that it could be otherwise. I cannot conceive of you fallen. It may be that it's because you are my son. The sons of others may fall, but not mine, just as we know that all others are doomed to die, but get into the habit of thinking ourselves immortal. So, I address this letter to you in the full belief that it will reach you somewhere, and that you will read it.

You know, of course, of our great loss at Vicksburg. It is disastrous but not irreparable. We still have a powerful army in the West, hardy, indomitable, one with which the enemy will have to reckon. As for myself I have been spared in many battles and I am well. It seems the sport of chance that you and I, while fighting on the same side, should have been separated in this war, you in the East and I in the West. But it has been done by One who knows best, and after all I am glad that you have been in such close contact with two of the greatest and highest-minded soldiers of the ages, Stonewall Jackson and Robert E. Lee. I do not think of them merely as soldiers, but as knights and champions with flaming swords. One of them, alas! is gone, but we have the other, and if man can conquer he will. Here in the West we repose our faith in Lee, as surely as do you in the East, you who see his face and hear his voice every day.

I have had two or three letters from Pendleton. That part of the State is for the present outside the area of conflict, though I hear that the guerrilla bands to the east in the mountains still vex and annoy, and that Skelly is growing bolder. I foresee the time when we shall have to reckon with this man, who is a mere brigand.

I hear that the prospects for fruit in our orchards were never finer. You will remember how you prowled in them when you were a little boy, Harry, and what a pirate you were among the apples and peaches and pears and good things that grew on tree and bush and briar in that beautiful old commonwealth of ours. I often upbraided you then, but I should like to see you now, far out on a bough as of old, reaching for a big yellow pear, or a red, red bunch of cherries! Alas! there are many lads who will never return, who will never see the pear trees and the cherry trees again, but I repeat I cannot feel that you will be among them. Who would ever have dreamed when this war began that it could go so far? More than two years of fierce and deadly battles and I can see no end. A deadlock and neither side willing to yield! How glad would be the men who made the war to see both sections back where they were two and a half years ago! and that's no treason.

Water rose in Harry's eyes. He knew how terribly his father's heart had been torn by the quarrel between North and South, and that he had thoughts which he did not tell to his son. Harry was beginning at last to think some of the same thoughts himself. If the South succeeded, then, after the war, what? Another war later on or reunion.

The rest of the letter was wholly personal, and in the end it directed Harry, when writing to him, to address his letters care of the Western Army under General Bragg. Harry was moved and he responded at once. He went to the hotel in which he had met the young men who constituted the leading lights in what was called the Mosaic Club, and, securing writing materials, made a long reply, which he posted with every hope that it would soon reach its destination.

Early in the evening he rejoined Dalton at the house of the Lanhams and they found that Mrs. Lanham had done wonders with their best uniforms. When they were dressed in them they felt that it was no harder to charge the Curtis house than to rush a battery.

"You young men go early," said Mr. Lanham. "Mrs. Lanham and I will appear later."

They departed, daring to practice their dance steps in the street to the delight of small boys who did not hesitate to chaff them. But Harry and Dalton did not care. They answered the chaff in kind, and soon approached the Curtis home, all the windows of which were blazing with light.

The house stood in extensive grounds, and lofty white pillars gave it an imposing appearance. Guests were arriving fast. Most of the men were military, but there was a fair sprinkling of civilians nevertheless. The lads saw their friends of the Mosaic Club pass in just ahead of them, all dressed with extreme care. Generals and colonels and other officers were in most favour now, but these men, with their swift and incisive wit and their ability to talk well about everything, fully made up for the lack of uniform.

Harry and Dalton, before passing through the side gateway that led to the house, paused awhile to look at those who came. Many people, and they ranked among the best in Richmond, walked. They had sent

135

all their horses to the front long ago to be ridden by cavalrymen or to draw cannon. Others, not so self-sacrificing, came in heavy carriages with negroes driving.

Harry noticed that in many cases the clothing of the men showed a little white at the seams, and there were cuffs the ends of which had been trimmed with great care. But it was these whom he respected most. He remembered that Virginia had not really wanted to go into the war, and that she had delayed long, but, being in it, she was making supreme sacrifices.

And there were many young girls who did not need elaborate dress. In their simple white or pink, often but cotton, their cheeks showing the delicate colour that is possessed only by the girls in the border states of the South, they seemed very beautiful to Harry and George, who had known nothing but camps and armies so long.

It was the healthy admiration of the brave youth of one sex for the fair youth of the other, but there was in it a deeper note, too. Age can stand misfortune. Youth wonders why it is stricken, and Harry felt as they passed by, bright of face and soft of voice, that the clouds were gathering heavily over them.

But he was too young himself for the feeling to endure long. Dalton was proposing that they go in and they promptly joined the stream of entering guests. Randolph soon found them and presented them to Mrs. Curtis, a large woman of middle years, and dignified manner, related to nearly all the old families of Virginia, and a descendant of a collateral branch of the Washingtons. Her husband, William Curtis, seemed to be of a different type, a man of sixty, tall, thin and more reserved than most Southerners of his time. His thin lips were usually compressed and his pale blue eyes were lacking in warmth. But the long strong line of his jaw showed that he was a man of strength and decision.

"A Northern bough on a Southern tree," whispered Dalton, as they passed on. "He comes from some place up the valley and they say that the North itself has not his superior in financial skill."

"I did not warm to him at first," said Harry, "but I respect him. As you know, George, we've put too little stress upon his kind of ability. We'll need him and more like him when the Confederacy is established. We'll have to build ourselves up as a great power, and that's done by trade and manufactures more than by arms."

"It's so, Harry. But listen to that music!"

A band of four pieces placed behind flowers and shrubbery was playing. Here was no blare of trumpets or call of bugles. It was the music of the dance and the sentimental old songs of the South, nearly all of which had a sad and wailing note. Harry heard the four black men play the songs that he had heard Samuel Jarvis sing, deep in the Kentucky mountains, and his heart beat with an emotion that he could not understand. Was it a cry for peace? Did his soul tell him that an end should come to fighting? Then throbbed the music of the lines:

Soft o'er the fountain lingering falls the Southern moon Far o'er the mountain breaks the day too soon. In thy dark eyes' splendour, where the moonlight loves to dwell Weary looks, yet tender, speak their fond farewell. Nita, Juanita! Ask thy soul if we should part, Nita, Juanita! Lean thou on my heart!

The music of the sad old song throbbed and throbbed, and sank deep into Harry's heart. At another time he might not have been stirred, but at this moment he was responsive in every fibre. He saw once more the green wilderness, and he heard once more the mellow tones of the singer coming back in far echoes from the gorges.

"Nita, Juanita! Ask thy soul if we should part," hummed Dalton, but Harry was still far away in the green wilderness, listening to the singer of the mountains. Then the singer stopped suddenly, and he was listening once more to the startling prediction of the old, old woman:

"I am proud that our house has sheltered you, but it is not for the last time. You will come again, and you will be thin and pale and in rags, and you will fall at the door. I see you coming with these two eyes of mine."

That prediction had been made a long time ago, years since, it seemed, but whenever it returned to him, and it returned at most unexpected times, it lost nothing of its amazing vividness and power; rather they were increased. Could it be true that the supremely old had a vision or second sight? Then he rebuked himself angrily. There was nothing supernatural in this world.

"Wake up, Harry! What are you thinking about?" whispered Dalton sharply. "You seem to be dreaming, and here's a house full of pretty girls, with more than a half-dozen looking at you, the gallant young officer of the Army of Northern Virginia, the story of whose romantic exploits had already reached Richmond."

"I was dreaming and I apologize," said Harry. That minute in which he had seen so much, so far away, passed utterly, and in another minute both he and Dalton were dancing with Virginia girls, as fair as dreams to these two, who had looked so long only upon the tanned faces of soldiers.

Both he and Dalton were at home in a half-hour. People in the Old South then, as in the New South now, are closely united by ties of kinship which are acknowledged as far as they run. One is usually a member of a huge clan and has all the privileges that clanship can confer. Kentucky was the daughter of Virginia, and mother and daughter were fond of each other, as they are to-day.

After the third dance Harry was sitting with Rosamond Lawrence of Petersburg in a window seat. She was a slender blonde girl, and the dancing had made the pink in her cheeks deepen into a flush.

"You're from Kentucky, I know," said Miss Lawrence, "but you haven't yet told me your town."

"Pendleton. It's small but it's on the map. My father is a colonel in the Western army."

"Aren't you a Virginian by blood? Most all Kentuckians are."

"Partly. My great grandfather, though, was born in Maryland."

"What was his name, Lieutenant Kenton?"

"Henry Ware!"

"Henry Ware! Kentucky's first and greatest governor."

"Yes, he was my great grandfather. I'm proud to be his descendant."

"I should think you would be."

"But his wife, who was Lucy Upton, my great grandmother, was of Virginia blood, and all of the next two generations intermarried with people of Virginia stock."

"Then you are a Kentuckian and a Virginian, too. I knew it! You have a middle name, haven't you?"

"Yes."

"Will you tell me what it is?"

"Cary."

The girl laughed.

"Harry Cary Kenton. Why Cary is one of our best old Virginia names. Will you tell me too what was your mother's name before she was married?"

"Parham."

"Another. Oh, all this unravels finely. And what was your grandmother's name?"

"Brent."

"Nothing could be more Virginian than Brent. Oh, you're one of us, Lieutenant Kenton, a real Virginian of the true blood."

"And heart and soul too!" giving her one of his finest young military glances.

She laughed. It was only quick friendship between them and no more, and a half-hour later he was dancing with another Virginia girl, not so blonde, but just as handsome, and their talk was quite as friendly.

Her name was Lockridge, and as they sat down near the musicians to rest, and listen a while, Harry saw a figure, slender and black-robed, pass. He knew at once who she was, and it had been predicted that he might meet her there, but she had stirred his curiosity a little, and thinking he might obtain further information he asked Miss Lockridge:

"Who is the woman who just passed us?"

"That's Miss Carden, Miss Henrietta Carden, a sewing woman, very capable too, who always helps at the big balls. Mrs. Curtis relies greatly upon her. The door through which she went leads to the ladies' dressing-room."

"A native of Richmond?"

"I don't know. But why are you so curious about a sewing woman, Lieutenant Kenton?"

Harry flushed. There was a faint tinge of rebuke in her words, and he knew that he merited it.

"It was just an idle question," he replied quickly, and with an air of indifference. "I noticed her on the train when we came into the capital, and we are so little used to women that we are inquisitive about every one whom we see. Why, Miss Lockridge, I didn't realize until I came to this ball that women could be so extraordinarily beautiful. Every one of you looks like an angel, just lowered gently from Heaven."

"If you're not merely a flatterer then it's long absence that gives charm. I assure you, Lieutenant Kenton, that we're very, very common clay. You should see us eat."

"I'll get you an ice at once."

"Oh, I don't mean that. I mean substantial things!"

"A healthy appetite doesn't keep a girl from being an angel."

"When men marry us they find out that we're not angels."

"The word 'angel' is with me merely a figure of speech. I don't want any real angel. I want my wife, if I ever marry, to be thoroughly human."

Harry's progress was rapid. A handsome figure and face, and an ingenuous manner made him a favourite. After midnight he wandered into a room where older men were smoking and talking. They were mostly officers, some of high rank, one a general, and they talked of that which they could never get wholly from their minds, the war. All knew Harry, and, as he wanted fresh air, they gave him a place by a window which looked upon a small court.

Harry was tired. In dancing he had been compelled to bring into play muscles long unused, and he luxuriated in the cushioned chair, while the pleasant night breeze blew upon him. They were discussing Lee's probable plans to meet Meade, who would certainly follow him in time across the Potomac. They spoke with weight and authority, because they were experienced men who had been in many battles, and they were here on furlough, most of them recovering from wounds.

Harry heard them, but their words were like the flowing of a river. He paid no heed. They did not bring the war back to him. He was thinking of the music and of the brilliant faces of the girls whom he loved collectively. What that Lawrence girl had said was true. He was a Virginian as well as a Kentuckian, and the Kentuckians and Virginians were all one big family. All those pretty Virginia girls were his cousins. It might run to the thirty-second degree, but they were his cousins just the same, and he would claim them with confidence.

He smiled and his eyelids drooped a little. It was rather dark outside, and he was looking directly into the court in which rosebushes and tall flowering plants grew. A shadow passed. He did not see whence it came or went, but he sat up and laughed at himself for dozing and conjuring up phantoms when he was at his first real ball in ages.

All the civilians had gone out and only five or six of the officers, the most important, were left. Their talk had grown more eager, and on the centre of the table around which they sat lay a large piece of white canvas upon which they were drawing a map expressing their collective opinion. Every detail was agreed upon, after much discussion, and Harry, as much interested as they, began to watch, while the lines grew upon the canvas. He ventured no opinion, being so much younger than the others.

"We don't know, of course, exactly what General Lee will do," said a colonel, "but we do know that he's always dangerous. He invariably acts on the offensive, even if he's retreating. I should think that he'd strike Meade about here."

"Not there, but not far from it," said the general. "Make a dot at that point, Bathurst, and make another dot here about twenty miles to the east, which represents my opinion."

Bathurst made the dots and the men, wholly absorbed, bent lower over their plans, which were growing almost unconsciously into a map, and a good one too. Harry was as much interested as they, and he still kept himself in the background, owing to his youth and minor rank.

The door to the room was open a little and the music, a waltz, came in a soft ripple from the drawing room. It was rhythmic and languorous, and Harry's feet would have moved to its tune at any other time, but he was too deeply absorbed in the conjectures and certainties that they were drawing with their pencils on the white canvas.

Many of the details, he knew, were absolutely true, and others he was quite sure must be true, because these were men of high rank who carried in their minds the military secrets of the Confederacy.

"I think we're pretty well agreed on the general nature of the plan," said Bathurst. "We differ only in details."

"That's so," said the general, "but we're lingering too long here. God knows that we see little enough of our women folks, and, when we have the chance to see them, and feel the touch of their hands, we waste our time like a lot of fools making military guesses. If I'm not too old to dance to the tune of the shells I'm not too old to dance to the tune of the fiddle and the bow. That's a glorious air floating in from the ballroom. I think I can show some of these youngsters like Kenton here how to shake a foot."

"After you, General," laughed Bathurst. "We know your capacity on both the field and the floor, and how you respond to the shell and the bow. Come on! The ballroom is calling to us, and I doubt whether we'll explain to the satisfaction of everybody why we've been away from it so long. You, too, Harry!"

They rose in a group and went out hastily. Harry was last, and his hand was on the bolt of the door, preparatory to closing it, when the general turned to Bathurst and said:

"You've that diagram of ours, haven't you, Bathurst? It's not a thing to be left lying loose."

"Why, no, sir, I thought you put it in your pocket."

The general laughed.

"You're suffering from astigmatism, Bathurst," he said. "Doubtless it was Colton whom you saw stowing it away. I think we'd better tear it into little bits as we have no further use for it."

"But I haven't it, sir," said Colton, a veteran colonel, just recovering from a wound in the arm. "I supposed of course that one of the others took it."

An uneasy look appeared in the general's eyes, but it passed in an instant.

"You have it, Morton?"

"No, sir. Like Bathurst I thought one of the others took it."

"And you, Kitteridge?"

"I did not take it, sir."

"You surely have it, Johnson?"

"No, sir, I was under the impression that you had taken it away with you."

"And you, McCurdy?"

McCurdy shook his head.

"Then Kenton, as you were the last to rise, you certainly have it."

"I was just a looker-on; I did not touch it," said Harry, whose hand was still on the bolt of the partly opened door.

The general laughed.

"Another case of everybody expecting somebody else to do a thing, and nobody doing it," he said. "Kenton, go back and take it from the table. In our absorption we've been singularly forgetful, and that plan must be destroyed at once."

Harry re-entered the room, and in their eagerness all of the officers followed. Then a simultaneous "Ah!" of dismay burst from them all. There was nothing on the table. The plan was gone. They looked at one another, and in the eyes of every one apprehension was growing.

"The window is partly open," said the general, affecting a laugh, although it had an uneasy note, "and of course it has blown off the table. We'll surely find it behind the sofa or a chair."

They searched the room eagerly, going over every inch of space, every possible hiding place, but the plan was not there.

"Perhaps it's in the court," said the general. "It might have fluttered out there. Raise the sash higher, Kenton. Let nobody make any noise. We must be as quiet as possible about this. Luckily there's enough moonlight now for us to find even a small scrap of paper in the court."

They stole through the window silently, one by one, and searched every inch of the court's space. But nothing was in it, save the grass and the flowers and the rosebushes that belonged there. They returned to the room, and once more looked at one another in dismay.

"Shut the window entirely and lock the door, Kenton," said the general.

Harry did so. Then the general looked at them all, and his face was set and very firm.

"We must all be searched," he said. "I know that every one of you is the soul of honour. I know that not one of you has concealed about his person this document which has suddenly become so valuable. I know that not one of you would smuggle through to the enemy such a plan at any price, no matter how large. Nevertheless we must know beyond the shadow of a doubt that none of us has the map. And I insist, too, that I be searched first. Bathurst, Colton, begin!"

They examined one another carefully in turn. Every pocket or possible place of concealment was searched. Harry was the last and when they were done with him the general heaved a huge sigh of relief.

"We know positively that we are not guilty," he said. "We knew it before, but now we've proved it. That is off our minds, but the mystery of the missing map remains. What a strange combination of circumstances. I think, gentlemen, that we had best say nothing about it to outsiders. It's certainly to the interest of every one of us not to do so. It's also to the interest of all of us to watch the best we can for a solution. You're young, Kenton, but from what I hear of you you're able to keep your own counsel."

"You can trust me, sir," said Harry.

"I know it, and now unlock the door. We've held ourselves prisoners long enough, and they'll be wondering about us in the ballroom."

Harry turned the key promptly enough and he was glad to escape from the room. He felt that he had left behind a sinister atmosphere. He had not mentioned to the older men the faint shadow that he thought he had seen crossing the courtyard. But then it was only fancy, nothing more, an idle figment of the brain! There was the music now, softer and more tempting than ever, an irresistible call to flying feet, and another dance with Rosamond Lawrence was due.

"I thought you weren't coming, Lieutenant Kenton," she said. "Some one said that you had gone into the smoking-room and that you were talking war with middle-aged generals and colonels."

"But I escaped as soon as I could, Miss Rosamond," he said—he was thinking of the locked door and the universal search.

"Well, you came just in time. The band is beginning and I was about to give your dance to that good-looking Lieutenant Dalton."

"You wouldn't treat me like that! Throw over your cousin in such a manner! I can't think it!"

"No, I wouldn't!"

Then the full swell of the music caught them both, and they glided away, as light and swift as the melody that bore them on.

CHAPTER 11

A Vain Pursuit

Youth was strong in Harry, and, while he danced and the music played, he forgot all about the incident in the smoking-room. With him it was just one pretty girl after another. He had heart enough for them all, and only one who was so young and who had been so long on battlefields could well understand what a keen, even poignant, pleasure it was to be with them.

Those were the days when a ball lasted long. Pleasures did not come often, but when they came they were to be enjoyed to the full. But as the morning hours grew the manner of the older people became slightly feverish and unnatural. They were pursuing pleasure and forgetfulness with so much zeal and energy that it bore the aspect of force rather than spontaneity. Harry noticed it and divined the cause. Beneath his high spirits he now felt it himself. It was that looming shadow in the North and that other in that far Southwest hovering over lost Vicksburg. Serious men and serious women could not keep these shadows from their eyes long.

The incident of the smoking-room and the missing map came back to him with renewed force. It could not have walked away. They had searched the room and the court so thoroughly that they would have found it, had it been there. The disappearance of a document, which men of authority and knowledge had built up almost unconsciously, puzzled and alarmed him.

It was almost day when he and Dalton left. They paid their respects to Mr. and Mrs. Curtis, and said many good-bys to "the girls they left behind them." Then they went out into the street, and inhaled great draughts of the cool night air.

"A splendid night," said Dalton.

"Yes, truly," said Harry.

"I hope you didn't propose to more than six girls."

"To none. But I love them all together."

"I'm glad to hear it, because you're entirely too young to marry, and your occupation is precarious."

"You needn't be so preachy. You're not more'n a hundred years old yourself."

"But I'm two months older than you are and often two months makes a vast difference, particularly in our cases. I notice about you, Harry, at times, a certain juvenility which I feel it my duty to repress."

"Don't do it, George. Let's enjoy it while we can, because as you say my occupation is precarious and yours is the same."

They stopped at the corner of the iron fence enclosing the Curtis home, in which many lights were still shining. It was near a dark alley opening on the street and running by this side of the house.

"I'm going to see what's behind Mr. Curtis's house," said Harry. Dalton stared at him.

"What's got into your head, Harry!" he exclaimed. "Do you mean to be a burglar prowling about the home of the man who has entertained you?"

Harry hesitated. He was sorry that Dalton was with him. Then he could have gone on without question, but he must make some excuse to Dalton.

"George," he said at last, "will you swear to keep a secret, a most important one which I am pledged to tell to nobody, but which I must confide in you in order to give a good reason for what I am about to do."

"If you are pledged to keep such a secret," replied Dalton, "then don't explain it to me. Your word is good enough, Harry. Go ahead and do what you want to do. I'll ask nothing about any of your actions, no matter how strange it may look."

"You're a man in a million, George. Come on, your confidence is going to be tested. Besides, you'll run the danger of being shot."

But Dalton followed him fearlessly as he led the way down the alley. Richmond was not lighted then, save along the main streets, and a few steps took them into the full dark. The brilliant windows threw bright bands across the lines, but they themselves were in darkness.

The alley ran through the next street and so did the Curtis grounds. They were as extensive in the rear of the house as in front, and contained small pines carefully trimmed, banks of roses and two grape arbours. Harry could hear no sound of any one stirring among them, but people, obviously the cooks and other servants, were talking in the big kitchen at the rear of the house.

145

The street itself running in the rear of the building was as well lighted as it was in front, but Harry saw no one in it save a member of the city police, who seemed to be keeping a good watch. But as he did not wish to be observed by the man he waited a little while in the mouth of the alley, until he had moved on and was out of sight.

"Now, George," he said, "you and I are going to do a little scouting. You know I'm descended from the greatest natural scout and trailer ever known in the West, one whose senses were preternaturally acute, one who could almost track a bird in the air by its flight."

"Yes, I've heard of the renowned Henry Ware, and I know that you've inherited a lot of his skill and intuition. Go ahead. I promised that I would help you and ask no questions. I keep my word."

Harry climbed silently over the low fence, and Dalton followed in the same manner. The light from the street and house did not penetrate the pines and rosebushes, where Harry quickly found a refuge, Dalton as usual following him.

"What next?" whispered Dalton.

"Now, I do my trailing and scouting, and you help me all you can, George, but be sure you don't make any noise. There's enough moonlight filtering through the pines to show the ground to me, but not enough to disclose us to anybody twenty feet away."

He dropped to his hands and knees, and, crawling back and forth, began to examine every inch of ground with minute care, while Dalton stared at him in amazement.

"I'd help," whispered Dalton, "if I only knew what you were doing."

"Suppose, George, that somebody wanted to see the Curtis house, and yet not be seen, wanted to observe as well as he could, without detection, what was going on there. He'd watch his chance, jump over the fence as we have done and enter this group of pines. He could ask no finer point of observation. We are perfectly hidden and yet we can see the whole rear of the house and one side of it."

"So we can. I infer that you are looking for some one who you think has been acting as a spy."

"Ah! here we are. The earth is a bit soft by this pine, and I see the trace of a footstep! And here is another trace, close by it, undoubtedly the imprint of the other foot. It's as plain as day."

Dalton knelt, looked at the traces, and shook his head. "I can't make out any of them," he said. "I see nothing but a slight displacement of the grass caused by the wind."

"That's because you haven't my keen eye, an inherited and natural ability as a trailer, although you may beat me out of sight in other things. The shape of these traces indicates that they were made by human feet, and their closeness together shows that the man stood looking at the house. If he had been walking along they would be much wider apart."

He examined the traces again with long and minute care.

"The toes point toward the house, consequently he was looking at it," he said. "He was a heavy man, and he stood here a long time, not moving from his tracks. That's why he left these traces, which are so clear and evident to me, George, although they're hidden from a blind man like you."

"Well, what of it?"

"Nothing much to you, but a lot to me."

He rose to his feet and examined the boughs of the pine.

"As I thought," he whispered with great satisfaction. "Despite his courage and power over himself, both of which were very great, he became a little excited. Doubtless he saw something that stirred him deeply."

"What under the stars are you talking about, Harry?"

"See, he broke off three twigs of the pine. Just snapped them in two with nervous fingers. Here are pieces lying on the ground. Now, a man does that sort of thing almost unconsciously. He will not reach up for the twig or down for it, but he breaks it because it presents itself to him at the corner of his eye. This man was six feet in height or more and built very powerfully. I think I know him! Yes, I'm sure I know him! Nor is it at all strange that he should be here."

"Shall we make a thorough search for him among the pines? You say he's tall and built powerfully. But maybe the two of us could master him, and if not we could call for help."

"Too late, George. He left a long time ago, and he took with him what he wanted. We needn't look any farther."

"Lead on, then, King of Trailers and Master of Secrets! If the mighty Caliph, Haroun al Kenton, wishes to prowl in these grounds, seeking the heart of some great conspiracy, it is not for his loyal vizier, the Sheikh Ul Dalton to ask him questions."

"I'm not certain that a vizier is a sheikh."

"Nor am I, but I'm certain that I want to go home and go to bed. Vikings of the land like ourselves can't stand much luxury. It weakens the tissues, made strong on the march and in the fields."

They left the grounds silently and unobserved and soon were in their own quarters, where they slept nearly the whole day. Then they spent three or four days more in the social affairs which were such a keen pleasure to them after such a long deprivation. But wherever they went, and they were in demand everywhere, Harry was always looking for somebody, a man, tall, heavy and broad shouldered, not a man who would come into a room where he was, or who would join a company of people that he had joined, but one who would hang upon the outskirts, and hide behind the corners of buildings or trees. He did not see the shadow, but once or twice he felt that it was there.

The officer, Bathurst, told him one night that some important papers had been stolen from the White House of the Confederacy itself.

"They pertain to our army," said Bathurst, "and they will be of value to the enemy, if they reach him."

"I'm quite certain that the most daring and dangerous of all northern spies is in Richmond," said Harry.

Then he told Bathurst of Shepard and of the trails that he had seen among the pines behind Curtis's house.

"Do you think this man got our map?" asked Bathurst.

"It may have been so. Perhaps he was hidden in the court and when he saw us go out, leaving the map on the table, he slipped in at the window and seized it."

"But the court was enclosed. He would have had to go with the paper through the house itself."

"That's where my theory fails. I can provide for his taking the paper, but I can't provide for his escape."

"I'll tell the General about it. I think you're right, Harry. I've heard of Shepard myself, and he's worth ten thousand men to the Yankees. It's more than that. At such a critical stage of our affairs he might ruin us. We'll make a general search for him. We'll rake the city with a fine tooth comb."

The search was made everywhere. Soldiers pried in every possible place, but they found nobody who could not give an adequate account of his presence in Richmond. Harry felt sure nevertheless that Shepard was somewhere in the capital, protected by his infinite daring and resource, and they received the startling news the next day after the search that a messenger sent northward with dispatches for Lee had been attacked only a short distance from the city. He had been struck from behind, and did not see his assailant, but the wound in the head—the man had been found unconscious—and the missing dispatches were sufficient proof.

A night later precious documents were purloined from the office of the Secretary of War and a list of important earthworks on the North and South Carolina coast disappeared from the office of the Secretary of the Navy. Alarm spread through all the departments of the Confederacy. Some one, spy and burglar too, had come into the very capital, and he was having uncommon success.

Harry had not the least doubt that it was Shepard, and he was filled with an ambition to capture this man, whom he really liked. If Shepard were caught he would certainly be hanged, but then a spy must take his chances.

They heard meanwhile that General Lee had gone to a former camp of his on the Opequan, but that later in response to manoeuvres by General Meade, he moved to a position near Front Royal. No orders came for Harry or Dalton to rejoin him, and, as a period of inactivity seemed to be at hand, they were glad to remain a while longer in Richmond. They still stayed with the Lanhams, who refused to take any pay, although the two young officers, chipping together, bought for Mrs. Lanham a little watch which had just come through the blockade from England.

Thus their days lengthened in Richmond, and, despite the shadow of the spy and his doings which was over Harry, they were still very pleasant. The members of the Mosaic Club, although older men, made much of them, and Harry and Dalton, being youths of sprightly wit, were able to hold their own in such company. The time had now passed into August, and they sat one afternoon in the lobby of the big hotel with their new friends. Richmond without was quiet and blazing in the sun. Harry had received a second letter from his father from an unnamed point in Georgia. It did not contain much news, but it was full of cheerfulness, and it intimated in more than one place that Bragg's army was going to strike a great blow.

All eyes were turned toward the West. The opinion had been spreading in the Confederacy that the chief danger was on that line. It seemed that the Army of Northern Virginia could take care of anything to the north and east, but in the south and west affairs did not go well.

"It's a pity that General Bragg is President Davis' brother-in-law," said Randolph.

"Why?" asked Daniel.

"Then he wouldn't be in command of our Western Army."

"Bragg's a fighter, though."

"But not a reaper."

"What do you mean?"

"He wins the victory, but lets the enemy take it."

"It may be so. But to come closer home, what about the Yankee spy in Richmond? It's an established fact that a man of most uncommon daring and skill is here."

"No doubt of it, what's the latest from him?"

"The house of William Curtis was entered last night and robbed."

"Robbed of what?"

"Papers. The man never takes any valuables."

"But Curtis is not in the government!"

"No, but he carries on a lot of blockade running, chiefly through Norfolk and Wilmington. I think the papers related to several blockade running vessels coming out from England, and of course the Yankee blockading ships will be ready for them. There's not a trace of the man who took them."

"Something is deucedly sinister about it," said Bagby. "It seems to be the work of one man, and he must have a hiding place in Richmond, but we can't find it. Kenton, you and Dalton are army officers, supposedly of intelligence. Now, why don't you find this mysterious terror? Ah, will you excuse me for a minute! I see Miss Carden leaving the counter with her basket, and there is no other seamstress in Richmond who can put the ruffles on a man's finest shirt as she can. She's been doing work for me for some time."

He arose, and, leaving them, bowed very politely to the seamstress. Her face, although thin and lined, was that of an educated woman of strong character. Harry thought it probable that she was a lady in the conventional meaning of the word. Many a woman of breeding and culture was now compelled to earn her own living in the South. She and Bagby exchanged only a few words, he returning to his chair, and she leaving the hotel at a side door, walking with dignity.

"I've seen Miss Carden three times before, once on the train, once at this hotel and once at Mr. Curtis's house; can you tell me anything about her?" said Harry.

"It's an ordinary tale," replied Bagby. "I think she lived well up the valley and her house being destroyed in some raid of the Federal troops she came down to the capital to earn a living. She's been doing work for me and others I know for a year past, and I know she's not been out of Richmond in that time."

The talk changed now to the books that had come through from Europe in the blockade runners. There was a new novel by Dickens and another by Thackeray, new at least to the South, and the members of the Mosaic Club were soon deep in criticism and defence.

Harry strolled away after a while. He did not tell his friends—nothing was to be gained by telling them—that he was absolutely sure of the identity of the spy, that it was Shepard. The question of identity did not matter if they caught him, and his old feeling that it was a duel between Shepard and himself returned. He believed that the duty to catch the man had been laid upon him.

He began to haunt Richmond at all hours of the night. More than once he had to give explanations to watchmen about public buildings, but he clung to the task that he had imposed upon himself. He explained to Dalton and the Virginian found no fault except for Harry's loss of time that might be devoted to amusement. Harry sometimes rebuked himself for his own persistency, but Bagby's taunt had stung a little, and he felt that it applied more to himself than to Dalton. He knew Shepard and he knew something of his ways. Moreover, his was the blood of the greatest of all trailers, and it was incumbent upon him to find the spy. Yet he was trailing in a city and not in a forest. In spite of everything he clung to his work.

On a later night about one o'clock in the morning he was near the building that housed army headquarters, and he noticed a figure come from some bushes near it. He instantly stepped back into the shadow and saw a man glance up and down the street, probably to see if it was clear. It was a night to favour the spy, dark, with heavy clouds and gusts of rain.

The figure, evidently satisfied that no one was watching, walked briskly down the street, and Harry's heart beat hard against his side. He knew that it was Shepard, the king of spies, against whom he had matched himself. He could not mistake, despite the darkness, his figure, his walk and the swing of his powerful shoulders.

His impulse was to cry for help, to shout that the spy was here, but at the first sound of his voice Shepard would at once dart into the shrubbery, and escape through the alleys of Richmond. No, his old feeling that it was a duel between Shepard and himself was right, and so they must fight it out.

Shepard walked swiftly toward the narrower and more obscure streets, and Harry followed at equal speed. The night grew darker and the rain, instead of coming in gusts, now fell steadily. Twice Shepard stopped and looked back. But on each occasion Harry flattened himself against a plank fence and he did not believe the spy had seen him.

Then Shepard went faster and his pursuer had difficulty in keeping him in view. He went through an alley, turned into a street, and Harry ran in order not to lose sight of him.

The alley came into the street at a right angle, and, when Harry turned the corner, a heavy, dark figure thrust itself into his path.

"Shepard!" he cried.

"Yes!" said the man, "and I hate to do this, but I must."

151

His heavy fist shot out and caught his pursuer on the jaw. Harry saw stars in constellations, then floated away into blackness, and, when he came out of it, found himself lying on a bed in a small room. His jaw was bandaged and very sore, but otherwise he felt all right. A candle was burning on a table near him and an unshuttered window on the other side of the room told him that it was still night and raining.

Harry looked leisurely about the room, into which he had been wafted on the magic carpet of the Arabian genii, so far as he knew. It was small and without splendour and he knew at once from the character of its belongings that it was a woman's room.

He sat up. His head throbbed, but touching it cautiously he knew that he had sustained no serious injury. But he felt chagrin, and a lot of it. Shepard had known that he was following him and had laid a trap, into which he had walked without hesitation. The man, however, had spared his life, although he could have killed him as easily as he had stunned him. Then he laughed bitterly at himself. A duel between them, he had called it! Shepard wouldn't regard it as much of a duel.

His head became so dizzy that he lay down again rather abruptly and began to wonder. What was he doing in a woman's room, and who was the woman and how had he got there? This would be a great joke for Dalton and St. Clair and Happy Tom.

He was fully dressed, except for his boots, and he saw them standing on the floor against the wall. He surveyed once more the immaculate neatness of the room. It was certainly a woman's, and most likely that of an old maid. He sat up again, but his head throbbed so fearfully that he was compelled to lie down quickly. Shepard had certainly put a lot in that right hand punch of his and he had obtained a considerable percentage of revenge for his defeat in the river.

Then Harry forgot his pain in the intensity of his curiosity. He had sustained a certain temporary numbing of the faculties from the blow and his fancy, though vivid now, was vague. He was not at all sure that he was still in Richmond. The window still showed that it was night, and the rain was pouring so hard that he could hear it beating against the walls. At all events, he thought whimsically, he had secured shelter, though at an uncommon high price.

He heard a creak, and a door at the end of the room opened, revealing the figure and the strong, haggard features of Henrietta Carden. Evidently she had taken off a hood and cloak in an outer room, as there were rain drops on her hair and her shoes were wet.

"How are you feeling, Mr. Kenton?" she asked.

"Full of aches and wonder."

"Both will pass."

She smiled, and, although she was not young, Harry thought her distinctly handsome, when she smiled.

"I seem to have driven you out of your room and to have taken your bed from you, Miss Carden," he said, "but I assure you it was unintentional. I ran against something pretty hard, and since then I haven't been exactly responsible for what I was doing."

She smiled again, and this time Harry found the smile positively winning.

"I'm responsible for your being here," she said.

Then she went back to the door and said to some one waiting in the outer room:

"You can come in, Lieutenant Dalton. He's all right except for his headache, and an extraordinary spell of curiosity."

Dalton stalked solemnly in, and regarded Harry with a stern and reproving eye.

"You're a fine fellow," he said. "A lady finds you dripping blood from the chin, and out of your head, wandering about the street in the darkness and rain. Fortunately she knows who you are, takes you into her own house, gives you an opiate or some kind of a drug, binds up your jaw where some man good and true has hit you with all his goodness and truth, and then goes for me, your guardian, who should never have let you out of his sight. I was awakened out of a sound sleep in our very comfortable room at the Lanham house, and I've come here through a pouring rain with Miss Carden to see you."

"I do seem to be the original trouble maker," said Harry. "How did you happen to find me, Miss Carden?"

"I was sitting at my window, working very late on a dress that Mrs. Curtis wants to-morrow. It was not raining hard then, and I could see very well outside. I saw a dark shadow in the street at the mouth of the alley. I saw that it was the figure of a man staggering very much. I ran out and found that it was you, Lieutenant Kenton. You were bleeding at the chin, where apparently some one had struck you very hard, and you were so thoroughly dazed that you did not know where you were or who you were."

"Yes, he hit me very hard, just as you supposed, Miss Carden," said Harry, feeling gently his sore and swollen chin.

"I half led and half dragged you into my house—there was nowhere else I could take you—and, as you were sinking into a stupor, I managed to make you lie down on my bed. I bound up your wound, while you were unconscious, and then I went for Lieutenant Dalton."

153

"And she saved your life, too, you young wanderer. No doubt of that," said Dalton reprovingly. "This is what you get for roaming away from my care. Lucky you were that an angel like Miss Carden saved you from dying of exposure. If I didn't know you so well, Harry, I should say that you had been in some drunken row."

"Oh, no! not that!" exclaimed Miss Carden. "There was no odour of liquor on his breath."

"I was merely joking, Miss Carden," said Dalton. "Old Harry here is one of the best of boys, and I'm grateful to you for saving him and coming to me. If there is any way we can repay you we'll do it."

"I don't want any repayment. We must all help in these times."

"But we won't forget it. We can't. How are you feeling, Harry?"

"My head doesn't throb so hard. The jarred works inside are gradually getting into place, and I think that in a half-hour I can walk again, that is, resting upon that stout right arm of yours, George."

"Then we'll go. I've brought an extra coat that will protect you from the rain."

"You are welcome to stay here!" exclaimed Miss Carden. "Perhaps you'd be wiser to do so."

"We thank you for such generous hospitality," said Dalton gallantly, "but it will be best for many reasons that we go back to Mrs. Lanham's as soon as we can. But first can we ask one favour of you, Miss Carden?"

"Of course."

"That you say nothing of Mr. Kenton's accident. Remember that he was on military duty and that in the darkness and rain he fell, striking upon his jaw."

"I'll remember it. Our first impression that he had been struck by somebody was a mistake, of course. You can depend upon me, both of you. Neither of you was ever in my house. The incident never occurred."

"But we're just as grateful to you as if it had happened."

A half-hour later they left the cottage, Miss Carden holding open the door a little to watch them until they were out of sight. But Harry had recovered his strength and he was able to walk without Dalton's assistance, although the Virginian kept close by his side in case of necessity.

"Harry," said Dalton, when they were nearly to the Lanham house, "are you willing to tell what happened?"

"As nearly as I know. I got upon the trail of that spy who has been infesting Richmond. I knew at the time that it couldn't have been any one else. I followed him up an alley, but he waited for me at the turn, and before I could defend myself he let loose with his right. When I came drifting back into the world I was lying upon the bed in Miss Carden's cottage."

"He showed you some consideration. He might have quietly put you out of the way with a knife."

"Shepard and I don't care to kill each other. Each wants to defeat the other's plans. It's got to be a sort of duel between us."

"So I see, and he has scored latest."

"But not last."

"We'd better stick to the tale about the fall. Such a thing could happen to anybody in these dark streets. But that Miss Carden is a fine woman. She showed true human sympathy, and what's more, she gave help."

"She's all that," agreed Harry heartily.

They had their own keys to the Lanham house and slipped in without awakening anybody. Their explanations the next day were received without question and in another day Harry's jaw was no longer sore, though his spirit was. Yet the taking of important documents ceased suddenly, and Harry was quite sure that his encounter with Shepard had at least caused him to leave the city.

CHAPTER 12

In Winter Quarters

Harry was sent a few days later with dispatches from the president to General Lee, who was still in his camp beside the Opequan. Dalton was held in the capital for further messages, but Harry was not sorry to make the journey alone. The stay in Richmond had been very pleasant. The spirits of youth, confined, had overflowed, but he was beginning to feel a reaction. One must return soon to the battlefield. This was merely a lull in the storm which would sweep with greater fury than ever. The North, encouraged by Gettysburg and Vicksburg, was gathering vast masses which would soon be hurled upon the South, and Harry knew how thin the lines there were becoming.

He thought, too, of Shepard, who was the latest to score in their duel, and he believed that this man had already sent to the Northern leaders information beyond value. Harry felt that he must strive in some manner to make the score even.

It was late in the summer when he rejoined the Army of Northern Virginia and delivered the letters to the commander-in-chief, who sat in the shade of a large tree. Harry observed him closely. He seemed a little greyer than before the Battle of Gettysburg, but his manner was as confident as ever. He filled to both eye and mind the measure of a great general. After asking Harry many questions he dismissed him for a while, to play, so he said. The young Kentuckian at once, and, as a matter of course, sought the Invincibles. St. Clair and Langdon hailed him with shouts of joy, but to his great surprise, Colonel Leonidas Talbot and Lieutenant-Colonel Hector St. Hilaire were not playing chess.

"We were getting on with the game last night, Harry," explained Colonel Talbot, "but we came to a point where we were about to develop heat over a projected move. Then, in order to avoid such a lamentable occurrence, we decided to postpone further play until tonight. But we find you looking uncommonly well, Harry. The flesh pots of Egypt have agreed with you."

"I had a good time in Richmond, sir, a fine one," replied Harry. "The people there have certainly been kind to me, as they are to all the officers of the Army of Northern Virginia."

"What have you done with the grave Dalton, who was your comrade on your journey to the capital?"

"They've kept him there for the present. They think he's stronger proof against the luxuries and temptations of a city than I am."

"Youth is youth, and I'm glad that you've had this little fling, Harry. Perhaps you'll have another, as I think you'll be sent back to Richmond very soon."

"What has been going on here, Colonel?"

"Very little. Nothing, in fact, of any importance. When we crossed the swollen Potomac, although threatened by an enemy superior to us in numbers, I felt that we would not be pushed. General Meade has been deliberate, extremely deliberate in his offensive movements. Up North they call Gettysburg a great victory, but we're resting here calmly and peacefully. Hector and I and our young friends have found rural peace and ease among these Virginia hills and valleys. You, of course, found Richmond very gay and bright?"

"Very gay and bright, Colonel, and full of handsome ladies."

Colonel Talbot sighed and Lieutenant-Colonel Hector St. Hilaire sighed also.

"Hector and I should have been there," said Colonel Talbot. "Although we've never married, we have a tremendous admiration for the ladies, and in our best uniforms we're not wholly unpopular among them, eh, Hector?"

"Not by any means, Leonidas. We're not as young as Harry here, but I know that you're a fine figure of a man, and you know that I am. Moreover, our experience of the dangerous sex is so much greater than that of mere boys like Harry and Arthur and Tom here, that we know how to make ourselves much more welcome. You talk to them about frivolous things, mere chit chat, while we explain grave and important matters to them."

"Are you sure, sir," asked St. Clair, "that the ladies don't really prefer chit chat?"

"I was not speaking of little girls. I was alluding to those ornaments of their sex who have arrived at years of discretion. Ah, if Leonidas and I were only a while in Richmond! It would be the next best thing to being in Charleston."

"Maybe the Invincibles will be sent there for a while."

"Perhaps. I don't foresee any great activity here in the autumn. How do they regard the Army of Northern Virginia in Richmond now, Harry?"

"With supreme confidence."

The talk soon drifted to the people whom Harry had met at the capital, and then he told of his adventure with Shepard, the spy.

"He seems to be a most daring man," said Talbot; "not a mere ordinary spy, but a man of a higher type. I think he's likely to do us great harm. But the woman, Miss Carden, was surely kind to you. If she hadn't found you wandering around in the rain you'd have doubtless dropped down and died. God bless the ladies."

"And so say we all of us," said Harry.

He returned to Richmond in a few days, bearing more dispatches, and to his great delight all that was left of the Invincibles arrived a week later to recuperate and see a little of the world. St. Clair and Happy Tom plunged at once and with all the ardour of youth into the gayeties of social life, and the two colonels followed them at a more dignified but none the less earnest pace. All four appeared in fine new uniforms, for which they had saved their money, and they were conspicuous upon every occasion.

Harry was again at the Curtis house, and although it was not a great ball this time the assemblage was numerous, including all his friends. The two colonels had become especial favourites everywhere, and they were telling stories of the old South, which Harry had divined was passing; passing whether the South won or not.

Although there had been much light talk through the evening and an abundance of real gayety, nearly every member of the company, nevertheless, had serious moments. The news from Tennessee and Georgia was heavy with import. It was vague in some particulars, but it was definite enough in others to tell that the armies of Rosecrans and Bragg were approaching each other. All eyes turned to the West. A great battle could not be long delayed, and a powerful division of the Army of Northern Virginia under Longstreet had been sent to help Bragg.

Harry found himself late at night once more in that very room in which the map had disappeared so mysteriously. The two colonels, St. Clair and Langdon, and one or two others had drifted in, and the older men were smoking. Inevitably they talked of the battle which they foresaw with such certainty, and Harry's anxiety about it was increased, because he knew his father would be there on one side, and the cousin, for whom he cared so much, would be on the other.

"If only General Lee were in command there," said Colonel Talbot, "we might reckon upon a great and decisive victory."

"But Bragg is a good general," said Lieutenant-Colonel St. Hilaire.

"It's not enough to be merely a good general. He must have the soul of fire that Lee has, and that Jackson had. Bragg is the Southern McClellan. He is brave enough personally, but he always overrates the strength of the enemy, and, if he is victorious on the field, he does not reap the fruits of victory."

"Where were the armies when we last heard from them?" asked a captain.

"Bragg was turning north to attack Rosecrans, who stood somewhere between him and Chattanooga."

"I'm glad that it's Rosecrans and not Grant who commands the Northern army there," said Harry.

"Why?" asked Colonel Talbot.

"I've studied the manner in which he took Vicksburg, and I've heard about him from my father, and others. He won't be whipped He isn't like the other Northern generals. He hangs on, whatever happens. I heard some one quoting him as saying that no matter how badly his army was suffering in battle, the army of the other fellow might be suffering worse. It seems to me that a general who is able to think that way is very dangerous."

"And so he is, Harry," said Colonel Talbot. "I, too, am glad that it's Rosecrans and not Grant. If there's any news of a battle, we're not in a bad place to hear it. It's said that Mr. Curtis always knows as soon as our government what's happened."

The talk drifted on to another subject and then a hum came from the larger room. A murmur only, but it struck such an intense and earnest note that Harry was convinced.

"It's news of battle! I know it!" he exclaimed.

They sprang to their feet and hurried into the ballroom. William Curtis, his habitual calm broken, was standing upon a chair and all the people had gathered in front of him. A piece of paper, evidently a telegram, was clutched in his hand.

"Friends," he said in a strained, but exultant voice, "a great battle has been fought near Chattanooga on a little river called the Chickamauga, and we have won a magnificent victory."

A mighty cheer came from the crowd.

"The army of Rosecrans, attacked with sudden and invincible force by Bragg, has been shattered and driven into Chattanooga."

Another cheer burst forth.

"No part of the Union army was able to hold fast, save one wing under Thomas."

A third mighty cheer arose, but this time Harry did not join in it. He felt a sudden sinking of the heart at the words, "save one wing under Thomas." Then the victory was not complete. It could be complete only when the whole Union army was driven from the field. As long as Thomas stood, there was a flaw in the triumph. He had heard many times of this man, Thomas. He had Grant's qualities. He was at his best in apparent defeat.

"Is there anything else, Mr. Curtis?" asked Colonel Talbot.

"That is all my agent sends me concerning its results, but he says that it lasted two days, and that it was fierce and bloody beyond all comparison with anything that has happened in the West. He estimated that the combined losses are between thirty and forty thousand men."

A heavy silence fell upon them all. The victory was great, but the price for it was great, too. Yet exultation could not be subdued long. They were soon smiling over it, and congratulating one another. But Harry was still unable to share wholly in the joy of victory.

"Why this gloom in your face, when all the rest of us are so happy?" asked St. Clair.

"My father was there. He may have fallen. How do I know?"

"That's not it. He always comes through. What's the real cause? Out with it!"

"You know that part of the dispatch saying, 'No part of the Union army was able to hold fast save one wing under Thomas.' How about that wing! You heard, too, what the colonel said about General Bragg. He always overestimates the strength of the enemy, and while he may win a victory he will not reap the fruits of it. That wing under Thomas still may be standing there, protecting all the rest of the Union army."

"Come now, old Sober Face! This isn't like you. We've won a grand victory! We've more than paid them back for their Gettysburg."

Harry rejoiced then with the others, but at times the thought came to him that Thomas with one wing might yet be standing between Bragg and complete victory. When he and Dalton went back home—they were again with the Lanhams—they found the whole population of Richmond ablaze with triumph. The Yankee army in the West had been routed. Not only was Chickamauga an offset for Gettysburg, but for Vicksburg as well, and once more the fortunes of the South were rising toward the zenith.

Dalton had returned from the army a little later this time than

160

Harry, but he had joined him at the Lanhams', and he too showed gravity amid the almost universal rejoicing.

"I see that you're afraid the next news won't be so complete, Harry," he said.

"That's it, George. We don't really know much, except that Thomas was holding his ground. Oh, if only Stonewall Jackson were there! Remember how he came down on them at the Second Manassas and at Chancellorsville! Thomas would be swept off his feet and as Rosecrans retreated into Chattanooga our army would pour right on his heels!"

They waited eagerly the next day and the next for news, and while Richmond was still filled with rejoicings over Chickamauga, Harry saw that his fears were justified. Thomas stood till the end. Bragg had not followed Rosecrans into Chattanooga. The South had won a great battle, but not a decisive victory. The commanding general had not reaped all the rewards that were his for the taking. Bragg had justified in every way Colonel Talbot's estimate of him.

And yet Richmond, like the rest of the South, felt the great uplift of Chickamauga, the most gigantic battle of the West. It told South as well as North that the war was far from over. The South could no longer invade the North, nor could the North invade the South at will. Even on the northernmost border of the rebelling section the Army of Northern Virginia under its matchless leader, rested in its camp, challenging and defiant.

Harry was glad to return with his friends to the army. His brief period of festival was over, and his fears for his father had been relieved by a letter, stating that he had received no serious harm in the great and terrible battle of Chickamauga.

After the failure of the armies of Lee and Meade to bring about a decisive battle at Mine Run, the Army of Northern Virginia established its autumn and winter headquarters on a jutting spur of the great range called Clarke's Mountain, Orange Court House lying only a few miles to the west. The huge camp was made in a wide-open space, surrounded by dense masses of pines and cedars. Tents were pitched securely, and, feeling that they were to stay here a long time many of the soldiers built rude log cabins.

General Lee himself continued to use his tent, which stood in the centre of the camp, the streets of tents and cabins radiating from it like the spokes of a wheel. Close about Lee's own tent were others occupied by Colonel Taylor, his adjutant general, Colonel Peyton, Colonel Marshall, and other and younger officers, including Harry and

Dalton. A little distance down one of the main avenues, which they were pleased to call Victory Street, the Invincibles were encamped, and Harry saw them almost every day.

The troops were well fed now, and the brooks provided an abundance of clear water. The days were still warm, but the evenings were cold, and, inhaling the healing odours of the pines and cedars, wounded soldiers returned rapidly to health.

It was a wonderful interval for Harry and his friends associated with him so closely. Save for the presence of armies, it seemed at times that there was no war. Deep peace prevailed along the Rapidan and the slopes of the mountain. It was the longest period of rest that he and his comrades were to know in the course of the mighty struggle. The action of the war was now chiefly in the Southwest, where Grant, taking the place of Rosecrans, was seeking to recover all that was lost at Chickamauga.

Harry had another letter from his father, telling him that his own had been received, and giving personal details of the titanic struggle on the Chickamauga. He did not speak out directly, but Harry saw in his words the vain regret that the great opportunity won at Chickamauga at such a terrible price had not been used. In his belief the whole Federal army might have been destroyed, and the star of the South would have risen again to the zenith.

Here Harry sighed and remembered his own forebodings. Oh, if only a Stonewall Jackson had been there! His mighty sweep would have driven Thomas and the rest in a wild rout. A tear rose in his eye as he remembered his lost hero. He sincerely believed then and always that the Confederacy would have won had he not fallen on that fatal evening at Chancellorsville. It was an emotion with him, a permanent emotion with which logic could not interfere.

Harry was conscious, too, that the long quiet on the Eastern front was but a lull. There was nothing to signify peace in it. If the North had ever felt despair about the war Gettysburg and Vicksburg had removed every trace of it. He knew that beyond the blue ranges of mountains, both to east and west, vast preparations were going forward. The North, the region of great population, of illimitable resources, of free access to the sea, and of mechanical genius that had counted for so much in arming her soldiers, was gathering herself for a supreme effort. The great defeats of the war's first period were to be ignored, and her armies were to come again, more numerous, better equipped and perhaps better commanded than ever.

Nevertheless, his mind was still the mind of youth, and he could not dwell continuously upon this prospect. The camp in the hills was pleasant. The heats had passed, and autumn in the full richness of its colouring had come. The forests blazed in all the brilliancy of red and yellow and brown. The whole landscape had the colour and intensity that only a North American autumn can know, and the October air had the freshness and vitality sufficient to make an old man young.

The great army of youth—it was composed chiefly of boys, like the one opposing it—enjoyed itself during these comparatively idle months. The soldiers played rural games, marbles even, pitching the horseshoe, wrestling, jumping and running. It was to Harry like Hannibal in winter quarters at Capua, without the Capua. There was certainly no luxury here. While food was more abundant than for a long time, it was of the simplest. Instead of dissipation there was a great religious revival. Ministers of different creeds, but united in a common object, appeared in the camp, and preached with power and energy. The South was emotional then and perhaps the war had made it more so. The ministers secured thousands of converts. All day long the preaching and singing could be heard through the groves of pine and cedar, and Harry knew that when the time for battle came they would fight all the better because of it. Yielding to the enemy was no part of the Christianity that these ministers preached.

Harry also saw the growth of the hero-worship accorded to his great commander. He did not believe that any other general, except perhaps Napoleon in his earlier career, had ever received such trust and admiration. Many soldiers who had felt his guiding hand in battle now saw him for the first time. He had an appearance and manner to inspire respect, and, back of that, was something much greater, a firm conviction in the minds of all that he had illimitable patience, a willingness to accept responsibility, and a military genius that had never been surpassed. Such was the attitude of the Southern people toward their great leader then, and, to an even greater degree now, when his figure, like that of Lincoln, instead of becoming smaller grows larger as it recedes into the past.

Harry often rode with him. He seemed to have an especial liking for the very young members of his staff, or for old private soldiers, bearded and grey like himself, whom he knew by name. Far in October he rode down toward the Rapidan where Stuart was encamped, taking with him only Harry and Dalton. He was mounted on his great white war horse, Traveller, which the soldiers knew from afar. Cheering arose, but when he raised his hand in a deprecating way the soldiers, obedient to his wish, ceased, and they heard only the murmur of many voices, as they went on. The general made the lads ride, one on his right and the other on his left hand, and brilliant October colouring and crisp air seemed to put him in a mood that was far from war.

"I pine for Arlington," he said at length to Harry, "that ancestral home of mine that is held by the enemy. I should like to see the ripening of the crops there. We Virginians of the old stock hold to the land, and you Kentuckians, who are really of the same race, hold to it, too."

"It is true, sir," said Harry. "My father loves the land. After his retirement from the army, following the Mexican war, he worked harder upon our place in Kentucky than any slave or hired man. He was going to free his slaves, but I suppose, sir, that the war has made him feel different about it."

"Yes, we're often willing to do things by our own free will, but not under compulsion. The great Washington himself wrote of the evils of slave labour. The 'old fields' scattered all over Virginia show what it has done for this noble commonwealth."

Harry remembered quite well similar "old fields" in Kentucky. Slaves were far less numerous there than in Virginia, and he was old enough to have observed that, in addition to the wrong of slavery, they were a liability rather than an asset. But he too felt anew the instinctive rebellion against being compelled to do what he would perhaps do anyhow.

General Lee talked more of the land and Harry and Dalton listened respectfully. Harry saw that his commander's heart turned strongly toward it. He knew that Jefferson had dreamed of the United States as an agricultural community, having no part in the quarrels of other nations, but he knew that it was only a dream. The South, the section that had followed Jefferson's dream, was now at a great disadvantage. It had no ships, and it did not have the mills to equip it for the great war it was waging. He realized more keenly than ever the one-sided nature of the South's development.

The general turned his horse toward the banks of the Rapidan, and a resplendent figure came forward to meet him. It was that incarnation of youth and fantastic knighthood, Jeb Stuart, who had just returned from a ride toward the north. He wore a new and brilliant uniform and the usual broad yellow sash about his waist. His tunic was embroidered, too, and his epaulets were heavy with gold. The thick gold braid about his hat was tied in a gorgeous loop in front. His hands were encased in long gloves of the finest buckskin, and he tapped the high yellow tops of his riding boots with a little whip.

Harry always felt that Stuart did not really belong to the present.

His place was with the medieval knights who loved gorgeous armour, who fought by day for the love of it and who sat in the evening on the castle steps with fair ladies for the love of it, and who in the dark listened to the troubadours below, also for the love of it. A great cavalry leader, he shone at his brightest in the chase, and, when there was no fighting to be done, his were the spirits of a boy, and he was as quick for a prank as any lad under his own command.

But Stuart, although he had joked with Jackson, never took any liberties with Lee. He instantly swept the ground with his plumed hat and said in his most respectful manner:

"General, will you honour us by dining with us? We've just returned from a long ride northward and we've made some captures."

Lee caught a twinkle in his eye, and he smiled.

"I see no prisoners, General Stuart," he replied, "and I take it that your captures do not mean human beings."

"No, sir, there are other things just now more valuable to us than prisoners. We raided a little Yankee outpost. Nobody was hurt, but, sir, we've captured some provisions, the like of which the Army of Northern Virginia has not tasted in a long time. Would you mind coming with me and taking a look? And bring Kenton and Dalton with you, if you don't mind, sir."

"This indeed sounds tempting," said the commander-in-chief of the Army of Northern Virginia. "I accept your invitation, General Stuart, in behalf of myself and my two young aides."

He dismounted, giving the reins of Traveller to an orderly, and walked toward Stuart's tent, which was pitched near the river. The "captures" were heaped in a grassy place.

"Here, sir," said General Stuart, "are twenty dozen boxes of the finest French sardines. I haven't tasted sardines in a year and I love them."

"I've always liked them," said General Lee.

"And here, sir, are several cases of Yorkshire ham, brought all the way across the sea—and for us. It isn't as good as our Virginia ham, which is growing scarce, but we'll like it. And cove oysters, cases and cases of 'em. I like 'em almost as well as sardines."

"Most excellent."

"And real old New England pies, baked, I suppose, in Washington. We can warm 'em over."

"I see that you have the fire ready."

"And jars of preserves, a half-dozen kinds at least, and all of 'em look as if two likely youngsters like Kenton and Dalton would be anxious to get at 'em."

"You judge us rightly, General," said Harry. "We'll show no mercy to such prisoners as we have here."

"You wouldn't be boys and you wouldn't be human if you did," rejoined Stuart, "would they, General?"

"They would not," replied Lee. "One of the principal recollections of my boyhood is that I was always hungry. Our regular three meals a day were not enough for us, however much we ate at one time. Virginia, like your own Kentucky, Harry, is full of forage, and we moved in groups. Now, didn't you find a lot of food in the woods and fields?"

"Oh, yes, sir," rejoined Harry with animation. "I was hungry all the time, too. An hour after breakfast I was hungry again, and an hour after dinner, which we had in the middle of the day, I was hungry once more."

"But you knew where to go for supplies."

"Yes, sir; we had berries, strawberries, blackberries, raspberries, gooseberries, dewberries, cherries, all of them growing wild although some of them started tame. And then we could forage for pears, peaches, plums, damsons, all kinds of apples, paw paws, and then later for the nuts, hickory nuts, walnuts, chestnuts, hazel nuts, chinquapins, and a lot more. We could have almost lived in the woods and fields from early spring until late fall."

"We did the same in Virginia," said the commander-in-chief. "I've often thought that our forest Indians did not develop a higher civilization, because it was so easy for them to live, save in the depths of a hard winter. They had most of the berries and fruits and nuts that we white boys had. The woods were full of game, and the lakes and rivers full of fish. They were not driven by the hard necessity that creates civilization."

"Dinner is ready, sir," announced General Stuart, who had been directing the orderlies. "I can offer you and the others nothing but boxes and kegs to sit on, but I can assure you that this Northern food, some of which comes in cans, is excellent."

The two lads and General Stuart fell to work with energy. General Lee ate more sparingly. Stuart was a boy himself, talking much and running over with fun.

"Have you heard what happened to General Early, sir?" he asked the commander-in-chief.

"Not yet."

"But you will, sir, to-morrow. Early will be slow in sending you that dispatch. He hasn't had time to write it yet. He's not through swearing."

"General Early is a valiant and able man, but I disapprove of his swearing."

"Why, sir, 'Old Jube' can't help it. It's a part of his breathing, and man cannot live without breath. He sent one of his best aides with a dispatch to General Hill, who is posted some distance away. Passing through a thick cedar wood the aide was suddenly set upon by a genuine stage villain, large, dark and powerful, who clubbed him over the head with the butt of a pistol, and then departed with his dispatch."

"And what happened then?"

"The aide returned to General Early with his story, but without his dispatch. The general believed his account, of course, but he called him names for allowing himself to be surprised and overcome by a single Yankee. He cursed until the air for fifty yards about him smelled strongly of sulphur and brimstone."

"Did he do anything more?"

"Yes, General. He sent a duplicate of the dispatch by an aide whom he said he could trust. In an hour the second man came back with the same big lump on his head and with the same story. He had been ambushed at the crossing of a ravine full of small cedars, and the highwayman was undoubtedly the same, too, a big, powerful fellow, as bold as you please."

Harry's pulse throbbed hard for a few moments, when he first heard mention of the man. The description, not only physical, but of manner and action as well, answered perfectly. He had not the slightest doubt that it was Shepard.

"A daring deed," said General Lee. "We must see that it is not repeated."

"But that wasn't all of the tale, sir. While the second man was sitting on the bank, nursing his broken head, the Yankee Dick Turpin read the dispatch and saw that it was a duplicate of the first. He became red-hot with wrath, and talked furiously about the extra and unnecessary work that General Early was forcing upon him. He ended by cramming the dispatch into the man's hands, directing him to take it back, and to tell General Early to stop his foolishness. The aide was a bit dazed from the blow he received and he delivered that message word for word. Why, sir, General Early exploded. People who have heard him swear for years and who know what an artist he is in swearing, heard him then utter swear words that they had never heard before, words invented on the spur of the moment, and in the heat of passion, words full of pith and meaning."

"And that was all, I suppose?"

"Not by any means, sir. General Early picked two sharpshooters and sent them with another copy of the dispatch. They passed the place of the first hold-up, and next the ravine without seeing anybody. But as they were riding some distance further on both of their horses were killed by shots from a small clump of pines. Before they could regain their feet Dick Turpin came out and covered them with his rifle—it seems that he had one of those new repeating weapons.

"The men saw that his eye was so keen and his hand so steady that they did not dare to move a hand to a pistol. Then as he looked down the sights of his rifle he lectured them. He told them they were foolish to come that way, when the two who came before them had found out that it was a closed road. He said that real soldiers learned by experience, and would not try again to do what they had learned to be impossible.

"Then he said that after all they were not to blame, as they had been sent by General Early, and he made one of them who had the stub of a pencil write on the back of the dispatch these words: 'General Jubal Early, C. S. A.: This has ceased to be a joke. After your first man was stopped, it was not necessary to do anything more. I have the dispatch. Why insist on sending duplicate after duplicate?' And the two had to walk all the way back to General Early with that note, because they didn't dare make away with the dispatch.

"I have a certain respect for that man's skill and daring, but General Early had a series of spells. He retired to his tent and if the reports are not exaggerated, a continuous muttering like low thunder came from the tent, and all the cloth of it turned blue from the lightnings imprisoned inside."

General Lee himself smiled.

"It was certainly annoying," he said. "I hope the dispatch was not of importance."

"It contained nothing that will help the Yankees, but it shows that the enemy has some spies—or at least one spy—who are Napoleons at their trade."

CHAPTER 13

The Coming of Grant

The little dinner ended. Despite his disapproval of General Early's swearing, General Lee laughed heartily at further details of the strange Yankee spy's exploits. But it was well known that in this particular General Early was the champion of the East. Harry did not know that in the person of Colonel Charles Woodville, his cousin, Dick Mason, had encountered one of equal ability in the Southwest.

Presently General Lee and his two young aides mounted their horses for the return. The commander-in-chief seemed gayer than usual. He was always very fond of Stuart, whose high spirits pleased him, and before his departure he thanked him for his thoughtfulness.

"Whenever we get any particularly choice shipments from the North I shall always be pleased to notify you, General, and send you your share," said Stuart, sweeping the air in front of him again with his great plumed hat. With his fine, heroic face and his gorgeous uniform he had never looked more a knight of the Middle Ages.

General Lee smiled and thanked him again, and then rode soberly back, followed at a short distance by his two young aides. Although the view of hills and mountains and valleys and river and brooks was now magnificent, the sumach burning in red and the leaves vivid in many colours, Lee, deeply sensitive, like all his rural forbears, to rural beauty, nevertheless seemed not to notice it, and soon sank into deep thought.

It is believed by many that Lee knew then that the Confederacy had already received a mortal blow. It was not alone sufficient for the South to win victories. She must keep on winning them, and the failure at Gettysburg and the defeat at Vicksburg had put her on the defensive everywhere. Fewer blockade runners were getting through. Above all, there was less human material upon which to draw. But he roused himself presently and said to Harry:

"There was something humorous in the exploits of the man who held up General Early's messengers, but the fellow is dangerous, exceedingly dangerous at such a time."

"I've an idea who he is, sir," said Harry.

"Indeed! What do you know?"

Then Harry told nearly all that he knew about Shepard, but not all—that struggle in the river, and his sparing of the spy and the filching of the map at the Curtis house, for instance—and the commander-in-chief listened with great attention.

"A bold man, uncommonly bold, and it appears uncommonly skilled, too. We must send out a general alarm, that is, we must have all our own scouts and spies watching for him."

Harry said nothing, but he did not believe that anybody would catch Shepard. The man's achievements had been so startling that they had created the spell of invincibility. His old belief that he was worth ten thousand men on the Northern battle line returned. No movement of the Army of Northern Virginia could escape him, and no lone messenger could ever be safe from him.

Lee returned to his camp on Clarke's Mountain, and, a great revival meeting being in progress, he joined it, sitting with a group of officers. Fitzhugh Lee, W. H. F. Lee, Jones, Rosser, Wickham, Munford, Young, Wade Hampton and a dozen others were there. Taylor and Marshall and Peyton of his staff were also in the company.

The preacher was a man of singular power and earnestness, and after the sermon he led the singing himself, in which often thirty or forty thousand voices joined. It was a moving sight to Harry, all these men, lads, mostly, but veterans of many fields, united in a chorus mightier than any other that he had ever heard. It would have pleased Stonewall Jackson to his inmost soul, and once more, as always, a tear rose to his eye as he thought of his lost hero.

Harry and Dalton left their horses with an orderly and came back to the edge of the great grove, in which the meeting was being held. They had expected to find St. Clair and Happy Tom there, but not seeing them, wandered on and finally drifted apart. Harry stood alone for a while on the outskirts of the throng. They were all singing again, and the mighty volume of sound rolled through the wood. It was not only a singular, it was a majestic scene also to Harry. How like unto little children young soldiers were! and how varied and perplexing were the problems of human nature! They were singing with the utmost fervour of Him who had preached continuously of peace, who was willing to turn one cheek when the other was smitten, and because of their religious zeal they would rush the very next day into battle, if need be, with increased fire and zeal.

He saw a heavily built, powerful man on the outskirts, but some distance away, singing in a deep rolling voice, but something vaguely familiar in the figure drew his glance again. He looked long and well and then began to edge quietly toward the singer, who was clothed in the faded butternut uniform that so many of the Confederate soldiers wore.

The fervour of the singer did not decrease, but Harry noticed that he too was moving, moving slowly toward the eastern end of the grove, the same direction that Harry was pursuing. Now he was sure. He would have called out, but his voice would not have been heard above the vast volume of sound. He might have pointed out the singer to others, but, although he felt sure, he did not wish to be laughed at in case of mistake. But strongest of all was the feeling that it had become a duel between Shepard and himself.

He walked slowly on, keeping the man in view, but Shepard, although he never ceased singing, moved away at about the same pace. Harry inferred at once that Shepard had seen him and was taking precautions. The temptation to cry out at the top of his voice that the most dangerous of all spies was among them was almost irresistible, but it would only create an uproar in which Shepard could escape easily, leaving to him a load of ridicule.

He continued his singular pursuit. Shepard was about a hundred yards away, and they had made half the circuit of this huge congregation. Then the spy passed into a narrow belt of pines, and when Harry moved forward to see him emerge on the other side he failed to reappear. He hastened to the pines, which led some distance down a little gully, and he was sure that Shepard had gone that way. He followed fast, but he could discover no sign. He had vanished utterly, like thin smoke swept away by a breeze.

He returned deeply stirred by the appearance and disappearance—easy, alike—of Shepard. His sense of the man's uncanny powers and of his danger to the Confederacy was increased. He seemed to come and go absolutely as he pleased. It was true that in the American Civil War the opportunities for spies were great. All men spoke the same language, and all looked very much alike. It was not such a hard task to enter the opposing lines, but Shepard had shown a daring and success beyond all comparison. He seemed to have both the seven league boots and the invisible cloak of very young childhood. He came as he pleased, and when pursuit came he vanished in thin air.

Harry bit his lips in chagrin. He felt that Shepard had scored on him again. It was true that he had been victorious in that fight in the river, when victory meant so much, but since then Shepard had triumphed, and it was bitter. He hardened his determination, and resolved that he would always be on the watch for him. He even felt a certain glow, because he was one of two in such a conflict of skill and courage.

The meeting having been finished, he went down one of the streets of tents to the camp of the Invincibles. Colonel Leonidas Talbot and Lieutenant-Colonel Hector St. Hilaire were not playing chess. Instead they were sitting on a pine log with Happy Tom and St. Clair and other officers, listening to young Julien de Langeais, who sat on another log, playing a violin with surpassing skill. Lieutenant-Colonel St. Hilaire, knowing his prowess as a violinist, had asked him to come and play for the Invincibles. Now he was playing for them and for several thousand more who were gathered in the pine woods.

Young de Langeais sat on a low stump, and the great crowd made a solid mass around him. But he did not see them, nor the pine woods nor the heavy cannon sitting on the ridges. He looked instead into a region of fancy, where the colours were brilliant or gay or tender as he imagined them. Harry, with no technical knowledge of music but with a great love of it, recognized at once the touch of a master, and what was more, the soul of one.

To him the violin was not great, unless the player was great, but when the player was great it was the greatest musical instrument of all. He watched de Langeais' wrapt face, and for him too the thousands of soldiers, the pines and the cannon on the ridges melted away. He did not know what the young musician was playing, probably some old French air or a great lyric outburst of the fiery Verdi, whose music had already spread through America.

"A great artist," whispered Lieutenant-Colonel St. Hilaire in his ear. "He studied at the schools in New Orleans and then for two years in Paris. But he came back to fight. Nothing could keep Julien from the army, but he brought his violin with him. We Latins, or at least we who are called Latins, steep our souls in music. It's not merely intellectual with us. It's passion, fire, abandonment, triumph and all the great primitive emotions of the human race."

Harry's feelings differed somewhat from those of Lieutenant-Colonel St. Hilaire—in character but not in power—and as young de Langeais played on he began to think what a loss a stray bullet could make. Why should a great artist be allowed to come on the battle line? There were hundreds of thousands of common men. One could replace another,

172

but nobody could replace the genius, a genius in which the whole world shared. It was not possible for either drill or training to do it, and yet a little bullet might take away his life as easily as it would that of a ploughboy. They were all alike to the bullets and the shells.

De Langeais finished, and a great shout of applause arose. The cheering became so insistent that he was compelled to play again.

"His family is well-to-do," said Lieutenant-Colonel St. Hilaire just before he began playing once more, "and they'll see that he goes back to Paris for study as soon as the war is over. If they didn't I would."

It did not seem to occur to Lieutenant-Colonel St. Hilaire that young de Langeais could be killed, and Harry began to share his confidence. De Langeais now played the simple songs of the old South, and there was many a tear in the eyes of war-hardened youth. The sun was setting in a sea of fire, and the pine forests turned red in its blaze. In the distance the waters of the Rapidan were crimson, too, and a light wind out of the west sighed among the pines, forming a subdued chorus to the violin.

De Langeais began to play a famous old song of home, and Harry's mind travelled back on its lingering note to his father's beautiful house and grounds, close by Pendleton, and all the fine country about it, in which he and Dick Mason and the boys of their age had roamed. He remembered all the brooks and ponds and the groves that produced the best hickory nuts. When should he see them again and would his father be there, and Dick, and all the other boys of their age! Not all! Certainly not all, because some were gone already. And yet this plaintive note of the homes they had left behind, while it brought a tear to many an eye, made no decrease in martial determination. It merely hardened their resolution to win the victory all the sooner, and bring the homecoming march nearer.

De Langeais ended on a wailing note that died like a faint sigh in the pine forest. Then he came back to earth, sprang up, and put his violin in its case. Applause spread out and swelled in a low, thunderous note, but de Langeais, who was as modest as he was talented, quickly hid himself among his friends.

The sun sank behind the blue mountains, and twilight came readily over the pine and cedar forests. Colonel Talbot and Lieutenant-Colonel St. Hilaire, who had a large tent together, invited the youths to stay awhile with them as their guests and talk. All the soldiers dispersed to their own portions of the great camp, and there would be an hour of quiet and rest, until the camp cooks served supper.

It had been a lively day for Harry, his emotions had been much stirred, and now he was glad to sit in the peace of the evening on a stone near the entrance of the tent, and listen to his friends. War drew comrades together in closer bonds than those of peace. He was quite sure that St. Clair, Dalton and Happy Tom were his friends for life, as he was theirs, and the two colonels seemed to have the same quality of youth. Simple men, of high faith and honour, they were often child-like in the ways of the world, their horizons sometimes not so wide as those of the lads who now sat with them.

"As I told Harry," said Lieutenant-Colonel St. Hilaire to Julien, "you shall have that talent of yours cultivated further after the war. Two years more of study and you will be among the greatest. You must know, lads, that for us who are of French descent, Paris is the world's capital in the arts."

"And for many of English blood, too," said Colonel Talbot.

Then they talked of more immediate things, of the war, the armies and the prospect of the campaigns. Harry, after an hour or so, returned to headquarters and he found soldiers making a bed for the commander-in-chief under the largest of the pines. Lee in his campaigns always preferred to sleep in the open air, when he could, and it required severe weather to drive him to a tent. Meanwhile he sat by a small fire—the October nights were growing cold—and talked with Peyton and other members of his staff.

Harry and Dalton decided to imitate his example and sleep between the blankets under the pines. Harry found a soft place, spread his blankets and in a few minutes slept soundly. In fact, the whole Army of Northern Virginia was a great family that retired early, slept well and rose early.

The next morning there was frost on the grass, but the lads were so hardy that they took no harm. The autumn deepened. The leaves blazed for a while in their most vivid colours and then began to fall under the strong west winds. Brown and wrinkled, they often whirled past in clouds. The air had a bite in it, and the soldiers built more and larger fires.

The Army of Northern Virginia never before had been quiescent so long. The Army of the Potomac was not such a tremendous distance away, but it seemed that neither side was willing to attack, and as the autumn advanced and began to merge into winter the minds of all turned toward the Southwest.

For the valiant soldiers encamped on the Virginia hills the news was not good. Grant, grim and inflexible, was deserving the great name that was gradually coming to him. He had gathered together all the broken parts of the army defeated at Chickamauga and was turning Union defeat into Union victory.

Winter closed in with the knowledge that Grant had defeated the

South disastrously on Lookout Mountain and all around Chattanooga. Chickamauga had gone for nothing, the whole flank of the Confederacy was turned and the Army of Northern Virginia remained the one great barrier against the invading legions of the North. Yet the confidence of the men in that army remained undimmed. They felt that on their own ground, and under such a man as Lee, they were invincible.

In the course of these months Harry, as a messenger and often as a secretary, was very close to Lee. He wrote a swift and clear hand, and took many dispatches. Almost daily messages were sent in one direction or another and Harry read from them the thoughts of his leader, which he kept locked in his breast. He knew perhaps better than many an older officer the precarious condition of the Confederacy. These letters, which he took from dictation, and the letters from Richmond that he read to his chief, told him too plainly that the limits of the Confederacy were shrinking. Its money declined steadily. Happy Tom said that he had to "swap it pound for pound now to the sutlers for groceries." Yet it is the historical truth that the heart of the Army of Northern Virginia never beat with more fearless pride, as the famous and "bloody" year of '63 was drawing to its close.

The news arrived that Grant, the Sledge Hammer of the West, had been put by Lincoln in command of all the armies of the Union, and would come east to lead the Army of the Potomac in person, with Meade still as its nominal chief, but subject, like all the others, to his command.

Harry heard the report with a thrill. He knew now that decisive action would come soon enough. He had always felt that Meade in front of them was a wavering foe, and perhaps too cautious. But Grant was of another kind. He was a pounder. Defeats did not daunt him. He would attack and then attack again and again, and the diminishing forces of the Confederacy were ill fitted to stand up against the continued blows of the hammer. Harry's thrill was partly of apprehension, but whenever he looked at the steadfast face of his chief his confidence returned.

Winter passed without much activity and spring began to show its first buds. The earth was drying, after melting snows and icy rains, and Harry knew that action would not be delayed much longer. Grant was in the East now. He had gone in January to St. Louis to visit his daughter, who lay there very ill, and then, after military delays, he had reached Washington.

Harry afterward heard the circumstances of his arrival, so characteristic of plain and republican America. He came into Washington by train as a simple passenger, accompanied only by his son, who was but fourteen years of age. They were not recognized, and arriving at a hotel, valise in hand, with a crowd of passengers, he registered in his turn: "U. S. Grant and son, Galena, Ill." The clerk, not noticing the name, assigned the modest arrival and his boy to a small room on the fifth floor. Then they moved away, a porter carrying the valise. But the clerk happened to look again at the register, and when he saw more clearly he rushed after them with a thousand apologies. He did not expect the victor of great battles, the lieutenant-general commanding all the armies of the Union, a battle front of more than a million men, to come so modestly.

When Harry heard the story he liked it. It seemed to him to be the same simple and manly quality that he found in Lee, both worthy of republican institutions. But he did not have time to think about it long. The signs were multiplying that the advance would soon come. The North had never ceased to resound with preparations, and Grant would march with veterans. All the spies and scouts brought in the same report. Butler would move up from Fortress Monroe toward Richmond with thirty thousand men and Grant with a hundred and fifty thousand would cross the Rapidan, moving by the right flank of Lee until they could unite and destroy the Confederacy. Such was the plan, said the scouts and spies in grey.

Longstreet with his corps had returned from the West and Lee gathered his force of about sixty thousand men to meet the mighty onslaught—he alone perhaps divined how mighty it would be—and when he was faced by the greatest of his adversaries his genius perhaps never shone more brightly.

May and the full spring came. It was the third day of the month, and the camp of the Army of Northern Virginia was as usual. Many of the young soldiers played games among the trees. Here and there they lay in groups on the new grass, singing their favourite songs. The cooks were preparing their suppers over the big fires. Several bands were playing. Had it not been for the presence of so many weapons the whole might have been taken for one vast picnic, but Harry, who sat in the tent of the commander-in-chief, was writing as fast as he could dispatch after dispatch that the Southern leader was dictating to him. He knew perfectly well, of course, that the commander-in-chief was gathering his forces and that they would move quickly for battle. He knew, too, how inadequate was the equipment of the army. Only a short time before he had taken from the dictation of his chief a letter to the President of the Confederacy a part of which ran:

My anxiety on the subject of provisions for the army is so great that I cannot refrain from expressing it to your Excellency. I cannot see how we can operate with our present supplies. Any derangement in their arrival or disaster to the railroad would render it impossible for me to keep the army together and might force a retreat into North Carolina. There is nothing to be had in this section for men or animals. We have rations for the troops to-day and to-morrow. I hope a new supply arrived last night, but I have not yet had a report.

Harry had thought long over this letter and he knew from his own observation its absolute truth. The depleted South was no longer able to feed its troops well. The abundance of the preceding autumn had quickly passed, and in winter they were mostly on half rations.

Lee, better than any other man in the whole South, had understood what lay before them, and his foes both of the battlefield and of the spirit have long since done him justice. Less than a week before this eve of mighty events he had written to a young woman in Virginia, a relative:

I dislike to send letters within reach of the enemy, as they might serve, if captured, to bring distress on others. But you must sometimes cast your thoughts on the Army of Northern Virginia, and never forget it in your prayers. It is preparing for a great struggle, but I pray and trust that the great God, mighty to deliver, will spread over it His Almighty arms and drive its enemies before it.

Harry had seen this letter before its sending, and he was not surprised now when Lee was sending messengers to all parts of his army. With all the hero-worshiping quality of youth he was once more deeply grateful that he should have served on the staffs and been brought into close personal relations with two men, Stonewall Jackson and Lee, who seemed to him so great. As he saw it, it was not alone military greatness but greatness of the soul, which was greater. Both were deeply religious—Lee, the Episcopalian, and Jackson, the Presbyterian, and it was a piety that contained no trace of cant.

Harry felt that the crisis of the great Civil War was at hand. It had been in the air all that day, and news had come that Grant had broken up his camps and was crossing the Rapidan with a huge force. He knew how small in comparison was the army that Lee could bring against him, and yet he had supreme confidence in the military genius of his chief.

He had written a letter with which an aide had galloped away, and then he sat at the little table in the great tent, pen in hand and ink and paper before him, but Lee was silent. He was dressed as usual with great neatness and care, though without ostentation. His face had its usual serious cast, but tinged now with melancholy. Harry knew that he no longer saw the tent and those around him. His mind dwelled for a few moments upon his own family and the ancient home that he had loved so well.

The interval was very brief. He was back in the present, and the principal generals for whom he had sent were entering the tent. Hill, Longstreet, Ewell, Stuart and others came, but they did not stay long. They talked earnestly with their leader for a little while, and then every one departed to lead his brigades.

The secretaries put away pen, ink and paper. Twilight was advancing in the east and night suddenly fell outside. The songs ceased, the bands played no more, and there was only the deep rumble of marching men and moving cannon.

"We'll ride now, gentlemen," said Lee to his staff.

Traveller, saddled and bridled, was waiting and the commander-in-chief sprang into the saddle with all the agility of a young man. The others mounted, too, Harry and Dalton as usual taking their places modestly in the rear. A regiment, small in numbers but famous throughout the army for valour, was just passing, and its colonel and its lieutenant-colonel, erect men, riding splendidly, but grey like Lee, drew their swords and gave the proud and flashing salute of the sabre as they went by. Lee and his staff almost with involuntary impulse returned the salute in like fashion. Then the Invincibles passed on, and were lost from view in the depths of the forest.

Harry felt a sudden constriction of the heart. He knew that he might never see Colonel Leonidas Talbot nor Lieutenant-Colonel Hector St. Hilaire again, nor St. Clair, nor Happy Tom either.

But his friends could not remain long in his mind at such a time. They were marching, marching swiftly, the presence of the man on the great white horse seeming to urge them on to greater speed. As the stars came out Lee's brow, which had been seamed by thought, cleared. His plan which he had formed in the day was moving well. His three corps were bearing away toward the old battlefield of Chancellorsville. Grant would be drawn into the thickets of the Wilderness as Hooker had been the year before, although a greater than Hooker was now leading the Army of the Potomac.

Harry, who foresaw it all, thrilled and shuddered at the remembrance. It was in there that the great Jackson had fallen in the hour of supreme triumph. Not far away were the heights of Fredericksburg, where Burnside had led the bravest of the brave to unavailing slaughter. As Belgium had been for centuries the cockpit of Europe, so the wild and sterile region in Virginia that men call the Wilderness became the cockpit of North America.

While Lee and his army were turning into the Wilderness Grant and the greatest force that the Union had yet assembled were seeking him. It was composed of men who had tasted alike of victory and defeat, veterans skilled in all the wiles and stratagems of war, and with hearts to endure anything. In this host was a veteran regiment that had come East to serve under Grant as it had served under him so valiantly in the West. Colonel Winchester rode at its head and beside him rode his favourite aide, young Richard Mason. Not far away was Colonel Hertford, with a numerous troop of splendid cavalry. Grant, alert and resolved to win, carried in his pocket a letter which he had received from Lincoln, saying:

> Not expecting to see you before the spring campaign opens, I wish to express in this way my entire satisfaction with what you have done up to this time, so far as I understand it. The particulars of your plans I neither know nor seek to know. You are vigilant and self-reliant, and, pleased with this, I wish not to obtrude any constraints or restraints upon you. While I am very anxious that any great disaster or the capture of our men in great numbers should be avoided, I know these points are less likely to escape your attention than they would mine. If there is anything wanting which is within my power to give, do not fail to let me know it. And now, with a brave army and a just cause, may God sustain you.

A noble letter, breathing the loftiest spirit, and showing that moral grandeur which has been so characteristic of America's greatest men. He had put all in Grant's hands and he had given to him an army, the like of which had never been seen until now on the American continent. Never before had the North poured forth its wealth and energy in such abundance.

Four thousand wagons loaded with food and ammunition followed the army, and there was a perfect system by which a wagon emptied of its contents was sent back to a depot to be refilled, while a loaded wagon took its place at the front. Complete telegram equipments, poles, wires, instruments and all were carried with every division. The wires could be strung easily and the lieutenant-general could talk to every part of his army. There were, also, staffs of signalmen, in case the wires should fail at any time. Grant held in his hand all the resources of the North, and if he could not win no one could.

All through the night the hostile armies marched, and before them went the spies and scouts.

CHAPTER 14

The Ghostly Ride

Harry and Dalton kept close together during the long hours of the ghostly ride. Just ahead of them were Taylor and Marshall and Peyton, and in front Lee rode in silence. Now and then they passed regiments, and at other times they would halt and let regiments pass them. Then the troops, seeing the man sitting on the white horse, would start to cheer, but always their officers promptly subdued it, and they marched on feeling more confident than ever that their general was leading them to victory.

Many hours passed and still the army marched through the forests. The trees, however, were dwindling in size and even in the night they saw that the earth was growing red and sterile. Dense thickets grew everywhere, and the marching became more difficult. Harry felt a sudden thrill of awe.

"George," he whispered, "do you know the country into which we're riding?"

"I think I do, Harry. It's the Wilderness."

"It can't be anything else, George, because I see the ghosts."

"What are you talking about, Harry? What ghosts?"

"The thousands and thousands who have fallen in that waste. Why the Wilderness is so full of dead men that they must walk at night to give one another room. I only hope that the ghost of Old Jack will ride before us and show us the way."

"I almost feel like that, too," admitted Dalton, who, however, was of a less imaginative mind than Harry. "As sure as I'm sitting in the saddle we're bound for the Wilderness. Now, what is the day going to give us?"

"Marching mostly, I think, and with the next noon will come battle. Grant doesn't hesitate and hold back. We know that, George."

"No, it's not his character."

Morning came and found them still in the forests, seeking the deep thickets of the Wilderness, and Grant, warned by his scouts and spies, and most earnestly by one whose skill, daring and judgment were unequalled, turned from his chosen line of march to meet his enemy. Once more Lee had selected the field of battle, where his inferiority in numbers would not count so much against him.

It was nearly morning when the march ceased, and officers and troops, save those on guard, lay down in the forest for rest. Harry, a seasoned veteran, could sleep under any conditions and with a blanket over him and a saddle for a pillow closed his eyes almost immediately. Lee and his older aides, Taylor and Peyton and Marshall, slept also. Around them the brigades, too, lay sleeping.

A while before dawn a large man in Confederate uniform, using the soft, lingering speech of the South, appeared almost in the centre of the army of Northern Virginia. He knew all the pass words and told the officers commanding the watch that the wing under Ewell was advancing more rapidly than any of the others. Inside the line he could go about almost as he chose, and one could see little of him, save that he was large of figure and deeply tanned, like all the rest.

He approached the little opening in which Lee and his staff lay, although he kept back from the sentinels who watched over the sleeping leader. But Shepard knew that it was the great Confederate chieftain who lay in the shadow of the oak and he could identify him by the glances of the sentinels so often directed toward the figure.

There were wild thoughts for a moment or two in the mind of Shepard. A single bullet fired by an unerring hand would take from the Confederacy its arm and brain, and then what happened to himself afterward would not matter at all. And the war would be over in a month or two. But he put the thought fiercely from him. A spy he was and in his heart proud of his calling, but no such secret bullet could be fired by him.

He turned away from the little opening, wandered an hour through the camp and then, diving into the deep bushes, vanished like a shadow through the Confederate lines, and was gone to Grant to report that Lee's army was advancing swiftly to attack, and that the command of Ewell would come in touch with him first.

Not long after dawn Harry was again on the march, riding behind his general. From time to time Lee sent messengers to the various divisions of his army, four in number, commanded by Longstreet, Early, Hill and Stuart, the front or Stuart's composed of cavalry. Harry's own time came, when he received a dispatch of the utmost importance to

181

take to Ewell. He memorized it first, and, if capture seemed probable, he was to tear it into bits and throw it away. Harry was glad he was to go to Ewell. In the great campaign in the valley he had been second to Jackson, his right arm, as Jackson had been Lee's right arm. Ewell had lost a leg since then, and his soldiers had to strap him in the saddle when he led them into battle, but he was as daring and cheerful as ever, trusted implicitly by Lee.

Harry with a salute to his chief rode away. Part of the country was familiar to him and in addition his directions were so explicit that he could not miss the way.

The four divisions of the army were in fairly close touch, but in a country of forests and many waters Northern scouts might come between, and he rode with caution, his hand ever near the pistol in his belt. The midday sun however clouded as the afternoon passed on. The thickets and forests grew more dense. From the distance came now and then the faint, sweet call of a trumpet, but everything was hidden from sight by the dense tangle of the Wilderness, a wilderness as wild and dangerous as any in which Henry Ware had ever fought. How it all came back to him! Almost exactly a year ago he had ridden into it with Jackson and here the armies were gathering again.

Imagination, fancy, always so strong in him, leaped into vivid life. The year had not passed and he was riding to meet Stonewall Jackson, who was somewhere ahead, preparing for his great curve about Hooker and the lightning stroke at Chancellorsville. Rabbits sprang out of the undergrowth and fled away before his horse's hoofs. In the lonely wilderness, which nevertheless had little to offer to the hunter, birds chattered from every tree. Small streams flowed slowly between dense walls of bushes. Here and there in the protection of the thickets wild flowers were in early bloom.

It was spring, fresh spring everywhere, but the bushes and the grass alike were tinged with red for Harry. The strange mental illusion that he was riding to Chancellorsville remained with him and he did not seek to shake it off. He almost expected to see Old Jack ahead on a hill, bent over a little, and sitting on Little Sorrel, with the old slouch hat drawn over his eyes. They had talked of the ghost of Jackson leading them in the Wilderness. He shivered. Could it be so? All the time he knew it was an illusion, but he permitted it to cast its spell over him, as one who dreams knowingly.

And Harry was dreaming back. Old Jack, the earlier of his two heroes, was leading them. He foresaw the long march through the thickets of the Wilderness, Stonewall forming the line of battle in the deep roads late in the evening, almost in sight of Hooker's camp, the sudden rush of his brigades and then the terrible battle far into the night.

He shook himself. It was uncanny. The past was the past. Dreams were thin and vanished stuff. Once more he was in the present and saw clearly. Old Jack was gone to take his place with the great heroes of the past, but the Army of Northern Virginia was there, with Lee leading them, and the most formidable of all the Northern chiefs with the most formidable of all the Northern armies was before them.

He heard the distant thud of hoofs and with instinctive caution drew back into a dense clump of bushes. A half-dozen horsemen were near and their eager looks in every direction told Harry that they were scouts. There was little difference then between a well worn uniform of blue or grey, and they were very close before Harry was able to tell that they belonged to Grant's army.

He was devoutly glad that his horse was trained thoroughly and stood quite still while the Northern scouts passed. A movement of the bushes would have attracted their attention, and he did not wish to be captured at any time, least of all on the certain eve of a great battle. After a battle he always felt an extra regret for those who had fallen, because they would never know whether they had won or lost.

They were alert, keen and vigorous men, or lads rather, as young as himself, and they rode as if they had been Southern youths almost born in the saddle. Harry was not the only one to notice how the Northern cavalry under the whip hand of defeat had improved so fast that it was now a match, man for man, for that of the South.

The young riders rode on and the tread of their hoofs died in the undergrowth. Then Harry emerged from his own kindly clump of bushes and increased his speed, anxious to reach Ewell, without any more of those encounters. He made good progress through the thickets, and soon after sundown saw a glow which he took to be that of campfires. He advanced cautiously, met the Southern sentinels and knew that he was right.

The very first of these sentinels was an old soldier of Jackson, who knew him well.

"Mr. Kenton!" he exclaimed.

"Yes, Thorn! It's you!" said Harry without hesitation.

The soldier was pleased that he should be recognized thus in the dusk, and he was still more pleased when the young aide leaned down and shook his hand.

"I might have known, Thorn, that I'd find you here, rifle on your arm, watching," he said.

"Thank you, Mr. Kenton. You'll find the general over there on a log by the fire."

Harry dismounted, gave his horse to a soldier and walked into the glade. Ewell sat alone, his crutch under his arms, his one foot kicking back the coals, his bald head a white disc in the glow.

"General Ewell, sir," said Harry.

General Ewell turned about and when he saw Harry his face clearly showed gladness. He could not rise easily, but he stretched out a welcoming hand.

"Ah! Kenton," he said, "you're a pleasant sight to tired eyes like mine. You bring back the glorious old days in the valley. So it's a message from the commander-in-chief?"

"Yes, sir. Here it is."

Ewell read it rapidly by the firelight and smiled.

"He tells us we're nearest to the enemy," he said, "and to hold fast, if we're attacked. You're to remain with us and report what happens, but doubtless you knew all this."

"Yes, I had to commit it to memory before I started."

"Then stay here with me. I may want to report to General Lee at any time. The enemy is in our front only three or four miles away. He knows we're here and it was a villainous surprise to him to find us in his way. They say this man Grant is a pounder. So is Lee, when the time comes to pound, but he's that and far more. I tell you, young man, that General Lee has had to trim a lot of Northern generals. McClellan and Pope and Burnside and Hooker and Meade have been going to school to him, and now Grant is qualifying for his class."

"But Grant is a great general. So our men in the West themselves say."

"He may be, but Lee is greater, greatest. And, Harry, you and I, who knew him and loved him, wish that another who alone was fit to ride by his side was here with him."

"I wish it from the bottom of my heart," said Harry.

"Well, well, regrets are useless. Help me up, Harry. I'm only part of a man, but I can still fight."

"We saw you do that at Gettysburg," said Harry, as he put his arm under Ewell's shoulder. Then Ewell took his crutch and they walked to the far side of the glade, where several officers of his staff gathered around him.

"Lieutenant Kenton, whom you all know," said General Ewell, "has brought a message from the commander-in-chief that we will be attacked first, and to be on guard. We consider it an honour, do we not, my lads?"

"Yes, let them come," they said.

"Harry, you may want to see the enemy. Clayton, you and Campbell take him forward through the pickets. But don't go too far. We don't want to lose three perfectly good young officers before the battle begins. After that it may be your business to get yourselves shot."

The two rode nearly two miles to the crest of a hill and then, using their strong glasses in the moonlight, they were able to see the lights of a vast camp.

"We hear that it is Warren's corps," said Clayton. "As General Ewell doubtless has told you, the enemy know that we're in front, but I don't believe they know our exact location. I believe we'll be in battle with those men in the morning."

Harry thought so too. In truth, it was inevitable. Warren would advance and Ewell would stand in his way. Yet he slept soundly when he went back to camp, although he was awakened long before dawn the next day. Then he ate breakfast, mounted and sat his horse not far away from Ewell, whom two soldiers had strapped into his saddle, and who was watching with eager eyes for the sunrise. Harry, listening intently, heard no sound in front of them, save the wind rippling through the dwarfed forests of the Wilderness, and he knew that no battle had yet begun elsewhere. Sound would come far on that placid May morning, and it was a certainty that Ewell was nearest to contact with the enemy.

But Ewell did not yet move. All his men had been served with early breakfast, such as it was, and remained in silent masses, partly hidden by the forest and thickets. The dawn was cold, and Harry felt a little chill, but it soon passed, as the red edge of the sun showed over the eastern border of the Wilderness. Then the light spread toward the zenith, but the golden glow failed to penetrate the sombre thickets.

"It's going to be a good day," said Harry to an aide.

"A good day for a battle."

"We'll hear from the Yankees soon. They can't fail to discover our exact location by sunrise, and they'll fight. Be sure of that."

It was now nearly six o'clock, and General Ewell, growing impatient, rode forward a little. Harry followed with his staff. A half-dozen Southern sharpshooters rose suddenly out of the thickets, and one of them dared to lay his hands on the reins of the general's horse. But Ewell was not offended. He looked down at the man and said:

"What is it, Strother?"

"Riflemen of the enemy are not more than three or four hundred yards away. If you go much farther, General, they will certainly see you and fire upon you."

"Thanks, Strother. So they've located us?"

"They're about to do it. They're feeling around. We've seen 'em in the bushes. We ask you not to go on, General. We wouldn't know what to do without you. There, sir! They're firing on our pickets!"

A half-dozen shots came from the front, and then a half-dozen or so in reply. Harry saw pink flashes, and then spirals of smoke rising. More shots were fired presently on their right, and then others on their left. The Northern riflemen were evidently on a long line, and intended to make a thorough test of their enemy's strength. Harry had no doubt that Shepard was there. He would surely come to the point where his enemy was nearest, and his eyes and ears would be the keenest of all.

The little skirmish continued for a few minutes, extending along a winding line of nearly a mile through the thickets. Only two or three were wounded and nobody killed on the Southern side. Harry understood thoroughly, as Ewell had said, that the sharpshooters of the enemy were merely feeling for them. They wanted to know if a strong force was there, and now they knew.

The firing ceased, not in dying shots, but abruptly. The Wilderness in front of them returned to silence, broken only by the rippling leaves. Harry knew that the Northern sharpshooters had discovered all they wanted, and were now returning to their leaders.

Ewell turned his horse and rode back toward the main camp, his staff following. The cooking fires had been put out, the lines were formed and every gun was in position. As little noise as possible was allowed, while they waited for Grant; not for Grant himself, but for one of his lieutenants, pushed forward by his master hand.

Harry and most of the staff officers dismounted, holding their horses by the bridle. The young lieutenant often searched the thickets with his glasses, but he saw nothing. Nevertheless he knew that the enemy would come. Grant having set out to find his foe, would never draw back when he found him.

A much longer period of silence than he had expected passed. The sun, flaming red, was moving on toward the zenith, and no sounds of battle came from either right or left. The suspense became acute, almost unbearable, and it was made all the more trying by the blindness of that terrible forest. Harry felt at times as if he would rather fight in the open fields; but he knew that his commander-in-chief was right when he drew Grant into the shades of the Wilderness.

When the suspense became so great that heavy weights seemed to be pressing upon his nerves, rifle shots were fired in front, and skirmishers uttered the long, shrill rebel yell. Then above both shots and shouts rose the far, clear call of a bugle.

"Here they come!" Harry heard Ewell say to himself, and the next moment the sound of human voices was drowned in the thunder of great guns and the crash of fifty thousand rifles. The battle was so sudden and the charge so swift that it seemed to leap into full volume in an instant. Warren, a resolute and daring general, led the Northern column and it struck with such weight and force that the Southern division was driven back. Harry felt it yielding, as if the ground were sliding under his feet.

There was so much flame and smoke that he could not see well, but the sensation of slipping was distinct. General Ewell was near him, shouting orders. His hat had fallen off, and his round, bald head had turned red, either from the rush of blood or the cannon's glare. It shone like a red dome, but Harry knew that there was no better man in such a crisis than this veteran lieutenant of Stonewall Jackson.

The Wilderness, usually so silent, was an inferno now. The battle, despite its tremendous beginning, increased in violence and fury. Although Grant himself was not there, the spirit that had animated him at Shiloh and Vicksburg was. He had communicated it to his generals, and Warren brought every ounce of his strength into action. The long line of his bayonets gleamed through the thickets and the Northern artillery, superb as usual, rained shells upon the Southern army.

Ewell's men, fighting with all the courage and desperation that they had shown on so many a field, were driven back further and further. Ewell, strapped in his saddle, flourishing his sword, his round, bald head glowing, rode among them, bidding them to stand, that help would soon come. They continued to go backward, but those veterans of so many campaigns never lost cohesion nor showed sign of panic. Their own artillery and rifles replied in full volume. The heads of the charging columns were blown away, but other men took their places, and Warren's force came on with undiminished fire and strength.

Harry wondered if the attack at other points had been made with such impetuosity, but there was such a roar and crash about him that it was impossible to hear sounds of battle elsewhere. Men were falling very fast, but the general was unharmed, and neither the young lieutenant nor his horse was touched.

A sudden shout arose, and it was immediately followed by the piercing rebel yell, swelling wild and fierce above the tumult of the battle. Help was coming. Regiments in grey were charging down the paths and on the left flank rose the thunder of hoofs as a formidable body of cavalry under Sherburne, sabres aloft, swept down on the Northern flank.

Ewell's entire division stopped its retreat and, reinforced by the new men, charged directly upon the Northern bayonets. Men met almost face to face. The saplings and bushes were mown down by cannon and rifles and the air was full of bursting shells. From time to time Ewell's men uttered their fierce, defiant yell, and with a great bound of the heart Harry saw that they were gaining. Warren was being driven back. Two of his cannon were captured already, and the Southern men, feeling the glow of the advance after retreat, charged again and again, reckless of death. But Harry soon saw that ultimate victory here would rest with the South. The troops of Warren, exhausted by their early rush, were driven from one position to another by the seasoned veterans who faced them. The Confederates retained the captured cannon and thrust harder and harder. It became obvious that Warren must soon fall back to the main Northern line, and though the battle was still raging with great fury Ewell beckoned Harry to him.

"Don't stay here any longer," he shouted in his ear. "Ride to General Lee and tell him we're victorious at this point for the day at least!"

Harry saluted and galloped away through the thickets. Behind him the battle still roared and thundered. A stray shell burst just in front of him, and another just behind him, but he and his horse were untouched. Once or twice he glanced back and it looked as if the Wilderness were on fire, but he knew that it was instead the blaze of battle. He saw also that Ewell was still moving forward, winning more ground, and his heart swelled with gladness.

How proud Jackson would have been had he been able to see the valour and skill of his old lieutenant! Perhaps his ghost did really hover over the Wilderness, where a year before he had fallen in the moment of his greatest triumph! Harry urged his horse into a gallop. All his faculties now became acute. He was beyond the zone of fire, but the roar of the battle behind him seemed as loud as ever. Yet it was steadily moving back on the main Union lines, and there could be no doubt of Ewell's continued success.

The curves of the low hills and the thick bushes hid everything from Harry's sight, as he rode swiftly through the winding paths of the Wilderness. When the tumult sank at last he heard a new thunder in front of him, and now he knew that the Southern centre under Hill had been attacked also, and with the greatest fierceness.

As Harry approached, the roar of the second battle became terrific. Uncertain where General Lee would now be, he rode through the sleet of steel, and found Hill engaged with the very flower of the Northern army. Hancock, the hero of Gettysburg, was making desperate exertions to crush him, pouring in brigade after brigade, while Sheridan, regardless of thickets, made charge after charge with his numerous cavalry.

Harry remained in the rear on his horse, watching this furious struggle. The day had become much darker, either from clouds or the vast volume of smoke, and the thickets were so dense that the officers often could not see their enemy at all, only their own men who stood close to them. The struggle was vast, confused, carried on under appalling conditions. The charging horsemen were sometimes swept from the saddle by bushes and not by bullets. Infantrymen stepped into a dark ooze left by spring rains, and pulling themselves out, charged, black to the waist with mud. Sometimes the field pieces became mired, and men and horses together dragged them to firmer ground.

Grant here, as before Ewell, continually reinforced his veterans, but Hill, although he was not able to advance, held fast. The difficult nature of the ground that Lee had chosen helped him. In marsh and thickets it was impossible for the more numerous enemy to outflank him. Harry saw Hill twice, a slender man, who had suffered severe wounds but one of the greatest fighters in the Southern army. He had been ordered to hold the centre, and Harry knew now that he would do it, for the day at least. Night was not very far away, and Grant was making no progress.

He rode on in search of Lee and before he was yet beyond the range of fire he met Dalton, mounted and emerging from the smoke.

"The commander-in-chief, where is he?" asked Harry.

"On a little hill not far from here, watching the battle. I'm just returning with a dispatch from Hill."

"I saw that Hill was holding his ground."

"So my dispatch says, and it says also that he will continue to hold it. You come from Ewell?"

"Yes, and he has done more than stand fast. He was driven back at first, but when reinforcements came he drove Warren back in his turn, and took guns and prisoners."

"The chief will be glad to hear it. We'll ride together. Look out for your horse! He may go knee deep into mire at any time. Harry, the Wilderness looks even more sombre to me than it did a year ago when we fought Chancellorsville."

"I feel the same way about it. But see, George, how they're fighting! General Hill is making a great resistance!"

"Never better. But if you look over those low bushes you can see General Lee on the hill."

Harry made out the figure of Lee on Traveller, outlined against the sky, with about a dozen men sitting on their horses behind him. He hurried forward as fast as he could. The commander-in-chief was reading a dispatch, while the fierce struggle in the thickets was going on, but when Harry saluted and Marshall told him that he had come to report the general put away the dispatch and said:

"What news from General Ewell?"

"General Ewell was at first borne back by the enemy's numbers, but when help came he returned to the charge, and has been victorious. He has gained much ground."

A gleam of triumph shot from Lee's eyes, usually so calm.

"Well done, Ewell!" he said. "The loss of a leg has not dimmed his ardour or judgment. I truly believe that if he were to lose the other one also he would still have himself strapped into the saddle and lead his men to victory. We thank you for the news you have brought, Lieutenant Kenton."

He put his glasses to his eyes and Harry and Dalton as usual withdrew to the rear of the staff. But they used their glasses also, bringing nearer to them the different phases of the battle, which now raged through the Wilderness. They saw at some points the continuous blaze of guns, and the acrid powder smoke, lying low, was floating through all the thickets.

But Harry now knew that the combat, however violent and fierce, was only a prelude. The sun was already setting, and they could not fight at night in those wild thickets, where men and guns would become mired and tangled beyond extrication. The great struggle, with both leaders hurling in their full forces, would come on the morrow.

The sun already hung very low, and in the twilight and smoke the savagery of the Wilderness became fiercer than ever. The dusk gathered around Lee, but his erect figure and white horse still showed distinctly through it. Harry, his spirit touched by the tremendous scenes in the very centre of which he stood, regarded him with a fresh measure of respect and admiration. He was the bulwark of the Confederacy, and he did not doubt that on the morrow he would stop Grant as he had stopped the others.

The darkness increased, sweeping down like a great black pall over the Wilderness. The battle in the centre and on the left died. Lee and his staff dismounting, prepared for the labours of the night.

CHAPTER 15

The Wilderness

When night settled down over the Wilderness the two armies lay almost face to face on a long line. The preliminary battle, on the whole, had favoured the Confederacy. Hill had held his ground and Ewell had gained, but Grant had immense forces, and, though naturally kind of heart, he had made up his mind to strike and keep on striking, no matter what the loss. He could afford to lose two men where the Confederacy lost one.

Harry, like many others, felt that this would be the great Northern general's plan. To-morrow's battle might end in Southern success, but Grant would be there to fight the following day with undiminished resolution. He was as sure of this as he was sure that the day would come.

The night itself was sombre and sinister, the heavens dusky and a raw chill in the air. Heavy vapours rose from the marshes, and clouds of smoke from the afternoon's battle floated about over the thickets, poisoning the air as if with gas, and making the men cough as they breathed it. It made Harry's heart beat harder than usual, and his head felt as if it were swollen. Everything seemed clothed in a black mist with a slightly reddish tint.

A small fire had been built in a sheltered place for the commander-in-chief and his staff, and the cooks were preparing the supper, which was of the simplest kind. While they ate the food and drank their coffee, the darkness increased, with the faint lights of other fires showing here and there through it. Around the muddy places frogs croaked in defiance of armies, and, from distant points, came the crackling fire of skirmishers prowling in the dusk.

Harry's horse, saddled and bridled, was tied to a bush not far away. He knew that it was to be no night of rest for him, or any other member of the staff. Lee would be sending messages continually. Longstreet, although he had been marching hard, was not yet up on the right, and he and his veterans must be present when the shock of Grant's mighty attack came in the morning.

Hill, thin and pale, yet suffering from the effects of his wounds, but burning as usual with the fire of battle, rode up and consulted long and earnestly with Lee. Presently he went back to his own place nearer the centre, and then Lee began to send away his staff one by one with messages. Harry was among the last to go, but he bore a dispatch to Longstreet.

He had heard that Longstreet had criticized Lee for ordering Pickett's famous charge at Gettysburg, but if so, Lee had taken no notice of it, and Longstreet had proved himself the same stalwart fighter as of old. He and the prompt arrival of his veterans had enabled Bragg to win Chickamauga, and it was not Longstreet's fault that the advantage gained there was lost afterward. Now Harry knew that he would be up in time with his seasoned veterans.

As the young lieutenant rode away he saw General Lee walking back and forth before the low fire, his hands clasped behind him, and his eyes as serious as those of any human being could be. Harry appreciated the immensity of his task, and in his heart was a sincere pity for the man who bore so great a burden. He was familiar with the statement that to Lee had been offered the command of the Northern armies at the beginning of the war, but believing his first duty was to his State he had gone with Virginia when Virginia reluctantly went out of the Union. Truly no one could regret the war more than he, and yet he had struck giant blows for its success.

A moment more and the tall figure standing beside the low fire was lost to sight. Then Harry rode among the thickets in the rear of the Confederate line and it was a weird and ghastly ride. Now and then his horse's feet sank in mud, and the frogs still dared to croak around the pools, making on such a night the most ominous of all sounds. It seemed a sort of funeral dirge for both North and South, a croak telling of the ruin and death that were to come on the morrow.

Damp boughs swept across his face, and the vapours, rising from the earth and mingled with the battle smoke, were still bitter to the tongue and poisonous to the breath. Rotten logs crushed beneath his horse's feet and Harry felt a shiver as if the hoofs had cut through a body of the dead. Riflemen rose out of the thickets, but he always gave them the password, and rode on without stopping.

Then came a space where he met no human being, the gap between Hill and Longstreet, and now the Wilderness became incredibly lonely and dreary. Harry felt that if ever a region was haunted by ghosts it was this. The dead of last year's battle might be lying everywhere, and as the breeze sprang up the melancholy thickets waved over them.

He was two-thirds of the way toward the point where he expected to find Longstreet when he heard the sough of a hoof in the mud behind him.

Harry listened and hearing the hoof again he was instantly on his guard. He did not know it, but the character of the night and the wild aspect of the Wilderness were bringing out all the primeval and elemental qualities in his nature. He was the great borderer, Henry Ware, in the Indian-haunted forest, feeling with a sixth sense, even a seventh sense, the presence of danger.

He was following a path, scarcely traceable, used by charcoal burners and wood-cutters, but when he heard the hoof a second time he turned aside into the deepest of the thickets and halted there. The hoofbeat came a third time, a little nearer, and then no more. Evidently the horseman behind him knew that he had turned aside, and was waiting and watching. He was surely an enemy of great skill and boldness, and it was equally sure that he was Shepard. Harry never felt a doubt that he was pursued by the formidable Union spy, and he felt too that he had never been in greater danger, as Shepard at such a moment would not spare his best friend.

But he was not afraid. Danger had become so common that one looked upon it merely as a risk. Moreover, he was never cooler or more ample of resource. He dismounted softly, standing beside his horse's head, holding the reins with one hand and a heavy pistol with the other. He suspected that Shepard would do the same, but he believed that his eyes and ears were the keener. The man must have been inside the Confederate lines all the afternoon. Probably he had seen Harry riding away, and, deftly appropriating a horse, had followed him. There was no end to Shepard's ingenuity and daring.

Harry's horse was trained to stand still indefinitely, and the young man, with the heavy pistol, who held the reins was also immovable. The silence about him was so deep that Harry could hear the frogs croaking at a distant pool.

He waited a full five minutes, and now, like the wild animals, he relied more upon ear than eye. He had learned the faculty of concentration and he bent all his powers upon his hearing. Not the slightest sound could escape the tightly drawn drums of his ears.

He was motionless a full ten minutes. Nor did the horse beside him stir. It was a test of human endurance, the capacity to keep himself absolutely silent, but with every nerve attuned, while he waited for an invisible danger. And those minutes were precious, too. The value of not a single one of them could have been measured or weighed. It was his duty to reach Longstreet at speed, because the general and his veterans must be in line in the morning, when the battle was joined. Yet the incessant duel between Shepard and himself was at its height again, and he did not yet see how he could end it.

Harry felt that it must be essentially a struggle of patience, but when he waited a few minutes longer, the idea to wait with ears close to the earth, one of the oldest devices of primitive man, occurred to him. It was fairly dry in the bushes, and he lay down, pressing his ear to the soil. Then he heard a faint sound, as if some one crawling through the grass, like a wild animal stalking its prey. It was Shepard, of course, and then Harry planned his campaign. Shepard had left his horse, and was endeavouring to reach him by stealth.

Leaving his own horse, he crept a little to the right, and then rising carefully in another thicket he picked out every dark spot in the gloom. He made out presently the figure of a riderless horse, standing partly behind the trunk of an oak, larger than most of those that grew in the Wilderness.

Harry knew that it was Shepard's mount and that Shepard himself was some distance in front of it creeping toward the thicket which he supposed sheltered his foe. There was barely enough light for Harry to see the horse's head and regretfully he raised his heavy pistol. But it had to be done, and when his aim was true he pulled the trigger.

The report of the pistol was almost like the roar of a cannon in the desolate Wilderness and made Harry himself jump. Then he promptly threw himself flat upon his face. Shepard's answering fire came from a point about thirty yards in front of the horse, and the bullet passed very close over Harry's head. It was a marvellous shot to be made merely at the place from which a sound had come. It all passed in a flash, and the next moment Harry heard the sound of a horse falling and kicking a little. Then it too was still.

He remained only a half minute in the grass. Then he began to creep back, curving a little in his course, toward his own horse. He did not believe that Shepard's faculty of hearing was as keen as his own, and he moved with the greatest deftness. He relied upon the fact that Shepard had not yet located the horse, and if Harry could reach it quickly it would not be hard for him, a mounted man, to leave behind Shepard, dismounted. It might be possible, too, that Shepard had gone back to see about his own horse, not knowing that it was slain.

He saw the dusky outline of his horse, and, rising, made two or three jumps. Then he snatched the rein loose, sprang upon his back, and lying down upon his neck to avoid bullets, crashed away, reckless of bushes and briars. He heard one bullet flying near him, but he laughed in delight and relief as his horse sped on toward Longstreet.

He did not diminish his speed until he had gone two or three miles, and then, knowing that Shepard had been left hopelessly behind, even if he had attempted pursuit, he brought his horse down to a walk, and laughed. There was a bit of nervous excitement in the laugh. He had outwitted Shepard again. He had never seen the man, but it did not enter his mind that it was not he. Each had scored largely over the other from time to time, but Harry believed that he was at least even.

He steadied his nerves now and rode calmly toward Longstreet, coming soon upon his scouts, who informed him that the heavy columns were not far behind, marching with stalwart step to their appointed place in the line. But it was Harry's business to see Longstreet himself, and he continued his way toward the centre of the division, where they told him the general could be found.

He rode forward and in the moonlight recognized Longstreet at once, a heavy-set, bearded man, mounted on a strong bay horse. He had a very small staff, and he was first to notice the young lieutenant advancing. He knew Harry well, having seen him with Lee at Gettysburg and with Jackson before. He stopped and said abruptly:

"You come from the commander-in-chief, do you not?"

"Yes, sir," replied Harry, "and I've been coming as fast as I could."

He did not deem it necessary to say anything about his encounter with Shepard.

"There has been heavy fighting. What are his orders?"

Harry told him, also giving him a written message, which the general read by the light of a torch an aide held.

"You can tell General Lee that all my men will be in position for battle before dawn," said the Georgian crisply.

Even as he spoke, Harry heard the heavy, regular tread of the brigades marching forward through the Wilderness. He saluted General Longstreet.

"I shall return at once with your message," he said.

But Harry, having had one such experience, was resolved not to risk another. He would make a wider circuit in the rear of the army. Shepard, on foot, and anxious to avenge his defeat, might be waiting for him, but he would go around him. So when he started back he made a wide curve, and soon was in the darkness and silence again.

He had a good horse and his idea of direction being very clear he rode swiftly in the direction he had chosen. But his curve was so great that when he reached the centre of it he was so far in the rear of the army that no sound came from it. If the skirmishers were still firing the reports of their rifles were lost in the distance. Where he rode the only noises were those made by the wild animals that inhabited the Wilderness, creatures that had settled back into their usual haunts after the armies had passed beyond.

Once a startled deer sprang from a clump of bushes and crashed away through the thickets. Rabbits darted from his path, and an owl, wondering what all the disturbance was about, hooted mournfully from a bough.

Long before dawn Harry reached the Southern sentinels in the centre and was then passed to General Lee, who remained at the same camp, sitting on a log by some smothered coals. Several other members of his staff had returned already, and the general, looking up when Harry came forward, merely said:

"Well!"

"I have seen General Longstreet, sir," said Harry, "and he bids me tell you that he and his men will be in position before dawn. He was nearly up when I left, and he has also sent you this note."

He handed the note to General Lee, who, bending low over the coals, read it.

"Everything goes well," he said with satisfaction. "We shall be ready for them. What time is it, Peyton?"

"Five minutes past four o'clock, sir."

"Then I think the attack should come within an hour."

"Perhaps before daybreak, sir."

"Perhaps. And even after the sun begins to rise it will be like twilight in this gloomy place."

Grant, in truth, prompt and ready as always, had ordered the advance to be begun at half-past four, but Meade, asking more time for arrangements and requesting that it be delayed until six, he had consented to a postponement until five o'clock and no more.

Harry had one more message to carry, a short distance only, and on his return he found the Invincibles posted on the commander-in-chief's right, and not more than two hundred yards away.

"You must be a body guard for the general," he said to Colonel Leonidas Talbot.

"There could be no greater honour for the Invincibles, nor could General Lee have a better guard."

"I'm sure of that, sir."

"What's happening, Harry? Tell us what's been going on in the night!"

"Our line of battle has been formed. General Longstreet and his men on the right are soon to be in touch with General Hill. I returned from him a little while ago. I can't yet smell the dawn, but I think the battle will come before then."

Harry rode back and resumed his place beside Dalton. The troops everywhere were on their feet, cannon and rifles ready, because it was a certainty that the two armies would meet very early.

In fact, the Army of Northern Virginia began to slide slowly forward. It was not the habit of these troops to await attack. Lee nearly always had taken the offensive, and the motion of his men was involuntary. They felt that the enemy was there and they must go to meet him.

"What time is it now?" whispered Dalton.

Harry was barely able to discern the face of his watch.

"Ten minutes to five," he replied.

"And the dawn comes early. It won't be long before Grant comes poking his nose through the Wilderness."

Harry was silent. A few minutes more, and there was a sudden crackle of rifles in front of them.

"The dawn isn't here, but Grant is," said Harry.

The crackling fire doubled and tripled, and then the fire of the Southern rifles replied in heavy volume. The lighter field guns opened with a crash, and the heavier batteries followed with rolling thunder. Leaves and twigs fell in showers, and men fell with them. The deep Northern cheer swelled through the Wilderness and the fierce rebel yell replied.

Grey dawn, rising as if with effort, over the sodden Wilderness found two hundred thousand men locked fast in battle. It might have been a bright sun elsewhere, but not here among the gloomy shades and the pine barrens. The firing was already so tremendous that the smoke hung low and thick, directly over the tops of the bushes, and the men, as they fought, breathed mixed and frightful vapours.

Both sides fought for a long time in a heavy, smoky dusk, that was practically night. Officers coming from far points, led, compass in hand, having no other guide save the roar of battle. As the Southern leaders had foreseen, Grant was throwing in the full strength of his powerful army, hoping with superior numbers and better equipment to crush Lee utterly that day.

The great Northern artillery was raking the whole Southern front. Hancock, the superb, was hurling the heavy Northern masses directly upon the main position of the South. He had half the Army of the Potomac, and at other points Warren, Wadsworth, Sedgwick and Burnside were advancing with equal energy and contempt of death. Fiercer and fiercer grew the conflict. Hancock, remembering how he had held the fatal hill at Gettysburg, and resolved to win a complete victory now, poured in regiment after regiment. But in all the fire and smoke and excitement and danger he did not neglect to keep a cool head. Hearing that a portion of Longstreet's corps was near, he sent a division and numerous heavy artillery to attack it, driving it back after a sanguinary struggle of more than an hour.

Then he redoubled his attack upon the Southern centre, compelling it to give ground, though slowly. Harry felt that gliding movement backward and a chill ran through his blood. The heavy masses of Grant and his powerful artillery were prevailing. The strongest portion of the Southern army was being forced back, and a gap was cut between Hill and Longstreet. Had Hancock perceived the gap that he had made he might have severed the Southern army, inflicting irretrievable retreat, but the smoke and the dusk of the Wilderness hid it, and the moment passed into one of the great "Ifs" of history.

Harry, on horseback, witnessed this conflict, all the more terrible because of the theatre in which it was fought. The batteries and the riflemen alike were frequently hidden by the thickets. The great banks of smoke hung low, only to be split apart incessantly by the flashes of fire from the big guns. But the bullets were more dangerous than the cannon balls and shells. They whistled and shrieked in thousands and countless thousands.

Lee sat on his horse impassive, watching as well as he could the tide of battle. Messengers covered with smoke and sweat had informed him of the gap between Hill and Longstreet, and he was dispatching fresh troops to close it up. Harry saw the Invincibles march by. The two colonels at their head beheld Lee on his white horse, and their swords flew from their scabbards as they made a salute in perfect unison. Close behind them rode St. Clair and Happy Tom, and they too saluted in like manner. Lee took off his hat in reply and Harry choked. "About to die, we salute thee," he murmured under his breath.

Then with a shout the Invincibles, their officers at their head, plunged into the fire and smoke, and were lost from Harry's view. But he could not stay there long and wonder at their fate. In a few minutes he was riding to Longstreet with a message for him to bear steadily toward Hill, that the gap might be closed entirely, and as soon as possible.

He galloped behind the lines, but bullets fell all around him, and often a shell tore the earth. The air had become more bitter and poisonous. Fumes from swamps seemed to mingle with the smoke and odours of burned gunpowder. His lips and his tongue were scorched. But he kept on, without exhaustion or mishap, and reached Longstreet, who had divined his message.

"The line will be solid in a few minutes," he said, and while the battle was still at its height on the long front he touched hands with Hill. Then both drove forward with all their might against Hancock, rushing to the charge, with the Southern fire and recklessness of death that had proved irresistible on so many fields. The advance, despite the most desperate efforts of Hancock and his generals, was stopped. Then he was driven back. All the ground gained at so much cost was lost and the Southern troops, shouting in exultation, pushed on, pouring in a terrible rifle fire. Longstreet, in his eagerness, rode a little ahead of his troops to see the result. Turning back, he was mistaken in the smoke by his own men for a Northern cavalryman, and they fired upon him, just as Jackson had been shot down by his own troops in the dusk at Chancellorsville.

The leader fell from his horse, wounded severely, and the troops advancing to victory became confused. The rumour spread that Longstreet had been killed. There was no one to give orders, and the charge stopped. Harry and a half-dozen others who had seen the accident or heard of it, galloped to Lee, who at once rode into the very thick of the command, giving personal orders and sending his aides right and left with others. The whole division was reformed under his eye, and he sent it anew to the attack.

The battle now closed in with the full strength of both armies. Hancock strove to keep his place. The valiant Wadsworth had been killed already. The dense thickets largely nullified Grant's superior numbers. Lee poured everything on Hancock, who was driven from every position. Fighting furiously behind a breastwork built the night before, he was driven from that too.

Often in the dense shades the soldiers met one another face to face and furious struggles hand-to-hand ensued. Bushes and trees, set on fire by the shells, burned slowly like torches put there to light up the ghastly scene of man's bravery and folly. Jenkins, a Confederate general, was killed and colonels and majors fell by the dozen. But neither side would yield, and Grant hurried help to his hard-pressed troops.

Harry had been grazed on the shoulder by a bullet, but his horse was unharmed, and he kept close to Lee, who continued to direct the battle personally. He knew that they were advancing. Once more the genius of the great Confederate leader was triumphing. Grant, the redoubtable and tenacious, despite his numbers, could set no trap for him! Instead he had been drawn into battle on a field of Lee's own choosing.

The conflict had now continued for a long time, and was terrible in all its aspects. It was far past noon, and for miles a dense cloud of smoke hung over the Wilderness, which was filled with the roar of cannon, the crash of rifles and the shouts of two hundred thousand men in deadly conflict. The first meeting of the two great protagonists of the war, Lee and Grant, was sanguinary and terrible, beyond all expectation.

Hundreds fell dead, their bodies lying hidden under the thickets. The forest burned fiercely here and there, casting circles of lurid light over the combatants, while the wind rained down charred leaves and twigs. The fires spread and joined, and at points swept wide areas of the forest, yet the fury of the battle was not diminished, the two armies forgetting everything else in their desire to crush each other.

Harry's horse was killed, as he sat near Lee, but he quickly obtained another, and not long afterward he was sent with a second message to Ewell. He rode on a long battle front, not far behind the lines, and he shuddered with awe as he looked upon the titanic struggle. The smoke was often so heavy and the bushes so thick that he could not see the combatants, except when the flame of the firing or the burning trees lighted up a segment of the circle.

Halfway to Ewell and he stopped when he saw two familiar figures, sitting on a log. They were elderly men in uniforms riddled by bullets. The right arm of one and the left leg of the other were tightly bandaged. Their faces were very white and it was obvious that they were sitting there, because they were not strong enough to stand.

Harry stopped. No message, no matter how important, could have kept him from stopping.

"Colonel Talbot! Colonel St. Hilaire!" he cried.

"Yes, here we are, Harry," replied Colonel Leonidas Talbot in a voice, thin but full of courage. "Hector has been shot through the leg and has lost much blood, but I have bound up his wound, and he has done as much for my arm, which has been bored through from side to side by a bullet, which must have been as large as my fist."

"And so for a few minutes," said Lieutenant-Colonel St. Hilaire, valiantly, "we must let General Lee conduct the victory alone."

"And the Invincibles!" exclaimed Harry, horrified. "Are they all gone but you?"

"Not at all," replied Colonel Talbot. "There is so much smoke about that you can't see much, but if it clears a little you will behold Lieutenant St. Clair and the youth rightly called Happy Tom and some three score others, lying among the bushes, not far ahead of you, giving thorough attention to the enemy."

"And is that all that's left of the Invincibles?"

"It's a wonder that they're so many. You were right about this man, Grant, Harry. He's a fighter, and their artillery is numerous and wonderful. John Carrington himself must be in front of us. We have not seen him, but the circumstantial evidence is conclusive. Nobody else in the world could have swept this portion of the Wilderness with shell and shrapnel in such a manner. Why, he has mowed down the bushes in long swathes as the scythe takes the grass and he has cut down our men with them. How does the battle go elsewhere?"

"We're succeeding. We're driving 'em back. I can stop only a moment now. I'm on my way to General Ewell."

"Then hurry. Don't be worried about us. I'll help Hector and Hector will help me. And do you curve further to the rear, Harry. The worst thing that a dispatch bearer can do is to get himself shot."

Waving his hand in farewell Harry galloped away. He knew that Colonel Talbot had given him sound advice, and he bore back from the front, coming once more into lonely thickets, although the flash of the battle was plainly visible in front of him, and its roar filled his ears. Yet when he rode alone he almost expected to see Shepard rise up before him, and bid him halt. His encounters with this man had been under such startling circumstances that it now seemed the rule, and not the exception, for him to appear at any moment.

But Shepard did not come. Instead Harry began to see the badly wounded of his own side drifting to the rear, helping one another as hurt soldiers learn to do. Two of them he allowed to hang on his stirrups a little while.

"They're fighting hard," said one, a long, gaunt Texan, "an' they're so many they might lap roun' us. This man of theirs, Grant, ain't much of a fellow to get scared, but I guess Marse Bob will take care of him just ez he has took care of the others who came into Virginia."

"They're led in the main attack by Hancock," said the other, a Virginian. "I caught a glimpse of him through the smoke, just as I had a view of him for a minute back there by the clump of trees on the ridge at Gettysburg."

"Are you one of Pickett's men?" asked Harry.

"I am, sir, one of the few that's left. I went clear to the clump of trees

201

and how I got back I've never known. It was a sort of red dream, in which I couldn't pick out anything in particular, but I was back with the army, carrying three bullets that the doctors took away from me, and here I've gathered up two more they'll rob me of in just the same way."

He spoke quite cheerfully, and when Harry, curving again, was compelled to release them, both, although badly wounded, wished him good luck.

He found General Ewell in front, stamping back and forth on his crutches, watching the battle with excitement.

"And so you're here again, Harry. Well it's good news at present!" he cried. "It seems that their man, Grant, is going to school to Lee just like the others."

"But some pupils learn too fast, sir!"

"That's so, but, Harry, I wish I could see more of the field. An invisible battle like this shakes my nerves. Batteries that we can't see send tornadoes of shot and shell among us. Riflemen, by the thousands, hidden in the thickets rain bullets into our ranks. It's inhuman, wicked, and our only salvation lies in the fact that it's as bad for them as it is for us. If we can't see them they can't see us."

"You can hold your ground here?"

"Against anything and everything. Tell General Lee that we intend to eat our suppers on the enemy's ground."

"That's all he wants to know."

As Harry rode back he saw that the first fires were spreading, passing over new portions of the battlefield. Sparks flew in myriads and fine, thin ashes were mingled with the powder smoke. The small trees, burnt through, fell with a crash, and the flames ran as if they were alive up boughs. Other trees fell too, cut through by cannon balls, and some were actually mown down by sheets of bullets, as if they had been grass.

His way now led through human wreckage, made all the more appalling by an approaching twilight, heavy with fumes and smoke, and reddened with the cannon and rifle blaze. His frightened horse pulled wildly at the bit, and tried to run away, but Harry held him to the path, although he stepped more than once in hot ashes and sprang wildly. The dead were thick too and Harry was in horror lest the hoof of his horse be planted upon some unheeding face.

He knew that the day was waning fast and that the dark was due in some degree to the setting sun, and not wholly to the smoke and ashes. Yet the fury of the battle was sustained. The southern left maintained the ground that it had gained, and in the centre and right it could not be driven back. It became obvious to Grant that Lee was not to be beaten in the Wilderness. His advance suffered from all kinds of disadvantages. In the swamps and thickets he could mass neither his guns nor his cannon. Communications were broken, the telegraph wires could be used but little and as the twilight darkened to night he let the attack die.

Harry was back with the commander-in-chief, when the great battle of the Wilderness, one of the fiercest ever fought, sank under cover of the night. It was not open and spectacular like Gettysburg, but it had a gloomy and savage grandeur all its own. Grant had learned, like the others before him, that he could not drive headlong over Lee, but sitting in silence by his campfire, chewing his cigar, he had no thought, unlike the others, of turning back. Nearly twenty thousand of his men had fallen, but huge resources and a President who supported him absolutely were behind him and he was merely planning a new method of attack.

In the Southern camp there was exultation, but it was qualified and rather grim. These men, veterans of many battles and able to judge for themselves, believed that they had won the victory, but they knew that it was by no means decisive. The numerous foe with his powerful artillery was still before them. They could see his campfires shining through the thickets, and their spies told them that, despite his great losses, there was no sign of retreat in Grant's camp.

An appalling night settled down on the Wilderness. The North American Continent never saw one more savage and terrible. Twenty thousand wounded were scattered through the thickets and dense shades, and spreading fires soon brought death to many whom the bullets had not killed at once. The smoke, the mists and vapours gathered into one dense cloud, that hung low and made everything clammy to the touch.

Lee stood under the boughs of an oak, and ate food that had been prepared for him hastily. But, as Harry saw, the act was purely mechanical. He was watching as well as he could what was going on in front, and he was giving orders in turns to his aides. Harry's time had not yet come, and he kept his eyes on his chief.

There was no exultation in the face of Lee. He had drawn Grant into the Wilderness and then he had held him fast in a battle of uncommon size and fierceness. But nothing was decided. He had studied the career of Grant, and he knew that he had a foe of great qualities with whom to deal. He would have to fight him again, and fight very soon. He heard too with a sorrow, hard to conceal, the reports of his own losses. They were heavy enough and the gaps now made could never be refilled. The Army of Northern Virginia, which had been such a powerful instrument in his hands, must fight with ever diminishing numbers.

Harry was sent to inquire into the condition of Longstreet, whom he found weak physically and suffering much pain. But the veteran was upborne by the success of the day and his belief in ultimate victory. He bade Harry tell the commander-in-chief that his men were fit to fight again and better than ever, at the first shoot of dawn.

Harry rode back in the night, the burning trees serving him for torches. Nearly all the soldiers were busy. Some were gathering up the wounded and others were building breastworks. His eyes were reddened by the powder-smoke, and often the heavy black masses of vapour were impenetrable, save where the forest burned. Now he came to a region where the dead and wounded were so thick that he dismounted and led his horse, lest a hoof be planted upon any one of them. But he noticed that here as in other battles the wounded made but little complaint. They suffered in silence, waiting for their comrades to take them away.

Then he passed around a section of forest that was burning fiercely. Here Southern and Union soldiers had met on terms of peace and were making desperate efforts to save their helpless comrades. Harry would have been glad to give aid himself, but he was too well trained now to turn aside when he rode for Lee.

He saw many dark figures passing before the flaming background, and as he walked more slowly than he thought, he saw one that looked remarkably familiar to him. It was impossible to see the face, but he knew the walk and the lift of the shoulders. Discipline gave way to impulse now, and he ran forward crying:

"Dick! Dick!"

Dick Mason, who had just dragged a wounded man beyond the range of the flames, turned at the sound of the voice. Even had Harry seen his face at first he would not have known him nor would Dick have known Harry. Both were black with ashes, smoke and burned gunpowder. But Dick knew the voice in an instant. Once more were the two cousins to meet in peace on an unfinished battlefield.

Each driven by the same impulse stepped forward, and their hands met in the strong grasp of blood kindred and friendship, which war itself could not sever.

"You're alive, Harry!" said Dick. "It seems almost impossible after what has happened to-day."

"And you too are all right. Not harmed, I see, though your face is an African black."

"I should call your own colour dark and smoky."

"I wasn't sure that you were in the East. When did you come?"

"With General Grant, and I knew that you were on General Lee's staff. I've a message to give him by you. Oh! you needn't laugh. It's a good straight talk."

"Go ahead then and say it to me."

"You say to General Lee that it's all over. Tell him to quit and send his soldiers home. If he doesn't he'll be crushed."

Harry laughed again and waved his finger at the sombre battlefield, upon which he stood.

"Does this look like it?" he asked. "We're farther forward to-night than we were this morning. Wouldn't General Grant be glad if he could say as much?"

"It makes no difference. I know you don't believe me, but it's so. The North is prepared as it never was before. And Grant will hammer and hammer forever. We know what a man Lee is. The whole North admits it, but I tell you the sun of the South is setting."

"You're growing poetical and poetry is no argument."

"But unlimited men, unlimited cannon and rifles, unlimited ammunition and supplies and a general who is willing to use them, are. Of course I know that you can't carry any such message to General Lee, but I feel it to be the truth."

"We've a great general and a great army that say, no."

Nobody paid any attention to the two. It was merely another one of those occasions when men of the opposing sides stood together amid the dead and wounded, and talked in friendly fashion. But Harry knew that he could not delay long.

"I've got to go, Dick," he said. "And I've a message too, one that I want you to deliver to General Grant."

"What is it?"

"Tell him that we've more than held our own to-day, and that we'll thrash him like thunder to-morrow, and whenever and wherever he may choose, no matter what the odds are against us."

Dick laughed.

"I see that you won't believe even a little bit of what I tell you," he said "and maybe if I were in your place I wouldn't either. But it's true all the same. Good-by, Harry."

The two hands, covered with battle grime, met again in the strong grasp of blood kindred and friendship.

"Take care of yourself, old man!"

The words, exactly alike, were uttered by the two simultaneously.

Both were stirred deeply. Harry sprang on his horse, looked back once, waving his hand, and rode rapidly to General Lee. Later in the night, he received permission to hunt up the Invincibles, his heart full of fear that they had perished utterly in the gloomy pit called the Wilderness, lit now only by the fire of death.

He left his horse with an orderly and walked toward the point where he had last seen them. He passed thousands of soldiers, many wounded, but silent as usual, while the unhurt were sleeping where they had dropped. The Invincibles were not at the point where he had seen them last, and the colonels of several scattered regiments could not tell him what had become of them. But he continued to seek them although the fear was growing in his heart that the last man of the Invincibles had died under the Northern cannon.

His search led toward the enemy's lines. Almost unconsciously he went in that direction, however, his knowledge of the two colonels telling him that they would take the same course. He turned into a little cove, partly sheltered by the dwarfed trees and he heard a thin voice saying:

"Nonsense, Leonidas. I scarcely felt it, but yours, old friend, is pretty bad. You must let me attend to it. Keep still! I'll adjust the bandage."

"Hector, why do you make a fuss over me, when I'm only slightly hurt, and sacrifice yourself, a severely injured man!"

"With all due respect you'd better let me attend to you both," said a voice that Harry recognized as St. Clair's.

"And maybe I could help a little," said another that he knew to be Happy Tom's. But their voices, like those of the colonels, were weak. Still he had positive proof that they were alive, and, as his heart gave a joyful throb or two, he stepped into the glade. There was enough light for him to see Colonel Leonidas Talbot, and Lieutenant-Colonel Hector St. Hilaire, sitting side by side on the grass with their backs against the earthly wall, very pale from loss of blood, but with heads erect and eyes shining with a certain pride. St. Clair and Langdon lay on the grass, one with an old handkerchief, blood-soaked, bound about his head and the other with a bandage tightly fastened over his left shoulder. Beyond them lay a group of soldiers.

"Good evening, heroes!" said Harry lightly as he stepped forward.

He was welcomed with an exclamation of joy from them all.

"We meet again, Harry," said Colonel Talbot, "and it is the second time since morning. I fancy that second meetings to-day have not been common. We have the taste of success in our mouths, but you'll excuse us for not rising to greet you. We are all more or less affected by the missiles of the enemy and for some hours at least neither walking nor standing will be good for us."

"Mohammed must come to all the mountains," said St. Clair, weakly holding out a hand.

Harry greeted them all in turn, and sat down with them. He was overflowing with sympathy, but it was not needed.

"A glorious day," said Colonel Leonidas Talbot.

"Truly," said Harry.

"A most glorious day," said Lieutenant-Colonel Hector St. Hilaire.

"Most truly," said Harry.

"An especially glorious day for the Invincibles," said Colonel Talbot.

"The most glorious of all possible days for the Invincibles," said Lieutenant-Colonel Hector St. Hilaire.

There was an especial emphasis to their words that aroused Harry's attention.

"The Invincibles have had many glorious days," he said. "Why should this be the most glorious of them all?"

"We went into battle one hundred and forty-seven strong," replied Colonel Talbot quietly, "and we came out with one hundred and forty-seven casualties, thirty-nine killed and one hundred and eight wounded. We lay no claim to valour, exceeding that of many other regiments in General Lee's glorious army, but we do think we've made a fairly excellent record. Do you see those men?"

He pointed to a silent group stretched upon the turf, and Harry nodded.

"Not one of them has escaped unhurt, but most of us will muster up strength enough to meet the enemy again to-morrow, when our great general calls."

Harry's throat contracted for a moment.

"I know it, Colonel Talbot," he said. "The Invincibles have proved themselves truly worthy of their name. General Lee shall hear of this."

"But in no boastful vein, Harry," said Colonel Talbot. "We would not have you to speak thus of your friends."

"I do not have to boast for you. The simple truth is enough. I shall see that a surgeon comes here at once to attend to your wounded. Good night, gentlemen."

"Good night," said the four together. Harry walked back toward General Lee's headquarters, full of pride in his old comrades.

CHAPTER 16

Spottsylvania

Harry secured a little sleep toward morning, and, although his nervous tension had been very great, when he lay down, he felt greatly strengthened in body and mind. He awakened Dalton in turn, and the two, securing a hasty breakfast, sat near the older members of the staff, awaiting orders. The commander-in-chief was at the edge of the little glade, talking earnestly with Hill, and several other important generals.

Harry often saw through the medium of his own feelings, and the rim of the sun, beginning to show over the eastern edge of the Wilderness, was blood red. The same crimson and sinister tinge showed through the west which was yet in the dusk. But in east and west there were certain areas of light, where the forest fires yet smouldered.

Both sides had thrown up hasty breastworks of earth or timber, but the two armies were unusually silent. A space of perhaps a mile and a half lay between them, but as the light increased neither moved. There was no crackle of rifle fire along their fronts. The skirmishers, usually so active, seemed to be exhausted, and the big guns were at rest. The fierce and tremendous fighting of the two days before seemed to have taken all the life out of both North and South.

Harry, inured to war, understood the reasons for silence and lack of movement. Grant had been drawn into a region that he did not like, where he could not use his superior numbers to advantage, and he must be shuddering at the huge losses he had suffered already. He would seek better ground. Lee too, was in no condition to take advantage of his successful defence. The old days when he could send Jackson on a great turning movement, to fall with all the crushing impact of a surprise upon the Northern flank, were gone forever. Stuart, the brilliant cavalryman, was there, but his men were not numerous enough, and, however brilliant, he was not Jackson.

The sun rose higher. Midmorning came, and the two armies still lay close. Harry grew stronger in his opinion that they would not fight again that day, although he watched, like the others, for any sign of movement in the Northern camp.

Noon came, and the same dead silence. The fires had burned themselves out now and the dusk that had reigned over the Wilderness, before the battle, recovered its ground, thickened still further by the vast quantities of smoke still hanging low under a cloudy sky. But the aspect of the Wilderness itself was more mournful than ever. Coals smouldered in the burned areas, and now and then puffs of wind picked up the hot ashes and sent them in the faces of the soldiers. Thickets and bushes had been cut down by bullets and cannon balls, and lay heaped together in tangled confusion. Back of the lines, the surgeons, with aching backs, toiled over the wounded, as they had toiled through the night.

Harry saw nearly the whole Southern front. The members of Lee's staff were busy that day, carrying orders to all his generals to rectify their lines, and to be prepared, to the last detail, for another tremendous assault. It was not until the afternoon that he was able to look up the Invincibles again. The two colonels and the two lieutenants were doing well, and the colonels were happy.

"We've already been notified," said Colonel Talbot, "that we're to retain our organization as a regiment. We're to have about a hundred new men now, the fragments of destroyed regiments. Of course, they won't be like the veterans of the Invincibles, but a half-dozen battles like that of yesterday should lick them into shape."

"I should think so," said Harry.

"Do you believe that Grant is retreating?" asked Lieutenant-Colonel St. Hilaire.

"Our scouts don't say so."

"Then he is merely putting off the evil day. The sooner he withdraws the more men he will save. No Yankee general can ever get by General Lee. Keep that in your mind, Harry Kenton."

Harry was silent, but rejoicing to find that his friends would soon recover from their wounds, he went back to his place, and saw all the afternoon pass, without any movement indicating battle.

Night came again and the scouts reported to Lee that the Union army was breaking camp, evidently with the intention of getting out of the Wilderness and marching to Fredericksburg. Harry was with the general when he received the news, and he saw him think over it long. Other scouts brought in the same evidence.

Harry did not know what the general thought, but as for himself, although he was too young to say anything, it was incredible that Grant should retreat. It was not at all in accordance with his character, now tested on many fields, and his resources also were too great for withdrawal.

But the night was very dark and no definite knowledge yet came out of it. Lee stayed by his little campfire and received reports. Far after dusk Harry saw the look of doubt disappear from his eyes, and then he began to send out messengers. It was evident that he had formed his opinion, and intended to act upon it at once.

He beckoned to Harry and Dalton, and bade them go together with written instructions to General Anderson, who had taken the place of General Longstreet.

"You will stay with General Anderson subject to his orders," he said, as Harry and Dalton, saluting, rode toward Anderson's command.

Their way led through torn, tangled and burned thickets. Sometimes a horse sprang violently to one side and neighed in pain. His hoof had come down on earth, yet so hot that it scorched like fire. Now and then sparks fell upon them, but they pursued their way, disregarding all obstacles, and delivered their sealed orders to General Anderson, who at once gathered up his full force, and marched away from the heart of the Wilderness toward Spottsylvania Court House.

Harry surmised that Grant was attempting some great turning movement, and Lee, divining it, was sending Anderson to meet his advance. He never knew whether it was positive knowledge or a happy guess.

But he was quite sure that the night's ride was one of the most singular and sinister ever made by an army. If any troops ever marched through the infernal regions it was they. In this part of the Wilderness the fires had been of the worst. Trees still smouldered. In the hollows, where the bushes had grown thickest, were great beds of coals. The smoke which the low heavy skies kept close to the earth was thick and hot. Gusts of wind sent showers of sparks flying, and, despite the greatest care to protect the ammunition, they marched in constant danger of explosion.

Harry thought at one time that General Anderson intended to camp in the Wilderness for the night, but he soon saw that it was impossible. One could not camp on hot ground in a smouldering forest.

"I believe it's a march till day," he said to Dalton. "It's bound to be. If a man were to lie down here, he'd find himself a mass of cinders in the morning, and it will take us till daylight and maybe past to get out of the Wilderness."

"If he didn't burn to death he'd choke to death. I never breathed such smoke before."

"That's because it's mixed with ashes and the fumes of burned gunpowder. A villainous compound like this can't be called air. How long is it until dawn?"

"About three hours, I think."

"You remember those old Greek stories about somebody or other going down to Hades, and then having a hard climb out again. We're the modern imitators. If this isn't Hades then I don't know what it is."

"It surely is. Phew, but that hurt!"

"What happened?"

"I brushed my hand against a burning bush. The result was not happy. Don't imitate me."

Dalton's horse leaped to one side, and he had difficulty in keeping the saddle. His hoof had been planted squarely in the midst of a mass of hot twigs.

"The sooner I get out of this Inferno or Hades of a place the happier I'll be!" said Dalton.

"I've never seen the like," said Harry, "but there's one thing about it that makes me glad."

"And what's the saving grace?"

"That it's in Virginia and not in Kentucky, though for the matter of that it couldn't be in Kentucky."

"And why couldn't it be in Kentucky?"

"Because there's no such God-forsaken region in all that state of mine."

"It certainly gets upon one's soul," said Dalton, looking at the gloomy region, so terribly torn by battle.

"But if we keep going we're bound to come out of it some time or other."

"And we're not stopping. A man can't make his bed on a mass of coals, and there'll be no rest for us until we're clear out of the Wilderness."

They marched on a long time, and, as day dawned, hundreds of voices united in a shout of gladness. Behind them were the shades of the Wilderness, that dismal region reeking with slaughter and ruin, and before them lay firm soil, and green fields, in all the flush of a brilliant May morning.

"Well, we did come out of Hades, Harry," said Dalton.

"And it does look like Heaven, but the trouble with our Hades, George, is that the inmates will follow us. Put your glasses to your eyes and look off there."

"Horsemen as sure as we're sitting in our own saddles."

"And Northern horsemen, too. Their uniforms are new enough for me to tell their colour. I take it that Grant's vanguard has moved by our right flank and has come out of the Wilderness."

"And our surmises that we were to meet it are right. Spottsylvania Court House is not far away, and maybe we are bound for it."

"And maybe the Yankees are too."

Harry's words were caused by the sound of a distant and scattering fire. In obedience to an order from Anderson, he and Dalton galloped forward, and, from a ridge, saw through their glasses a formidable Union column advancing toward Spottsylvania. As they looked they saw many men fall and they also saw flashes of flame from bushes and fences not far from its flank.

"Our sharpshooters are there," said Harry. And he was right. While the Union force was advancing in the night Stuart had dismounted many of his men and using them as skirmishers had incessantly harassed the march of Grant's vanguard led by Warren.

"Each army has been trying to catch the other napping," said Dalton.

"And neither has succeeded," said Harry.

"Now we make a race for the Spottsylvania ridge," said Dalton. "You see if we don't! I know this country. It's a strong position there, and both generals want it."

Dalton was right. A small Union force had already occupied Spottsylvania, but the heavy Southern division crossing the narrow, but deep, river Po, drove it out and seized the defensive position.

Here they rested, while the masses of the two armies swung toward them, as if preparing for a new battlefield, one that Harry surveyed with great interest. They were in a land of numerous and deep rivers. Here were four spreading out, like the fingers of a human hand, without the thumb, and uniting at the wrist. The fingers were the Mat, the Ta, the Po, and the Nye, and the unit when they united was called the Mattopony.

Lee's army was gathering behind the Po. A large Union force crossed it on his flank, but, recognizing the danger of such a position, withdrew. Lee himself came in time. Hill, overcome by illness and old wounds, was compelled to give up the command of his division, and Early took his place. Longstreet also was still suffering severely from his injuries. Lee had but few of the able and daring generals who had served him in so many fields. But Stuart, the gay and brilliant, the medieval knight who had such a strong place in the commander-in-chief's affections, was there. Nor was his plumage one bit less splendid.

The yellow feather stood in his hat. There was no speck or stain on the broad yellow sash and his undimmed courage was contagious.

But Harry with his sensitive and imaginative mind, that leaped ahead, knew their situation to be desperate. His opinion of Grant had proved to be correct. Although he had found in Lee an opponent far superior to any other that he had ever faced, the Union general, undaunted by his repulse and tremendous losses in the Wilderness, was preparing for a new battle, before the fire from the other had grown cold.

He knew too that another strong Union army was operating far to the south of them, in order to cut them off from Richmond, and scouts had brought word that a powerful force of cavalry was about to circle upon their flank. The Confederacy was propped up alone by the Army of Northern Virginia, which having just fought one great battle was about to begin another, and by its dauntless commander.

The Southern admiration for Lee, both as the general and as the man, can never be shaken. How much greater then was the effect that he created in the mind of impressionable youth, looking upon him with youth's own eyes in his moments of supreme danger! He was in very truth to Harry another Hannibal as great, and better. The long list of his triumphs, as youth counted them, was indeed superior to those of the great Carthaginian, and he believed that Lee would repel this new danger.

Nearly all that day the two armies constructed breastworks which stood for many years afterward, but neither made any attempt at serious work, although there was incessant firing by the skirmishers and an occasional cannon shot. Harry, whether carrying an order or not, had ample chance to see, and he noted with increasing alarm the growing masses of the Union army, as they gathered along the Spottsylvania front.

"Can we beat them?" "Can we beat them?" was the question that he continually asked himself. He wondered too where the Winchester regiment and Dick Mason lay, and where the spy, Shepard, was. But Shepard was not likely to remain long in one place. Skill and courage such as his would be used to the utmost in a time like this. Doubtless he was somewhere in the Confederate lines, discovering for Grant the relatively small size of the army that opposed him.

Near dusk and having the time he followed his custom and sought the Invincibles. Both colonels had recovered considerable strength, and, although one of them could not walk, he would be helped upon his horse whenever the battle began, and would ride into the thick of it. But the faces of St. Clair and Happy Tom glowed and their wounds apparently were forgotten.

"Lieutenant Arthur St. Clair and Lieutenant Thomas Langdon are gone forever," said Colonel Talbot. "In their places we have Major Arthur St. Clair and Captain Thomas Langdon. All our majors and captains have been killed, and with our reduced numbers these two will fill their places, as best they can; and that they can do so most worthily we all know. They received their promotions this afternoon."

Harry congratulated them both with the greatest warmth. They were very young for such rank, but in this war the toll of officers was so great that men sometimes became generals when they were but little older.

"Is it to be to-morrow?" asked Colonel Talbot.

"I think it likely that we'll fight again then," said Harry.

"And Grant has not yet had enough. He wants a little more of the same, does he!"

"It would appear so, sir."

"Then I take it without consulting General Lee that he is ready to deal with the Yankees as he dealt with them in the Wilderness."

"I hope so. Good night."

"Good night!" they called to him, and Harry returned to the staff. Taylor, the adjutant general, told him and Dalton to lie down and seek a little sleep. Harry was not at all averse, as he was completely exhausted again after the tremendous excitement of the battle, and the long hours of strain and danger. But his nerves were so much on edge that he could not yet sleep. His eyes were red and smarting from the smoke and burned powder, and he felt as if accumulated smoke and dust encased him like a suit of armour.

"I'd give a hundred dollars for a good long drink, just as long as I liked to make it," he groaned, "and I mean a drink of pure cold water, too."

"Confederate paper or money?" said Dalton.

"I mean real money, but at the same time you oughtn't to make invidious comparisons."

"Then the money's mine, but you can pay me whenever you feel like it, which I suppose will be never. There's a spring in the thick woods just back of your quarters. It flows out from under rocks, at the distance of several yards makes a deep pool, and then the overflow of the pool goes on through the forest to the Po. Come on, Harry! We'll luxuriate and then tell the others."

Harry found that it was a most glorious spring, indeed; clear and cold. He and Dalton drank slowly at first, and then deeply.

"I didn't know I could hold so much," said Dalton.

"Nor I," said Harry.

"Let's take another."

"I'm with you."

"Let's make it two more."

"I still follow you."

"Horace wrote about his old Falernian, and the other wines which he enjoyed, as he and the leading Roman sports sat around the fountain, flirting with the girls," said Dalton, "but I don't believe any wine ever brewed in Latium was the equal of this water."

"I've always had an idea that Horace wasn't as gay as he pretended to be, else he wouldn't have written so much about Chloe and her comrades. I imagine that an old Roman boy would keep pretty quiet about his dancing and singing, and not publish it to the public."

"Well, let him be. He's dead and the Romans are dead, and the Americans are doing their best to kill off one another, but let's forget it for a few minutes. That pool there is about four feet deep, the water is clear and the bottom is firm ground; now do you know what I'm going to do?"

"Yes, and I'm going to do the same. Bet you even that I beat you into the water."

"Taken."

They threw off their clothes rapidly, but the splashes were simultaneous as their bodies struck the water. Although the limits of the pool were narrow they splashed and paddled there for a while, and it was a long time since they had known such a luxury. Then they walked out, dried themselves and spread the good news. All night long the pool was filled with the bathers, following one another in turn.

The water taken internally and externally soothed Harry's nerves. His excitement was gone. A great army with which they were sure to fight on the morrow was not far away, but for the time he was indifferent. The morrow could take care of itself. It was night, and he had permission to go to sleep. Hence he slumbered fifteen minutes later.

He slept almost through the night, and, when he was awakened shortly before dawn, he found that his strength and elasticity had returned. He and Dalton went down to the spring again, drank many times, and then ate breakfast with the older members of the staff, a breakfast that differed very little from that of the common soldiers.

Then a day or two of waiting, and watching, and of confused but terrible fighting ensued. The forests were again set on fire by the bursting shells and they were not able to rescue many of the wounded from the flames. Vast clouds again floated over the whole region, drawing a veil of dusk between the soldiers and the sun. But neither army was willing to attack the other in full force.

Grant commanding all the armies of the East was moving meanwhile. A powerful cavalry division, he heard, had got behind Beauregard, who was to protect Richmond, and was tearing up an important railway line used by the Confederacy. The daring Sheridan with another great division of cavalry had gone around Lee's left and was wrecking another railway, and with it the rations and medical supplies so necessary to the Confederates. Grant, recognizing his antagonist's skill and courage and knowing that to succeed he must destroy the main Southern army, resolved to attack again with his whole force.

The day had been comparatively quiet and the Army of Northern Virginia had devoted nearly the whole time to fortifying with earthworks and breastworks of logs. The young aides, as they rode on their missions, could easily see the Northern lines through their glasses. Harry's heart sank as he observed their extent. The Southern army was sadly reduced in numbers, and Grant could get reinforcement continually.

But such is the saving grace of human nature that even in these moments of suspense, with one terrible battle just over and another about to begin, soldiers of the Blue and Grey would speak to one another in friendly fashion in the bushes or across the Po. It was on the banks of this narrow river that Harry at last saw Shepard once more. He happened to be on foot that time, the slope being too densely wooded for his horse, and Shepard hailed him from the other side.

"Good day, Mr. Kenton. Don't fire! I want to talk," he said, holding up both hands as a sign of peace.

"A curious place for talking," Harry could not keep from saying.

"So it is, but we're not observed here. It was almost inevitable while the armies remained face to face that we should meet in time. I want to tell you that I've met your cousin, Richard Mason, here, and his commanding officer, Colonel Winchester. Oh, I know much more about you and your relationships than you think."

"How is Dick?"

"He has not been hurt, nor has Colonel Winchester. Mr. Mason has received a letter from his home and your home in Pendleton in Kentucky. The outlaws to the eastward are troublesome, but the town is occupied by an efficient Union garrison and is in no danger. His mother and all of his and your old friends, who did not go to the war, are in good health. He thought that in my various capacities as ranger, scout and spy I might meet you, and he asked me, if it so happened, to tell these things to you."

"I thank you," said Harry very earnestly, "and I'm truly sorry, Mr. Shepard, that you and I are on different sides."

"I suppose it's too late for you to come over to the Union and the true cause."

Harry laughed.

"You know, Mr. Shepard, there are no traitors in this war."

"I know it. I was merely jesting."

He slipped into the underbrush and disappeared. Harry confessed to himself once more that he liked Shepard, but he felt more strongly than ever that it had become a personal duel between them, and they would meet yet again in violence.

That night he had little to do. It was a typical May night in Virginia, clear and beautiful with an air that would have been a tonic to the nerves, had it not been for the bitter smoke and odours that yet lingered from the battle of the Wilderness.

Before dawn the scouts brought in a rumour that there was a heavy movement of Federal troops, although they did not know its meaning. It might portend another flank march by Grant, but a mist that had begun to rise after midnight hid much from them. The mist deepened into a fog, which made it harder for the Southern leaders to learn the meaning of the Northern movement.

Just as the dawn was beginning to show a little through the fog, Hancock and Burnside, with many more generals, led a tremendous attack upon the Southern right centre. They had come so silently through the thickets that for once the Southern leaders were surprised. The Union veterans, rushing forward in dense columns, stormed and took the breastworks with the bayonet.

Many of the Southern troops, sound asleep, awoke to find themselves in the enemy's hands. Others, having no time to fire them, fought with clubbed rifles.

Harry, dozing, was awakened by the terrific uproar. Even before the dawn had fairly come the battle was raging on a long front. The centre of Lee's army was broken, and the Union troops were pouring into the gap. Grant had already taken many guns and thousands of prisoners, and the bulldog of Shiloh and Vicksburg and Chattanooga was hurrying fresh divisions into the combat to extend and insure his victory. Through the forests swelled the deep Northern cry of triumph.

Harry had never before seen the Southern army in such danger, and he looked at General Lee, who had now mounted Traveller. The turmoil and confusion in front of them was frightful and indescribable. The Union troops had occupied an entire Confederate salient, and their generals, feeling that the moment was theirs, led them on, reckless of life, and swept everything before them.

Harry never took his eyes from Lee. The rising sun shot golden beams through the smoke and disclosed him clearly. His face was calm and his voice did not shake as he issued his orders with rapidity and precision. The lion at bay was never more the lion.

A new line of battle was formed, and the fugitives formed up with it. Then the Southern troops, uttering once more the fierce rebel yell, charged directly upon their enemy and under the eye of the great chief whom they almost worshipped. Now Harry for the first time saw his general show excitement. Lee galloped to the head of one of the Virginia regiments, and ranging his horse beside the colours snatched off his hat and pointed it at the enemy. It was a picture which with all the hero worship of youth he never forgot. It did not even grow dim in his memory—the great leader on horseback, his hat in his hand, his eyes fiery, his face flushed, his hand pointing the way to victory or death.

It was an occasion, too, when the personal presence of a leader meant everything. Every man knew Lee and tremendous rolling cheers greeted his arrival, cheers that could be heard above the thunder of cannon and rifles. It infused new courage into them and they gathered themselves for the rush upon their victorious foe.

Gordon of Georgia, spurring through the smoke, seized Lee's horse by the bridle. He did not mean to have their commander-in-chief sacrificed in a charge.

"This is no place for you, General Lee!" he cried. "Go to the rear!"

Lee did not yet turn, and Gordon shouted:

"These men are Virginians and Georgians who have never failed. Go back, I entreat you!"

Then Gordon turned to the troops and cried, as he rose on his toes in his stirrups:

"Men, you will not fail now!"

Back came the answering shout:

"No! No!" and the whole mass of troops burst into one thunderous, echoing cry:

"Lee to the rear! Lee to the rear! Lee to the rear!"

Nor would they move until Lee turned and rode back. Then, led by Gordon, they charged straight upon their foe, who met them with an equal valour. All day long the battle of Spottsylvania, equal in fierceness and desperation to that of the Wilderness, swayed to and fro. To Harry as he remembered them they were much alike. Charge and defence, defence and charge. Here they gained a little, and there they lost a little. Now they were stumbling through sanguinary thickets, and then they rushed across little streams that ran red.

The firing was rapid and furious to an extraordinary degree. The air rained shell and bullets. Areas of forest between the two armies were mowed down. More than one large tree was cut through entirely by rifle bullets. Other trees here, as in the Wilderness, caught fire and flamed high.

Midnight put an end to the battle, with neither gaining the victory and both claiming it. Harry had lost another horse, killed under him, and now he walked almost dazed over the terrible field of Spottsylvania, where nearly thirty thousand men had fallen, and nothing had yet been decided.

Yet in Harry's heart the fear of the grim and silent Grant was growing. The Northern general had fought within a few days two battles, each the equal of Waterloo, and Harry felt sure that he was preparing for a third. The combat of the giants was not over, and with an anxious soul he waited the next dawn. They remained some days longer in the Wilderness, or the country adjacent to it, and there was much skirmishing and firing of heavy artillery, but the third great pitched battle did not come quite as soon as Harry expected. Even Grant, appalled by the slaughter, hesitated and began to manoeuvre again by the flank to get past Lee. Then the fighting between the skirmishers and heavy detached parties became continuous.

During the days that immediately followed Harry was much with Sherburne. The brave colonel was one of Stuart's most trusted officers. Despite the forests and thickets there was much work for the cavalry to do, while the two armies circled and circled, each seeking to get the advantage of the other.

Sheridan, they heard, was trying to curve about with his horsemen and reach Richmond, and Stuart, with his cavalry, including Sherburne's, was sent to intercept him, Harry riding by Sherburne's side. It was near the close of May, but the air was cool and pleasant, a delight to breathe after the awful Wilderness.

Stuart, despite his small numbers, was in his gayest spirits, and when he overtook the enemy at a little place called Yellow Tavern he attacked with all his customary fire and vigour. In the height of the charge, Harry saw him sink suddenly from his horse, shot through the body. He died not long afterward and the greatest and ⸱ brilliant horseman of the South passed away to join Jackson and had gone before. Harry was one of the little group v news to Lee, and he saw how deeply the great leader many of his brave generals had fallen that he was li⸍ family, bereft.

Nevertheless the lion still at bay was great and terrible to strike. It was barely two weeks after Spottsylvania when Lee took up a strong position at Cold Harbor, and Grant, confident in his numbers and powerful artillery, attacked straightaway at dawn.

Harry was in front during that half-hour, the most terrible ever seen on the American continent, when Northern brigade after brigade charged to certain death. Lee's men, behind their earthworks, swept the field with a fire in which nothing could live. The charging columns fairly melted away before them and when the half-hour was over more than twelve thousand men in blue lay upon the red field.

Grant himself was appalled, and the North, which had begun to anticipate a quick and victorious end of the war, concealed its disappointment as best it could, and prepared for another campaign.

Grant and Lee, facing each other, went into trenches along the lines of Cold Harbor, and the hopes of the young Southern soldiers after the victory there rose anew. But Harry was not too sanguine, although he kept his thoughts to himself.

The officers of the Invincibles had recovered from their wounds, and Colonel Leonidas Talbot and Lieutenant-Colonel Hector St. Hilaire, sitting in a trench, resumed their game of chess.

Colonel Talbot took a pawn, the first man captured by either since early spring.

"That was quite a victory," he said.

"Not important! Not important, Leonidas!"

"And why not, Hector?"

"Because you've left the way to your king easier. I shall promptly move along that road."

"As Grant moved through the Wilderness."

"Don't depreciate Grant, Leonidas. He never stops pounding. We've fought two great battles with him in the Wilderness and a third at Cold Harbor, but he's still out there facing us. Can't you see the Yankees with your glasses, Harry?"

"Yes, sir, quite clearly. They're about to fire a shot from a big gun in a wood. There it goes!"

The deep note of the cannon came to them, passed on, and then rolled back in echoes like a threat.

The Tree of Appomattox

A Story of the Civil War's Close

Characters in the Civil War Novels

Principal Characters

Harry Kenton	a lad who fights on the Southern side
Dick Mason	cousin of Harry Kenton, who fights on the Northern side
Colonel George Kenton	father of Harry Kenton
Mrs Mason	mother of Dick Mason
Juliana	Mrs Mason's devoted coloured servant
Colonel Arthur Winchester	Dick Mason's regimental commander
Colonel Leonidas Talbot	commander of the Invincibles, a Southern regiment
Lieutenant Colonel Hector St Hilaire	second in command of the Invincibles
Alan Hertford	a Northern cavalry leader
Philip Sherburne	a Southern cavalry leader
William J Shepard	a Northern spy
Daniel Whitley	a Northern sergeant and veteran of the plains
George Warner	a Vermont youth who loves mathematics
Frank Pennington	a Nebraska youth, friend of dick mason
Arthur St Clair	a native of Charleston, friend of Harry Kenton
Tom Langdon	friend of Harry Kenton
George Dalton	friend of Harry Kenton
Bill Skelly	mountaineer and guerrilla
Tom Slade	a guerrilla chief
Sam Jarvis	the singing mountaineer

Ike Simmons	Jarvis' nephew
Aunt "Suse"	a centenarian and prophetess
Bill Petty	a mountaineer and guide
Julien de Langeais	a musician and soldier from Louisiana
John Carrington	famous Northern artillery officer
Dr Russell	principal of the Pendleton School
Arthur Travers	a lawyer
James Bertrand	a messenger from the South
John Newcomb	a Pennsylvania colonel
John Markham	a Northern officer
John Watson	a Northern contractor
William Curtis	a Southern merchant and blockade runner
Mrs Curtis	wife of William Curtis
Henrietta Garden	a seamstress in Richmond
Dick Jones	a North Carolina mountaineer
Victor Woodville	a young Mississippi officer
John Woodville	father of Victor Woodville
Charles Woodville	uncle of Victor Woodville
Colonel Bedford	a Northern officer
Charles Gordon	a Southern staff officer
John Lanham	an editor
Judge Kendrick	a lawyer
Mr Culver	a state senator
Mr Bracken	a tobacco grower
Arthur Whitridge	a state senator

HISTORICAL CHARACTERS

Abraham Lincoln	President of the United States
Jefferson Davis	President of the Southern Confederacy
Judah P Benjamin	member of the Confederate cabinet
U S Grant	Northern commander
Robert B Lee	Southern commander
Stonewall Jackson	Southern general
Philip H Sheridan	Northern general
George H Thomas	"the Rock of Chickamauga"

Albert Sidney Johnston	Southern general
A P Hill	Southern general
W S Hancock	Northern general
George B Mc Clellan	Northern general
Ambrose B Burnside	Northern general
Turner Ashby	Southern cavalry leader
J E B Stuart	Southern cavalry leader
Joseph Hooker	Northern general
Richard S Ewell	Southern general
Jubal Early	Southern general
William S Rosecrans	Northern general
Simon Bolivar Buckner	Southern general
Leonidas Polk	Southern general and bishop
Braxton Bragg	Southern general
Nathan Bedford Forrest	Southern cavalry leader
John Morgan	Southern cavalry leader
George J Meade	Northern general
Don Carlos Buell	Northern general
W T Sherman	Northern general
James Longstreet	Southern general
P G T Beauregard	Southern general
William L Yancey	Alabama orator
James A Garfield	Northern general, afterwards President of the United States

.... and many others

IMPORTANT BATTLES DESCRIBED IN THE CIVIL WAR SERIES

Bull Run	Kernstown	Cross Keys
Winchester	Port Republic	The Seven Days
Mill Spring	Fort Donelson	Shiloh
Perryville	Stone River	The Second Manassas
Antietam	Fredericksburg	Chancellorsville
Gettysburg	Champion Hill	Vicksburg
Chickamauga	Missionary Ridge	The Wilderness
Spottsylvania	Cold Harbor	Fisher's Hill
Cedar Creek	Appomattox	

Foreword

The Tree of Appomattox concludes the series of connected romances dealing with the Civil War, begun in *The Guns of Bull Run*, and continued successively through *The Guns of Shiloh*, *The Scouts of Stonewall*, *The Sword of Antietam*, *The Star of Gettysburg*, *The Rock of Chickamauga* and *The Shades of the Wilderness* to the present volume. It has been completed at the expense of vast labour, and the author has striven at all times to be correct, wherever facts are involved. So far, at least, no historic detail has been challenged by critic or reader.

More than half a century has passed since the Civil War's close. Not many of the actors in it are left. It was one of the most tremendous upheavals in the life of any nation, and it was the greatest of all struggles, until the World War began, but scarcely any trace of partisan rancour or bitterness is left. So, it has become easier to write of it with a sense of fairness and detachment, and the lapse of time has made the perspective clear and sharp.

However lacking he may be in other respects, the author perhaps had an advantage in being born, and having grown up in a border state, where sentiment was about equally divided concerning the Civil War. He was surrounded during his early youth by men who fought on one side or the other, and their stories of camp, march and battle were almost a part of the air he breathed. So he hopes that this circumstance has aided him to give a truthful colour to the picture of the mighty combat, waged for four such long and terrible years.

CHAPTER 1

The Apple Tree

Although he was an officer in full uniform he was a youth in years, and he had the spirits of youth. Moreover, it was one of the finest apple trees he had ever seen and the apples hung everywhere, round, ripe and red, fairly asking to be taken and eaten. Dick Mason looked up at them longingly. They made him think of the orchards at home in his own state, and a touch of coolness in the air sharpened his appetite for them all the more.

"If you want 'em so badly, Dick," said Warner, "why don't you climb the tree and get 'em? There's plenty for you and also for Pennington and me."

"I see. You're as anxious for apples as I am, and you wish me to gather 'em for you by making a strong appeal to my own desires. It's your clever New England way."

"We're forbidden to take anything from the people, but it won't hurt to keep a few apples from rotting on the ground. If you won't get 'em Pennington will."

"I understand you, George. You're trying to play Frank against me, while you keep yourself safe. You'll go far. Never mind. I'll gather apples for us all."

He leaped up, caught the lowest bough, swung himself lightly into the fork, and then climbing a little higher, reached for the reddest and ripest apples, which he flung down in a bountiful supply.

"Now, gluttons," he said, "satiate yourselves, but save a lot for me."

Then he went up as far as the boughs would sustain him and took a look over the country. Apple trees do not grow very tall, but Dick's tree stood on the highest point in the orchard, and he had a fine view, a view that was in truth the most remarkable the North American continent had yet afforded.

He always carried glasses over his shoulder, and lately Colonel Winchester had made him a gift of a splendid pair, which he now put into use, sweeping the whole circle of the horizon. With their powerful aid he was able to see the ancient city of Petersburg, where Lee had thrown himself across Grant's path in order to block his way to Richmond, the Southern capital, and had dug long lines of trenches in which his army lay. It was Lee who first used this method of defence for a smaller force against a larger, and the vast trench warfare of Europe a half century later was a repetition of the mighty struggle of Lee and Grant on the lines of Petersburg.

Dick through his glasses saw the trenches, lying like a brown bar across the green country, and opposite them another brown bar, often less than a hundred yards away, which marked where the Northern troops also had dug in. The opposing lines extended a distance of nearly forty miles, and Richmond was only twenty miles behind them. It was the nearest the Army of the Potomac had come to the Southern capital since McClellan had seen the spires of its churches, and that was more than two years away. Warner and Pennington were lying on the ground, eating big red apples with much content and looking up lazily at Mason.

"You're curving those glasses about a lot. What do you see, Dick?" asked Pennington at length.

"I see Petersburg, an old, old town, half buried in foliage, and with many orchards and gardens about it. A pity that two great armies should focus on such a pleasant place."

"No time for sentiment, Dick. What else do you see?"

"Jets of smoke and flame from the trenches, an irregular sort of firing, sometimes a half-dozen shots at one place, and then a long and peaceful break until you come to another place, where they're exchanging bullets."

"What more do you see, Brother Richard?"

"I see a Johnny come out of his trench hands up and advance toward one of our Yanks opposite, who also has come out of his trench hands up."

"What are they trading?" asked Warner.

"The Reb offers a square of plug tobacco, and the Yank a bundle of newspapers. Now they've made the exchange, now they've shaken hands and each is going back to his own trench."

"It's a merry world, my masters, as has been said before," resumed Warner, "but I should add that it's also a mad wag of a world. Here we are face to face for forty miles, at some points seeking to kill one another in a highly impersonal way, and at other points conducting sale and barter according to the established customs of peace. People at home wouldn't believe it, and later on a lot more won't believe it, when the writers come to write about it. But it's true just the same. What else do you see from the apple tower, Brother Richard?"

"A long line of wagons approaching a camp some distance behind the Confederate trenches. They must be loaded pretty heavily, because the drivers are cracking their whips over the horses and mules."

"That's bad. Provisions, I suppose," said Warner. "The more these Johnnies get to eat the harder they fight, and they're not supposed to be receiving supplies now. Our cavalry ought to have cut off that wagon train. I shall have to speak to Sheridan about it. This is no way to starve the Johnnies to death. Seest aught more, Brother Richard?"

"I do! I do! Jump up, boys, and use your own glasses! I behold a large man on a gray horse, riding slowly along, as if he were inspecting troops away behind the trenches. Wherever he passes the soldiers snatch off their caps and, although I can't hear 'em, I know they're cheering. It's Lee himself!"

Both Warner and Pennington swung themselves upon the lower boughs of the tree and put their glasses to their eyes.

"It's surely Lee," said Warner. "I'm glad to get a look at him. He's been giving us a lot of trouble for more than three years now, but I think General Grant is going to take his measure."

"They're terribly reduced," said Pennington, "and if we stick to it we're bound to win. Still, you boys will recall for some time that we've had a war. What else do you see from the heights of the apple tree, Dick?"

"Distant dust behind our own lines, and figures moving in it dimly. Cavalry practicing, I should say. Have you fellows fruit enough?"

"Plenty. You can climb down and if the farmer hurries here with his dog to catch you we'll protect you."

"This is a fine apple tree," said Dick, as he descended slowly. "Apple trees are objects of beauty. They look so well in the spring all in white bloom, and then they look just as well in the fall, when the red or yellow apples hang among the leaves. And this is one of the finest I've ever seen."

He did not dream then that he should remember an apple tree his whole life, that an apple tree, and one apple tree in particular, should always call to his mind a tremendous event, losing nothing of its intensity and vividness with the passing years. But all that was in the future, and when he joined his comrades on the ground he made good work with the biggest and finest apple he could find.

"Early apples," he said, looking up at the tree. "It's not the end of July yet."

"But good apples, glorious apples, anyhow," said Pennington, taking another. "Besides, it's fine and cool like autumn."

"It won't stay," said Dick. "We've got the whole of August coming. Virginia is like Kentucky. Always lots of hot weather in August. Glad there's no big fighting to be done just now. But it's a pity, isn't it, to tear up a fine farming country like this. Around here is where the United States started. John Smith and Rolfe and Pocahontas and the rest of them may have roamed just where this orchard stands. And later on lots of the great Americans rode about these parts, some of the younger ones carrying their beautiful ladies on pillions behind them. You are a cold-blooded New Englander, Warner, and you believe that anyone fighting against you ought to burn forever, but as for me I feel sorry for Virginia. I don't care what she's done, but I don't like to see the Old Dominion, the Mother of Presidents, stamped flat."

"I'm not cold-blooded at all, but I don't gush. I don't forget that this state produced George Washington, but I want victory for our side just the same, no matter how much of Virginia we may have to tread down. Is that farm house over there still empty?"

"Of course, or we wouldn't have taken the apples. It belongs to a man named Haynes, and he left ahead of us with his family for Richmond. I fancy it will be a long time before Haynes and his people sleep in their own rooms again. Come, fellows, we'd better be going back. Colonel Winchester is kind to us, but he doesn't want his officers to be prowling about as they please too long."

They walked together toward the edge of the orchard and looked at the farm house, from the chimneys of which no smoke had risen in weeks. Dick felt sure it would be used later on as headquarters by some general and his staff, but for the present it was left alone. And being within the Union lines no plunderer had dared to touch it.

It was a two-story wooden house, painted white, with green shutters, all closed now. The doors were also locked and sealed until such time as the army authorities wished to open them, but on the portico, facing the Southern lines were two benches, on which the three youths sat, and looked again over the great expanse of rolling country, dotted at intervals by puffs of smoke from the long lines of trenches. Where they sat it was so still that they could hear the faint crackle of the distant rifles, and now and then the heavier crash of a cannon.

Dick's mind went back to the Wilderness and its gloomy shades, the sanguinary field of Spottsylvania, and then the terrific mistake of

Cold Harbor. The genius of Lee had never burned more brightly. He had handled his diminishing forces with all his old skill and resolution, but Grant had driven on and on. No matter what his losses the North always filled up his ranks again, and poured forward munitions and supplies in a vast and unbroken stream. A nation had summoned all its powers for a supreme effort to win, and Dick felt that the issue of the war was not now in doubt. The genius of Lee and the bravery of his devoted army could no longer save the South. The hammer strokes of Grant would surely crush it.

And then what? He had the deepest sympathy for these people of Virginia. What would become of them after the war? Defeat for the South meant nearer approach to destruction than any nation had suffered in generations. To him, born south of the Ohio River, and so closely united by blood with these people, victory as well as defeat had its pangs.

Warner and Pennington rose and announced that they would return to the regiment which was held in reserve in a little valley below, but Dick, their leave not having run out yet, decided to stay a while longer.

"So long," said Warner. "Let the orchard alone. Leave apples for others. Remember that they are protected by strict orders against all wandering and irresponsible officers, but ourselves."

"Yes, be good, Dick," said Pennington, and the two went down the slope, leaving Dick on the portico. He liked being alone at times. The serious cast of mind that he had inherited from his famous great grandfather, Paul Cotter, demanded moments of meditation. It was peaceful too on the portico, and a youth who had been through Grant's Wilderness campaign, a month of continuous and terrible fighting, was glad to rest for a while.

The distant rifle fire and the occasional cannon shot had no significance and did not disturb him. They blended now with the breeze that blew among the leaves of the apple trees. He had never felt more like peace, and the pleasant open country was soothing to the eye. What a contrast to that dark and sodden Wilderness where men fought blindly in the dusk. He shuddered as he remembered the forests set on fire by the shells, and burning over the fallen.

A light step aroused him and a large man sat down on the bench beside him. Dick often wondered at the swift and almost noiseless tread of Shepard, with whom he was becoming well acquainted. He was tall, built powerfully and must have weighed two hundred pounds, yet he moved with the ease and grace of a boy of sixteen. Dick thought it must come from his trade.

"I don't want to intrude, Mr. Mason," said Shepard, "but I saw you sitting here, looking perhaps too grave and thoughtful for one of your years."

"You're most welcome, Mr. Shepard, and I was thinking, that is in a vague sort of way."

"I saw your face and you were wondering what was to become of Virginia and the Virginians."

"So I was, but how did you know it?"

"I didn't know it. It was just a guess, and the guess was due to the fact that I was having the same thoughts myself."

"So you regard the war as won?" asked Dick, who had a great respect for Shepard's opinion.

"If the President keeps General Grant in command, as he will, it's a certainty, but it will take a long time yet. We can't force those trenches down there. Remember what Cold Harbor cost us."

Dick shuddered.

"I remember it," he said.

"It would be worse if we tried to storm Lee's lines. After Cold Harbor the general won't attempt it, and I see a long wait here. But we can afford it. The South grows steadily weaker. Our blockade clamps like a steel band, and presses tighter and tighter all the time. Food is scarce in the Confederacy. So is ammunition. They receive no recruits, and every day the army of Lee is smaller in numbers than it was the day before."

"You go into Richmond, Mr. Shepard. I've heard from high officers that you do. How do they feel there with our army only about twenty miles away?"

"They're quiet and seem to be confident, but I believe they know their danger."

"Have you by any chance seen or heard of my cousin, Harry Kenton, who is a lieutenant on the staff of the Southern commander-in-chief?" Shepard smiled, as if the question brought memories that pleased him.

"A fine youth," he said. "Yes, I've seen him more than once. I'm free to tell you, Lieutenant Mason, that I know a lot about this rebel cousin of yours. He and I have come into conflict on several occasions, and I did not win every time."

"Nobody could beat Harry always," exclaimed Dick with youthful loyalty. "He was always the strongest and most active among us, and the best in forest and water. He could hunt and fish and trail like the scouts of our border days."

"I found him in full possession of all these qualities and he used them against me. I should grieve if that cousin of yours were to fall, Mr. Mason. I want to know him still better after the war."

Dick would have asked further questions about the encounters between Harry and the spy, but he judged that Shepard did not care to answer them, and he forbore. Yet the man aroused the most intense curiosity in him. There were spies and spies, and Shepard was one of them, but he was not like the others. He was unquestionably a man of great mental power. His calm, steady gaze and his words to the point showed it. No one patronized Shepard.

"I should like to go into Richmond with you some dark night," said Dick, who hid a strong spirit of adventure under his quiet exterior.

"You're not serious, Lieutenant Mason?"

"I wasn't, maybe, when I began to say it, but I believe I am now. Why shouldn't I be curious about Richmond, a place that great armies have been trying to take for three years? Just at present it's the centre of the world to me in interest."

"You must not think of such a thing, Mr. Mason. Detection means certain death."

"No more for me than for you."

"But I have had a long experience and I have resources of which you can't know. Don't think of it again, Mr. Mason."

"I was merely jesting. I won't," said Dick.

He involuntarily looked toward the point beyond the horizon where Richmond lay, and Shepard meanwhile studied him closely. Young Mason had not come much under his notice until lately, but now he began to interest the spy greatly. Shepard observed what a strong, well-built young fellow he was, tall and slender but extremely muscular. He also bore a marked resemblance to his cousin, Harry Kenton, and such was the quality of Shepard that the likeness strongly recommended Dick to him. Moreover, he read the lurking thought that persisted in Dick's mind.

"You mustn't dream of such a thing as entering Richmond, Mr. Mason," he said.

"It was just a passing thought. But aren't you going in again?"

"Later on, no doubt, but not just now. I understand that we're planning some movement. I don't know what it is, but I'm to wait here until it's over. Good-by, Mr. Mason. Since things are closing in it's possible that you and I will see more of each other than before."

"Of course, when I'm personally conducted by you on that trip into Richmond."

Shepard, who had left the portico, turned and shook a warning finger. "Dismiss that absolutely and forever from your mind, Mr. Mason," he said.

Dick laughed, and watched the stalwart figure of the spy as he strode away. Again the singular ease and lightness of his step struck him. To the lad's fancy the grass did not bend under his feet. Upon Dick as upon Harry, Shepard made the impression of power, not only of strength but of subtlety and courage.

"I'm glad that man's on our side," said Dick to himself, as Shepard's figure disappeared among the trees. Then he left the portico and went down in the valley to Colonel Winchester's regiment, where he was received with joyous shouts by several young men, including Warner and Pennington, who had gone on before. Colonel Winchester himself smiled and nodded, and Dick saluted respectfully.

The Winchesters, as they loved to call themselves, were faring well at this particular time. Like the Invincibles on the other side, this regiment had been decimated and filled up again several times. It had lost heavily in the Wilderness and at Spottsylvania, but its colonel had escaped without serious hurt and had received special mention for gallantry and coolness. It had been cut up once more at Cold Harbor, and because of its great services and losses it was permitted to remain a while in the rear as a reserve, and obtain the rest it needed so sorely.

The brave youths were recovering fast from their wounds and exertions. Their camp was beside a clear brook and there were tents for the officers, though they were but seldom used, most of them, unless it should be raining, preferring to sleep in their blankets under the trees. The water was good to drink, and farther down were several deep pools in which they bathed. Food, as usual in the Northern army, was good and plentiful, and for the Winchesters it seemed more a period of play than of war.

"What did you see at the house, Dick?" asked Colonel Winchester.

"The spy, Shepard. I talked a while with him. He says the Confederacy is growing weaker every day, but if we try to storm Lee's lines we'll be cut to pieces."

"I think he's right in both respects, although I feel sure that some kind of a movement will soon be attempted. But Dick, a mail from the west has arrived and here is a letter for you."

He handed the lad a large square envelope, addressed in tall, slanting script, and Dick knew at once that it was from his mother. He seized it eagerly, and Colonel Winchester, suppressing the wish to know what was inside, turned away.

* * * * * * * *

I have not heard from my dearest boy since the terrible battles in the east [Mrs. Mason wrote], but I hope and pray that you have come safely through them. You have escaped so many dangers that I feel you must escape all the rest. The news reaches us that the fighting in Virginia has been of the most dreadful character, but when it arrives in Pendleton it has two meanings. Those of our little town who are for the Confederacy say General Grant's losses have been so enormous that he can go no farther, and that the last and greatest effort of the North has failed.

Those who sympathize with the Union say General Lee has been reduced so greatly that he must be crushed soon and with him the Confederacy. As you know, I wish the latter to be true, but I suspect that the truth is somewhere between the two statements.

But the truth either way brings me great grief. I cannot hate the Southern people. We are Southern ourselves in all save this war, and, although our dear little town is divided in feeling, I have received nothing but kindness from those on the other side. Dr. Russell often asks about you. He says you were the best Latin scholar in the Academy, and he expects you to have a great future, as a learned man, after the war. He speaks oftenest of you and Harry Kenton, and I believe that you two were his favourite pupils. He says that Harry's is the best mathematical mind he has ever found in his long years of teaching.

Your room remains just as it was when you left. Juliana brushes and airs it every day, and expects at any time to see her young Master Dick come riding home. She keeps in her mind two pictures of you, absolutely unlike. In one of these pictures you are a great officer, carrying much of the war's weight on your shoulders, consulted continually by General Grant, who goes wrong only when he fails to take your advice. In the other you are a little boy whom she alternately scolds and pets. And it may be that I am somewhat like Juliana in this respect.

The garden is very fine this year. The vegetables were never more plentiful, and never of a finer quality. I wish you were here for your share. It must be a trial to have to eat hard crackers and tough beef and pork day after day. I should think that you would grow to hate the sight of them. Sam, the coloured man who has been with us so long, has proved as faithful and trustworthy as Juliana. He makes a most excellent farmer, and the yield of corn in the bottom land is going to be amazing.

They say that since the Federal successes in the West the operations of Skelly's band of guerrillas have become bolder, but he has not threatened Pendleton again. They say also that a little farther south a band of like character, who call themselves Southern, under a man named Slade, are ravaging, but I suppose that you, who see great generals and great armies daily, are not much concerned about outlaws.

Always keep your feet dry and warm if you can, and never fail to spread a blanket between you and the damp grass. Give my respects to Colonel Winchester. Tell him that we hear of him now and then in Kentucky and that we hear only good. Don't forget about the blanket.

* * * * * * * *

There was more, but it was these passages over which Dick lingered longest.

He read the letter three times—letters were rare in those years, and men prized them highly—and put it away in his strongest pocket. Colonel Winchester was standing by the edge of the brook, and Dick, saluting him, said:

"My mother wishes me to deliver to you her respects and best wishes."

A flush showed through the tan of the colonel's face, and Dick, noticing it, was startled by a sudden thought. At first his feeling was jealousy, but it passed in an instant, never to come again. There was no finer man in the world than Colonel Winchester.

"She is well," he added, "and affairs could go no better at Pendleton."

"I am glad," said Colonel Winchester simply. Then he turned to a man with very broad shoulders and asked:

"How are the new lads coming on?"

"Very well, sir," replied Sergeant Daniel Whitley. "Some of 'em are a little awkward yet, and a few are suffering from change of water, but they're good boys and we can depend on 'em, sir, when the time comes."

"Especially since you have been thrashing 'em into shape for so many days, sergeant."

"Thank you, sir."

An orderly came with a message for Colonel Winchester, who left at once, but Dick and the sergeant, his faithful comrade and teacher, stood beside the stream. They could easily see the bathers farther down, splashing in the water, pulling one another under, and, now and then, hurling a man bodily into the pool. They were all boys to the veteran. Many of them had been trained by him, and his attitude toward them was that of a school teacher toward his pupils.

"You have ears that hear everything, sergeant," said Dick. "What is this new movement that I've heard two or three men speak of? Something sudden they say."

"I've heard too," replied Sergeant Whitley, "but I can't guess it. Whatever it is, though, it's coming soon. There's a lot of work going on at a point farther down the line, but it's kept a secret from the rest of us here."

The sergeant went away presently, and Dick, going down stream, joined some other young officers in a pool. He lay on the bank afterward, but, shortly after dark, Colonel Winchester returned, gave an order, and the whole regiment marched away in the dusk. Dick felt sure that the event Sergeant Whitley had predicted was about to happen, but the colonel gave no hint of its nature, and he continued to wonder, as they advanced steadily in the dusk.

CHAPTER 2

The Woman at the House

The men marched on for a long time, and, after a while, they heard the hum of many voices and the restless movements that betokened the presence of numerous troops. Dick, who had dismounted, walked forward a little distance with Colonel Winchester, and, in the moonlight, he was able to see that a large division of the army was gathered near, resting on its arms. It was obvious that the important movement, of which he had been hearing so much, was at hand, but the colonel volunteered nothing concerning its nature.

The troops were allowed to lie down, and, with the calmness that comes of long experience, they soon fell asleep. But the officers waited and watched, and Dick saw other regiments arriving. Warner, who had pushed through some bushes, came back and said in a whisper:

"I've seen a half-dozen great mounds of fresh earth."

"Earth taken out to make a trench, no doubt," said Dick.

But Warner shook his head.

"There's too much of it," he said, "and it's been carried too far to the rear. In my opinion extensive mining operations have been going on here."

"For what?" asked Pennington. "Not for silver or gold. We're no treasure hunters, and besides, there's none here."

Warner shook his head again.

"I don't know," he replied, "but I'm quite sure that it has something to do, perhaps all to do, with the movement now at hand. To the right of us, regiments, including several of coloured troops, are already forming in line of battle, and I've no doubt our turn will come before long."

"We must be intending to make an attack," said Dick, "but I don't suppose we'll move until day."

He had learned long since that night attacks were very risky. Friend was likely to fire into friend and the dusk and confusion invariably forbade victory. But the faculties that create anxiety and alarm had been dulled for the time by immense exertions and dangers, and he placidly awaited the event, whatever it might be.

"What time is it?" asked Pennington.

"Half past three in the morning," replied Dick, who was able to see the face of his watch.

"Not such a long wait then. Day comes early this time of the year."

"You lads can sit down and make yourselves comfortable," said Colonel Winchester. "It's desirable for you to be as fresh as possible when you're wanted. I'm glad to see the men sleeping. They'll receive a signal in ample time."

The young officers followed his suggestion, but they kept very wide awake, talking for a little while in whispers and then sinking away into silence. The noise from the massed troops near them decreased also and Dick's curiosity began to grow again. He stood up, but he saw no movement, nothing to indicate the nature of any coming event. He looked at his watch again. Dawn was almost at hand. A narrow band of gray would soon rim the eastern hills. An aide arrived, gave a dispatch to Colonel Winchester, and quickly passed on.

The men were awakened and stood up, shaking the sleep from their eyes and then, through habit, looking to their arms and ammunition. The thread of gray showed in the east.

"Whatever it is, it will come soon," whispered Warner to Dick.

The gray thread broadened and became a ribbon of silver. The silver, as it widened, was shot through with pink and red and yellow, the colours of the morning. Dick caught a glimpse of massed bayonets near him, and of the Southern trenches rising slowly out of the dusk not far away. Then the earth rocked.

He felt a sudden violent and convulsive movement that nearly threw him from his feet, and the whole world in front of him blazed with fire, as if a volcano, after a long silence, had burst suddenly into furious activity. Black objects, the bodies of men, were borne upon the mass of shooting flames, and the roar was so tremendous that it was heard thirty miles away.

Dick had been expecting something, but no such red dawn as this, and when the fires suddenly sank, and the world-shaking crash turned to echoes he stood for a few moments appalled. He believed at first that a magazine had exploded, but, as the dawn was rapidly advancing, he beheld in front of them, where Southern breastworks had stood, a vast pit two or three hundred feet long and more than thirty feet deep. At the bottom of it, although they could not be seen through the smoke, lay the fragments of Confederate cannon and Confederate soldiers who had been blown to pieces.

"A mine breaking the rebel line!" cried Warner, "and our men are to charge through it!"

Trumpets were already sounding their thrilling call, and blue masses, before the smoke had lifted, were rushing into the pit, intending to climb the far side and sever the Southern line. But Colonel Winchester did not yet give the word to his own regiment, and Dick knew that they were to be held in reserve.

Into the great chasm went white troops and black troops, charging together, and then Dick suddenly cried in horror. Those were veterans on the other side, and, recovering quickly from the surprise, they rushed forward their batteries and riflemen. Mahone, a little, alert man, commanded them, and in an instant they deluged the pit, afterward famous under the name of "The Crater," with fire. The steep slope held back the Union troops and from the edges everywhere the men in gray poured a storm of shrapnel and canister and bullets into the packed masses.

Colonel Winchester groaned aloud, and looked at his men who were eager to advance to the rescue, but it was evident to Dick that his orders held him, and they stood in silence gazing at the appalling scene in the crater. A tunnel had been run directly under the Confederates, and then a huge mine had been exploded. All that part was successful, but the Union army had made a deep pit, more formidable than the earthwork itself.

Never had men created a more terrible trap for themselves. The name, the crater, was well deserved. It was a seething pit of death filled with smoke, and from which came shouts and cries as the rim of it blazed with the fire of those who were pouring in such a stream of metal. Inside the pit the men could only cower low in the hope that the hurricane of missiles would pass over their heads.

"Good God!" cried Dick. "Why don't we advance to help them!"

"Here we go now, and we may need help ourselves!" said Warner.

Again the trumpets were sending forth their shrill call to battle and death, and, as the colonel waved his sword, the regiment charged forward with others to rescue the men in the crater. A bright sun was shining now, and the Southern leaders saw the heavy, advancing column. They were rapidly bringing up more guns and more riflemen, and, shifting a part of their fire, a storm of death blew in the faces of those who would go to the rescue.

As at Cold Harbor, the men in blue could not live before such a fire at close quarters, and the regiments were compelled to recoil, while those who were left alive in the crater surrendered. The trumpets sounded the unwilling call to withdraw, and the Winchester men, many of them shedding tears of grief and rage, fell back to their old place, while from some distant point, rising above the dying fire of the cannon and rifles, came the long, fierce rebel yell, full of defiance and triumph.

The effect upon Dick of the sight in the crater was so overwhelming that he was compelled to lie down.

"Why do we do such things?" he exclaimed, after the faintness passed. "Why do we waste so many lives in such vain efforts?"

"We have to try," replied Warner, gloomily. "The thing was all right as far as it went, but it broke against a hedge of fire and steel, crowning a barrier that we had created for ourselves."

"Let's not talk about it," said Pennington, who had been faint too. "It's enough to have seen it. I am going to blot it out of my mind if I can."

But not one of the three was ever able wholly to forget that hideous dawn. Luckily the Winchesters themselves had suffered little, but they were quite content to remain in their old place by the brook, where the next day a large man in civilian dress introduced himself to Dick.

"Perhaps you don't remember me, Mr. Mason," he said, "but in such times as these it's easy to forget chance acquaintances."

Dick looked at him closely. He was elderly, with heavy pouches under his eyes and a rotund figure, but he looked uncommonly alert and his pale blue eyes had a penetrating quality. Then Dick recalled him.

"You're Mr. Watson, the contractor," he said.

"Right. Shake hands."

Dick shook his hand, and he noticed that, while it was fat, it was strong and dry. He hated damp hands, which always seemed to him to have a slimy touch, as if their owner were reptilian.

"I suppose business is good with you, Mr. Watson," he said.

"It couldn't be better, and such affairs as the one I witnessed this morning mean more. But doubtless I have grieved over it as much as you. I may profit by the great struggle, but I have not wished either the war or its continuance. Someone must do the work I am doing. You're a bright boy, Lieutenant Mason, and I want you still to bear in mind the hint that I gave you once in Washington."

"I don't recall it, this instant."

"That to go into business with me is a better trade than fighting."

"I thank you for the offer, but my mind turns in other directions. I'm not depreciating your occupation, Mr. Watson, but I'm interested in something else."

"I knew that you were not, Lieutenant Mason. You have too much sense. Your kind could not fight if my kind did not find the sinews, and after the war the woods will be full of generals, and colonels and majors who will be glad to get jobs from men like me."

"I've no doubt of it," said Dick, "but what happened this morning made me think the war is yet far from over."

"We shall see what we shall see, but if you ever want a friend write to me in Washington. General delivery, there will do. Good-by."

"Good-by," said Dick, and, as he watched the big man walk away, he felt that he was beginning to understand him. He had never been interested greatly in mercantile pursuits. Public and literary life and the soil were the great things to him. Now he realized that the vast strength of the North, a strength that could survive any number of defeats, lay largely in her trade and commerce. The South, almost stationary upon the soil, had fallen behind, and no amount of skill and courage could save her.

Colonel Winchester gave the young officers who had been awake all night permission to sleep, and Dick was glad to avail himself of it. He still felt weak, and ill, and, with a tender smile, remembering his mother's advice about the blanket, he spread one in the shade of a small oak and lay down upon it.

Despite the terrible repulse of the morning most of the men had regained their usual spirits. Several were playing accordions, and the others were listening. The Winchesters were known as a happy regiment, because they had an able colonel, strong but firm, efficient and tactful minor officers. They seldom got into mischief, and always they pooled their resources.

One lad was reading now to a group from a tattered copy of *Les Miserables*, which had just reached them. He was deep in Waterloo and Dick heard their comments.

"You wait till the big writers begin to tell about Chickamauga and Gettysburg and Shiloh," said one. "They'll class with Waterloo or ahead of it, and the French and English never fought any such campaign as that when Grant came down through the Wilderness. What's that about the French riding into the sunken road? I'm willin' to bet it was nothing but a skirmish beside Pickett's charge at Gettysburg."

"And both failed," said Warner. "There are always brave men on every side in any war. I don't know whether Napoleon was right or wrong—I suppose he was wrong at that time—but it always makes me feel sad to read of Waterloo."

"Just as a lot of our own people were grieved at the death of Stonewall Jackson, although next to Lee he was our most dangerous foe," said Pennington.

The reader resumed, and, although he was interrupted from time to time by question or comment, his monotone was pleasant and soothing, and Dick fell asleep. When he awoke his nerves were restored, and he could think of the crater without becoming faint again.

That night Colonel Hertford of the cavalry came to their camp and talked with Colonel Winchester in the presence of Dick and his comrades of the staff. The disastrous failure of the morning, so the cavalryman said, had convinced all the generals that Lee's trenches could not be forced, and the commander-in-chief was turning his eye elsewhere. While the deadlock before Petersburg lasted he would push the operations in some other field. He was watching especially the Valley of Virginia, where Early, after his daring raid upon the outskirts of Washington, was being pursued by Sheridan, though not hard enough in the opinion of General Grant.

"It's almost decided that help will be sent to Sheridan," said Hertford, "and in that event my regiment is sure to go. Yours has served as a mounted regiment, and I think I have influence enough to see that it is sent again as cavalry, if you wish."

Colonel Winchester accepted the offer gladly, and his young officers, in all eagerness, seconded him. They were tiring of inactivity, and of the cramped and painful life in the trenches. To be on horseback again, riding over hills and across valleys, seemed almost Heaven to them, and, as Colonel Hertford walked away, earnest injunctions to use his influence to the utmost followed him.

"It will take the sight of the crater from my mind," said Warner. "That's one reason why I want to go."

Dick, searching his own mind, concluded it was the chief reason with him, although he, too, was eager enough for a more spacious life than that of the trench.

"I'm going to wish so hard for it," said Pennington, "that it'll come true."

Whether Pennington's wish had any effect or not, they departed two days later, three mounted regiments under the general command of Hertford, his right as a veteran cavalry leader. All regiments, despite new men, had been reduced greatly by the years of fighting, and the three combined did not number more than fifteen hundred horse. But there was not one among them from the oldest to the youngest who did not feel elation as they rode away on the great curve that would take them into the Valley of Virginia.

"It's glorious to be on a horse again, with the world before you," said Pennington. "I was born horseback, so to speak, and I never had to do any walking until I came to this war. The great plains and the free winds that blow all around the earth for me."

"But you don't have rivers and hills and forests like ours," said Dick.

"I know it, but I don't miss them. I suppose it's what you're used to that you like. I like a horizon that doesn't touch the ground anywhere within fifteen or eighteen miles of me. And think of seeing a buffalo herd, as I have, that's all day passing you, a million of 'em, maybe!"

"And think of being scalped by the Sioux or Cheyennes, as your people out there often are," said Warner.

Pennington took off his cap and disclosed an uncommonly thick head of hair.

"You see that I haven't lost mine yet," he said. "If a fellow can live through big battles as I've lived through 'em he can escape Sioux and Cheyennes."

"So you should. Look back now, and you can see the armies face to face."

They were on the highest hill, and all the cavalry had turned for a last glance. Dick saw again the flashes from occasional rifle fire, and a dark column of smoke still rising from a spot which he knew to be the crater. He shuddered, and was glad when the force, riding on again, passed over the hill. Before them now stretched a desolated country, trodden under foot by the armies, and his heart bled again for Virginia, the most reluctant of all the states to secede, and the greatest of them all to suffer.

Colonel Hertford, Colonel Winchester, and the colonel of the third regiment, a Pennsylvanian named Bedford, rode together and their young officers were just behind. All examined the country continually through glasses to guard against ambush. Stuart was gone and Forrest was far away, but they knew that danger from the fierce riders of the South was always present. Just when the capital seemed safest Early's men had appeared in its very suburbs, and here in Virginia, where the hand of every man and of every woman and child also was against them, it was wise to watch well.

As they rode on the country was still marked by desolation. The fields were swept bare or trampled down. Many of the houses and barns and all the fences had been burned. The roads had been torn up by the passage of artillery and countless wagons. All the people seemed to have gone away.

But when they came into rougher and more wooded regions they were shot at often by concealed marksmen. A half-dozen troopers were killed and more wounded, and, when the cavalrymen forced a path through the brush in pursuit of the hidden sharpshooters, they found nothing. The enemy fairly melted away. It was easy enough for a rifleman, knowing every gully and thicket, to send in his deadly bullet and then escape.

"Although it's merely the buzzing and stinging of wasps," said Warner, "I don't like it. They can't stop our advance, but I hate to see any good fellow of ours tumbled from his horse."

"Makes one think of that other ride we took in Mississippi," said Dick.

"In one way, yes, but in others, no. This is hard, firm ground, and we're not persecuted by mosquitoes. Nor is the country suitable for an ambush by a great force. Ouch, that burnt!"

A bullet fired from a thicket had grazed Warner's bridle hand. Dick was compelled to laugh.

"You're free from mosquitoes, George," he said, "but there are still little bullets flying about, as you see."

A dozen cavalrymen were sent into the thicket, but the sharp-shooter was already far away. Colonel Hertford frowned and said:

"Well, I suppose it's the price we have to pay, but I'd like to see the people to whom we have to pay it."

"Not much chance of that," said Colonel Winchester. "The Virginians know their own ground and the lurking sharpshooters won't fire until they're sure of a safe retreat."

But as they advanced the stinging fire became worse. There was no Southern force in this part of the country strong enough to meet them in open combat, but there was forest and thicket sufficient to shelter many men who were not only willing to shoot, but who knew how to shoot well. Yet they never caught anybody nor even saw anybody. A stray glimpse or two of a puff of smoke was the nearest they ever came to beholding an enemy.

It became galling, intolerable. Three more men were killed and the number of wounded was doubled. The three colonels held a consultation, and decided to extend groups of skirmishers far out on either flank. Dick was chosen to lead a band of thirty picked men who rode about a mile on the right, and he had with him as his second, and, in reality, as his guide and mentor in many ways, the trusty

Sergeant Whitley. It was altogether likely that Colonel Winchester would not have sent Dick unless he had been able to send the wise sergeant with him.

"While you are guarding us from ambush," he said to Dick, "be sure you don't fall into an ambush yourself."

"Not while Whitley, here, is with us," replied Dick. "He learned while out on the plains, not only to have eyes in the back of his head, but to have 'em in the sides of it as well. In addition he can hear the fall of a leaf a mile away."

The sergeant shook his head and uttered an emphatic no in protest, but in his heart he was pleased. He was a sergeant who liked being a sergeant, and he was proud of all his wilderness and prairie lore.

Dick gave the word and the little troop galloped away to the right, zealous in its task and beating up every wood and thicket for the hidden riflemen who were so dangerous. At intervals they saw the cavalry force riding steadily on, and again they were hidden from it by forest or bush. More than an hour passed and they saw no foe. Dick concluded that the sharpshooters had been scared off by the flanking force, and that they would have no further trouble with them. His spirits rose accordingly and there was much otherwise to make them rise.

It was like Heaven to be on horseback in the pleasant country after being cramped up so much in narrow trenches, and there was the thrill of coming action. They were going to join Sheridan and where he rode idle moments would be few.

"Ping!" a bullet whistled alarmingly near his head and then cut leaves from a sapling beyond him. The young lieutenant halted the troop instantly, and Sergeant Whitley pointed to a house just visible among some trees.

"That's where it came from, and, since it hasn't been followed by a second, it's likely that only one man is there, and he is lying low, waiting a chance for another bullet," he said.

"Then we'll rout him out," said Dick.

He divided his little troop, in order that it could approach the house from all sides, and then he and the sergeant and six others advanced directly in front. He knew that if the marksman were still hidden inside he would not fire now, but would seek rather to hide, since he could easily observe from a window that the building was surrounded.

It was a small house, but it was well built and evidently had been occupied by people of substance. It was painted white, except the shutters which were green, and a brick walk led to a portico, with fine and lofty columns. There was nobody outside, but as the shutters were open it was probable that someone was inside.

Dick disliked to force an entrance at such a place, but he had been sent out to protect the flank and he could not let a rifleman lie hidden there, merely to resume his deadly business as soon as they passed on. They pushed the gate open and rode upon the lawn, an act of vandalism that he regretted, but could not help. They reached the door without any apparent notice being taken of them, and as the detachments were approaching from the other sides, Dick dismounted and knocked loudly. Receiving no answer, he bade all the others dismount.

"Curley, you hold the horses," he said, "and Dixon, you tell the men in the other detachments to seize anybody trying to escape. Sergeant, you and I and the others will enter the house. Break in the lock with the butt of your rifle, sergeant! No, I see it's not locked!"

He turned the bolt, and, the door swinging in, they passed into an empty hall. Here they paused and listened, which was a wise thing for a man to do when he entered the house of an enemy. Dick's sense of hearing was not much inferior to that of the sergeant, and while at first they heard nothing, they detected presently a faint click, click. He could not imagine what made the odd sound, and, listening as hard as he could, he could detect no other with it.

He pushed open a door that led into the hall and he and his men entered a large room with windows on the side, opening upon a rose garden. It was a pleasant room with a high ceiling, and old-fashioned, dignified furniture. A blaze of sunlight poured in from the windows, and, where a sash was raised, came the faint, thrilling perfume of roses, a perfume to which Dick was peculiarly susceptible. Yet, for years afterward, the odour of roses brought back to him that house and that room.

He thought at first that the room, although the faint clicking noise continued, contained no human being. But presently he saw sitting at a table by the open window a woman whose gray dress and gray hair blended so nearly with the gray colours of the chamber that even a soldier could have been excused for not seeing her at once. Her head and body were perfectly still, but her hands were moving rapidly. She was knitting, and it was the click of her needles that they had heard.

She did not look up as Dick entered, and, taking off his cap, he stood, somewhat abashed. He knew at once by her dress and face, and the dignity, disclosed even by the manner in which she sat, that she was a great lady, one of those great ladies of old Virginia who were great ladies in fact. She was rather small, Martha Washington might have looked much like her, and she knitted steadily on, without showing by the least sign that she was aware of the presence of Union soldiers.

A long and embarrassed silence followed. Dick judged that she was about sixty-five years of age, though she seemed strong and he felt that she was watching them alertly from covert eyes. There was no indication that anyone else was in the building, but it did not seem likely that a great lady of Virginia would be left alone in her house, with a Union force marching by.

He approached, bowed and said:

"Madame!"

She raised her head and looked at him slowly from head to foot, and then back again. They were fierce old eyes, and Dick felt as if they burned him, but he held his ground knowing that he must. Then she turned back to her knitting, and the needles clicked steadily as before.

"Madame!" repeated Dick, still embarrassed.

She lifted the fierce old eyes.

"I should think," she said, "that the business of General Grant's soldiers was to fight those of General Lee rather than to annoy lone women."

Dick flushed, but angry blood leaped in his veins.

"Pardon me, madam," he said, "but we have not come here to annoy a woman. We were fired upon from this house. The man who did it has had no opportunity to escape, and I'm sure that he's still concealed within these walls."

"Seek and ye shall—not find," she half quoted.

"I must search the house."

"Proceed."

"First question her," the sergeant whispered in the young lieutenant's ear.

Dick nodded.

"Pardon me, madam," he said, "but I must obtain information from you. This is war, you know."

"I have had many rude reminders that it is so."

"Where is your husband?"

She pointed upward.

"Forgive me," said Dick impulsively. "I did not intend to recall a grief."

"Don't worry. You and your comrades will never intrude upon him there."

"Perhaps you have sons here in this house?"

"I have three, but they are not here."

"Where are they?"

"One fell with Jackson at Chancellorsville. It was a glorious death, but he is not dead to me. I shall always see him, as he was when he went away, a tall, strong man with brown hair and blue eyes. Another fell in Pickett's charge at Gettysburg. They told me that his body lay across one of the Union guns on Cemetery Hill. That, too, was a glorious death, and like his brother he shall live for me as long as I live. The third is alive and with Lee."

She had stopped knitting, but now she resumed it, and, during another embarrassed pause, the click, click of the needles was the only sound heard in the room.

"I regret it, madam," resumed Dick, "but we must search the house thoroughly."

"Proceed," she said again in that tone of finality.

"Take the men and look carefully through every room," said Dick to the sergeant. "I will remain here."

Whitley and the troopers withdrew quietly. When the last of them had disappeared he walked to one of the windows and looked out. He saw his mounted men beyond the rose garden on guard, and he knew that they were as vigilant on the other sides of the house. The sharpshooter could not escape, and he was firmly resolved not to go without him. Yet his conscience hurt him. It was hard, too, to wait there, while the woman said not a word, but knitted on as placidly as if he did not exist.

"Madame," he said at last, "I pray that you do not regard this as an intrusion. The uses of war are hard. We must search. No one can regret it more than I do, in particular since I am really a Southerner myself, a Kentuckian."

"A traitor then as well as an enemy."

Dick flushed deeply, and again there was angry blood in his veins, but he restrained his temper.

"You must at least allow to a man the liberty of choice," he said.

"Provided he has the intelligence and honesty to choose right."

Dick flushed again and bit his lip. And yet he felt that a woman who had lost two sons before Northern bullets might well be unforgiving. There was nothing more for him to say, and while he turned back to the window the knitting needles resumed their click, click.

He waited a full ten minutes and he knew that the sergeant and his men were searching the house thoroughly. Nothing could escape the notice of Whitley, and he would surely find the sharpshooter. Then he heard their footsteps on a stairway and in another minute they entered the great room. The face of the sergeant clearly showed disappointment.

251

"There's nobody in the house," he said, "or, if he is he's so cleverly hidden, that we haven't been able to find him—that is so far. Perhaps Madame here can tell us something."

"I know nothing," she said, "but if I knew anything I would not tell it to you."

The sergeant smiled sourly, but Dick said:

"We must look again. The man could not have escaped with the guard that we've set around the house."

The sergeant and his men made another search. They penetrated every place in which a human being could possibly hide. They thrust their rifle barrels up the chimneys, and they turned down the bed covers, but again they found nothing. Dick meanwhile remained as before in the large room, covertly watching the woman, lest she give a signal to the rifleman who must be somewhere.

All the while the perfume of the roses was growing stronger and more penetrating, a light wind that had sprung up bringing it through the open window. It thrilled Dick in some singular manner, and the strangeness of the scene heightened its effect. It was like standing in a room in a dim old castle to which he had been brought as a prisoner, while the terrible old woman was his jailer. Then the click of the knitting needles brought him back to the present and reality, but reality itself, despite the sunshine and the perfume of the roses, was heavy and oppressive.

Dick apparently was looking from the window at the garden, brilliant with flowers, but in fact he was closely watching the woman out of the corner of his eye. He had learned to read people by their own eyes, and he had seen how hers burned when she looked at them. Strength of will and intent lie in the human eye. Unless it is purposely veiled it tells the mind and power that are in the brain back of it.

A fear of her crept slowly over him. Perhaps the fear came because, obviously, she had no fear at all of him, or of Whitley or of the soldiers. After their short dialogue she had returned to her old immobility. Neither her body nor her head moved, only her hands, and the motion was wholly from the wrists. She was one of the three Fates, knitting steadily and knitting up the destiny of men.

He shook himself. His was a sound and healthy mind, and he would allow no taint of morbidness to enter it. He knew that there was nothing supernatural in the world, but he did believe that this woman with the gray hair, the burning eyes and the sharp chin, looking as if it had been cut from a piece of steel, was the possessor of uncanny wisdom. Beyond a doubt she knew where the marksman was hidden, and, unless he watched her ceaselessly, she would give him a signal of some kind.

Perhaps he was hidden in the garden among the rose bushes, and he would see her hand, if it was raised ever so slightly. Maybe that was why the window was open, because the clearest glass even could obscure a signal meant to be faint, unnoticed by all except the one for whom it was intended. He would have that garden searched thoroughly when the sergeant returned, and his heart beat with a throb of relief when he heard the stalwart Whitley's footstep once more at the door.

"We have found nothing, sir," said the sergeant. "We've explored every place big enough to hide a cat."

"Search the garden out there," said Dick. "Look behind every vine and bush."

"You will at least spare my roses," said the woman.

"They shall not be harmed," replied the lieutenant, "but my men must see what, if anything, is in the garden."

She said no more. She had not even raised her head when she spoke, and the sergeant and his men went into the garden. They looked everywhere but they damaged nothing. They did not even break off a single flower for themselves. Dick had felt confident that after the failure to find the sharpshooter in the house he would be discovered there, but his net brought in no fish.

He glanced at the sergeant, who happened to glance at him at the same time. Each read the look in the eyes of the other. Each said that they had failed, that they were wasting time, that there was nothing to be gained by hunting longer for a single enemy, that it was time to ride on, as flankers on the right of the main column.

"Madame," said Dick politely, "we leave you now. I repeat my regret at being compelled to search your house in this manner. My duty required it, although we have found nobody."

"You found nobody because nobody is here."

"Evidently it is so. Good-by. We wish you well."

"Good-by. I hope that all of you will be shot by our brave troops before night!"

The wish was uttered with the most extraordinary energy and fierceness. For the first time she had raised her level tone, and the lifted eyes that looked into Dick's were blazing with hate. He uttered an exclamation and stepped back. Then he recovered himself and said politely:

"Madame, I do not wish any such ill to you or yours."

But she had resumed her knitting, and Dick, without another word, walked out of the house, followed by the sergeant and his men.

"I did not know a woman could be so vindictive," he said.

"Our army has killed two of her sons," said the sergeant. "To her we, like all the rest of our troops, are the men who killed them."

"Perhaps that is so," said Dick thoughtfully, as he remounted.

They rode beside the walk and out at the open gate. Dick carried a silver whistle, upon which he blew a signal for the rest of his men to join them, and then he and the sergeant went slowly up the road. He was deeply chagrined at the escape of the rifleman, and the curse of the woman lay heavily upon him.

"I don't see how it was done," he said.

"Nor I," said the sergeant, shaking his head.

There was a sharp report, the undoubted whip-like crack of a rifle, and a man just behind, uttering a cry, held up a bleeding arm. Dick had a lightning conviction that the bullet was intended for himself. It was certain also that the shot had come from the house.

"Back with me, sergeant!" he exclaimed. "We'll get that fellow yet!"

They galloped back, sprang from their horses, and rushed in, followed by the original little troop that had entered, Dick shouting a direction to the others to remain outside. The fierce little old woman was sitting as before by the table, knitting, and she had never appeared more the great lady.

"Once was enough," she said, shooting him a glance of bitter contempt.

"But twice may succeed," Dick said. "Sergeant, take the men and go through all the house again. Our friend with the rifle may not have had time to get back into his hidden lair. I will remain here."

The sergeant and his men went out and he heard their boots on the stairway and in the other rooms. The window near him was still open and the perfume of the roses came in again, strangely thrilling, overpowering. But something had awakened in Dick. The sixth, and even the germ of a seventh sense, which may have been instinct, were up and alive. He did not look again at the rose garden, nor did he listen any longer to the footsteps of his men.

He had concentrated all his faculties, the known, and the unknown, which may have been lying dormant in him, upon a single object. He heard only the click of the knitting needles, and he saw only the small, strong hands moving swiftly back and forth. They were very white, and they were firm like those of a young woman. There were none of the heavy blue veins across the back that betoken age.

The hands fascinated him. He stared at them, fairly pouring his gaze upon them. They were beautiful, as the hands of a great lady should be kept, and it was all the more wonderful then that the right should have across the back of it a faint gray smudge, so tiny that only an eye like his, and a concentrated gaze like his, could have seen it.

He took four swift steps forward, seized the white hand in his and held it up.

"Madame," he said, and now his tone was as fierce as hers had ever been, "where is the rifle?"

She made no attempt to release her hand, nor did she move at all, save to lift her head. Then her eyes, hard, defiant and ruthless, looked into his. But his look did not flinch from hers. He knew, and, knowing, he meant to act.

"Madame," he repeated, "where is the rifle? It is useless for you to deny."

"Have I denied?"

"No, but where is the rifle?"

He was wholly unconscious of it, but his surprise and excitement were so great that his hand closed upon hers in a strong muscular contraction. Thrills of pain shot through her body, but she did not move.

"The rifle! The rifle!" repeated Dick.

"Loose my hand, and I will give it to you."

His hand fell away and she walked to the end of the room where a rug, too long, lay in a fold against the wall. She turned back the fold and took from its hiding place a slender-barrelled cap-and-ball rifle. Without a word she handed it to Dick and he passed his hand over the muzzle, which was still warm.

He looked at her, but she gave back his gaze unflinching.

"I could not believe it, were it not so," he said.

"But it is so. The bullets were not aimed well enough." Dick felt an emotion that he did not wholly understand.

"Madame," he said, "I shall take the rifle, and again say good-by. As before, I wish you well."

She resumed her seat in the chair and took up the knitting. But she did not repeat her wish that Dick and all his men be shot before night. He went out in silence, and gently closed the door behind him. In the hall he met Sergeant Whitley and said:

"We needn't look any farther. I know now that the man has gone and we shall not be fired upon again from this house."

The sergeant glanced at the rifle Dick carried and made no comment. But when they were riding away, he said:

"And so that was it?"

"Yes, that was it."

255

CHAPTER 3

Over the Hills

Dick and his little troop rode on through the silent country, and they were so watchful and thorough that they protected fully the right flank of the marching column. One or two shots were fired, but the reports came from such distant points that he knew the bullets had fallen short.

But while he beat up the forests and fields for sharpshooters he was very thoughtful. He had a mind that looked far ahead, even in youth, and the incident at the house weighed upon him. He foresaw the coming triumph of the North and of the Union, a triumph won after many great disasters, but he remembered what an old man at a blacksmith shop in Tennessee had told him and his comrades before the Battle of Stone River. Whatever happened, however badly the South might be defeated, the Southern soil would still be held by Southern people, and their bitterness would be intense for many a year to come. The victor forgives easily, the vanquished cannot forget. His imagination was active and vivid, often attaining truths that logic and reason do not reach, and he could understand what had happened at the house, where the ordinary mind would have been left wondering.

It is likely also that the sergeant had a perception of it, though not as sharp and clear as Dick's.

"When the war is over and the soldiers all go back, that is them that's livin'," he said, "it won't be them that fought that'll keep the grudge. It's the women who've lost their own that'll hate longest."

"I think what you say is true, Whitley," said Dick, "but let's not talk about it any more. It hurts."

"Me too," said the sergeant. "But don't you like this country that we're ridin' through, Mr. Mason?"

"Yes, it's fine, but most of it has been cropped too hard. I remember reading somewhere that George Washington himself said, away back in the last century, that slave labour, so careless and reckless, was ruining the soil of Virginia."

"Likely that's true, sir, but it won't have much chance to keep on ruinin' it. Wouldn't you say, sir, that was a Johnny on his horse up there?"

"I can soon tell you," said Dick, unslinging his glasses.

On their right was a hill towering above the rest. The slopes were wooded densely, but the crest was quite bare. Upon it sat a solitary figure on horseback, evidently watching the marching column.

Dick put his glasses to his eyes. The hill and the lone sentinel enlarged suddenly and came nearer. The pulses in his temples beat hard. Although he could not see the watcher's face clearly, because he too was using glasses, he knew him instantly. He would have known that heroic figure and the set of the shoulders and head anywhere. He felt astonishment at first, but it passed quickly. It was likely that they should meet again some time or other, since the field of battle had narrowed so much.

Sergeant Whitley, who invariably saw everything, had seen Dick's slight start.

"Someone you know, sir?" he asked.

"Yes, sergeant. It's my cousin, Harry Kenton. You've heard me talk of him often. A finer and braver and stronger fellow never lived. He's using glasses too and I've no doubt he's recognized me."

Dick suddenly waved his glasses aloft, and Harry Kenton replied in like manner.

"He sees and knows me!" cried Dick.

But the sergeant was very sober. He foresaw that these youths, bound by such ties of blood and affection, might come into battle against each other. The same thought was in Dick's mind, despite his pleasure at the distant view of Harry.

"We exchanged shots in the Manassas campaign," said Dick. "We were sheltered and we didn't know each other until several bullets had passed."

"Three more horsemen have joined him," said the sergeant.

"Those are his friends," said Dick, who had put the glasses back to his eyes. "Look how they stand out against the sun!"

The four horsemen in a row, at equal distances from one another, were enlarged against a brilliant background of red and gold. Their attitude was impressive, as they sat there, unmoving, like statues cut in stone. They were in truth Harry and Dalton, St. Clair and Happy Tom, and farther on the Invincibles were marching, the two colonels at their head, to the Valley of Virginia to reinforce Early, and to make headway, if possible, against Sheridan.

Harry was deeply moved. Kinship and the long comradeship of youth count for much. Perhaps for more in the South than anywhere else. Stirred by a sudden emotion he took off his cap and waved it as a signal of hail and farewell. The four removed their own caps and waved them also. Then they turned their horses in unison, rode over the hill and were gone from Dick's sight.

Sergeant Whitley was not educated, but his experience was vast, he knew men and he had the gift of sympathy. He understood Dick's feelings.

"All civil wars are cruel," he said. "The killing of one's own people is worst of all."

But as they went on, Dick's melancholy fell from him, and he had only pleasant recollections of the meeting. Besides, the continued movement and freedom were inspiriting in the highest degree to youth. Although it was August the day was cool, and the blue sky of Virginia was never brighter. A refreshing breeze blew from dim, blue mountains that they could see far ahead, and, as they entered a wide stretch of open country where ambush was impossible, the trumpets called in the flankers.

"We shall make the lower mountains about midnight, and we'd better camp then until dawn. Don't you think so, gentlemen?" asked Colonel Hertford of his associate colonels, Winchester and Bedford.

"The plan seems sound to me," replied Bedford, the Pennsylvanian. "Of course, we want to reach Sheridan as soon as possible, but if we push the horses too hard we'll break them down."

Dick had dropped back with Warner and Pennington, but he heard the colonels talking.

"We all saw General Sheridan at the great battles in the West," he said. "I particularly remember how he planted himself and the batteries at Perryville and saved us from defeat, but he seems to be looming up so much more now in the East."

"He's become the Stuart of our side," said Warner. "I've heard some of the people at Washington don't believe in him, but he has General Grant's confidence and that's enough for me. Not that I put military authority over civil rule, but war has to be fought by soldiers. I look for lively times in the Valley of Virginia."

"Anyway, the Lord has delivered me from the trenches at Petersburg," said Pennington. "Think of me, used to roaming over a thousand miles of plains, shut up between mud walls only four or five feet apart."

"I believe that, with Sheridan, you're going to have all the roaming you want," said Dick.

They passed silent farm houses, but took nothing from them. Ample provision was carried on extra horses or their own, and the three colonels were anxious not to inflame the country by useless seizures. Twilight came, and the low mountains sank away in the dusk. But they had already reached a higher region where nearly all the hills were covered with forest, and Colonel Hertford once more spread out the flankers, Dick and the sergeant, as before, taking the right with their little troop.

The night was fortunately clear, almost as light as day, with a burnished moon and brilliant stars, and they did not greatly fear ambush. Dick shrewdly reckoned that Early would need all his men in the valley, and, after the first day at sharpshooting, they would withdraw to meet greater demands.

Nevertheless he took a rather wide circuit and came into a lonely portion of the hills, where the forest was unbroken, save for the narrow path on which they rode. The sergeant dismounted once and examined the ground.

"Nothing has passed here," he said, "and the woods and thickets are so dense that men can't ride through 'em."

The path admitted of only two abreast, and the forest was so heavy that it shut out most of the moonlight. But they rode on confidently, Dick and the sergeant leading. If it had not been for the size of the trees, Dick would have thought that he was back in the Wilderness. They heard now and then the wings of night birds among the leaves, and occasionally some small animal would scuttle across the path. They forded a narrow but deep stream, its waters black from decayed vegetation, and continued to push on briskly through the unbroken forest, until the sergeant said in a low voice to Dick:

"I think I hear something ahead of us."

They pulled back on the reins so suddenly that those behind almost rode into them. Then they sat there, a solid, compact little group, while Dick and the sergeant listened intently.

"It's hoofbeats," said Dick, "very faint, because they are far away."

"I think you are right, sir," said the sergeant.

"But they're coming this way."

"Yes, and at a steady pace. No stops and no hesitation."

"Which shows that it's somebody who doesn't fear any harm."

"The beats are pretty solid. A heavy man on a heavy horse."

"About three hundred yards away, don't you think?"

"About that, sir."

"Maybe a farmer going home?"

"Maybe, but I don't think so, sir."

"At any rate, we'll soon see, because our unknown comes on without a break. There he is now!"

They had a comparatively clear view straight ahead, and the figure of a man and a horse emerged from the shadows.

The sergeant raised his rifle, but, as the man came on without fear, he dropped it again. Some strange effect of the moonlight exaggerated the rider and his horse, making both look gigantic, blending them together in such manner that a tremendous centaur seemed to be riding them down. In an instant or two the general effect vanished and as a clear beam fell upon the man's face Dick uttered an exclamation of relief.

"Shepard!" he said, and he felt then that he should have known before that it was Shepard who was coming. He, alone of all men, seemed to have the gift of omniscience and omnipresence. The spy drew his horse to a halt directly in front of him and saluted:

"Lieutenant Mason, sir?" he said.

"I'm glad it's you, Mr. Shepard," said Dick. "I think that in this wood we'll need the hundred eyes that once belonged to Argus, but which he has passed on to you."

"Thank you, sir," said Shepard.

But the man at whom he looked most was the sergeant, and the sergeant looked most at him. One was a sergeant and the other was a spy, but each recognized in the other a king among men. Eyes swept over powerful chests and shoulders and open, bold countenances, and signified approval. They had met before, but they were more than well met here in the loneliness and the dark, amid dangers, where skill and courage, and not rank, counted. Then they nodded without speaking, as an Indian chief would to an Indian chief, his equal.

"You were coming to meet us, Mr. Shepard?" said Dick.

"I expected to find you on this path."

"And you have something to tell?"

"A small Confederate force is in the mountains, awaiting Colonel Hertford. It is inferior to his in numbers, but it knows the country thoroughly and has the sympathy of all the inhabitants, who bring to it news of everything."

"Do you know these Confederate troops?"

"Yes, sir. Their corps is a regiment called in General Lee's army the Invincibles, but it includes two other skeleton regiments. Colonel

Talbot who leads the Invincibles is the commander of them all. He has, I should say, slightly less than a thousand men."

"You know a good deal about this regiment called the Invincibles, do you not, Mr. Shepard?"

"I do, sir. Its colonel, Talbot, and its lieutenant-colonel, St. Hilaire, are as brave men as any that ever lived, and the regiment has an extraordinary reputation in the Southern army for courage. Two of General Lee's young staff officers are also with them now."

"Who are they?"

"Lieutenant Harry Kenton and Lieutenant George Dalton."

Dick with his troop rode at once to Colonel Hertford and reported. Colonel Hertford listened and then glanced at Dick.

"Kenton is your cousin, I believe," he said.

"Yes, sir," replied Dick. "He has been in the East all the time. Once in the second Manassas campaign we came face to face and fired at each other, although we did not know who was who then."

"And now here you are in opposing forces again. With the war converging as it is, it was more than likely that you should confront each other once more."

"But I don't expect to be shooting at Harry, and I don't think he'll be shooting at me."

"Will you ride into the woods again on the right, Mr. Shepard?" said Colonel Hertford. "Perhaps you may get another view of this Confederate force. Dick, you go with him. Warner, you and Pennington come with me."

Dick and Shepard entered the woods side by side, and the youth who had a tendency toward self-analysis found that his liking and respect for the spy increased. The general profession of a spy might be disliked, but in Shepard it inspired no repulsion, rather it increased his heroic aspect, and Dick found himself relying upon him also. He felt intuitively that when he rode into the forest with Shepard he rode into no danger, or if by any chance he did ride into danger, they would, under the guidance of the spy, ride safely out of it again.

Shepard turned his horse toward the deeper forest, which lay on the left, and very soon they were out of sight of the main column, although the sound of hoofs and of arms, clinking against one another, still came faintly to them. Yet peace, the peace for which Dick longed so ardently, seemed to dwell there in the woods. The summer was well advanced and as the light winds blew, the leaves, already beginning to dry, rustled against one another. The sound was pleasant and soothing. He and Harry Kenton and other lads of their age had often heard it on autumn nights, when they roamed through the forests around Pendleton in search of the raccoon and the opossum. It all came back to him with astonishing vividness and force.

He was boy and man in one. But he could scarcely realize the three years and more of war that had made him a man. In one way it seemed a century, and in another it seemed but yesterday. The water rose in his eyes at the knowledge that this same cousin who was like a brother to him, one with whom he had hunted, fished, played and swum, was there in the woods less than a mile away, and that he might be in battle with him again before morning.

"You were thinking of your cousin, Mr. Kenton," said Shepard suddenly.

"Yes, but how did you know?" asked Dick in surprise.

"Because your face suddenly became melancholy—the moonlight is good, enabling me to read your look—and sadness is not your natural expression. You recall that your cousin, of whom you think so much, is at hand with your enemies, and the rest is an easy matter of putting two and two together."

"You're right in all you say, Mr. Shepard, but I wish Harry wasn't there."

Shepard was silent and then Dick added passionately:

"Why doesn't the South give up? She's worn down by attrition. She's blockaded hard and fast! When she loses troops in battle she can't find new men to take their places! She's short in food, ammunition, medicines, everything! The whole Confederacy can't be anything but a shell now! Why don't they quit!"

"Pride, and a lingering hope that the unexpected will happen. Yes, we've won the war, Mr. Mason, but it's yet far from finished. Many a good man will fall in this campaign ahead of us in the valley, and in other campaigns too, but, as I see it, the general result is already decided. Nothing can change it. Look between these trees, and you can see the Southern force now."

Dick from his horse gazed into a valley down which ran a good turnpike, looking white in the moonlight. Upon this road rode the Southern force in close ranks, but too far away, for any sound of their hoof beats to come to the watchers. The moon which was uncommonly bright now coloured them all with silver, and Dick, with his imaginative mind, easily turned them into a train of the knights of old, clad in glittering mail. They created such a sense of illusion and distance, time as well as space, that the peace of the moment was not disturbed. It was a spectacle out of the past, rather than present war.

"You are familiar with the country, of course," said Dick.

"Yes," replied Shepard. "Our road, as you know, is now running parallel with that on which the Southern force is travelling, with a broad ridge between. But several miles farther on the ridge becomes narrower and the roads merge. We're sure to have a fight there. Like you, I'm sorry your cousin Harry Kenton is with them."

"It seems that you and he know a good deal of each other."

"Yes, circumstances have brought us into opposition again and again from the beginning of the war, but the same circumstances have made me know more about him than he does about me. Yet I mean that we shall be friends when peace comes, and I don't think he'll oppose my wish."

"He won't. Harry has a generous and noble nature. But he wouldn't stand being patronized, merely because he happened to be on the beaten side."

"I shouldn't think of trying to do such a thing. Now, we've seen enough, and I think we'd better go back to the colonels, with our news."

They rode through the woods again, and, for most of the distance, there was no sound from the marching troops. The wonderful feeling of peace returned. The sky was as blue and soft as velvet. The great stars glittered and danced, and the wind among the rustling leaves was like the soft singing of a violin. At one point they crossed a little brook which ran so swiftly down among the trees that it was a foam of water. They dismounted, drank hastily, and then let the horses take their fill.

"I like these hills and forests and their clear waters," said Dick, "and judging by the appearance it must be a fine country to which we're coming."

"It is. It's something like your Kentucky Blue Grass, although it's smaller and it's hemmed in by sharper and bolder mountains. But I should say that the Shenandoah Valley is close to a hundred and twenty miles long, and from twenty-five to forty miles wide, not including its spur, the Luray Valley, west of the Massanuttons."

"As large as one of the German Principalities."

"And as fine as any of them."

"It's where Stonewall Jackson made that first and famous campaign of his."

"And it's lucky for us that we don't have to face him there now. Early is a good general, they say, but he's no Stonewall Jackson."

"And we're to be led by Sheridan. I think he saved us at Perryville in Kentucky, but they say he's become a great cavalry commander. Do you know him, Mr. Shepard?"

"Well. A young man, and a little man. Why, you'd overtop him more than half a head, Mr. Mason, but he has a great soul for battle. He's the kind that will strike and strike, and keep on striking, and that's the kind we need now."

"Here are our own men just ahead. I see the three colonels riding together."

They went forward swiftly and told what they had seen, Shepard also describing the nature of the ground ahead, and the manner in which the two roads converged.

"Which column do you think will reach the junction first?" asked Colonel Hertford.

"They'll come to it about the same time," replied Shepard.

"And so a clash is unavoidable. It was not our purpose to fight before we reached General Sheridan, but since the enemy wants it, it must be that way."

Orders were issued for the column to advance as quietly as possible, while skirmishers were thrown out to prevent any ambush. Shepard rode again into the forest but Dick remained with Warner and Pennington. Warner as usual was as cool as ice, and spoke in the precise, scholarly way that he liked.

"We march parallel with the enemy," he said, "and yet we're bound to meet him and fight. It's a beautiful mathematical demonstration. The roads are not parallel in an exact sense but converge to a point. Hence, it is not our wish, but the convergence of these roads that brings us together in conflict. So we see that the greatest issues of our life are determined by mathematics. It's a splendid and romantic study. I wish you fellows would pay more attention to it."

"Mathematics beautiful and romantic!" exclaimed Pennington. "Why, George, you're out of your head! There's nothing in the world I hate more than the sight of an algebra!"

"The trouble is with you and not with the algebra. You were alluding in a depreciatory manner to my head but it's your own head that fails. When I said algebra was a beautiful and romantic study I used the adjectives purposely. Out of thousands of adjectives in the dictionary I selected those two to fit the case. What could be more delightful than an abstruse problem in algebra? You never know along what charming paths of the mind it will lead you. Moreover there is over it a veil of mystery. You can't surmise what delightful secrets it will reveal later on. What will the end be? What a powerful appeal such a question will always make to a highly intelligent and imaginative mind like mine! No poetry! No beauty! Why every algebraic problem from the very nature of its being is surcharged with it! It's like the mystery of life itself, only in this case we solve the mystery! And if I may change the metaphor, an algebraic formula is like a magnificent diamond, cutting its way through the thick and opaque glass, which represents the unknown! I long for the end of the war for many reasons, but chief among them is the fact that I may return to the romantic and illimitable fields of the mathematical problem!"

"I didn't know anyone could ever become dithyrambic about algebra," said Dick.

"What's dithyrambic?" asked Pennington.

"Spouting, Frank. But George, as we know, is a queer fellow. They grow 'em in Vermont, where they love steep mountains, deep ravines and hard mathematics."

They had been speaking in low tones, but now they ceased entirely. Shepard had come back from the forest, reporting that the junction of the roads was near, and the Confederate force was marching toward it at the utmost speed.

The hostile columns might be in conflict in a half hour now, and the men prepared themselves. Innumerable battles and skirmishes could never keep their hearts from beating harder when it became evident that they were to go under fire once more. After the few orders necessary, there was no sound save that of the march itself. Meanwhile the moon and stars were doing full duty, and the night remained as bright as ever.

CHAPTER 4

The Fight at the Crossways

Colonel Hertford was near the head of the Union column, while the three youths rode a little farther back with Colonel Winchester, the regiment of Colonel Bedford bringing up the rear. Just behind Dick was Sergeant Whitley, mounted upon a powerful bay horse. The sergeant had shown himself such a woodsman and scout, and he was so valuable in these capacities that Colonel Winchester had practically made him an aide, and always kept him near for orders.

Dick noticed now that the sergeant leaned a little forward in his saddle and was using his eyes and ears with all the concentration of the great plainsman that he was. In that attitude he was a formidable figure, and, though he lacked the spy's subtlety and education, he seemed to have much in common with Shepard.

As for Dick himself his nerves had not been so much on edge since he went into his first battle, nor had his heart beat so hard, and he knew it was because Harry Kenton and those comrades of his would be at the convergence of the roads, and they would meet, not in the confused conflict of a great battle, when a face might appear and disappear the next second, but man to man with relatively small numbers. The moon was dimmed a little by fleecy clouds, but the silvery colour, instead of vanishing was merely softened, and when Dick looked back at the Union column it, like the troop of the South, had the quality of a ghostly train. But the clouds floated away and then the light gleamed on the barrels of the short carbines that the horsemen carried. From a point on the other side of the forest came the softened notes of a trumpet and the great pulse in Dick's throat leaped. Only a few minutes more and they would be at the meeting of the ways.

Colonel Hertford sent a half dozen mounted skirmishers into the road, but the column moved forward at its even pace, still silvered in the moonlight, but ready for battle, wounds and death. Sergeant Whitley whispered to Dick:

"Other men than our own are moving in the forest. I can hear the tread of horses' hoofs on the dry leaves and twigs at the far edge. Our scouts should meet them in a moment or two."

It came as the sergeant had predicted, and Dick saw a tiny flash of fire, not much larger than a pink dot in the woods, heard the sharp report of a rifle and then the crack of another rifle in reply. Silence followed for an instant, but it was evident that the hostile forces were in touch and then in another moment or two the horses of the scouts crashed in the brush, as they rode back to the main column. They had seen enough.

Colonel Hertford gave the order and the entire Union force now advanced at a gallop. Through the woods, narrowing so rapidly, came the swift beat of hoofs on the other side, and it was apparent that coincidence would bring the two forces to the point of convergence at the same time. The moonlight seemed to Dick to grow so bright and intense that it had almost the quality of sunlight. Nature, in the absence of day, was making the field of battle as light as possible.

"What's the lay of the land at the point of meeting?" he whispered hurriedly to Shepard who had ridden up by his side.

"Almost level," came the quick response.

A few more rapid hoofbeats and the shrouding woods between disappeared. One column saw another column, both clad in the moonlight, in Dick's fancy, all in silver mail. The two forces wheeled and faced each other across the open space, their horses staring with red eyes, and the men looking intently at their opponents. Both were oppressed for an instant or two by a deep and singular silence.

Dick's eyes swept fearfully along the gray column of the South, and he saw the one whom he did not wish to see—at least not there—Harry Kenton himself, sitting on his bay horse with his friends around him. The two elderly men must be Colonel Leonidas Talbot and Lieutenant-Colonel Hector St. Hilaire, and the three youths beside Harry were surely St. Clair, Langdon and Dalton.

As he looked, Colonel Leonidas Talbot raised his sword, and at the same time came the sharp command of Colonel Hertford. Rifles and carbines flashed from either side across the open space, and two streams of bullets crossed. In an instant the silver of the moonlight was hidden by clouds of smoke through which flashed the fire from hundreds of rifles and carbines. All around Dick's ears was the hissing sound of bullets, like the alarm from serpents.

The fire at close range was so deadly to both sides that holes were smashed in the mounted ranks. The shrill screams of wounded horses, far more terrible than the cries of wounded men, struck like knife points on the drums of Dick's ears. He saw Shepard's horse go down, killed instantly by a heavy bullet, but the spy himself leaped clear, and then Dick lost him in the smoke. A bullet grazed his own wrist and he glanced curiously at the thin trickle of blood that came from it. Yet, forgetting it the next instant, he waved his sabre above his head, and began to shout to the men.

Rifles and pistols emptied, the Southern horsemen were preparing to charge. The lifting smoke disclosed a long line of tossing manes and flashing steel. At either end of the line a shrill trumpet was sounding the charge, and the Northern bugles were responding with the same command. The two forces were about to meet in that most terrible of all combats, a cavalry charge by either side, when enemies looked into the eyes of one another, and strong hands swung aloft the naked steel, glittering in the moonlight.

"Bend low in the saddle," exclaimed the sergeant, "and then you'll miss many a stroke!"

Dick obeyed promptly and their whole line swept forward over the grass to meet the men in gray who were coming so swiftly against them. He saw a thousand sabres uplifted, making a stream of light, and then the two forces crashed together. It seemed to him that it was the impact of one solid body upon another as solid, and then so much blood rushed to his head that he could not see clearly. He was conscious only of a mighty crash, of falling bodies, sweeping sabres, that terrible neigh again of wounded horses, of sun-tanned faces, and of fierce eyes staring into his own, and then, as the red mist thinned a little, he became conscious that someone just before him was slashing at him with a long, keen blade. He bent yet lower, and the sword passed over him, but as he rose a little he cut back. His edge touched only the air, but he uttered a gasp of horror as he saw Harry Kenton directly before him, and knew that they had been striking at each other. He saw, too, the appalled look in Harry's eyes, who at the same time had recognized his opponent, and then, in the turmoil of battle, other horsemen drove in between.

That shiver of horror swept over Dick once more, and then came relief. The charging horsemen had separated them in time, and he did not think it likely that the chances of battle would bring Harry and him face to face more than once. Then the red blur enclosed everything and he was warding off the sabre strokes of another man. The air was yet filled with the noise of shouting men, and neighing horses, of heavy falls and the ring of steel on steel. Neither gave way and neither could advance. The three Union colonels rode up and down their lines encouraging their men, and the valiant Talbot and St. Hilaire were never more valiant than on that night.

A combat with sabres cannot last long, and cavalry charges are soon finished. North and South had met in the centre of the open space, and suddenly the two, because all their force was spent, fell back from that deadly line, which was marked by a long row of fallen horses and men. They reloaded their rifles and carbines and began to fire at one another, but it was at long range, and little damage was done. They fell back a bit farther, the firing stopped entirely, and they looked at one another.

It was perhaps the effect of the night, with its misty silver colouring, and perhaps their long experience of war, giving them an intuitive knowledge, that made these foes know nothing was to be gained by further combat. They were so well balanced in strength and courage that they might destroy one another, but no one could march away from the field victorious. Perhaps, too, it was a feeling that the God of Battles had already issued his decree in regard to this war, and that as many lives as possible should now be spared. But whatever it was, the finger fell away from the trigger, the sabre was returned to the scabbard, and they sat on their horses, staring at one another.

Dick took his glasses from his shoulder and began to scan the hostile line. His heart leaped when he beheld Harry in the saddle, apparently unharmed, and near him three youths, one with a red bandage about his shoulder. Then he saw the two colonels, both erect men with long, gray hair, on their horses near the centre of the line, and talking together. One gestured two or three times as he spoke, and he moved his arm rather stiffly.

The three Union colonels were in a little group not far from Dick, and they also were talking with one another. Dick wondered what they would do, but he was saved from long wonderment by the call of a trumpet from the Southern force, and the appearance of a horseman not older than himself riding forward and bearing a white flag.

"They want a truce," said Colonel Hertford. "Go and meet them, Mason."

Dick, willing enough, turned his horse toward the young man who, heavily tanned, was handsome, well-built and dressed with scrupulous care in a fine gray uniform.

"My name is St. Clair," he said, "and I'm an officer on the staff of Colonel Leonidas Talbot, who commands the force behind me."

"I think we've met once before," said Dick. "My name is Mason, Richard Mason, and I am with Colonel Arthur Winchester, who commands one of the regiments that has just been fighting you."

"It's so! Upon my life it's so, and you're the same Dick Mason that's the cousin of our Harry Kenton, the fellow he's always talking about! He's on General Lee's staff, but he's been detached for temporary duty with us. He's over there all right. But I've come to tell you that Colonel Talbot, who commands us, offers a flag of truce to bury the dead. He sees that neither side can win, that to continue the battle would only involve us in mutual destruction. He wishes, too, that I convey to your commander his congratulations upon his great skill and courage. I may add, myself, Mr. Mason, that Colonel Talbot knows a brave man when he sees him."

"I've no doubt the offer will be accepted. Will you wait a moment?"

"Certainly," replied St. Clair, giving his most elegant salute with his small sword.

Dick went back to the Union colonels, and they accepted at once. That long line of dead and wounded, and the mournful song of the wind through the trees, affected the colonels on both sides. More flags of truce were hoisted, and the officers in blue or gray rode forward to meet one another, and to talk together as men who bore no hate in their hearts for gallant enemies.

The troopers rapidly dug shallow graves with their bayonets in the soft soil, and the dead were laid away. The feeling of friendship and also of curiosity among these stern fighters grew. They were anxious to see and talk a little with men who had fought one another so hard more than three years. Nearly all of them had lost blood at one time or another, and the venom of hate had gone out with it.

Dick found Harry dismounted and standing with a group of officers, among whom were St. Clair and Langdon. The two cousins shook hands with the greatest warmth.

"Well, Dick," said Harry, "we didn't think to meet again in this way, did we?"

"No, but both of us at least have come out of it alive, and unwounded. I'm sorry to see that your friend there is hurt."

"It's nothing," said Langdon, whose left arm was in a hasty bandage. "A scratch only. I'll be able to use my arm as well as ever three days from now."

"Your force," said St. Clair, "was marching to reinforce General Sheridan in the Valley of Virginia. I'm not asking for information, which of course you wouldn't give. I'm merely stating the fact."

"And yours," said Dick, "was marching to reinforce General Early in the same valley. I, like you, am just making a statement."

"We've met, but you haven't been able to stop us."

"Nor have you been able to stop *us*."

"And so it's checkmate."

"Checkmate it is."

"Why don't you fellows give up and go home?" exclaimed Dick, moved by an irresistible impulse. "You know that your armies are wearing out, while ours are growing stronger!"

"We couldn't think of such a thing," replied St. Clair, in a tone of cool assurance. "My friend Langdon here, has taken an oath to sleep in the White House. We also intend to make a triumphal march through Philadelphia, and then down Broadway in New York. You would not have us break our oaths or change our purposes."

"It's true, Dick," said Harry, "we can't do either. We'd like to oblige you Yankees, but we must make those triumphal parades through Philadelphia and New York."

"I should have known that I couldn't reason with you Johnny Rebs," said Dick, smiling, "but I hope that none of you will get killed, and here and now I make you a promise."

"What is it, Dick?" asked Harry.

"When you suffer your final defeat, and all of you become my prisoners, I'll treat you well. I'll turn you loose in a Blue-grass pasture, and you can roam as you please within its limits."

"Thank you," said Happy Tom, "but I'm no Nebuchadnezzar. I can't live on grass. If I become a prisoner at any time I demand the very best of food, especially as you Yankees already have more than your share."

"There go the trumpets recalling us," said St. Clair. "The men have finished the gruesome task. I want you to know, Mr. Mason, that we bear you no animosity, and we're quite sure that you bear us none."

He extended his hand and Dick's met it in a warm grasp. Langdon also shook hands with him, and as his eyes twinkled he said:

"Don't fail to notice my haughty bearing when I march at the head of a triumphal troop down Broadway!"

"I promise," said Dick. Then he and Harry gave each other the final clasp. But with the pride of the young they strove not to show emotion.

"Take care of yourself, Dick, old man!" said Harry. "Don't get in the way of bullets and shell. Remember they're harder than you are."

"The same to you, Harry. It's not worth while to take any more risks than necessary."

Then, obeying the call of the trumpets, they mounted and rode to their own commands. There was something strange in this brief half hour of friendship, when they buried the dead together. Blue and gray formed again in long lines facing one another, but midway between was another long line of fresh earth, and it rose up suddenly, an impassable barrier to a charge by either force.

"We can't beat them and they can't beat us. That's been proved," said Colonel Hertford to Colonel Winchester and Colonel Bedford.

"So it has," said Colonel Winchester, "and I'd like to march from here. I don't care for any more fighting on this spot."

"Nor I. Hark, they've decided it for us!"

The Southern trumpet sounded another call, and the line of men in gray, turning away, began to march into the southwest. Colonel Hertford promptly gave an order, the Union trumpet sounded also, and the men in blue, curving also, rode toward the northwest.

Dick and his comrades were silent a long time. Their feelings were perhaps the same. To youth a year is a long time, and two years are almost a life time. Three years and more of it had made war to them a normal state. They had not thought much before of an end to the great struggle between North and South, and of what was to come after. Now they realized that peace, not war, was normal, and that it must return.

The moonlight faded and then the stars were dimmed, as the darkness that precedes the dawn came. The silvery veil that had been thrown over them vanished and the column became a ghostly train riding in the dusk. But the road into which Shepard guided them led over a pleasant land of hills and clear streams. Although the scouts on their flanks kept vigilant watch, many of the men slept soundly in their saddles. Dick himself dozed awhile, and slept awhile, and, when he roused himself from his last nap, the dawn was breaking over the brown hills and the column was halting for food and a little rest.

It was August, the time of great heat in Virginia, but they were already building fires to cook the breakfast and make coffee, and most of the men had dismounted. Dick sprang down also and turned his horse loose to graze with the others. Then he joined Warner and Pennington and fell hungrily to work. When he thought of it afterward he could scarcely remember a time in the whole war when he was not hungry.

The sense of unreality disappeared with the brilliant dawn, though the night itself with the battle in the moonlight seemed to be almost a dream. Yet the combat had been fought, and he had met Harry Kenton and his friends. The empty saddles proved it.

"I see a great country opening out before us," said Warner. "I suppose it's this Valley of Virginia, of which we've all heard and seen so much, and in which once upon a time Stonewall Jackson thumped us so often."

"It's a branch of it," said Pennington, "but Stonewall Jackson is gone, God rest his soul—I say that from the heart, even if he was against us—and I've an idea that instead of getting thumped we're going to do the thumping. There's something about this man Sheridan that appeals to me. We've seen him in action with artillery, but now he's a cavalry commander. They say he rides fast and far and strikes hard. People are beginning to talk about Little Phil. Well, I approve of Little Phil."

"He'll be glad to hear of it," said Dick. "It will brace him up a lot."

"He may be lucky to get it," replied Pennington calmly. "There are many generals in this war, and two or three of them have been commander-in-chief, of whom I don't approve at all. I think you'll find, too, that history will have a habit of agreeing with me."

"But don't make predictions," said Dick. "There have been no genuine, dyed-in-the-wool prophets since those ancient Hebrews were gathered to their fathers, and that was a mighty long time ago."

"There you're wrong, Dick," said Warner, earnestly. "It's all a matter of mathematics, the scientific application of a romantic and imaginative science to facts. Get all your premises right, arrange them correctly, and the result follows as a matter of course."

The trumpet sounded boots and saddles, and cut him short. In a few more minutes they were all up and away, riding over the hills and across the dips toward the main sweep of the famous valley which played such a great part in the tactics and fighting of the Civil War. It had already been ravaged much by march and battle and siege, but its heavier fate was yet to come.

But Dick did not think much of what might happen as he rode with his comrades across the broken country and saw, rising before them, the dim blue line of the mountains that walled in the eastern side of the valley. The day was not so warm as usual, and among the higher hills a breeze was blowing, bringing currents of fresh, cool air that made the lungs expand and the pulses leap. The three youths felt almost as if they had been re-created, and Pennington became vocal.

"Woe is the day!" he said. "I lament what I have lost!"

"If what you have lost was worth keeping I lament with you," said Dick. "O, woe is the day!"

"O, woe is the day for me, too!" said Warner, "but why do we utter cries of woe, Frank?"

"Because of the narrow, little, muddy little, ugly little, mean little trench we've left behind us! O, woe is me that I've left such a trench, where one could sit in mud to the knees and touch the mud wall on either side of him, for this open, insecure world, where there is nothing but fresh air to breathe, nothing but water to drink, nothing but food to eat, and no world but blue skies, hills, valleys, forests, fields, rivers, creeks and brooks!"

"O, woe is me!" the three chanted together. "We sigh for our narrow trench, and its muddy bottom and muddy sides and foul air and lack of space, and for the shells bursting over our heads, and for the hostile riflemen ready to put a bullet through us at the first peep! Now, do we sigh for all those blessings we've left behind us?"

"Never a sigh!" said Dick.

"Not a tear from me," said Pennington.

"The top of the earth for me," said Warner.

Their high spirits spread to the whole column. So thoroughly inured were they to war that their losses of the night before were forgotten, and they lifted up their voices and sang. Youth and the open air would have their way and the three colonels did not object. They preferred men who sang to men who groaned.

"Do you know just where we're going, and where we expect to find this Little Phil of yours?" asked Warner.

"I've heard that we're to report to him at Halltown, a place south of the Potomac, and about four miles from Harper's Ferry," replied Dick.

"As that's a long distance, we'll have a long ride to reach it," said Warner, "and I'm glad of it. I'm enjoying this great trail, and I hope we won't meet again those fire-eating friends of yours, Dick, who gave us so much trouble last night."

"I hope so too," said Dick, "for their sake as well as ours. I don't like fighting with such close kin. They must be well along on the southwestern road now to join Early."

"There's no further danger of meeting them, at least before this campaign opens," said Warner. "Shepard has just come back from a long gallop and he reports that they are now at least twenty miles away, with the distance increasing all the time."

Dick felt great relief. He was softening wonderfully in these days, and while he had the most intense desire for the South to yield he had no wish for the South to suffer more. He felt that the republic had been saved and he was anxious for the war to be over soon. His heart swelled with pride at the way in which the Union states had stood fast, how they had suffered cruel defeats, but had come again, and yet again, how mistakes and disaster had been overcome by courage and tenacity.

"A Confederate dollar for your thoughts," said Warner.

"You can have 'em without the dollar," replied Dick. "I was thinking about the end of the war and after. What are all the soldiers going to do then?"

"Go straight back to peace," replied Warner promptly. "I know my own ambition. I've told you already that I intend to be president of Harvard University, and, barring death, I'm bound to succeed. I give myself twenty-five years for the task. If I choose my object now and bend every energy toward it for twenty-five years I'm sure to obtain it. It's a mathematical certainty."

"I'm going to be a great ranchman in Western Nebraska with my father," said Pennington. "He's under fifty yet, and he's as strong as a horse. The buffalo in Western Nebraska must go and then Pennington and Son will have fifty thousand fine cattle in their place. And you, Dick, have you already chosen the throne on which you're going to sit?"

"Yes, I've been thinking about it for some time. I've made up my mind to be an editor. After the war I'm going to the largest city in our state, get a place on a newspaper there and strive to be its head. Then I'll try to cement the reunion of North and South. That will be my greatest topic. We soldiers won't hate one another when the war is over, and maybe the fact that I've fought through it will give weight to my words."

"I'll tell you what I'll do," said Warner. "When I'm president of Harvard I'll invite the great Kentucky editor, Richard Mason, to deliver the annual address to my young men. I like that idea of yours about making the Union firmer than it was before the war. Since the Northern States and the Southern States must dwell together the more peace and brotherly love we have the better it will be for all of us."

"When you give me that invitation, George, you'd better ask my cousin, Harry Kenton, at the same time, because it's almost a certainty that he will then be governor of Kentucky. His great grandfather, the famous Henry Ware, was the greatest governor the state ever had, and, as I know that Harry intends to study law and enter politics, he's bound to follow in his footsteps."

"Of course I'll ask him," said Warner in all earnestness, "and he shall speak too. You can settle it between you who speaks first. It will be an exceedingly effective scene, the two cousins, the great editor who fought on the Northern side and the great governor who fought on the Southern side, speaking from the same stage to the picked youth of New England. Pennington, the representative of the boundless West, shall be there too, and if the owner of fifty thousand fine cattle roaming far and wide wants to make an address he shall do so."

"I don't think I'd care to speak, George," said Pennington. "I'm not cut out for oratory, but I certainly accept right now your invitation to come. I'll sit on the stage with Dick and the Johnny Reb, his cousin Harry, and I'll smile and smile and applaud and applaud, and after it's all over I'll choose a few of your picked youth of New England, take 'em out west with me, teach 'em how to rope cattle, how to trail stray steers and how to take care of themselves in a blizzard. Oh, I'll make men of 'em, I will! Now, what is that on the high hill to the south?"

The three put their glasses to their eyes and saw a man on horseback waving a flag. The head of the horse was turned toward some hill farther south, and the man was evidently making signals to another patrol there.

"A Johnny," said Pennington. "I suppose they're sending the word on toward Early that we're passing."

"From hill to hill," said Dick. "A message can be sent a long way in that manner."

"I don't think it will interfere with us," said Warner. "They're merely telling about us. They don't intend to attack us. They haven't the men to spare."

"No, they won't attack, they know I'm here," said Pennington.

The three colonels did not stop the column, but they watched the signals as they rode. Nobody was able to interpret them, not even Shepard, but they felt that they could ignore them. Colonel Hertford, nevertheless, sent off a strong scouting party in that direction, but as it approached the horseman on the hill rode over the other side and disappeared.

All that day they advanced through a lonely and hostile country. It was a region intensely Southern in its sympathies, and it seemed that everybody, including the women and children, had fled before them. Horses and cattle were gone also and its loneliness was accentuated by the fact that not so long before it had been a well-peopled land, where now the houses stood empty and silent. They saw no human beings, save other watchmen on the hills making signals, but they were far away and soon gone.

By noon both horses and men showed great fatigue. They had slept but little the night before, and, toughened as they were by war, they had reached the limit of endurance. So the trumpet sounded the halt in a meadow beside a fine stream, and all, save those who were to ride on the outskirts and watch for the enemy, dismounted gladly. A vast drinking followed. The water was clear, running over clean pebbles, and a thousand men knelt and drank again and again. Then the horses were allowed to drink their fill, which they did with mighty gurglings of satisfaction, and the men cooked their midday meal.

Meanwhile they talked of Sheridan. All expected battle and then battle again when they joined him, and they looked forward to a great campaign in the valley. That valley was not so far away. The blue walls of the mountains that hemmed its eastern edge were very near now. Dick looked at them through his glasses, not to find an enemy, but merely for the pleasure of bringing out the heavy forests on their slopes. It was true that the leaves were already touched by the summer's heat, but in the distance at least the mass looked green. He knew also that under the screen of the leaves the grass preserved its freshness and there were many little streams, foaming in white as they rushed down the steep slopes. It was a marvellously pleasing sight to him, and, as the wilderness thus called, he was once more deeply grateful that he had escaped from the muddy trench

"We'll pass through a gap, sir, tomorrow morning," said Sergeant Whitley, "and go into the main valley."

"The gap would be the place for the Southern force to meet us."

But Sergeant Whitley shook his head.

"There are too many gaps and too few Southern troops," he said. "I think we'll find this one clear. Besides, Colonel Hertford is sure to send a scouting party ahead tonight. But if you don't mind taking a little advice from an old trooper, sir, I'd lie on the grass and sleep while we're here. An hour even will do a lot of good."

Dick followed his advice gladly and thanked him. He was always willing to receive instruction from Sergeant Whitley, who had proved himself his true friend and who in reality was able to teach men of much higher rank. He lay down upon the brown grass, and despite all the noise, despite all the excitement of past hours, fell fast asleep in a few minutes. He slept an hour, but it seemed to him that he had scarcely closed his eyes, when the trumpets were calling boots and saddles again. Yet he felt refreshed and stronger when he sprang up, and Sergeant Whitley's advice, as always, had proved good.

The column resumed its march before mid-afternoon, continuing its progress through a silent and empty country. The blue wall came closer and closer and Dick and his comrade saw the lighter line, looking in the distance like the slash of a sword, that marked the gap. Shepard, who rode a very swift and powerful horse, came back from another scouting trip and reported that there was no sign of the enemy, at least at the entrance to the gap.

Later in the afternoon, as they were passing through a forest several shots were fired at them from the covert. No damage was done beyond one man wounded slightly, and Dick, under orders, led a short pursuit. He was glad that they found no one, as prisoners would have been an encumbrance, and it was not the custom in the United States to shoot men not in uniform who were defending the soil on which they lived. He had no doubt that those who had fired the shots were farmers, but it had been easy for them to make good their escape in the thickets.

He thought he saw relief on Colonel Hertford's face also, when he reported that the riflemen had escaped, and, after spreading out skirmishers a little farther on either flank, the column, which had never broken its march, went on at increased pace. It was growing warm now, and the dust and heat of the long ride began to affect them. The blue line of the mountains, as they came close, turned to green and Dick, Warner and Pennington looked enviously at the deep shade.

"Not so bad," said Warner. "Makes me think a little of the Green Mountains of Vermont, though not as high and perhaps not as green."

"Of course," said Dick. "Nothing outside of Vermont is as good as anything inside of it."

"I'm glad you acknowledge it so readily, Dick. I have found some people who would not admit it at first, and I was compelled to talk and persuade them of the fact, a labour that ought to be unnecessary. The truth should always speak for itself. Vermont isn't the most fertile state in the Union and it's not the largest, but it's the best producer of men, or I should say the producer of the best men."

"What will Massachusetts say to that? I've read Daniel Webster's speech in reply to Hayne."

"Oh, Massachusetts, of course, has more people, I'm merely speaking of the average."

"Nebraska hasn't been settled long," said Pennington, "but you just wait. When we get a population we'll make both Vermont and Massachusetts take a back seat."

"And that population, or at least the best part of it," rejoined the undaunted Warner, "will come from Vermont and Massachusetts and other New England states."

"Sunset and the gap together are close at hand," said Dick, "and however the mountains of Virginia may compare with those of Vermont, it's quite certain that the sun setting over the two states is the same."

"I concede that," said Warner; "but it looks more brilliant from the Vermont hills."

Nevertheless, the sun set in Virginia in a vast and intense glow of colour, and as the twilight came they entered the gap.

CHAPTER 5

An Old Enemy

Despite the brilliant sunset the night came on very dark and heavy with damp. The road through the gap was none too good and the lofty slopes clothed in forest looked menacing. Many sharpshooters might lurk there, and the three colonels were anxious to reach Sheridan with their force intact, at least without further loss after the battle with Colonel Talbot's command.

The column was halted and it was decided to send out another scouting party to see if the way was clear. Twenty men, of whom the best for such work were Shepard and Whitley, were chosen, and Dick, owing to his experience, was put in nominal command, although he knew in his heart that the spy and the sergeant would be the real leaders, a fact which he did not resent. Warner and Pennington begged to go too, but they were left behind.

Shepard had received a remount, and, as all of them rode good horses, they advanced at a swift trot through the great gap. The spy, who knew the pass, led the way. The column behind, although it was coming forward at a good pace, disappeared with remarkable quickness. Dick, looking back, saw a dusky line of horsemen, and then he saw nothing. He did not look back again. His eyes were wholly for Shepard and the dim path ahead.

The aspect of the mountains, which had been so inviting before they came to them, changed wholly. Dick did not long so much for green foliage now, as a chill wind began to blow. All of them carried cloaks or overcoats rolled tightly and tied to their saddles, which they loosed and put on. The wind rose, and, confined within the narrow limits of the pass, it began to groan loudly. A thin sheet of rain came on its edge, and the drops were almost as cold as those of winter.

Dick's first sensation of uneasiness and discomfort disappeared quickly. Like his cousin, Harry, he had inherited a feeling for the wilderness. His own ancestor, Paul Cotter, had been a great woodsman too, and, as he drew on the buckskin gauntlets and wrapped the heavy cloak about his body, his second sensation was one of actual physical pleasure. Why should he regard the forest with a hostile eye? His ancestors had lived in it and often its darkness had saved them from death by torture.

He looked up at the dark slopes, but he could see only the black masses of foliage and the thin sheets of driven rain. For a little while, at least, his mind reproduced the wilderness. It was there in all its savage loneliness and majesty. He could readily imagine that the Indians were lurking in the brush, and that the bears and panthers were seeking shelter in their dens. But his own feeling of safety and of mental and physical pleasure in the face of obstacles deepened.

"I've been just that way myself," said Sergeant Whitley, who was riding beside him and who could both see and read his face. "On the plains when we were so well wrapped up that the icy winds whistling around us couldn't get at us then we felt all the better. But it was best when we were inside the fort and the winter blizzard was howling."

"A lot of us were talking a little while back about what they were going to do after the war. What's your plan, sergeant, if you have any?"

"I do have a plan, Mr. Mason. I was a lumberman, as you know, before I entered the regular army, and when the fighting's done I think I'll go back to it. I can swing an axe with the best of 'em, but I mean after a while to have others swinging axes for me. If I can I'm going to become a big lumberman. I'd rather be that than anything else."

"It's a just and fine ambition, sergeant, I feel sure that you're going to become a man of money and power. Mr. Warner means to become president of Harvard, twenty or twenty-five years from now, and my cousin Harry Kenton, a reconstructed rebel, is going to deliver an address there to the new president's young men, while Mr. Pennington and I, as the president's guests, are going to sit on the stage and smile. Right now, and with authority from Mr. Warner, I'm going to invite you as the lumber king of the Northwest to sit on the stage with us on that occasion, as the guest of President Warner, and smile with us."

"If I become what you predict I'll accept," said the sergeant.

The chances were a thousand to one against the prophecy, but it all came true, just as they wished.

The rain increased a little, although it was not yet able to penetrate Dick's heavy coat, but they were compelled to go more slowly on account of the thickening darkness. They reached very soon the crest of the pass and halted there a little while to see or hear any sign of a human being. But no sound came to them and they resumed the scout in the darkness, riding now down the slope which would end before long in a great valley.

The ground softened by the rain deadened the footsteps of their horses, and they made little noise as they rode down the narrow pass, examining as well as they could the dripping forest on either side of the road. Shepard was a bit ahead, and Dick and the sergeant, riding side by side, came next. Behind were the troopers, a small picked band, daring horsemen, used to every kind of danger.

They did not really anticipate the presence of an enemy in the pass. They knew that Colonel Talbot's command had turned toward the southwest. All the other Confederate forces must be gathering far up the valley to meet Sheridan, and the South was too much reduced to raise new men. Yet after a half hour's moderate riding down the slope Dick became sure that some one was in the narrow belt of forest on their right, where the slope was less steep than on their left.

At first it seemed to be an intuition, merely a feeling brought on waves of air that men, enemies, were in the wood. Then he knew that the feeling was due to sounds as of someone moving lightly through a wet thicket, but unable to keep the boughs from giving forth a rustle. He was about to call to Shepard, but before he could do so the spy stopped. Then all the others stopped also.

"Did you hear it?" Dick whispered to Sergeant Whitley.

"Yes," replied the sergeant. "Men are moving in the thicket on our right. I couldn't hear much, but they must be as numerous as we are. They're enemies or they'd have come out. They're on foot, too, as they couldn't manage horses in those deep woods. Likely they've left their mounts with a guard on top of a ridge, as men on foot wouldn't be abroad at such a time on such a night."

"Then it's an ambush!" said Dick, and he added in a sharp voice: "Pull away to the left, men, under cover!"

Shepard was the first to turn and all the others followed instantly. Three jumps of the horses and they were among the bushes and trees on the left. It was lucky for them that they had heard the sound of the wet bushes rustling together, as a dozen rifles flashed in the dusk on the other side of the road. Bullets cut the leaves about them. Two or three buried themselves with a plunk in the trunks of trees, one killed a horse, the trooper springing clear without hurt, and one man was wounded slightly in the arm.

"Take cover," called Dick, "but don't lose your horses!"

281

They dismounted and concealed themselves behind the trunks of trees. Some hastily tethered their horses to bushes, but others hung the bridle over an arm. They knew that if a combat was to occur it must be fought on foot, but, for the present, they were compelled to wait. Yet if their enemy was hidden from them they also were hidden from him. All the conditions of an old Indian battle in darkness and ambush were reproduced, and Dick was deeply grateful that he had at his elbow two redoubtable champions like Whitley and Shepard. They were peculiarly fitted for such work as that which lay before them, and he was ready and willing to take advice from either.

"It's a small party," whispered Shepard, "probably not much larger than ours. They must have expected to make a complete ambush, but we heard them too soon."

"It's surely not a part of Colonel Talbot's command," said Dick. "If so, Harry Kenton and his friends would certainly be there and I shouldn't like to be in battle with them again."

"Never a fear of that," said Sergeant Whitley. "It's more likely to be some guerrilla band, roaming around as it pleases. The condition of the country and these mountains give such fellows a chance. I'm going to lie down and creep forward as we used to do on the plains. I want to get a sight of those fellows, that is, if you say so, sir."

"Of course," said Dick, "but don't take too big risks, sergeant. We can't afford to let you be shot."

"Never fear," said the sergeant, dropping almost flat upon his face, and creeping slowly forward.

The dusky figure worming itself through the bushes heightened the illusion of an old Indian combat. The sergeant was a scout and trailer feeling for the enemy and he reminded Dick of his famous ancestor, Paul Cotter. Several more shots were fired by the foe, but they did not hurt anybody, all of them flying overhead. Dick's men were anxious to send random bullets in reply into the thickets, but he restrained them. It would be only a waste, and while it was annoying to be held there, it could not be helped. Some of the horses reared and plunged with fright at the shots, but silence soon came.

Dick still watched the sergeant as he edged forward, inch by inch. Had not his eyes been following the dusky figure he could not have picked it out from the general darkness. But he still saw it faintly, a darker blur against the dark earth. Yielding a little to his own anxiety, he handed the bridle of his horse to his orderly, and moved toward the edge of the woodland strip, bending low, and using the tree trunks for shelter.

At the last tree he knelt and looked for those on the other side. The sergeant was already beyond cover, but he lay so low in the grass that Dick himself could scarcely discern him.

The wind was still driving the thin sheets of rain before it, and was keeping up a howling and whistling in the pass, a most sinister sound to one not used to the forest and darkness, although Dick paid no attention to it.

Twice the clouds parted slightly and showed a bit of moonlight, but the gleam was so brief that it was gone in a second or two. Nevertheless at the second ray Dick saw crouched beside a tree at the far side of the road a small hunched figure holding a rifle, the head crowned by an enormous flap-brimmed hat. His imagination also made him see small, close-set, menacing red eyes, and he knew at once that it was Slade, the same guerrilla leader who had once pursued him with such deadly vindictiveness through the Mississippi forest and swamps. He had heard that he had come farther north and had united his band with that of Skelly, who pretended to be on the other side. But one could never tell about these outlaws. When they were distant from the regular armies nobody was safe from them.

"Did you see?" whispered Dick to the sergeant who had crept to his side.

"Yes, I caught a glimpse of him. It was Slade, who tried so hard to kill you down there in the Vicksburg campaign. If we get another ray of the moonlight I'll pick him off, that is if you say so, sir."

"I've no objection, sergeant. Such a man as Slade cumbers the earth. Besides, he'll do everything he can now to kill us."

The sergeant knelt, carbine raised, and waited for the ray of moonlight. He was a dead shot, and he believed that he would not miss, but when the ray came at last Slade was not there. Whitley uttered a low exclamation of disgust.

"A good chance gone," he said, "and it may never come again. I'd have saved the lives of a lot of good men."

But a flash came from the thicket, and the sergeant from the grass replied. A cry followed his shot, showing that some one had received his bullet, but Dick knew instinctively that it was not Slade, the crafty leader he was sure now being safe behind the trunk of a tree.

Presently the sergeant fired from another point, and then crept hastily away lest the flash of his rifle betray him. A dozen shots were fired by Slade's band, but no harm was done, and then, the sergeant coming back, Dick held a consultation with his two lieutenants and advisers.

"Perhaps we may flank them," he said. "We can divide our force, and taking them by surprise drive them out of the wood."

But Sergeant Whitley, wary and weather-wise, was against it.

"The risk would be too great, sir," he said. "We can afford to wait while they can't. Our whole column will be up in time, while it's not likely that anybody can come to help Slade. It's true too, sir, that this rain is going to stop. The clouds are beginning to clear away, and when there's light we'll have a fair chance at 'em."

"I think," said Dick, "that it will be best for Mr. Shepard to return and hurry up a relieving column. What do you say?"

"I think so too, sir," said Shepard. "I can lead my horse back some distance through the forest, then mount and gallop up the road. They may be gone before I come again, but if they are not we can soon drive them away."

"We'll cover you with our rifles against any rush made by Slade's men," said Dick.

But it did not become necessary to fire. Shepard was able to lead his horse through the woods without noise, until he was at least three hundred yards on the return journey. Then he mounted and galloped at great speed up the pass. Dick heard the distant thud of hoofs growing fainter and fainter until they died away altogether, and he knew that Slade must have heard them too. And a man as acute and experienced as the guerrilla chief would easily divine their meaning.

The rain ceased, and the moaning and whistling of the wind in the pass became a murmur. The clouds parted and sank away toward every horizon, leaving the full dome of the sky, shot with a bright moon and millions of dancing stars. A silvery light over the woods and thickets drove away the deep darkness, and when Sergeant Whitley crept forward again to spy out the enemy he found that they were gone. He trailed them up the lofty slope and discovered, as he had surmised, that they had left their horses there while they attempted the ambush. He was sure now that they were far away, and he returned with his story, just as Shepard arrived with the vanguard of the column, led by Colonel Winchester.

"And so it was Slade!" said the Colonel.

"Undoubtedly, sir," said Dick. "I saw him plainly, and so did Sergeant Whitley."

"I'm not sorry he's here," said Colonel Winchester thoughtfully, "and I hope the story that he and Skelly have joined bands is true, because if they are in this region they're so far away from Pendleton that your people are safe from mischief at their hands."

"I hadn't thought of it in that way, sir, but it's just as you say. I'd rather have to fight them here than have them attacking our innocent people at home. In the early part of the war Skelly called himself a Unionist, did he not?"

"Yes, and he may do so yet, but names are nothing to him. He'd rob, and murder, too, with equal zest under either flag."

"It's so," said Dick, and he felt the full truth as he thought of Pendleton, and his beautiful young mother, alone in her house, save for the gigantic and faithful Juliana. But Juliana was an armed host herself, and Dick smiled at the recollection of the strong and honest black face that had bent over him so often. He prayed without words that these ruthless guerrillas, no matter what flag they bore, should never come to Pendleton.

"I don't think our column on its present march need fear anything from Slade and his band," said Colonel Winchester. "Such as he can operate only from ambush, and so far as Virginia is concerned, in the mountains. Shepard says we'll be out of the pass in another hour, and by that time it will be day. I'll be glad, too, as the cold rain and the darkness and the long ride are beginning to affect the men."

The column resumed its march, Dick rode by the side of Colonel Winchester. Time, propinquity, genuine esteem, and a fourth influence which Dick did not as yet suspect, were fast knitting these two, despite the difference in age, into a friendship which nothing could break. The meeting with Slade was forgotten quickly, by all except those concerned, and by most of those too, so vast was the war and so little space did it afford for the memory of brief events. Yet it lingered a while with Dick. Twice now he had met Slade and he felt that he would meet him yet again at points far apart.

Dawn came slow and gray in a cloudy sky, but the sun soon broke through. The heat returned and the earth began to dry. The three colonels felt it necessary to give their men rest and food, and let them dry their uniforms, which had become wet in many cases, despite their overcoats and heavy cloaks.

They were now in a deep cove of the great Valley of Virginia, with the steep mountains just behind them, and far beyond the dim blue outline of other mountains enclosing it on the west. As the fires blazed up and the men made coffee and cooked their breakfasts, Dick's heart leaped. This was the great valley once more, where so much history had been made. Lee and Grant were deadlocked in the trenches before Petersburg, but here in the valley history would be made again. It was the finest part of Virginia, the greatest state of the Confederacy, and Dick knew in his heart that some heavy blows would soon be struck, where fields already had been won and lost in desperate strife.

But the men were very cheerful. The little band of skirmishers or sharpshooters under Slade had been brushed aside easily, and now that they were in the valley they did not foresee any further attempt to stop their march to Sheridan. The three colonels shared in the view, and when the men had finished breakfast and dried themselves at their fires they remounted and rode away gaily. High spirits rose again in youthful veins, and some lad of a mellow voice began to sing. By and by all joined and a thousand voices thundered out:

"Oh, share my cottage, gentle maid,
"It only waits for thee
"To give a sweetness to its shade
"And happiness to me.
"Here from the splendid, gay parade
"Of noise and folly free
"No sorrows can my peace invade
"If only blessed with thee.
"Then share my cottage, gentle maid,
"It only waits for thee
"To give a sweetness to its shade
"And happiness to me."

Colonel Hertford made no attempt to check them as they rode across the fields, yet green here, despite the summer's heat.

"They're bravest when they sing," he said to Colonel Winchester.

"It encourages them," said Colonel Winchester, "and I like to hear it myself. It's a wonderful effect, a thousand or more strong lads singing, as they sweep over the valley toward battle."

Dick, Pennington and Warner had joined in the song, but the youth some distance ahead of them was leader. They finished *Gentle Maid* and then, with the same lad leading them, swung into a song that made Dick start and that for a moment made other mountains and another valley stand out before him, sharp and clear.

"Soft o'er the fountain, ling'ring falls the Southern moon
"Far o'er the mountain, breaks the day too soon.
"In thy dark eyes' splendour, where the warm light loves to dwell,
"Weary looks, yet tender, speak their fond farewell.
"Nita! Juanita!
"Ask thy soul if we should part,
"Nita! Juanita!

"Lean thou on my heart.

"When in thy dreaming moons like these shall shine again,

"And daylight beaming prove thy dreams are vain,

"Wilt thou not, relenting, for thy absent lover sigh?

"In thy heart consenting to a prayer gone by!

"Nita! Juanita!

"Let me linger by thy side.

"Nita! Juanita!

"Be my own fair bride."

They put tremendous heart and energy into the haunting old song as they sang, and Dick still saw Sam Jarvis, the singer of the hills, and his valley, where the paths of Harry Kenton and himself had crossed, though at times far apart.

"Now!" shouted the young leader, "The last verse again!" and with increased heart and energy they thundered out:

"When in thy dreaming moons like these shall shine again,

"And daylight beaming prove thy dreams are vain,

"Wilt thou not, relenting, for thy absent lover sigh?

"In thy heart consenting to a prayer gone by!

"Nita! Juanita!

"Let me linger by thy side.

"Nita! Juanita!

"Be my own fair bride." The mighty chorus sank away and the hills gave it back in echoes until the last one died.

"It's sung mostly in the South," said Dick to Warner and Pennington.

"True," said Warner, "but before the war songs were not confined to one section. They were the common property of both. We've as much right to sing Juanita as the Johnnies have."

All that day they rode and sang, going north toward Halltown, where the forces of Sheridan were gathering, and the valley, although lone and desolate, continually unfolded its beauty before them. The mountains were green near by and blue in the distance, and the fertile floor that they enclosed, like walls, was cut by many streams. Here, indeed, was a region that had bloomed before the war, and that would bloom again, no matter what war might do.

They found inhabited houses now and then, but all the men of military age were gone away and the old men, the women and the children would answer nothing. The women were not afraid to tell the Yankees what they thought of them, and in this war which was never a war on women the troopers merely laughed, or, if they felt anger, they hid it.

On they went through night and day, and now they drew near to Sheridan. Scouts in blue met them and the gallant column shook their sabres and saluted. Yes, it was true, they said, that Sheridan was gathering a fine army and he and all of his men were eager to march, but Colonel Hertford's force, sent by General Grant to help, would be welcomed with shouts. The fame of its three colonels had gone on before.

It was bright noon when they approached the northern end of the valley, and Dick saw a horseman followed by a group of about twenty men galloping toward them. The leader was a short, slender man, sitting firmly in his saddle.

"General Sheridan!" exclaimed Shepard.

Colonel Hertford instantly ordered his trumpeter to sound a signal, and the troopers, stopping and drawing up in a long line, awaited the man who was to command them, and who was coming on so fast. Again Dick examined him closely through his glasses, and he saw the young, tanned face under the broad brim of his hat, and the keen, flashing eyes. He noticed also how small he was. Sheridan was but five feet five inches in height and he weighed in the momentous campaign now about to begin, only one hundred and fifteen pounds! As slight as a young boy, he gave, nevertheless, an impression of the greatest vigour and endurance.

He reined in his horse a score of yards in front of the long line and was about to speak to Colonel Hertford, who sat his saddle before it, Colonel Winchester and Colonel Bedford on either side of him, but there was a sudden interruption.

Fifteen hundred sabres flashed aloft, the blazing sunlight glittering for a moment on their broad blades. Then they swept in mighty curves, all together, and from fifteen hundred throats thundered:

"Sheridan! Sheridan! Sheridan!"

The sabres made another flashing curve, sank back into their scabbards, and the men were silent.

Sheridan's tanned face flushed deeply, and a great light leaped up in his eyes, as he received the magnificent salute. His own sword sprang out, and made the salute in reply. Then, riding a little closer, he said in a loud, clear tone that all could hear:

"Men, I have been looking for you! I have come forward to meet you! I knew that you were great horsemen, gallant soldiers, but I see that you are even greater and more gallant men than I had hoped. The Army of the Potomac has sent its best as a gift to the Army of the Shenandoah. Men, I thank you for this welcome, the warmest I have ever received!"

Again the sabres flashed aloft, made their glittering curve, and again from muscular throats came the thunderous cheer:

"Sheridan! Sheridan! Sheridan!"

Then the young general shook hands heartily with the three colonels, the young aides were introduced, and with Sheridan himself at their head the whole column swept off toward the north, and to the camp of the Army of the Shenandoah which lay but a little distance away.

CHAPTER 6

The Fishermen

The welcome that the column found in Sheridan's camp was as warm as they had hoped, and more. Fifteen hundred sabres such as theirs were not to be valued lightly, and Sheridan knew well the worth of three such colonels as Hertford, Winchester and Bedford, with all three of whom he was acquainted personally, and with whose records he was familiar. Dick, Pennington and Warner also came in for his notice, and he recalled having seen Dick at the fierce battle of Perryville in Kentucky, a fact of which Dick was very proud.

"Now don't become too haughty because he remembers you," said Warner reprovingly. "Bear in mind that trifles sometimes stick longer in our minds than more important things."

"It's just jealousy on your part," said Dick. "You New Englanders are able people, but you can't bear for anybody else to achieve distinction."

"We don't have to feel that jealousy often," said Warner calmly.

"Merit like charity begins with you at home."

"And modesty can't keep us from admitting it, but you Kentuckians do fight well—under our direction."

"Don't talk with him, Dick," said Pennington. "Against his wall of mountainous conceit wisdom breaks in vain."

"I'm glad to see you expressing yourself so poetically, Frank," said Warner. "The New England seed planted in Nebraska will flower into bloom some day."

Sergeant Whitley came at that moment and asked them to go and see the new horses provided for them, and the three went with him, friends bound to one another by hooks of steel. The horses given to them by special favour of Sheridan in place of their worn-out mounts, were splendid animals, and Sergeant Whitley himself had prepared them for their first appearance before their new masters.

"They'll do! They'll do!" said Dick with enthusiasm. "Grand fellows! They ought to carry us anywhere!"

"Upon this point I must confess myself somewhat your inferior," said Warner in his precise manner. "The mountainous character of our state keeps us from making horses a specialty. You, I believe, in Kentucky, pay great attention to their breeding, and so I ask you, young Mr. Mason, if the horse chosen for me is all that he should be."

"He asks it as a matter of condescension, Dick, and not as a favour," said Pennington.

"It's all right any way you take it," laughed Dick. "Yes, George, your horse has no defect. You can always lead the charge on him against Early."

"If I'm not at the very front I expect to be somewhere near it," said Warner. "But don't you like the looks of this camp, boys? It shows order, method and precision. Everything has been done according to the best algebraic formulae. I call it mathematics, charged with fire. Our Little Phil is a great commander. One can feel his spirit in the air all about us."

Dick himself had noticed the military workmanship and that, too, of a high order, and he understood thoroughly that Sheridan had gathered a most formidable army. It was not much short of thirty thousand men, veteran troops, and he had with him Wright, Emory, Crook, Merritt, Averill, Torbert, Wilson and Grover, all able generals. Nor had Sheridan neglected to inform himself of the country over which he intended to march. With his lieutenant of engineers, Meigs, a man of great talent, he had spent days and nights studying maps of the valley. Now he knew all the creeks and brooks and roads and towns, and he understood the country as well as Early himself, who faced him with as large a Confederate force as he could gather.

Dick and his comrades expected immediate action, but it did not come. They lingered for days, due, they supposed, to orders from Washington, but they did not bother themselves about it, as they liked their new camp and were making many new friends. September days passed and they saw the summer turning into autumn. The mountains in the distance looked blue, but, near at hand, their foliage had turned brown. The great heat gave way to a crisper air and the lads who had come from the trenches before Petersburg enjoyed for a little while the luxury of early autumn and illimitable space.

They rode now and then with the cavalry outposts. Early and his men stretched across the valley to oppose them, and often Northern and Southern pickets were in touch, though they seldom fired upon one another. Dick, whenever he rode with the advanced guard, watched for Harry Kenton, St. Clair and Langdon, but it was nearly a week before he saw them. Then they rode with a small group, headed by two elderly but very upright men, whom he knew to be Colonel Leonidas Talbot and Lieutenant Colonel Hector St. Hilaire.

He felt genuine gladness, and, shouting at the top of his voice, he waved his hand. They recognized him, and all waved a welcome in return. He saw the two colonels studying him through their glasses, but he knew that no attack would be made upon him and the little party with which he rode. It was one of those increasing intervals of peace and friendship between battles. The longer the war and the greater the losses the less men troubled themselves to shoot one another save when real battle was joined.

They were about four hundred yards apart and Dick used his glasses also, enabling him to see that the young Southern officers were unwounded—Langdon's slight hurt had healed long since—and were strong and hearty. He thought it likely that they, as well as he, had found the brief period of rest and freedom from war a genuine luxury. He waved his hand once more, and they waved back as before. Then the course of the two little troops took them away from each other, and the Southerners were hid from his view by a belt of forest. But he was very glad that he had seen them. It had been almost as if there were no war.

Dick rode back to the camp, gave his horse to an orderly, and, walking toward his tent, was met by Warner and Pennington, carrying long slender rods on their shoulders—Warner in fact carrying two.

"What's this?" he exclaimed.

"We're going fishing," replied Warner. "We've permission for you also. There's a fine stream about a half mile west of us, running through the woods, and it's been fished in but little since the war started. Here, take your rod! You don't expect me to carry it for you any longer do you? It has a good hook and line and it's easy for us to find bait under a big stone on soft soil."

"Thank you, George," said Dick happily. "You couldn't keep me from going with you two. Do you know, I haven't been fishing in more than three years, and me not yet of age?"

"Well, now's your chance, and you may not have another until after the war is over. They say it's a fine stream, though, of course, it's not like the beautiful little rivers of Vermont, that come dashing down from the mountains all molten silver, where they're not white foam. Splendid fish! Splendid rivers! Splendid sport! Dick, do you think I'm facing now in the exact direction of Vermont?"

He had turned about and was gazing with a rapt look into the northeast.

"I should say," said Dick, "that if your gaze went far enough it would strike squarely upon the Green Mountains of Vermont."

Warner's hand rose in a slow and majestic salute.

"Great little state, mother of men, I salute thee!" he said. "Thou art stern and yet beautiful to the eye and thy sons love thee! I, who am but one among them, love all thy rocks, and clear streams, and noble mountains and green foliage! Here, from the battle fields and across the distance I salute thee, O great little state! O mother of men!"

"Quite dithyrambic," said Dick, "and now that your burst of rhetoric is over let's go on and catch our fish. Will you also use your romantic science of mathematics in fishing? By the way, what has become of that little algebra book of yours?"

"It's here," said Warner, taking it from the breast pocket of his tunic. "I never part with it and I most certainly expect to use its principles when I reach the fishing stream. Let x express my equipment and myself, let y equal skill and patience; x we shall say also equals the number 7, while y equals the number 5. Now the fish are represented by z which is equal to 12. It is obvious even to slow minds like yours and Pennington's that neither x nor y alone can equal z, the fish, otherwise 12, but when combined they represent that value exactly, that is x plus y equals 12. So, if I and my equipment coordinate perfectly with my skill and patience, which most certainly will happen, the fish are as good as caught by me already. The rest is a mere matter of counting."

"Best give in, Dick," said Pennington. "He'll always prove to you by his algebra that he knows everything, and that everything he does is right. Of course, he's the best fisherman in the world!"

"I'd have you to know, Francis Pennington," said Warner, with dignity, "that I was a very good fisherman when I was five years old, and that I've been improving ever since, and that Vermont is full of fine deep streams, in which one can fish with pleasure and profit. What do you know, you prairie-bred young ruffian, about fishing? I've heard that your creeks and brooks are nothing but strips of muddy dew. The Platte River itself, I believe, is nearly two inches deep at its deepest parts. I don't suppose there's another stream in America which takes up so much space on the map and so little on the ground."

"The Platte is a noble river," rejoined Pennington. "What it lacks in depth it makes up in length, and I'll not have it insulted by anybody in its absence."

While they talked they passed through the brown woods and came to the creek, flowing with a fine volume of water down from the mountains into one of the rivers of the valley.

"It's up to its advertisements," said Warner, looking at it with satisfaction. "It's clear, deep and it ought to have plenty of good fish. I see a snug place between the roots of that oak growing upon the bank, and there I sit."

"There are plenty of good places," said Dick, as they seated themselves and unwrapped their lines, "and I've a notion that our fishing is going to prove good. Isn't it fine? Why, it's like being back home!"

"Time's rolled back and we're just boys again," said Pennington.

"Don't try to be poetic, Frank," said Warner. "I've told you already that a man who has nothing but muddy streaks of dew to fish in can't know anything about fishing."

"Stop quarrelling, you two," said Dick. "Don't you know that such voices as yours raised in loud tones would scare away the boldest fish that ever swam?"

The three cast their lines out into the stream. They were of the old-fashioned kind, a hook, a lead sinker, and a cork on the line to keep it from sinking too far. Dick had used just such an equipment since he was eight years old, in the little river at Pendleton, and now he was anxious to prove to himself that he had not lost his skill. All three were as eager to catch a fish as they were to win a battle, and, for the time, the war was forgotten. It seemed to Dick as he sat on the brown turf between the enclosing roots of the tree, and leaning against its trunk, that his lost youth had returned. He was just a boy again, fishing and with no care save to raise something on his hook. The wood, although small, was dense, and it shut out all view of the army. Nor did any martial sounds come to them. The rustle of the leaves under the gentle wind was soothing. He was back at Pendleton. Harry Kenton was fishing farther up the stream, and so were other boys, his old friends of the little town.

The bit of forest was to all intents a wilderness just then, and it was so pleasant in the comfortable place between the supporting roots of the tree that Dick fell into a dreamy state, in which all things were delightful. It was perhaps the power of contrast, but after so much riding and fighting he felt a sheer physical pleasure in sitting there and watching the clear stream flow swiftly by. He smiled too at the way in which his cork bobbed up and down on the water, and he began to feel that it would not matter much whether he caught any fish or not. It was just enough to sit there and go through all the motions of fishing.

A shout from a point twenty yards below and he looked up, startled, from his dream.

"A bite!" exclaimed Warner, "I thought I had him, but he slipped off the hook! I raised him to the surface and I know he was two feet long!"

"Nine inches, probably," said Dick. "Allow at least fifteen inches for your imagination, George."

"I suppose you're right, Dick. At least, I have to do it down here. If it were a Vermont river he'd be really two feet long."

Dick heard his line and sinker strike the water again, and then silence returned to the little wood, but it did not endure long. From a point beyond Warner came a shout, and this was undeniably a cry of triumph. It was accompanied by a swishing through the air and the sound of an object striking the leaves.

"I got him! I got him! I got him!" exclaimed Pennington, dancing about as if he were only twelve years old.

Dick stood up and saw that Pennington, in truth, had caught a fine fish, at least a foot long, which was now squirming over the leaves, its silver scales gleaming.

"It seems to me," said Dick, "that the very young Territory of Nebraska has scored over the veteran State of Vermont."

"A victor merely in a preliminary skirmish," said Warner serenely. "The fish happened to be there. Frank's baited hook was close by. The fish was hungry and the result was a mathematical certainty. Frank is entitled to no credit whatever. As for me, I lure my fish within the catching area."

As Dick resumed his seat he felt a sharp pull at his own line, and drawing it in smartly he drew with it a fish as large as Pennington's, a fact that he announced with pride.

"I think, Frank," he called, "that this is not good old Vermont's day. Either we're more skilful or the fish like us better than they do Warner. Which do you think it is?"

"It's both, Dick."

"On second thought, I don't agree with you, Frank. The fish in this river are entirely new to us. They've never seen us before, and they know nothing about us by hearsay and reputation. It's a case of skill, pure skill, Frank. We've got Mr. Vermont down, and we're going to hold him down."

Warner said nothing, but Dick rose up a little and saw his face. It was red, the teeth clenched tightly, and the mouth drawn down at the corners. His eyes were fixed eagerly on his cork in the hope of seeing it bob for a moment and then be drawn swiftly under.

"Good old George," said Dick, under his breath. "He hates to be beaten—well, so do we all."

Pennington caught another fish and then Dick drew in his second. Warner did not have a bite since his first miss and his two comrades did not spare him. They insinuated that there were no fish in Vermont, and they doubted whether the state had any rivers either. In any event it was obvious that Warner had never fished before. For several minutes they carried on this conversation, the words, in a way, as they went back and forth, passing directly by his head. But Warner did not speak. He merely clenched his teeth more tightly and watched his floating cork. Meanwhile Dick caught his third fish and then Pennington equalled him. Now their taunts, veiled but little, became more numerous.

Warner never spoke, nor did he take his eyes from his cork. He had heard every word, but he would not show annoyance. He was compelled to see Dick draw in yet another fine fellow, while his own cork seemed to have all the qualities of a lifeboat. It danced and bobbed around, but apparently it had not the slightest intention of sinking. Why did he have such luck, or rather lack of it? Was fortune going to prove unkind to the good old rock-ribbed Green Mountain State?

There came a tremendous jerk upon the line! The cork shot down like a bullet, but Warner, making a mighty pull and snap with the rod, landed a glorious gleaming fish upon the bank, a full two feet in length, probably as large as any that had ever been caught in that stream. He detached the hook and looked down at his squirming prize, while Dick and Pennington also came running to see.

"I've been waiting for you, my friend," said Warner serenely to the fish. "Various small brothers of yours have come along and looked at my bait, but I've always moved it out of reach, leaving them to fall a prey to my friends who are content with little things. I had to wait for you some time, O King of Fishes, but you came at last and you are mine."

"You can't put him down, Dick, and it's not worth while trying," said Pennington, and Dick agreeing they went back to their own places.

The fishing now went on with uninterrupted success. Dick caught a big fellow too, and so did Pennington. Fortune, after wavering in her choice, decided to favour all three about equally, and they were content. The silvery heaps grew and they rejoiced over the splendid addition they would make to their mess. The colonels would enjoy this fine fresh food, and they were certainly enjoying the taking of it.

They ran out of chaff and fell into silence again, while they fished industriously. Dick, who was farthest up the stream, noticed a small piece of wood floating in the centre of the current. It seemed to have been cut freshly. "Loggers at work farther up," he said to himself. "May be cutting wood for the army."

He caught another fish and a fresh chip passed very near his line. Then came a second, and a third touched the line itself. Dick's curiosity was aroused. Loggers at such a time would not take the trouble to throw their chips into the stream. He lifted his line, caught an unusually large white chip on the hook and drew it to the land. When he picked it up and looked at it he whistled. Someone had cut upon its face with a sharp penknife these clear and distinct words:

Yankees Beware
This is our River Don't Fish in It These Fish are Ours.
JOHNNY REBS.

"Well, this is surely insolence," said Dick, and calling his comrades he showed them the chip. Both were interested, but Warner had admiration for its sender.

"It shows a due consideration for us," he said. "He merely warns us away as trespassers before shooting at us. And perhaps he's right. The river and the fish in it really belong to them. We're invaders. We came down here to crush rebellion, not to take away property."

"But I'm going to keep my fish, just the same," said Pennington. "You can't crush a rebellion without eating. Nor am I going to quit fishing either."

"Here comes another big white chip," said Dick.

Warner caught it on his hook and towed it in. It bore the inscription, freshly cut:

Let our river alone Take in your lines You're in danger, As you'll soon see.

It was unsigned and they stared at it in wonder.

"Do you think this is really a warning?" said Pennington, "or is it some of the fellows playing tricks on us?"

"I believe it's a warning," said Warner soberly. "Probably a farmer a little distance up the stream has been cutting wood, and these chips have come from his yard, but he didn't send them. Dick, can you tell handwriting when it's done with a knife?"

Dick looked at the chip long and critically.

"It may be imagination," he said, "but the words cut there bear some resemblance to the handwriting of Harry Kenton. He makes a peculiar L and a peculiar A and they're just the same way on this chip.

The writing is different on the other chip, but on this one I believe strongly that it's Harry's."

"It looks significant to me," said Warner thoughtfully. "A mile or two farther up, this stream, so I'm told, makes an elbow, and beyond that it comes with a rush out of the mountains. Its banks are lined with woods and thickets and some of the enemy may have slipped in and launched these chips. I've a sort of feeling, Dick, that it's really your cousin and his friends who have done it."

"I incline to that belief myself," said Dick. "You know they're ready to dare anything, and they don't anticipate any great danger, because we don't care to shoot at one another, until the campaign really begins."

"At least," said Warner, "it's best to apply to the problem a good algebraic formula. Here we are in a wood, some distance from our main camp. Messages, bearing a warning either in jest or in earnest, have come floating down from a point which may be within the enemy's country. One of the facts is x and the other is y, but what they amount to is an unknown quantity. Hence we are left in doubt, and when you're in doubt it's best to do the safe thing."

"Which means that we should go back to the camp," said Dick. "But we'll take our fish with us, that's sure."

They began to wind up their lines, but knowing that departure would be prudent they were yet reluctant to go in the face of a hidden danger, which after all might not be real.

"Suppose I climb this tree," said Pennington, indicating a tall elm, "and I may be able to get a good look over the country, while you fellows keep watch."

"Up you go, Frank," said Dick. "George and I will be on guard, pistols in one hand and fish in the other."

Pennington climbed the elm rapidly and then announced from the highest bough able to support him that he saw open country beyond, then more woods, a glimpse of the stream above the elbow, but no human being. He added that he would remain a few minutes in the tree and continue his survey of the country.

Dick's eyes had followed Frank's figure until it disappeared among the brown leaves, and he had listened to him carefully, while he was telling the result of his outlook, but his attention now turned back to the river. No more chips were floating down its stream. Nothing foreign appeared upon the clear surface of its waters, but Dick's sharp vision caught sight of something in a thicket on the far shore that made his heart beat.

It was but little he saw, merely the brown edge of an enormous flap-brimmed hat, but it was enough. Slade and his men undoubtedly were there—practically within the Union lines—and he was the danger! He called up the tree in a fierce sibilant whisper that carried amazingly far:

"Come down, Frank! Come down at once, for your life!"

It was a call so alarming and insistent that Pennington almost dropped from the tree. He was upon the ground, breathless, in a half minute, his fish in one hand and the pistol that he had snatched from his belt in the other.

"What is it?" exclaimed Warner, who had not yet seen anything.

"Slade and his men are in the bush on the other side of the river. The warning was real and I've no doubt Harry sent it. They've seen Frank come down the tree! Drop flat for your lives!"

Again his tone was so compelling that the other two threw themselves flat instantly, and Dick went down with them. They were barely in time. A dozen rifles flashed from the thickets beyond the stream, but all the bullets passed over their heads.

"Now we run for it!" exclaimed Dick, once more in that tone of compelling command. All three rose instantly, though not forgetting their fish and their fishing rods, and ran at their utmost speed for fifty or sixty yards, when at Dick's order they threw themselves flat again. Three or four more shots were fired from the thickets, but they did not come near their targets.

"Thank God for that little river in between us!" said Pennington, piously and sincerely. "Rivers certainly have their uses!"

Then they heard a sharp, shrill note blown upon a whistle.

"That's Slade recalling his men," said Dick. "I heard him use the same whistle in Mississippi and I know it. His wicked little scheme to slaughter us has failed and knowing it he prudently withdraws."

"For which, perhaps, we have a chip to thank," said Warner. "Shall we rise and run again?"

"Yes," said Dick. "I think they've gone, but fifty yards farther and nobody in those thickets can reach us."

They stooped as they ran, and they ran fast, but, when they dropped down again, it was behind a little hill, and they knew that all danger had passed. The thumping of their hearts ceased, and they looked thankfully at one another.

"Our lives were in danger," said Warner proudly, "but I didn't forget my fish. See, the silver beauties!"

"And here are mine too!" said Pennington, holding up his string.

"And mine also!" said Dick.

"I don't like the way we had to run," said Warner. "We were practically within our own lines and we were compelled to be undignified. I've been insulted by that flap-brimmed scoundrel, Slade, and I shall not forget it. If he hangs upon our flank in this campaign I shall make a point of it, if I am able, to present him with a bullet."

The sound of thudding hoofs came, and Colonel Winchester and a troop galloped up.

"We heard shots!" he exclaimed. "What was it?"

Dick held up his fish.

"We've been fishing, sir," he replied, "and as you can see, we've had success, but we were interrupted by the guerrilla Slade, whom I met in Mississippi, and his men. We got off, though, unhurt, and brought our fish with us."

Colonel Winchester's troop numbered more than a hundred men, and crossing the river they beat up the country thoroughly, but they saw no Confederate sign. When he came back Dick told him all the details of the episode, and Colonel Winchester agreed with him that Harry had sent the warning.

"You'd better keep it to yourself," he said. "It's too vague and mysterious to make a peg upon which to hang anything. Since we've cleared the bush of enemies we'll go eat the fish you and your friends have caught."

Sergeant Whitley cooked them, and, as Dick and a score of others sat around the fire and ate fish for supper, they were so exuberant and chaffed so much that he forgot for the time all about Slade.

CHAPTER 7

Sheridan's Attack

More days passed and the army of Sheridan lay waiting at the head of the valley, apparently without any aim in view. But Dick knew that if Little Phil delayed it was with good cause. As Colonel Winchester was high in the general's confidence Dick saw the commander every day. He soon learned that he was of an intensely energetic and active nature, and that he must put a powerful rein upon himself to hold back, when he had such a fine army to lead.

Many of the younger officers expressed impatience and Dick saw by the newspapers that the North too was chafing at the delay. Newspapers from the great cities, New York, Philadelphia and Boston, reached their camp and they always read them eagerly. Criticisms were levelled at Sheridan, and from the appearance of things they had warrant, but Dick had faith in their leader. Yet another period of depression had come in the North. The loss of life in Grant's campaign through the Wilderness had been tremendous, and now he seemed to be held indefinitely by Lee in the trenches before Petersburg. The Confederacy, after so many great battles, and such a prodigious roll of killed and wounded, was still a nut uncracked, and Sheridan, who was expected to go up the valley and turn the Southern flank, was resting quietly in his camp.

Such was the face of matters, but Dick knew that, beneath, great plans were in the making and that the armies would soon stir. The more he saw of Sheridan the more he was impressed by him. He might prove to be the Stonewall Jackson of the North. Young, eager, brave, he never fell into the fault some of the other Union commanders had of overestimating the enemy. He always had a cheery word for his young officers, and when he was not poring over the maps with his lieutenant of engineers, Meigs, he was inspecting his troops, and seeing that their equipment and discipline were carried to the highest pitch. He was the very essence of activity and the army, although not yet moving, felt at all times the tonic of his presence.

Cavalry detachments were sent out on a wider circle. Slade and his men had no opportunity to come so close again, but Shepard informed Dick that he was in the mountains hemming in the valley on the west, and that the statement of his having formed a junction with a band under Skelly from the Alleghenies was true. He had seen the big man and the little man together and they had several hundred followers.

Shepard in these days showed an almost superhuman activity. He would leave the camp, disguised as a civilian, and after covering a great distance and risking his life a dozen times he would return with precious information. A few hours of rest and he was gone again on a like errand. He seemed to be burning with an inward fire, not a fire that consumed him, but a fire of triumph. Dick, who had formed a great friendship with him and who saw him often, had never known him to speak more sanguine words. Always cautious and reserved in his opinions, he talked now of the certainty of victory. He told them that the South was not only failing in men, having none to fill up its shattered ranks, but that food also was failing. The time would come, with the steel belt of the Northern navy about it and the Northern armies pressing in on every side, when the South would face starvation.

But a day arrived when there were signs of impending movements in the great Northern camp. Long columns of wagons were made ready and orders were issued for the vanguard of cavalry to start at an appointed time. Then, to the intense disappointment of the valiant young troops, the orders were countermanded and the whole army settled back into its quarters. Dick, who persistently refused to be a grumbler, knew that a cause must exist for such an action, but before he could wonder about it long Colonel Winchester told him, Warner and Pennington to have their horses saddled, and be ready to ride at a moment's notice.

"We're to be a part of General Sheridan's escort," he said, "and we're to go to a little place called Charlestown."

The three were delighted. They were eager to move, and above all in the train of Sheridan. The mission must be of great importance or the commander himself would not ride upon it. Hence they saddled up in five minutes, hoping that the call would come in the next five.

"Did Colonel Winchester tell you why we were going to ride?" asked Warner of Dick.

"No."

"Then perhaps we're going to receive the surrender of Early and all his men."

Dick laughed.

"I've heard that old Jube Early is one of the hardest swearers in the Southern army," he said, "and I've heard, too, that he's just as hard a fighter. I don't think he'll be handing us his surrender on a silver platter at Charlestown or anywhere else."

"I know it," said Warner. "I was only joking, but I'm wondering why we go."

In ten minutes an orderly came with a message for them and they were in the saddle as quickly as if they intended to ride to a charge. Sheridan himself and his staff and escort were as swift as they, and the whole troop swept away with a thunder of hoofs and the blood leaping in their veins. It was now almost the middle of September, and the wind that blew down from the crest of the mountains had a cool breath. It fanned Dick's face and the great pulse in his throat leaped. He felt that this ride must portend some important movement. Sheridan would not gallop away from his main camp, except on a vital issue.

It was not a long distance to Charlestown, and when they arrived there they dismounted and waited. Dick saw Colonel Winchester's face express great expectancy and he must know why they waited, but the youth did not ask him any questions, although his own curiosity increased.

An hour passed, and then a short, thickset, bearded man, accompanied by a small staff, appeared. Dick drew a deep breath. It was General Grant, Commander-in-Chief of all the armies of the Union, and Sheridan hastened forward to meet him. Then the two, with several of the senior officers, went into a house, while the younger men remained outside, and on guard.

"I knew that we were waiting for somebody of importance," said Warner, "but I didn't dream that it was the biggest man we've got in the field."

"Didn't your algebra give you any hint of it?" asked Dick.

"No. An algebra reasons. It doesn't talk and waste its time in idle chatter."

The young officers with their horses walked back and forth a long time, while Grant and Sheridan talked. Dick, surprised that Grant had left the trenches before Petersburg and had come so far to meet his lieutenant, felt that the meeting must be momentous. But it was even more crowded with the beginnings of great events than he thought. Grant, as he wrote long afterward, had come prepared with a plan of campaign for Sheridan, but, as he wrote, "seeing that he was so clear and so positive in his views I said nothing about this and did not take it out of my pocket." It was a quality of Grant's greatness, like that of Lee, to listen to a lieutenant, and when he thought his plan was better than his own to adopt the lieutenant's and put his own away.

In that memorable interview, from which such stirring campaigns dated, Grant was impressed more and more by the earnestness and clearness of the famous Little Phil, and, when they parted, he gave him a free rein and an open road. Sheridan, when they rode away from the conference, was sober and thoughtful. He was to carry out his own plan, but the full weight of the responsibility would be his, and it was very great for a young man who was not much more than thirty.

But Dick and his comrades felt exultation, and did not try to hide it. Now that Grant himself had come to see Sheridan the army was bound to move. Pennington looked toward the South and waved his hand.

"You've been waiting for us a long time, old Jube," he said, "but we're coming. And you'll see and hear our resistless tread."

"But don't forget, Frank," said Warner soberly, "that we'll have a big bill of lives to pay. We don't ride unhurt over the Johnnies."

"Don't I know it?" said Pennington. "Haven't I been learning it every day for three years?"

Action was prompt as the young officers had hoped. The very next day after the meeting with his superior, Sheridan prepared to march, and the hopes of Dick and his friends rose very high. They did not know that daring Southern spies had learned of the meeting of Grant and Sheridan, and Early, judging that it portended a great movement against him, was already consolidating his forces and preparing to meet it. And Jubal Early was an able and valiant general.

Dick did not sleep that night. All had received orders to hold themselves in readiness for an instant march, and his blood tingled with expectancy. At midnight the Winchester regiment rode off to the left to join the cavalry under Wilson which was to lead the advance, moving along a pike road and then crossing the little river Opequan.

Dick rode close behind Colonel Winchester and Warner and Pennington were on either side of him. Not far away from them was Sergeant Whitley, ready for use as a scout. Shepard had disappeared already in the darkness. They joined Wilson's command and waited in silence. At three o'clock in the morning the word to advance was given and the whole division marched forward in the starlight.

They had not gone far before Shepard rode back telling them that the crossing of the Opequan was guarded by Confederate troops. The cavalry increased their speed. After the long period of inaction they were anxious to come to grips with their foe. Dick still rode knee to knee with Warner and Pennington, as they went on at a rapid pace in the starlight, the fields and strips of forest gliding past. Men on horseback talk less at night than in the day and moreover these had little to say. Their part was action, and they were waiting to see what the little Opequan would disclose to them.

"Do you think they'll have a big force at the river?" asked Pennington.

"No," replied Dick. "I fancy from what we've heard of Early's army that he won't have the men to spare."

"But we can look for a brush there," said Warner.

The night began to darken as a premonition of the coming dawn, a veil of vapour was drawn before the stars, trees blended together and the air became chill. Then the vapour was pierced in the east by a lance of light. The rift widened, and the pale light of the first dawn appeared over the hills. Dick, using his glasses, saw a flash which he knew was the Opequan. And with that silvery gleam of water came other flashes of red and rapid crackling reports. The Southern sharpshooters along the stream were already opening fire.

A great shout went up from the cavalry. All the forces restrained so long in these young men burst forth. The dawn was now deepening rapidly, its pallor turning to silver, and the river, for a long length, lay clear to view before them. Trumpets to right and left and in the centre sounded the charge, the mellow notes coming back in many echoes.

The horsemen firing their own carbines and swinging aloft their sabres, galloped forward in a mighty rush. The beat of hundreds of hoofs made a steady sound, insistent and threatening. The yellow light of the sun, replacing the silver of the first dawn, gilded them with gold, glittering on the upraised blades and tense faces. The bullets of the Southern sharpshooters, in the bushes and trees along the Opequan, crashed among them, and horses and men went down, but the mighty sweep of the mass was not delayed for an instant.

Dick was flourishing the cavalry sabre that he now carried and was shouting with the rest. Nearer and nearer came the belt of clear water, and the fire of the Southern skirmishers increased in volume and accuracy. No great Southern force was there, but the men were full of courage and activity. Their rifle fire emptied many of the Northern saddles. A bullet went through the sleeve of Dick's tunic and grazed the skin, but he only felt a slight burning touch and then soon forgot it.

Then the whole column started together, as they swept into the

Opequan, driving before them through sheer weight of mass the skirmishers and sharpshooters, who were hidden among the trees and thickets. The water itself proved but little obstacle. It was churned to foam by hundreds of trampling hoofs, and Dick felt it falling upon him like rain, but the drops were cool and refreshing.

Still at a gallop, they emerged from the river, wet and dripping, so much water had been dashed up by the beating hoofs, and charged straight on, driving the scattered Southern riflemen before them. Dick's exultation swelled, and so did that of Warner and Pennington. The young Nebraskan was compelled to give voice to his.

"Hurrah!" he shouted. "We'll gallop the whole length of the valley! Nothing can stop us!"

But Warner, naturally cautious, despite his rejoicings, would not go so far.

"Not the whole length of the valley, Frank!" he exclaimed. "Only half of it!"

"All or nothing!" shouted Pennington, carried away by his enthusiasm. "Hurrah! Hurrah!"

Before them now lay a small earthwork, from which field pieces began to send ugly gusts of fire, but so great was the sweep of the cavalry that they charged directly upon it. The defenders, too few to hold it, withdrew and retreated in haste, and in a few minutes the Northern cavalry were in possession.

"Didn't I tell you," exclaimed Pennington, "that we were going to gallop the whole length of the valley! We've taken a fort with horsemen!"

"Yes," said Warner, "but we'll stop here a while. Listen to the trumpets sounding the halt, and yonder you can see the main lines of the Johnnies."

It was obvious that it was unwise to go farther until the whole army came up, as they heard other trumpets calling now, and they were not their own but those of their enemies. Early had not been caught napping. The dark lines of his infantry were advancing to retake the little fort. The cavalry was reduced in an instant from the offensive to the defensive, and dismounting and sending their horses to the rear, where they were held by every tenth man, they waited with carbines ready, the masses of men in gray bearing down upon them. Dick wondered if the Invincibles were there before him. Second thought told him that it was unlikely, as the advancing troops were infantry, and he knew that the Invincibles were now mounted.

"Now, lads," said Colonel Winchester, going down the ranks, "ready with your rifles!"

The Southern infantry came on to the steady beating of a drum somewhere, but as they drew near the fort a sheet of bullets poured upon them, and drove them back, leaving the ground sprinkled with the fallen. Again and again they reformed and returned to the charge always to meet the same fate.

"Brave fellows!" exclaimed Warner, "but they can't retake this fort from us!"

After the last repulse Colonel Winchester drew out his men, mounted them, and charging the infantry in flank sent them far down the road toward Winchester, where heavy columns came to their support. But the Winchester men had time to breathe, and also to exult, as they had suffered but little loss. While they remained at the captured fort, awaiting further orders, they watched the battle elsewhere, flaring in a long irregular line across the valley.

The rifle fire was heavy and the big guns of Early were sweeping the roads with shell and grapeshot. As well as Dick could see through his glasses, the only success yet achieved was that of the cavalry at the fort. Sheridan himself had not yet appeared, and the hopes of the three sank a little. They had seen so many triumphs nearly achieved and then lost that they could believe in nothing until it was done.

But the morning was yet very young. While the east had long been full of light, the golden glow was just enveloping the west. The rifles crashed incessantly and the heavy thunder of the cannon gave the steady sound a deeper note. The fire of the defending Southern force made a red stream across the hills and fields.

"It's too early to have a battle," said Warner, looking at the sun, which was not yet far above the horizon.

"Too early for us or too early for the Johnnies?" said Pennington. "I think, Dick, I see those rebel friends of yours. Turn your glasses to the right, and look at that regiment of horses by the edge of the grove. I see at the head of it two men with longish hair. Apparently they are elderly, and they must be Colonel Talbot and Lieutenant Colonel St. Hilaire."

Dick turned his glasses eagerly and the officers of the Invincibles were at once recognizable to his more familiar eye. He could not mistake Colonel Leonidas Talbot and Lieutenant Colonel Hector St. Hilaire, both of whom were watching the progress of the battle through glasses, and he knew that the four young men who sat their horses just behind them were Harry, St. Clair, Dalton and Langdon.

As no further attack was made on the fort, and Colonel Winchester's troop remained stationary for the time, Dick kept his glasses bearing continually upon the Invincibles. The glasses were powerful and they told him much. He inferred from the manner in which the men were drawn up that they would charge soon. Near them a battery of four Confederate guns was planted on a hill, and it was firing rapidly and effectively, sending shell and shrapnel into advancing lines of blue infantry.

A singular feeling took hold of him, one of which he was not then conscious. He knew six of the officers who sat in the front of the Invincibles, and one of them was his own cousin, almost his brother. He did not know a soul in the blue columns advancing upon them, and his hopes and fears centred suddenly around that little group of six.

The wood was filled with Southern infantry, as it was now spouting flame, and the battery continued to thunder as fast as the men could reload and fire. The Invincibles who carried short rifles, much like the carbines of the North, raised them and pulled the triggers. Many in the blue column fell, but the others went on without faltering.

Dick knew from long experience what would follow, and he watched it alike with the eye and the mind that divines. Either his eye or his fancy saw the Invincibles lean forward a little, fasten their rifles, shake loose the reins with one hand, and drop the other hand to the hilt of the sabre. It was certain that in the next minute they would charge.

He saw a trumpeter raise a trumpet to his lips and blow, loud and shrill. Then the column of the Invincibles leaped forward, the necks of the horses outstretched, the men raising their sabres and flashing them above their heads. Dick drew deep breaths and his pulses beat painfully. Had he realized what his wishes were then he would have considered himself a traitor. In those swift moments his heart was with the Invincibles and not with the blue columns that stood up against them.

He saw the gray horsemen sweep forward into a cloud of fire and smoke, in which he caught the occasional flash of a sabre. The combat behind the veil lasted only a minute or two, though it seemed an hour to Dick, and then he saw the blue infantry reeling back, their advance checked by the charge of the Invincibles. A cheer rose in Dick's throat, but he checked it, and then, remembering, he trembled in a brief chill, as if shaken by the knowledge that for a few moments at least he had not been true to the cause for which he fought.

"A gallant charge those Johnnies made," said Warner, "and it's been effective, too. Our men are falling back, while the Johnnies are returning to their place near the wood."

Dick was straining his eyes through the glasses to see whether any one of the five whom he knew had fallen, but as the Invincibles returned from their victorious charge in a close mass it was impossible for him to tell. A number of saddles had been emptied, as riderless horses were galloping wildly over the plain. He sighed a little and replaced his glasses in their case.

"Here come more of our cavalry!" said Warner.

They heard the heavy beat of many hoofs and in an instant many horsemen swarmed about them. It was Sheridan himself who led them, his face flushed and eager and his eyes blazing. He was a little man, but he was electric in his energy, and his very presence seemed to communicate more spirit and fire to the troops. The officers crowded about him, and, while he swept the field with his glasses, he also gave a rapid command.

The Southern resistance, despite inferior numbers, was valiant and enduring. Their heavy guns were pouring a deadly fire upon the Northern centre. Beyond the taking of the fort by the cavalry the Army of the Shenandoah had made no progress, and the Southern troops were rapidly concentrating at every critical point. Old Jube Early, mighty swearer, was proving himself a master of men.

Dick could not watch Sheridan long, as the cavalry were quickly sent off to the left to clear away skirmishers, and let the infantry and artillery get up on that front. There were many groups of trees, and from every one of these the Southern riflemen sent swarms of bullets. It seemed to Dick that he was preserved miraculously. Many a bullet coming straight for his head must have turned aside at the last moment to seek a target elsewhere. To him at least these bullets were merciful that morning.

But they cleared the ground, though some of their own saddles were emptied, and the infantry and the artillery came up behind them. The big guns were planted and began to reply to those of the South. Yet the Confederate lines still held fast. Clouds of smoke floated over the field, but whenever they lifted sufficiently Dick saw the gray army maintaining all its positions. He looked for the Invincibles again but could not find them. Doubtless they were hid from his view by the hills.

"It's anybody's fight," said Warner, surveying the field with his cool, mathematical eye. "We have the greater numbers but our infantry are coming up slowly and, besides, the enemy has the advantage of interior lines."

"And the morning wanes," said Dick. "I thought we'd make a grand rush and sweep over 'em!"

"Oh, these Johnnies are tough. They have to be. There's not much marching over the other by either side in this war."

A heavy battle of cannon and rifles, with no advantage to either side, went on for a long time. Dick saw Sheridan galloping here and there, and urging on his troops, but the reserves were slow in coming and he was not yet able to hurl his full strength upon his enemy. Noon came, the battle already having lasted four or five hours, and Sheridan had no triumph to show, save the little fort that the cavalry had seized early in the morning.

"Do you think we'll have to draw off?" asked Pennington.

"Maybe we'll have to, but we won't," replied Dick. "Sheridan refuses to recognize necessities when they're not in his favour. You'll now see the difference between a man and men."

Colonel Winchester's regiment was sent off further to the left to prevent any flanking movement, but they could still see most of the field. For the moment they were not engaged, and they watched the thrilling and terrific panorama as it passed before them.

Colonel Winchester himself suddenly broke from his calm and pointed to the rear of the Union lines.

"Look!" he exclaimed. "All our reserves of artillery and infantry are coming up! The whole army will now advance!"

They saw very clearly the deepening of the lines in the centre. Sheridan was there massing the new troops for the attack, and soon the trumpets sounded the charge along the whole front. The Northern batteries redoubled their fire, and the South, knowing that a heavier shock of battle was coming, replied in kind.

"Here we go again!" cried Pennington, and the horsemen rode straight at their enemy. It seemed to Dick that the Southern regiments came forward to meet them and a battle long, fierce and wavering in its fortunes ensued. The wing to which the Winchesters belonged pressed forward, driving their enemy before them, only to be caught when they went too far by a savage flanking fire of artillery. Early had brought in his reserve guns, and so powerful was their attack that at this point the Northern line was almost severed, and a Southern wedge was driven into the gap.

But Sheridan did not despair. He had a keen eye and a collected mind, infused with a fiery spirit. Where his line had been weakened he sent new troops. With charge after charge he drove the Confederates out of the gap and closed it up. A whole division was then hurled with its full weight against the Southern line and broke it, although the gallant general who led the column fell shot through the heart.

But Early formed new lines. It was only a temporary success for Sheridan. An important division of cavalry sent on a wide flanking movement had not yet arrived, and he wondered why. Perhaps the thought came into his own dauntless heart that he might not succeed at all, but, if so, he hid it, and called up fresh resources of strength and courage. It was now far into the afternoon but he resolved nevertheless to win victory before the day was over. Everywhere the call for a new charge was sounded.

The Winchesters had a good trumpeter, a deep-chested young fellow who loved to blow forth mellow notes, and now as his brazen instrument sang the song that summoned men to death the young men unconsciously tightened the grip of the knee on their horses, and leaned a little forward, as if they would see the enemy more closely. To the right the fire grew heavier and heavier, and most of the field was hidden by a thick veil of smoke.

Dick saw other cavalry massing on either side of the Winchester regiment, and he knew their charge was to be one of great weight and importance.

"I feel that we're going to win or lose here," he said to Warner.

"Looks like it," replied the Vermonter, "but I think you can put your money on the cavalry today. It's Sheridan's great striking arm."

"It'll have to strike with all its might, that's sure," said Dick.

He did not know that the force in front of him was commanded by a general from his own state, Breckinridge, once Vice-President of the United States and also high in the councils of the Confederacy. Breckinridge was inspiring his command with the utmost vigour and already his heavy guns were sweeping the front of the Union cavalry, while the riflemen stood ready for the charge.

The great mass of Northern horsemen were eager and impatient. A thrill of anticipation seemed to run through them, as if through one body, and when the final command was given they swept forward in a mighty, irresistible line. In Dick's mind then anticipation became knowledge. He was as sure as he was of his own name that they were going to win.

Again he was knee to knee with Warner and Pennington, and with these good comrades on his right and left he rode into the Southern fire, among the shell and shrapnel and grapeshot and bullets that had swept so often around him. In spite of the most desperate courage, the Southern troops gave way before the terrific onset—they had to give ground or they would have been trampled under the feet of the horses. Cannon and many rifles were taken, and the whole Confederate division was driven in disorder down the road.

Warner's stern calm was broken, and he shouted in delight "We win! We win!" Then Dick and Pennington shouted with him: "We win! We win!" and as the smoke of their own battle lifted they saw that the Union army elsewhere was triumphant also. Sheridan along his whole line was forcing the enemy back toward Winchester, raking him with his heavy guns, and sending charge after charge of cavalry against him. Unable to withstand the weight hurled upon them the Southern troops gave ground at an increased rate.

Yet Early and his veterans never showed greater courage than on that day. His brave officers were everywhere, checking the fugitives and, his best division turning a front of steel to the enemy, covered the retreat. Neither infantry nor cavalry could break it, although every man in the Southern command knew that the battle was lost. Yet they were resolved that it should not become a rout, and though many were falling before the Union force they never shrank for a moment from their terrible task.

The Invincibles were in the division that covered the retreat, and they were exposed at all times to the full measure of the Union attack. Dalton had joined them that morning, but the bullets and shells seemed resolved to spare the four youths and the two colonels, or at least not to doom them to death. Nearly every one of them bore slight wounds, and often men had been killed only a few feet away, but the valiant band, led by its daring officers, fought with undimmed courage and resolution.

"I fear that we have been defeated, Hector," said Colonel Leonidas Talbot.

"Don't call it a defeat, Leonidas. It's merely a masterly retreat before superior numbers, after having inflicted great loss upon the enemy. As you see, we are protecting our withdrawal. Every attack of the enemy upon our division has been beaten back, and we will continue to beat him back as long as he comes."

"True, true, Hector, and the Invincibles are bearing a great part in this glorious feat of arms! But the Yankee general, Sheridan, is not like the other Yankee generals who operated in the valley earlier in the war. We're bound to admit that."

"We do admit it, Leonidas, and alas! we have now no Stonewall Jackson to meet him, brave and capable as General Early is!"

The two colonels looked at the setting sun, and hoped that it would go down with a rush. The division could not hold forever against the tremendous pressure upon it that never ceased, but darkness would put an end to the battle. The first gray of twilight was already showing on the eastern hills, and Early's men still held the broad turnpike leading into the South. Here, fighting with all the desperation of imminent need, they beat off every effort of the Northern cavalry to gain their ground, and when night came they still held it, withdrawing slowly and in good order, while Sheridan's men, exhausted by tremendous marches and heavy losses, were unable to pursue. Yet the North had gained a great and important victory.

* * * * * * * *

Darkness closed over a weary but exultant army. It had not destroyed the forces of Early, and it had been able to pursue only three miles. It had lost five thousand men in killed and wounded, but the results, nevertheless, were great and the soldiers knew it. The spell of Southern invincibility in the famous valley, where Jackson had won so often, was broken, and the star of Sheridan had flashed out with brilliancy, to last until the war's close. They knew, too, that they now held all of the valley north of Winchester, and they were soon to know that they would continue to hold it. They commanded also a great railway and a great canal, and the South was cut off from Maryland and Pennsylvania, neither of which it could ever invade again.

Although a far smaller battle than a dozen that had been fought, it was one of the greatest and most complete victories the North had yet won. After a long and seemingly endless deadlock a terrible blow had been struck at the flank of Lee, and the news of the triumph filled the North with joy. It was also given on this occasion to those who had fought in the battle itself to know what they had done. They were not blinded by the dust and shouting of the arena.

Dick with his two young comrades sat beneath an oak and ate the warm food and drank the hot coffee the camp cook brought to them. They had escaped without hurt, and they were very happy over the achievement of the day. The night was crisp, filled with starshine, and the cooking fires had been built along a long line, stretching away like a series of triumphant bonfires.

"I felt this morning that we would win," said Dick.

"I've felt several times that we would win, when we didn't," said Pennington.

"But this time I felt it right. They say that Stonewall Jackson always communicated electricity to his men, and I think our Little Phil has the same quality. Since we first came to him here I haven't doubted that we would win, and when I saw him and Grant talking I knew that we'd be up and doing."

"It's the spirit that Grant showed at Vicksburg," said Warner, seriously. "Little Phil—I intend to call him that when I'm not in his presence, because it's really a term of admiration—is another Grant, only younger and on horseback."

"It's fire that does it," said Dick. "No, Frank, I don't mean this material fire burning before us, but the fire that makes him see obstacles little, and advantages big, the fire that makes him rush over everything to get at the enemy and destroy him."

"Well spoken, Dick," said Warner. "A bit rhetorical, perhaps, but that can be attributed to your youth and the region from which you come."

"It's a great pity, George, about my youth and the region from which I come. If so many youths in blue didn't come from that same region the whole Mississippi Valley might now be in the hands of the Johnnies."

"Didn't I tell you, Dick, not to argue with him?" said Pennington. "What's the use? New England has the writers and when this war is ended victoriously they'll give the credit of all the fighting to New England. And after a while, through the printed word, they'll make other people believe it, too."

"Then you Nebraskans and Kentuckians should learn to read and write. Why blame me?" said Warner with dignity.

Colonel Winchester joined them at that moment, having returned from a brief council with Sheridan and his officers. Dick, without a word, passed him a plate of hot ham and a tin cup of sizzling coffee. The colonel, who looked worn to the bone but triumphant, ate and drank. Then he settled himself into an easy place before one of the fires and said:

"A messenger has gone to General Grant with the news of our victory, and it will certainly be a most welcome message. The news will also be sent to the nearest telegraph station, and then it will travel on hundreds of wires to every part of the North, but while it's flashing through space we'll be riding forward to new battle."

"I expected it, sir," said Dick. "I suppose we advance again at dawn."

"And maybe a little sooner. Now you boys must rest. You've had eighteen hours of marching and fighting. I've been very proud of my regiment today, and fortunately we have escaped without large losses."

"And you sleep, too, sir, do you not?" said Warner, respectfully. "If we've been marching and fighting for eighteen hours so have you."

"I shall do so a little later, but that's no reason why the rest of you should delay. How that coffee and ham refreshed me! I didn't know I was so nearly dead."

"Here's more, Colonel!"

"Thank you, Dick. I believe I will. But as I say, go to sleep. I want all my regiment to sleep. We don't know what is before us tomorrow, but whatever it is it won't be easy. Now you boys have had enough to eat and drink. Into the blankets with you!"

He did not wait to see his order obeyed, but strode away on another hasty errand. But it was obeyed and that, too, without delay. The young warriors rolled themselves in their blankets and hunted a soft place for their heads. But their nerves were not yet quiet, and sleep did not come for a little while. The long lines of fires still glowed, and the sounds of an army came to them. Dick looked up into the starshine. He was still rejoicing in the victory, not because the other side had lost, but because, in his opinion, it brought peace much nearer. He realized as he lay there gazing into the skies that the South could never win as long as the North held fast. And the North was holding fast. The stars as they winked at him seemed to say so.

He propped himself upon his elbow and said:

"George, does your little algebra tell you anything about the meaning of this victory?"

Warner tapped his breast.

"That noble book is here in the inside pocket of my tunic," he replied. "It's not necessary for me to take it out, but tucked away on the 118th page is a neat little problem which just fits this case. Let x equal the Army of Northern Virginia, let y equal the army of Early here in the valley, and let x plus y equal a possibly successful defence by the South. But when y is swept away it's quite certain that x standing alone cannot do so. My algebra tells you on the 118th page, tucked away neatly in a paragraph, that this is the beginning of the end."

"It sounds more like a formula than a problem, George, but still I'm putting my faith in your little algebra book."

"George's algebra is all right," said Pennington, "but it doesn't always go before, it often comes after. It doesn't show us how to do a thing, but proves how we've done it. As for me, I'm pinning my faith to Little Phil. He won a great victory today, when all our other leaders for years have been beaten in the Valley of Virginia, and sometimes beaten disgracefully too."

"Your argument is unanswerable, Frank," said Dick. "I didn't expect such logic from you."

"Oh, I think I'm real bright at times."

"Despite popular belief," said Warner.

"I don't advertise my talents," said Pennington.

"But you ought to. They need it."

Dick laughed.

"Frank," he said, "I give you your own advice to me. Don't argue with him. With him the best proof that he's always right is because he thinks he is."

"I think clearly and directly, which can be said of very few of my friends," rejoined Warner.

Then all three of them laughed and lay down again, resting their heads on soft lumps of turf.

They were under the boughs of a fine oak, on which the leaves were yet thick. Birds, hidden among the leaves, began to sing, and the three, astonished, raised themselves up again. It was a chorus, beautiful and startling, and many other soldiers listened to the sound, so unlike that which they had been hearing all day.

"Strange, isn't it?" said Pennington.

"But fine to hear," said Warner.

"Likely they were in the tree this morning when the battle began," said Dick, "and the cannon and the rifles frightened 'em so much that they stayed close within the leaves. Now they're singing with joy, because it's all over."

"A good guess, I think, Dick," said Warner, "but isn't it beautiful at such a time and such a place? How these little fellows must be swelling their throats! I don't believe they ever sang so well before."

"I didn't think today that I'd be sung to sleep tonight," said Dick, "but it's going to happen."

When his eyes closed and he floated away to slumberland it was to the thrilling song of a bird on a bough above his head.

CHAPTER 8

The Messenger from Richmond

It seemed that Dick and his comrades were to see an activity in the valley under Sheridan much like that which Harry and his friends had experienced under Stonewall Jackson earlier in the war. All of the men before they went to sleep that night had felt confirmed in the belief that a strong hand was over them, and that a powerful and clear mind was directing them. There would be no more prodigal waste of men and supplies. No more would a Southern general have an opportunity to beat scattered forces in detail. The Union had given Sheridan a splendid army and a splendid equipment, and he would make the most of both.

Their belief in Sheridan's activity and energy was justified fully, perhaps to their own discomfort, as the trumpets sounded before dawn, and they ate a hasty breakfast, while the valley was yet dark. Then they were ordered to saddle and ride at once.

"What, so early?" exclaimed Pennington. "Why, it's not daylight yet. Isn't this new general of ours overdoing it?"

"We wanted a general who would lead," said Warner, "and we've got him."

"But a battle a day! Isn't that too large an allowance?"

"No. We've a certain number of battles to fight, and the sooner we fight them the sooner the war will be over."

"Here comes the dawn," said Dick, "and the bugles are singing to us to march. It's the cavalry that are to show the way."

The long line of horsemen rode on southward, leaving behind them Winchester, the little city that had been beloved of Jackson, and approached the Massanuttons, the bold range that for a while divided the valley into two parts. The valley was twenty miles wide before they came to the Massanuttons, but after the division the western extension for some distance was not more than four miles across, and it was here that they were going. At the narrower part, on Fisher's Hill, Early had strong fortifications, defended by his finest infantry, and Colonel Winchester did not deem it likely that Sheridan would make a frontal attack upon a position so well defended.

It was about noon when the cavalry arrived before the Southern works. Dick, through his glasses, clearly saw the guns and columns of infantry, and also a body of Southern horse, drawn up on one flank of the hill. He fancied that the Invincibles were among them, but at the distance he could not pick them from the rest.

The regiment remained stationary, awaiting the orders of Sheridan, and Dick still used his glasses. He swept them again and again across the Confederate lines, and then he turned his attention to the mountains which here hemmed in the valley to such a straitened width. He saw a signal station of the enemy on a culminating ridge called Three Top Mountain, and as the flags there were waving industriously he knew that every movement of the Union army would be communicated to Early's troops below.

Yet the whole scene despite the fact that it was war, red war, appealed to Dick's sense of the romantic and beautiful. The fertile valley looked picturesque with its woods and fields, and on either side rose the ranges as if to protect it. Mountains like trees always appealed to him, and the steep slopes were wooded densely. Lower down they were brown, with touches of green that yet lingered, but higher up the glowing reds and golds of autumn were beginning to appear. The wind that blew down from the crests was full of life.

Sheridan arrived and, riding before the centre of his army, looked long and well at the Southern defences. Then he called his generals, and some of the colonels, including Winchester, and held a brief council.

"It means," said Warner, while the colonel was yet away at the meeting, "that we won't fight any this afternoon, but that we'll do a lot of riding tonight. That position is too strong to be attacked. It would cost us too many men to take it straight away, but having seen a specimen of Little Phil's quality we know that he'll try something else."

"You mean get on their flank," said Dick. "Maybe we can make a passage along the slopes of the mountains."

"As the idea has occurred to me I take it that it will occur to Little Phil also," said Warner.

"Are you sure that he hasn't thought of it first?"

"My politeness forbids an answer. I am but a lieutenant and he is our commander."

The rest of the day was spent in massing the troops across the valley, the Winchester regiment being sent further west until it was against the base of the Massanuttons. Here Shepard came in the twilight and conferred with Colonel Winchester, who called Dick.

"Dick," he said, "Mr. Shepard thinks he can obtain information of value on the mountain. He has an idea that some fighting may occur, and so it's better for a small detachment to go with him. I've selected you to lead the party, because you're at home in the woods."

"May I take Lieutenant Warner and Lieutenant Pennington with me? It would hurt their feelings to be left behind."

"Yes. Under no circumstances must the feelings of those two young men be hurt," laughed Colonel Winchester.

"And Sergeant Whitley, too? He's probably the best scout in our army. He can follow a trail where there is no trail. He can see in the pitchy dark, and he can hear the leaves falling."

"High recommendations, but they're almost true. Take the sergeant by all means. I fancy you'll need him."

The whole party numbered about a dozen, and Shepard was the guide. It was dismounted, of course, as the first slope they intended to carry was too steep for a horse to climb. They were also heavily armed, it being absolutely certain that Southern riflemen were on Massanutton Mountain.

Dick and Shepard were in the lead, and, climbing up at a sharp angle, they quickly disappeared from the view of those below. It was as if night and the wilderness had blotted them out, but every member of the little party felt relief and actual pleasure in the expedition. Something mysterious and unknown lay before them, and they were anxious to find out what it was.

Shepard whispered to Dick of the care that they must take against their foes, and Warner whispered to Pennington that the mountain was really fine, although finer ridges could be found in Vermont.

Two hundred yards up, and Shepard, touching Dick's shoulder, pointed to the valley. The whole party stopped and looked back. Although themselves buried in brown foliage they saw the floor of the valley all the way to the mountains on the other side, and it was a wonderful sight, with its two opposing lines of camp fires that shot up redly and glowed across the fields. Now and then they saw figures of men moving against a crimson background, but no sound of the armies came to them. Peace and silence were yet supreme on the mountain.

"It makes you feel that you're not only above it in the body, but that you are not a part of it at all," said Shepard.

Dick was not surprised at his words. He had learned long since that the spy was an uncommon man, much above most of those who followed his calling.

"It gives me a similar feeling of detachment," he said, "but we know just the same that they're going to fight again tomorrow, and that we'll probably be in the thick of it. I hope, Mr. Shepard, that our victory yesterday marks the beginning of the end."

"I think it does, Mr. Mason. If we clean up the valley, and we'll do it, Lee's flank and Richmond will be exposed. He'll have to come out of his trenches then, and that will give Grant a chance to attack him with an overwhelming force. The Confederacy is as good as finished, but I've never doubted the result for a moment."

"I've worried a little at times. It seemed to me now and then that all those big defeats in Virginia might make our people too weary to go on. Why is that light flaring so high on Fisher's Hill?"

"It may be a signal. Possibly the Southerners are replying to it with another fiery signal on this mountain. We can't see the crest of Massanutton from this slope."

"You seem to know every inch of the ground in this region. How did you manage to learn it so thoroughly?"

"I was born in the valley not far from here. I've climbed over Massanutton many a time. Not far above us is a grove of splendid nut trees, and along the edge of it runs a ravine. I mean to lead the way up the ravine, Mr. Mason. It will give us shelter from the scouts and spies of the enemy."

"Shelter is what we want. I've no taste for being shot obscurely here on the side of the mountain."

"Then keep close behind me, all of you," said Shepard. "We're above the steepest part now, and I know a little path that leads to the ravine. Don't stumble if you can help it."

The path was nothing more than a trace, but it sufficed to give them a surer footing, and in eight or ten minutes they reached the ravine which ran in a diagonal line across the face of the mountain, gradually ascending to the summit. The ravine itself was not more than three or four feet deep, but as its banks were thickly lined with dwarfed cedar they were completely hidden unless they should chance to meet the Southern riflemen, coming down the mountain by the same way.

The ravine at one point led out on a bare shoulder of the slope, and looking over the little pines they clearly saw a fire blazing on the crest and waving flags silhouetted before its glow. Far below, at Fisher's Hill, flags were waving also.

"Quite a lively talk," whispered Shepard. "I suppose the lookouts are telling a lot about our army."

"But it won't make much difference," said Dick. "By the time they've spelled out from the flags what Sheridan is doing he'll be doing something else."

They resumed their climb and the ravine led again into dense forest. Sergeant Whitley had moved up by the side of Shepard, as they were now near the enemy, and his great scouting abilities were needed. It was a wise precaution, as presently he held up his hand, and then, at a signal from him, the whole party climbed softly out of the ravine, and crouched among the little cedars.

Now Dick himself heard what the sergeant had heard perhaps a half minute earlier, that is, the footsteps of two men coming swiftly down the ravine. In another minute they came in sight, Confederate troopers, obviously scouting. Luckily, the ravine being stony and the light bad, they did not see any trail, left by Shepard's troop, and they went on down the ravine.

"Shall we go on?" asked Dick.

"Not yet, sir," replied Shepard. "They don't suspect that we're up here, and it's likely they're trying for a good view of our army. But I fancy they'll be returning in a few minutes. We'd best be very quiet, sir."

Dick cautioned the men, and they lay as still as wild animals in their coverts. In about ten minutes the two riflemen came back up the ravine, and the hidden troopers could hear them talking.

"We'll try some other part of the slope, Jack," said one.

"Yes, that was a bad view," rejoined the other. "We couldn't tell a thing about the Yankee movements from down there. We can leave the ravine higher up, and I know a path that leads toward the north."

"There's not much good in finding out about 'em anyway. That fellow Sheridan is going to press us hard, and they have everything, numbers, arms, food, while we have next to nothing."

"But we'll fight 'em anyhow. Still, I wish old Stonewall was here."

"But he ain't here, and we'll have to do the best we can without him."

Their voices were lost, as they passed up the ravine and disappeared. Then Dick and his little party came out cautiously, and followed.

"I gather from what those two said that Early's men are depressed," said Dick.

"They've a right to be," replied Shepard. "Their army is in bad shape, besides being small, and now that we have a real leader we are, I think, sure to clean up the valley."

"But there'll be plenty of hard fighting."

"Yes. We'll have to win what we get."

The ravine widened and deepened a little, and they stopped. Sergeant Whitley in his capacity of chief scout and trailer climbed up the rocky side and looked about a little, while the others waited. He returned in two or three minutes, and Dick saw, by the moonlight, that his face expressed surprise.

"What is it, sergeant?" asked Dick.

"A woman is on the mountain. She passed by the ravine not long since, perhaps not a half hour ago."

"A woman at such a time? Why, sergeant, it's impossible!"

"No, sir, it isn't. See here!"

He opened his left hand. Within the palm lay a tiny bit of thin gray cloth.

"There may not be more than a dozen threads here," he said, "but I found 'em sticking to a thorn bush not twenty yards away. A half hour ago they were a part of a woman's dress. A thorn bush grows among the cedars above. She was in a hurry, and when her dress caught in it she jerked it loose."

"But how do you know it was only a half hour or less ago?" asked Dick.

"Because she broke two 'or three of the thorns when she jerked, and it was so late that their wounds are still bleeding, that is, a faint bit of sap is oozing out at the fractures."

"That sounds conclusive," said Dick, "but likely it was a mountain woman who lives somewhere along the slope."

The sergeant shook his head.

"No, sir, it was no mountain woman," he said. "When I found the cloth on the thorns I knelt and looked for a trail. It's hard ground mostly, but I thought I might find the trace of a footstep somewhere. I found several, and not one of them was made by the flat, broad shoe that mountain women wear. I found small rounded heel prints which the shoes worn by city women make."

"If any city woman is on this mountain she's a long way from home," said Warner.

"But I'm quite sure of what I say, sir," said the sergeant.

"And so am I," said Shepard, who had been listening with the keenest attention. "Will you mind letting me lead the way for a little while, sir?"

"Go ahead, of course," said Dick. "In such work as this we rely upon the sergeant and you."

"Then I'd like to take a look at those heel prints also."

Dick thought he detected a quiver of excitement or emotion in the voice of Shepard, always so calm and steady hitherto, and he wondered. Nevertheless he asked no questions as he led the way out of the ravine.

The sergeant showed the heel prints to Shepard, and beyond question they had been made by a woman. By careful scrutiny they found a half dozen more leading in a diagonal direction up the side of the mountain, but beyond that the ground was so hard and rocky that they could discover no further traces.

"You agree with me that the tracks have just been made?" said the sergeant to Shepard.

"I do," replied the spy, his voice showing growing excitement, "and I think I know who made them. I didn't believe it at first. It seemed incredible. I want to try a little experiment. Will all of you remain perfectly still?"

"Of course," said Dick.

He took a small whistle from his pocket and blew upon it. The sound was not shrill like that of Slade's whistle, but was very low, soft and musical. He blew only a few notes. Then he took the whistle from his lips and waited. Dick saw that his excitement was growing. It showed clearly in the spy's eyes, and he felt his own excitement increasing, too. He divined that something extraordinary was going to happen.

Out of the cedars to their right and a little higher up the slope came the notes of a whistle, exactly similar, low, soft and musical.

"Ah, I knew it!" breathed Shepard. He waited perhaps half a minute and then blew again, notes similar and just the same in number. In a few moments came the reply, a precise duplicate.

"We'll wait," said Shepard. "She'll be here in a minute or two."

Dick and his comrades looked eagerly toward the point from which the sound of the second whistle had come. This was something amazing, something beyond their experience, but the excitement of Shepard seemed to have passed. His face had become a mask once more, and he was waiting with certainty.

Dick's sharp ear caught the sound of a light footstep approaching them, evidently coming straight and with confidence. He realized that until now he had not really believed, despite the footprints, despite everything, that a woman was on the mountain. But he knew at last. He even heard the swish of her skirts once or twice against the bushes. Then she came through the dwarfed cedars, stepping boldly, and stood before them.

The stranger stood full in the moonlight, and Dick saw her very clearly. She was thin, small and elderly, clothed in a gray riding suit, and with a sort of small gray turban on her head. But despite her smallness and thinness and years there was nothing insignificant in her appearance. As she stood there looking at them, she showed a pair of the brightest and most intelligent eyes that Dick had ever seen. Her small, pointed chin had the firmness of steel, and figure, manner and appearance alike betokened courage and resolution in the highest degree.

All these impressions were made upon Dick in a single instant, as if in a flash of light, and he also noticed in her face a resemblance to some one, although he could not recall, for a moment, who it was. But the silence that endured for a half minute, while the men regarded the woman and the woman regarded the men, was broken by Shepard, who uttered a low cry and strode forward.

"Henrietta," he exclaimed, "you here at such a time!"

He put his arms around her and kissed her.

She returned his kiss, laughed a little, and the two turned toward the others. Then Dick saw whom she resembled. As they stood side by side the likeness was marked, the same eyes, the same nose, the same mouth, the same chin, only hers were in miniature, in comparison with his, and in addition she was eight or ten years older.

"Mr. Mason," said Shepard, addressing himself directly to their nominal leader. "This is my sister. She also serves as I do, and for her, hardships and dangers are not less than mine for me. She works chiefly in Richmond itself. But as you see, she has now come alone into the mountains, and also into the very fringe of the armies."

"Then," said Dick, "she must come on a mission of great importance and it is for us to honour so brave a messenger."

He and all the others took off their caps in silence. They might have cheered, but every one knew that the foe was not far away in the thickets. There was sufficient light for him to see a little flush of pride appear for a moment on the face of the woman. Strange as her position was, she seemed easy and confident, lightly swinging in her hand a small riding whip.

"I'll not ask you for the present, Henrietta, how you come to be here," said Shepard, "but I'll ask instead what you've brought. These young men are Lieutenant Mason, Lieutenant Warner and Lieutenant Pennington. As I've indicated already, Lieutenant Mason leads us."

"I bring information," she replied, "information that you will be glad to carry to General Sheridan. As a woman I could go where men could not, and you remember, Brother William, that I know the country."

"Almost as well as I do," said Shepard. "As a girl you rode like a man and were afraid of nothing. Nor do you fear anything today."

"Tell General Sheridan," she said, turning to Dick, "that the Confederate numbers are even less than he thinks, that a large area at the base of Little North Mountain is wholly unoccupied."

"And if we get there," exclaimed Dick, eagerly, "we can crash in on the flank of Early."

"I'm not a soldier," she said, "but that plan was in my mind. A large division could be hidden in the heavy timber along Cedar Creek, and then, if the proper secrecy were observed, reach the Confederate flank tomorrow night, unseen."

"And that's on the other side of the valley," said Dick.

"But at this point it's only four or five miles across."

"I wasn't making difficulties, I was merely locating the places as you tell them."

"I've drawn a map of the Confederate position. It's in pencil, but it ought to help."

"It will be beyond price!" exclaimed Dick. "You will give it to me?"

"Of course! But you must wait a minute! Until I heard my brother's whistle I didn't know whether it was North or South that I was going to meet on the mountain."

She disappeared in the bushes, and Dick heard a light rustling, but in a few moments she returned and held out a broad sheet of heavy paper, upon which a map had been drawn with care and skill. He had divined already its great value, and now his opinion was confirmed.

"I can't thank you," he said, as he took it, "but General Sheridan and General Grant can. And I've no doubt they'll do it when the time comes."

Again the light flush appeared in her cheeks and she looked actually handsome.

"Since my present task is finished," she said, "I'd better go."

"Where did you leave your horse?" asked Shepard.

"He's tethered in the bushes about a hundred yards farther down the side of the mountain. I'll mount and ride back in the direction of Richmond. I know all the roads."

Sergeant Whitley, who had gone a little higher up and who was watching while they talked, whistled softly. Yet the whistle, low as it was, was undoubtedly a signal of alarm.

"Go at once, Henrietta," whispered Shepard, urgently. "It's important that you shouldn't be held here, that you be left with a free hand."

"It's so," she said.

He stooped and kissed her on the brow, and, without another word, she vanished among the cedars on the lower slope. Dick thought he heard a moment later the distant beat of hoofs and he felt sure she was riding fast and far. Then he turned his attention to the danger confronting them, because a danger it certainly was, and that, too, of the most formidable kind. But, first, he gave the map to Shepard to carry.

Sergeant Whitley came down the slope and joined them.

"I think we'd better lie down, all of us," he said.

Now the real leadership passed to the sergeant, scout, trailer and skilled Indian fighter. It passed to him, because all of them knew that the conditions made him most fit for the place. They knelt or lay but held their weapons ready. The sergeant knelt by Dick's side and the youth saw that he was tense and expectant.

"Is it a band of the Johnnies?" he whispered.

"I merely heard 'em. I didn't see 'em," replied the sergeant, "but I'm thinkin' from the way they come creepin' through the woods that it's Slade and his gang."

"If that's so we'd better look out. Those fellows are woodsmen and they'll be sure to see signs that we're here."

"Right you are, Mr. Mason. It's well the lady left so soon, and that we're between them and her."

"It looks as if this fellow Slade had set out to be our evil genius. We're always meeting him."

"Yes, sir, but we can take care of him. I don't specially mind this kind of fighting, Mr. Mason. We had to do a lot of it in the heavy timber on the slopes of some of them mountains out West, the names of which I don't know, and generally we had to go up against the Sioux and Northern Cheyennes, and them two tribes are king fighters, I can tell you. Man for man they're a match for anybody."

"Slade's men don't appear to be moving," said Shepard, who was on the other side of the sergeant.

"Not so's you could hear 'em," said Sergeant Whitley. "They heard us and they're creeping now so's to see what we are and then fall on us by surprise. Guess them that's kneeling had better bend down a little lower."

Warner, who had been crouched on his knees, lay down almost flat. He did not understand forests and darkness as Dick did, nor did he have the strong hereditary familiarity with them, and he felt uncomfortable and apprehensive.

"I don't like it," he said to Pennington. "I'd rather fight in the open."

"So would I," said Pennington. "It's awful to lie here and feel yourself being surrounded by dangers you can't see. I guess a man in the African wilderness stalked at night by a dozen hungry lions would feel just about as I do."

"I'm going to creep a little distance up the slope again," said the sergeant, "and try to spy 'em out."

"A good idea, but be very careful."

"I certainly will, Mr. Mason. I want to live."

He slid among the bushes so quietly that Dick did not hear the noise of him passing, nor was there any sound until he came back a few minutes later.

"I saw 'em," he whispered. "They're lying among the bushes, and they're not moving now, 'cause they're not certain what's become of us. It's Slade sure. I saw him sitting under a tree, wearing that big flap-brimmed hat, and sitting beside him was a great, black-haired, red-faced man, a most evil-looking fellow, too."

"Skelly! Bill Skelly, beyond a doubt!" said Dick.

"That's him! From what you said Skelly started out by being for the Union. Now, as we believed before, he's joined hands with Slade who's for the South."

"They're just guerrillas, sergeant. They're for themselves and no-body else."

"I reckon that's true, and they're expecting to get some plunder from us. But if you'll listen to me, Mr. Mason, we'll burn their faces while they're about it."

"You're our leader now, sergeant. Tell us what to do."

"Just to our right is a shallow gully, running through the cedars. We can take shelter in it, crawl up it, and open fire on 'em. They don't know our numbers, and if we take 'em by surprise maybe we can scatter 'em for the time."

"I suppose we'll have to. I'd like to get away with this map at once, but they'd certainly follow and force us to a fight."

"That's true. We must deal with 'em, now. I'll have to ask all of you to be very careful. Don't slip, and look out for the dead wood lying about. If a piece of it cracks under you Slade and Skelly will be sure to notice it, and it'll be all up with our surprise."

"You hear," whispered Dick to the others. "If you don't do as the sergeant says, very likely you'll get shot by Slade's men."

With life as the price it was not necessary to say anything more about the need of silence, and nobody slipped and no stick broke as they crept into the gully after the sergeant. The cedars and thickets almost met over the narrow depression, shutting out the moonlight, but every one was able to discern the man before him creeping forward like a wild animal. It was easy enough for Dick to imagine himself that famous great grandfather of his, Paul Cotter reincarnated, and that the days of the wilderness and the Indian war bands had come back again. He even felt exultation as he adapted himself so readily to the situation, and became equal to it. But Warner was grieved and exasperated. It hurt his dignity to prowl on his knees through the dark.

They advanced about two hundred yards in a diagonal course along the side of the mountain until they came to a point where the cedars thinned out a little. Then the sergeant whispered to the others to stop, rose from his knees, and Dick rose beside him.

"See!" he said, nodding his head in the direction in which he wished Dick to look.

Dick saw a number of dark figures standing among the trees. Two were in close conference, evidently trying to decide upon a plan. One, a giant in size, was Skelly, and the other, little, wizened and wearing an enormous flap-brimmed hat, could be none but Slade.

"A pretty pair," said Dick, "but I don't like to fire on 'em from ambush."

"Nor do I," said the sergeant, "but we've got to do it, or we won't get the surprise we need so bad."

But they were saved from firing the first shot as some one in the gully—they never knew or asked his name—stumbled at last. Slade and Skelly instantly sprang for the trees and Slade blew sharply upon his whistle. Twenty shots were fired in the direction of the gully, but they whistled harmlessly over the heads of its occupants.

It was Dick who gave the command for the return volley, and with a mighty shouting they swept the woods with their breech-loading rifles. They were not sure whether they hit anything, but as the gully blazed with fire they presented all the appearance of a formidable force that might soon charge.

"Cease firing!" said Dick, presently.

A cloud of smoke rose from the gully, and, as it lifted, they could see nothing in the woods beyond, but the sergeant announced that for an instant or two he heard the sound of running feet.

"It means they've gone," said Dick, "and that being the case we'll be off, too. I fancy we've a great prize in this map. Your sister, Mr. Shepard, must be a woman of extraordinary daring and ability."

"She's all that," replied the spy earnestly. "I think sometimes that God gave to me the size and physical strength of the family, but to her the mind. Think of her life there in Richmond, surrounded by dangers! She has done great service to our cause tonight, and she has done other services, equally as great, before."

Shepard was silent for a little while and then he began to chuckle to himself, almost under his breath, but Dick heard.

"What is it?" he asked.

"I was thinking of my sister," Shepard replied. "Your cousin, Harry Kenton, if you should ever meet him again—and I know that you will—could tell you a story of a dark night in Richmond, or at least a part of it, and he could also tell an interesting story, or a part of it, of another map, almost as valuable as this, which disappeared mysteriously from the house of a rich man in Richmond where he and other Southern officers were being entertained. It vanished almost from under their hands."

"Tell me now," said Dick, feeling great curiosity.

"I think I'd better wait, if you'll pardon me, sir," said Shepard.

"I'll have to wait anyhow," said Dick, "because I hear the tread of men coming toward us."

"But they're our own," said Sergeant Whitley, who was a little ahead, peering between the cedars.

"I suppose they heard the shots and are hurrying to our relief," said Dick. "But we routed the enemy, we did not lose a man, and we've brought away the prize."

The two forces joined and they were shortly back with Colonel Winchester, who fully appreciated the great value of the information obtained by such a remarkable coordination of effort.

"Dick," he said, "you and Mr. Shepard shall ride at once with me and this map to General Sheridan."

CHAPTER 9

At Grips With Early

Dick felt great excitement and elation as he rode before dawn with Colonel Winchester and the spy to see Sheridan. They found him sitting by a small fire receiving or sending reports, and talking with a half-dozen of his generals. It was not yet day, but the flames lighted up the commander's thin, eager face, and made him look more boyish than ever.

Dick felt as he had felt before that he was in the presence of a man. He had had the same impression when he stood near Grant and Thomas. Did strong men send off electric currents of will and power which were communicated to other men, by which they could know them, or was it the effect of deeds achieved? He could not decide the question for himself, but he knew that he believed implicitly in their leader.

Colonel Winchester paused near Sheridan, but the general's keen eye caught him at once.

"Good morning, Colonel Winchester!" he exclaimed. "You bring news of value. I can tell it by your face!"

"I do, sir," replied the colonel, "but it was Mr. Shepard here, whom you know, and Lieutenant Mason who obtained it. Mr. Shepard, show General Sheridan the map."

It was characteristic of Colonel Winchester, a man of the finest feelings, that he should have Shepard instead of himself carry the map to General Sheridan. He wanted the spy to have the full measure of credit, including the outward show, for the triumph he had achieved with the aid of his sister. And Shepard's swift glance of thanks showed that he appreciated it. He drew the map from his pocket and handed it to the general.

Sheridan held it down, where the full glow of the flames fell upon it, and he seemed to comprehend at once the meaning of the lines. A great light sprang up in his eyes.

"Ah!" he exclaimed. "The location of the Confederate forces and the openings between them and the mountains! This is important! Splendid! Did you make it yourself, Mr. Shepard?"

"No, sir. It was made by my sister who came from Richmond. We met her on the mountain."

Sheridan looked at Shepard and the eyes of general and spy met in complete understanding.

"I know of her," the general murmured. "A noble woman! There are many such as she who have done great service to our cause that can never be repaid! But this is a stroke of fortune!"

"Look, Merritt, Averill and all of you," he said aloud. "Here lies our path! Mr. Shepard, you will go over the details of this with us and, Colonel Winchester, you and your aide remain also to help."

Dick felt complimented, and so did Colonel Winchester. Sheridan knew how to handle men. While the sentinels, rifle on shoulder, walked up and down a little distance away, a dozen eager faces were soon poring over the map, Shepard filling in details as to the last little hill or brook.

"Since we know where they are and how many they are," said Sheridan, "we'll make a big demonstration in front of Fisher's Hill, where Early's works are too strong to be carried, and while we keep him occupied there we'll turn his left flank with a powerful force, marching it just here into the open space that Mr. Shepard's map shows. Tomorrow—or rather today, for I see the dawn comes—will be a day of great noise and of much burning of powder. But behind the curtain of smoke we'll make our movements. Merritt with his cavalry shall go to the right and Averill will go with him. Crook shall take his two divisions and hold the north bank of Cedar Creek, and later on Crook shall be the first to strike. Gentlemen, we've won one victory, and I know that all of you appreciate the value of a second and a third. The opportunity of the war lies here before us. We can uncover the entire left flank of the Confederacy here in Virginia, and who knows what will follow!"

He looked up, his eyes glowing and his confidence was communicated to them all. They were mostly young men and they responded in kind to his burning words. Sheridan knew that he could command from them the utmost fidelity and energy, and he uttered a little exclamation of confidence.

"I shall consider the victory already won," he said.

The generals left for their commands, and Sheridan again thanked Colonel Winchester, Dick and Shepard.

"I recommend that all three of you take some rest," he said, "you won't have much to do this morning."

They saluted, mounted and rode back. "You take his advice, Dick, and roll yourself in your blanket," said Colonel Winchester, when they were on the way.

"I will, sir," said Dick, "although I know that great history is being made now."

"I feel that way, too," said the colonel. "Look, the sun is coming up, and you can see the Confederate outposts."

The thin, clear air of September was brilliant with morning light, and through glasses the Confederate outposts and works around Fisher's Hill were quite clear and distinct. Some of the Northern and Southern sentinels were already exchanging compliments with one another, and they heard the faint popping of rifles. But Dick well knew from Sheridan's words that this early firing meant nothing. It would grow much heavier bye and bye and it would yet be but the cover for something else.

He found Warner and Pennington already sound asleep, and wrapping himself in his blanket he lay down under a tree and fell asleep to the distant crackle of rifles and the occasional thud of great guns. He slept on through the morning while the fire increased, and great volumes of smoke rolled, as the wind shifted up or down the valley. But it did not disturb him, nor did he dream. His slumbers were as sound as if he lay in his distant bed in Pendleton.

While Dick and his comrades slept Sheridan was moving the men on his chess board. Young in years, but great in experience, he was never more eager and never more clear of mind than on this, one of the most eventful days of his life. He saw the opportunity, and he was resolved that it should not escape him. Two great reputations were made in the valley by men very unlike, Stonewall Jackson and Little Phil Sheridan. In the earlier years of the war the Union armies had suffered many disasters there at the hands of the leader under the old slouch hat, and now Sheridan was resolved to retrieve everything, not with one victory alone, but with many.

There was firing in the valley all day long, the crackling of the rifles, the thudding of the great guns, and the occasional charge of horsemen. The curtain of smoke hung nearly always. Sometimes it grew thicker, and sometimes it became thinner, but Sheridan's mind was not upon these things, they were merely the veil before him, while behind it, as a screen, he arranged the men on his chess board. When night came his whole line was pushed forward. His vanguard held the northern part of the little town of Strasburg, while Early's held the southern part, only a few hundred yards away. In the night the large force under Crook was moved into the thick forest along Cedar Creek, where it was to lie silent and hidden until it received the word of command.

All the next day the movements were continued, while Crook's force, intended to be the striking arm, was still concealed in the timber. Yet before dark there was a heavy combat, in which the Southern troops were driven out of Strasburg, enabling the Northern batteries to advance to strong positions. That night Crook's whole strength was brought across Cedar Creek, but was hidden again in heavy timber. To the great pleasure of its colonel and other officers the Winchester regiment was sent to join it as a cavalry support.

It was quite dark when they rode their horses across the creek and Shepard was again with them as guide. Although he concealed it, the spy felt a great exultation. The map that he had brought from his sister had proved invaluable. Sheridan was using it every hour, and Shepard was giving further assistance through his thorough knowledge of the ground. Dick was glad to ride beside him and whisper with him, now and then.

"I haven't known things to go so well before," Dick said, when they were across the creek.

"They're going well, Mr. Mason," said Shepard, "because everything is arranged. There is provision against every unlucky chance. It's leadership. The difference between a good general and a bad general is about fifty thousand men."

The entire division moved forward in the dusk at a fair pace, but so many troops with cavalry and guns could not keep from making some noise. Dick with Shepard and the sergeant rode off in the woods towards the open valley to see if the enemy were observing them. Dick's chief apprehensions were in regard to Slade and Skelly, but they found no trace of the guerrillas, nor of any other foes.

The night was fairly bright, and from the edge of the wood they saw far over hills and fields, dotted with two opposing lines of camp fires. A dark outline was Fisher's Hill, and lights burned there too. From a point in front of it a gun boomed now and then, and there was still an intermittent fire of skirmishers and sharpshooters.

"That hill will be ours inside of twenty-four hours," said Shepard. "We'll fall upon Early from three sides and he'll have to retreat to save himself. He hasn't numbers enough to stand against an army driven forward by a hand like that of General Sheridan."

* * * * * * * *

While Dick, the sergeant and the spy looked from the woods upon the lights of Fisher's Hill the Invincibles lay in an earthwork before it facing their enemy. Harry Kenton sat with St. Clair, Langdon and Dalton. The two colonels were not far away. For almost the first time, Harry's heart failed him. He did not wish to depreciate Early, but he felt that he was not the great Jackson or anything approaching him. He knew that the troops felt the same way. They missed the mighty spirit and the unfaltering mind that had led them in earlier years to victory. They were ragged and tired, too, and had but little food.

Happy Tom, who concealed under a light manner uncommonly keen perceptions, noticed Harry's depression.

"What are you thinking about, Harry?" he asked.

"Several things, Happy. Among them, the days when we rode here with Stonewall from one victory to another."

"We'll have to think of something else. Cheer up. Remember the old saying that the darkest hour is just before the dawn."

"Whose dawn?"

"That's not like you, Harry. You've usually put up the boldest front of us all."

"Happy's giving you good advice," said St. Clair.

"So he is," said Harry, as he shook himself. "We'll fight 'em off tomorrow. They can't beat us again. The spirit of Old Jack will hover over us."

"If we only had more men," said Dalton. "Then we could spread out and cover the slopes of the mountains on either side. I wish I knew whether those dark fringes hid anything we ought to know."

"They hide rabbits, squirrels, raccoons, birds and maybe a black bear or two," said Happy Tom. "When we shatter Sheridan's army and drive the fragments across the Potomac I think I'll come back here and do a little hunting, leaving to Lee the task of cleaning up the Army of the Potomac."

"I'd like to come with you," said St. Clair, "but I wouldn't bring any gun. I'd just roam through the woods for a week and disturb nothing. If I saw a bear I'd point my finger at him and say: 'Go away, young fellow, I won't bother you if you won't bother me,' and then he'd amble off peacefully in one direction, and I'd amble off peacefully in another. I wouldn't want to hear a gun fired during all that week. I'd just rest, rest, rest my nerves and my soul. I wouldn't break a bough or a bush. I'd even be careful how hard I stepped on the leaves. Birds

334

could walk all over me if they liked. I'd drink from those clear streams, and I'd sleep in my blanket on a bed of leaves."

"But suppose it rained, Arthur?"

"I wouldn't let it rain in that enchanted week of mine. Nothing would happen except what I wanted to happen. It would be a week of the most absolute peace and quiet the world has ever known. There wouldn't be any winds, they would be zephyrs. The skies would all be made out of the softest and finest of blue satin and any little clouds that floated before 'em would be made of white satin of the same quality. The nights would be clear with the most wonderful stars that ever shone. Great new stars would come out for the first time, and twinkle for me, and the man in the most silvery moon known in the history of time would grin down at me and say without words: 'St. Clair, old fellow, this is your week of peace, everything has been fixed for you, so make the most of it.' And then I'd wander on. The birds would sing to me and every one of 'em would sing like a prima donna. Wherever I stepped, wild flowers would burst into bloom as I passed, and if a gnat should happen to buzz before my face I wouldn't brush him away for fear of hurting him. The universe and I would be at peace with each other."

"Hear him! O, hear him!" exclaimed Happy Tom. "Old Arthur grows dithyrambic and hexametrical. He fairly distils the essence of highfalutin poetry."

"I don't know that he's so far fetched," said sober Dalton. "I feel a good deal that way myself. I suppose, Thomas Langdon, that the colours of the world depend upon one's own eyes. What I call green may appear to you like the colour of blue to me. Now, Arthur really sees all these things that he's telling about, because he has the eye of the mind with which to see them. I've quit saying that people don't see things, because I don't see 'em myself."

"Good for you, Professor," said Langdon. "That's quite a lecture you gave me, long though not windy, and I accept it. Those Elysian fields that Arthur was painting are real and he's going to have his enchanted week as he calls it. Arthur is a poet, sure enough."

"I have written a few little verses which were printed in the Charleston Mercury," said St. Clair.

"What's this? What's this?" asked a mellow voice. "Can it be possible that young gentlemen are discussing poetry between battles and with the enemy in sight?"

It was Colonel Leonidas Talbot, coming down the trench, and Lieutenant Colonel Hector St. Hilaire was just behind him. The young officers rose and saluted promptly, but they knew there was no reproof in Colonel Talbot's tone.

"We had to do it, sir," said Harry respectfully. "Something struck Arthur here, and like a fountain he gushed suddenly into poetry. He had a most wonderful vision of the Elysian fields and of himself wandering through them for a week, knee deep in flowers, and playing the softest of music on a guitar."

"He's put that in about the guitar," protested St. Clair. "I never mentioned such a thing, but all the rest is true."

"Well, if I had my way," said the colonel, "you should have a guitar, too, if you wanted it, and I like that idea of yours about a week in the Elysian fields. We'll join you there and we'll all walk around among the flowers, and Hector's relative, that wonderful musician, young De Langeais, shall play to us on his violin, and maybe the famous Stonewall will come walking to us through the flowers, and he'll have with him Albert Sidney Johnston, and Turner Ashby and all the great ones that have gone."

The colonel stopped, and Harry felt a slight choking in his throat.

"In the course of this lull, Leonidas and I had some thought of resuming our unfinished game of chess," said Lieutenant Colonel St. Hilaire, "but the time is really unpropitious and too short. It may be that we shall have to wait until the war is over to conclude the match. The enemy is pressing us hard, and I need not conceal from you lads that he will press us harder tomorrow."

"So he will," agreed Colonel Talbot. "There was some heavy and extremely accurate artillery fire from his ranks this afternoon. The way the guns were handled and the remarkable rapidity and precision with which the discharges came convinces me that John Carrington is here in the valley, ready to concentrate all the fire of the Union batteries upon us. It is bad, very bad for us that the greatest artilleryman in the world should come with Sheridan, and yet we shall have the pleasure of seeing how he achieves wonders with the guns. It was in him, even in the old days at West Point, when we were but lads together, and he has shown more than once in this war how the flower that was budding then has come into full bloom."

As if in answer to his words the deep boom of a cannon rolled over the hills, and a shell burst near the earthwork.

"That, I think, was John talking to us," said Colonel Talbot. "He was saying to us: 'Beware of me, old friends. I'm coming tomorrow, not with one gun but with many!' Well, be it so. We shall give John and Sheridan a warm welcome, and we shall try to make it so very warm that it will prove too hot for them. Now, my lads, there is no immediate duty for you, and if you can sleep, do so. Good-night."

They rose and saluted again as the two colonels went back to their own particular place.

"I hope those two will be spared," said St. Clair. "I want them to finish their chess game, and I'd like, too, to see their meeting after the war with their old friend, John Carrington."

"It will all come to pass," said Harry. "If Arthur is a poet as he seems to be, then I'm a prophet, as I know I am."

"At least you're an optimist," said Dalton.

"Go to sleep, all of you, as the colonel told you to do," said Harry. "If you don't stop talking you'll keep the enemy awake all night."

But Harry himself was the last of them to sleep. He could not keep from rising at times, and, in the starlight, looking at the fires of the foe and the dark slopes of the mountains. His glasses passed more than once over the forests along Cedar Creek, but no prevision, no voice out of the dark, told him that Dick was there, one of a formidable force that was lying hidden, ready to strike the fatal blow. His last dim sight, as he fell asleep, was a spectacle evoked from the past, a vision of Old Jack riding at the head of his phantom legions to victory.

* * * * * * * *

At dawn all of Crook's forces marched out of the woods along Cedar Creek, the Winchester men, Shepard at their head, leading, but they still kept to the shelter of the forest and wide ravines along the lower slopes of the mountain. The sun was not clear of the eastern hills before the heavy thudding of the great guns and the angry buzz of the rifles came from the direction of Fisher's Hill.

The demonstration had begun and it was a big one, big enough to make the defenders think it was reality and not a sham. Before Early's earthworks a great cloud of smoke was gathering. Dick looked over his shoulder at it. It gave him a curious feeling to be marching past, while all that crash of battle was going on in the valley. It almost looked as if they were deserting their general.

"How far are we going?" he asked Warner.

"I don't know," replied the Vermonter, "but I fancy we'll go far enough. My little algebra, although it remains unopened in my pocket, tells me that we shall continue our progress unseen until we reach the desired point. These woods have grown up and these gullies have been furrowed at a very convenient time for us."

The light was yet dim in the forests along the slopes, but the valley itself was flooded with the sun's rays. The echoes of the firing rolled continuously through the gorges and multiplied it. Despite the clouds about the earthworks and the hill, Dick saw continual flashes of light, and he knew now that the battle below was a reality and not a sham. Early and all his men would be kept too busy to see the march of Crook and his force on his flank, and Dick, like Warner, became sure that the great movement would be a success.

But their progress, owing to the nature of the ground and the need to keep under cover, was slow. It seemed to Dick that they marched an interminable time under the trees, while the battle flashed and roared in the plain. He saw noon pass and the sun rise to the zenith. He saw the brilliant light dim on the eastern mountains, and they were still marching through the forests.

The battle was now behind them and the sun was very low, but the command halted and turned toward the east. Nevertheless, they were still hidden by the woods and the low hills of the valley. Yet they lay behind and on the side of their enemy who would speedily be exposed where he was weakest, to their full weight. The long flanking movement had been a complete success so far.

Little of the day was left. The sun was almost hidden behind the eastern mountains but it still flamed in the west, glittering along the bayonets of the men in the forest, and showing their eager faces. Dick's heart throbbed. In that moment of anticipated victory he forgot all about Harry and his friends who were in the closing trap. Then trumpets sang the charge, and the cavalry thundered out of the wood, followed by the infantry and the artillery.

At the same time, another powerful division that had been moved forward by Sheridan, charged, while those in front increased their fire. The unfortunate Southern army was overwhelmed by troops who had moved forward in such complete unison. They were swept out of their earthworks, driven from their fortified hill, and those who did not fall or were not taken were sent in rapid flight down the valley.

The battle was short. Completeness of preparation and superiority in numbers and resources made it so. Early and what was left of his army had no choice but the flight they made. The sun had nearly set when the deadly charge issued from the wood, and, by the time it had set, the pursuit was thundering along the valley, the Winchester men in the very forefront of it. Long after dark it continued. Several miles from the field the fragments of the Invincibles and some others rallied on a hill, posted two cannon and made a desperate resistance. But the attack upon them was so fierce that they were compelled to retreat again, and they did not have time to take the guns with them.

It was a strange night to Dick, alike joyous and terrible. He believed that the army of the enemy was practically destroyed, and yet he had a great sympathy for some who were in it. He was in constant fear lest he should find them dead, or wounded mortally. But he had no time to look for them. Sheridan was pressing the pursuit to the utmost. Midnight did not stop it. Fugitives were captured continually. Here and there an abandoned cannon was taken. Rifles flashed all through the darkness, and the horses of the Union cavalry were driven to the utmost.

Neither Dick nor his companions felt exhaustion. Their excitement was too great, and the taste of triumph was too strong. They had seen no such victory before, and eager and willing they still led the advance. Midnight passed and the pursuit never ceased until it reached Woodstock, ten miles from Fisher's Hill. By that time Sheridan's infantry was exhausted, and as Early was beginning to draw together the remains of his force he would prove too strong for the cavalry alone.

At dawn the army of Sheridan stopped, the troopers almost falling from their horses in exhaustion, while Early used the opportunity to escape with what was left of his men, leaving behind many prisoners and twenty cannon. Yet the triumph had been great, and again, when the telegraph brought the news of it, the swell of victory passed through the North.

The Winchester regiment was drawn up near Woodstock, already dismounted, the men standing beside their horses. The camp cooks were lighting the fires for breakfast, but many of the young cavalrymen fell asleep first. Dick managed to keep awake long enough for his food, and then, at the order of the colonel, he slept on the ground, awaiting the command of Sheridan which might come at any moment.

CHAPTER 10

An Unbeaten Foe

Dick's belief that he would not be allowed to sleep long was justified. In three or four hours the whole Winchester regiment was up, mounted and away again. Early and his army left the great valley pike, and took a road leading toward the Blue Ridge, where he eventually entered a gap, and fortified to await supplies and fresh men from Richmond, leaving all the great Valley of Virginia, where in former years the Northern armies had suffered so many humiliations, in the possession of Sheridan. It was the greatest and most solid triumph that the Union had yet achieved and Dick and the youths with him rejoiced.

After many days of marching and fighting they lay once more in the shadow of the mountains, within a great grove of oak and beech, hickory and maple. The men and then the horses had drunk at a large brook flowing near by, and both were content. The North, as always, sent forward food in abundance to its troops, and now, just as the twilight was coming, the fires were lighted and the pleasant aromas of supper were rising. Colonel Winchester and his young staff sat by one of the fires near the edge of the creek. They had not taken off their clothes in almost a week, and they felt as if they had been living like cave-men. Nevertheless the satisfaction that comes from deeds well done pervaded them, and as they lay upon the leaves and awaited their food and coffee they showed great good humour.

"Have you any objection, sir, to my taking a census?" said Warner to Colonel Winchester.

"No, Warner, but what kind of a census do you mean?"

"I want to count our wounds, separately and individually and then make up the grand total."

"All right, George, go ahead," said Colonel Winchester, laughing.

"Dick," said Warner, "what hurts have you sustained in the past week?"

"A bullet scratch on the shoulder, another on the side, a slight cut from a sabre on my left arm, about healed now, a spent bullet that hit me on the head, raising a lump and ache for the time being, and a kick from one of our own horses that made me walk lame for a day."

"The kick from a horse, as it was one of our horses, doesn't go."

"I didn't put it forward seriously. I withdraw my claim on its account."

"That allows you four wounds. Now, Pennington, how about you?"

"First I had a terrible wound in the foot," replied the Nebraskan. "A bullet went right through my left shoe and cut the skin off the top of my little toe."

"Leave out the 'terrible.' That's no dreadful wound."

"No, but it burned like the sting of a wasp and bled in a most disgraceful manner all over my sock. Then my belt buckle was shot away."

"That doesn't count either. A wound's a wound only when you're hit yourself, not when some piece of your clothing is struck."

"All right. The belt buckle's barred, although it gave me a shock when the bullet met it. A small bullet went through the flesh of my left arm just above the elbow. It healed so fast that I've hardly noticed it, due, of course, to the very healthy and temperate life I've led. I suppose, George, it would have laid up a fellow of your habits for a week."

"Never mind about my habits, but go on with the list of your wounds. A great beauty of mathematics is that it compels you to keep to your subject. When you're solving one of those delightful problems in mathematics you can't digress and drag in irrelevant things. Algebra is the very thing for a confused mind like yours, Frank, one that doesn't coordinate. But get on with your list."

"When we were in pursuit my horse stumbled in a gully and fell so hard that I was thrown over his shoulder, giving my own shoulder a painful bruise that's just getting well."

"We'll allow that, since it happened in battle. What else now? Speak up!"

"That's all. Three good wounds, according to your own somewhat severe definition of a wound. I'm one behind Dick, but I believe that when I was thrown over my horse's head I was hurt worse than he was at any time."

"Frank Pennington, you're a good comrade, but you're a liar, an unmitigated liar."

"George, if I weren't so tired and so unwilling to be angry with anybody I'd get up and belt you on the left ear for that."

"But you're a liar, just the same. You're holding something back."

"What are you driving at, you chattering Green Mountaineer?"

"Why don't you tell something about the time the trooper fell from his horse wounded, and you, dismounting under the enemy's fire, helped him on your own horse, although you got two wounds in your body while doing it, and brought him off in safety? Didn't I say that you were a liar, a convicted liar from modesty?"

Pennington blushed.

"I didn't want to say anything about that," he muttered. "I had to do it."

"Lots of men wouldn't have had to do it. You go down for five good wounds, Frank Pennington."

"Now, then, what about yourself, George?" asked Dick.

"One in the arm, one on the shoulder and one across the ankle. I don't waste time in words, like you two, my verbose friends. That gives the three of us combined twelve wounds, a fair average of four apiece."

"And it's our great good luck that not one of the twelve is a disabling hurt," said Dick.

"But we get the credit for the full twelve, all the same," said Warner, "and we maintain our prestige in the army. Our consciences also are satisfied. But the last two or three weeks of battles and marches have fairly made me dizzy. I can't remember them or their sequence. All I know is that we've cleaned up the valley, and here we are ready at last to take a couple of minutes of well earned rest."

"Do you know," said Pennington, "there were times when I clear forgot to be hungry, and I've been renowned in our part of Nebraska for my appetite. But nature always gets even. For all those periods of forgetfulness memory is now rushing upon me. I'm hungry not only for the present but from the past. It'll take a lot to satisfy me."

The briskness of the night also sharpened Pennington's appetite. They were deep in autumn, and the winds from the mountains had an edge. The foliage had turned and it glowed in vivid reds and yellows on the slopes, although the intense colours were hidden now by the coming of night.

The wind was cold enough to make the fires feel good to their relaxed systems, and they spread out their hands to the welcome flames, as they had often done at home on wintry nights, when children. Beyond the trees the horses, under guard, were grazing on what was left of the late grass, but within the wood the men themselves, save those who were preparing food, were mostly lying down on the dry leaves or their blankets, and were talking of the things they had done, or the things they were going to do.

"I wonder what the bill of fare will be tonight," said Pennington, who was growing hungrier and hungrier.

"I had several engraved menus," said Warner, "but I lost them, and so we won't be able to order. We'll just have to take what they offer us."

"A month or so later they'll be having fresh sausage and spare ribs in old Kentucky," said Dick, "and I wish we had 'em here now."

"And a month later than that," said Pennington, "they'll be having a roasted bull buffalo weighing five thousand pounds for Christmas dinner in Nebraska."

"Nonsense!" exclaimed Warner. "No buffalo ever weighed five thousand pounds."

Pennington looked at him pityingly.

"You have no romance or poetry after all, George," he said. "Why can't you let me put on an extra twenty-five hundred or three thousand pounds for the sake of effect?"

"Besides, you don't roast buffaloes whole and bring them in on a platter!"

"No, we don't, but that's no proof that we can't or won't. Now, what would you like to have, George?"

"After twelve or fifteen other things, I'd like to finish off with a whole pumpkin pie, and a few tin cups of cider would go along with it mighty well. That's the diet to make men, real men, I mean."

"Any way," said Dick, raising a tin cup of hot coffee, "here's to food. You may sleep without beds, and, in tropical climates, you may go without clothes, but in whatever part of the world you may be, you must have food. And it's best when you've ridden hard all day, and, in the cool of an October evening, to sit down by a roaring fire in the woods with the dry leaves beneath you, and the clear sky above you."

"Hear! hear!" said Warner. "Who's dithyrambic now? But you're right, Dick. War is a terrible thing. Besides being a ruthless slaughter it's an economic waste,—did you ever think of that, you reckless youngsters?—but it has a few minor compensations, and one of them is an evening like this. Why, everything tastes good to us. Nothing could taste bad. Our twelve wounds don't pain us in the least, and they'll heal absolutely in a few days, our blood being so healthy. The air we breathe is absolutely pure and the sky over our heads is all blue and silver, spangled with stars, a canopy stretched for our especial benefit, and upon which we have as much claim of ownership as anybody else has. We've lived out of doors so much and we've been through so much hard exercise that our bodies are now pretty nearly tempered steel. I doubt whether I'll ever be able to live indoors again, except in winter."

"I'm the luckiest of all," said Pennington. "Out on the plains we don't have to live indoors much anyway. I've lived mostly in the saddle since I was seven or eight years old, but the war has toughened me just the same. I'll be able to sleep out any time, except in the blizzards."

"As soon as you finish devouring the government stores," said a voice behind them, "it would be well for all of you to seek the sleep you're telling so much about."

It was Colonel Winchester who spoke, and they looked at him, inquiringly.

"Can I ask, sir, which way we ride?" said Dick.

"Northward with General Sheridan," replied the Colonel.

"But there is no enemy to the north, sir!"

"That's true, but we go that way, nevertheless. Although you're discreet young officers I'm not going to tell you any more. Now, as you've eaten enough food and drunk enough coffee, be off to your blankets. I want all of you to be fresh and strong in the morning."

Fresh and strong they were, and promptly General Sheridan rode away, taking with him all the cavalry, his course taking him toward Front Royal. The news soon spread among the horsemen that from Front Royal the general would go on to Washington for a conference with the War Department, while the cavalry would turn through a gap in the mountains, and then destroy railroads in order to cut off General Early's communications with Richmond.

"We're to be an escort and then a fighting and destroying force," said Dick. "But it's quite sure that we'll meet no enemy until we go through the gap. Meanwhile we'll enjoy a saunter along the valley."

But when they reached Front Royal a courier, riding hard, overtook them. He demanded to be taken at once to the presence of General Sheridan, and then he presented a copy of a dispatch which read:

To Lieutenant-General Early:

Be ready to move as soon as my forces join you, and we will crush Sheridan. Longstreet, Lieutenant-General.

Sheridan read the dispatch over and over again, and pondered it gravely. The courier informed him that it was the copy of a signal made by the Confederate flags on Three Top Mountain, and deciphered by Union officers who had obtained the secret of the Confederate code. General Wright, whom he had left in command, had sent it to him in all haste for what it was worth.

The young general not only pondered the message gravely, but he pondered it long. Finally he called his chief officers around him and consulted with them. If the grim and bearded Longstreet were really coming into the valley with a formidable force, then indeed it would be the dance of death. Longstreet, although he did not have the genius of Stonewall Jackson, was a fierce and dangerous fighter. All of them knew how he had come upon the field of Chickamauga with his veterans from Virginia, and had turned the tide of battle. His presence in the valley might quickly turn all of Sheridan's great triumphs into withered laurels.

But Sheridan had a great doubt in his mind. The Confederate signal from Three Top Mountain that his own officers had read might not be real. It might have been intended to deceive, Early's signalmen learning that the Union signalmen had deciphered their code, or it might be some sort of a grim joke. He did not believe that the Army of Northern Virginia could spare Longstreet and a large force, as it would be weakened so greatly that it could no longer stand before Grant, even with the aid of the trenches.

His belief that this dispatch, upon which so much turned, as they were to learn afterward, was false, became a conviction and most of his officers agreed with him. He decided at last that the coming of Longstreet with an army into the valley was an impossibility, and he would go on to Washington. But Sheridan made a reservation, and this, too, as the event showed, was highly important. He ordered all the cavalry back to General Wright, while he proceeded with a small escort to the capital.

It was Dick who first learned what had happened, and soon all knew. They discussed it fully as they rode back on their own tracks, and on the whole they were glad they were to return.

"I don't think I'd like to be tearing up railroads and destroying property," said Dick. "I prefer anyhow for the valley to be my home at present, although I believe that dispatch means nothing. Why, the Confederates can't possibly rally enough men to attack us!"

"I think as you do," said Warner. "I suppose it's best for the cavalry to go back, but I wish General Sheridan had taken me on to Washington with him. I'd like to see the lights of the capital again. Besides, I'd have given the President and the Secretary of War some excellent advice."

"He isn't jesting. He means it," said Pennington to Dick.

"Of course I do," said Warner calmly. "When General Sheridan failed to take me with him, the government lost a great opportunity."

But their hearts were light and they rode gaily back, unconscious of the singular event that was preparing for them.

* * * * * * * *

The army of Early had not been destroyed entirely. Sheridan, with all his energy, and with all the courage and zeal of his men could not absolutely crush his foe. Some portions of the hostile force were continually slipping away, and now Early, refusing to give up, was gathering them together again, and was meditating a daring counter stroke. The task might well have appalled any general and any troops, but if Early had one quality in pre-eminence it was the resolution to fight. And most of his officers and men were veterans. Many of them had ridden with Jackson on his marvellous campaigns. They were familiar with the taste of victory, and defeat had been very bitter to them. They burned to strike back, and they were willing to dare anything for the sake of it.

Orders had already gone to all the scattered and ragged fragments, and the men in gray were concentrating. Many of them were half starved. The great valley had been stripped of all its live stock, all its grain and of every other resource that would avail an army. Nothing could be obtained, except at Staunton, ninety miles back of Fisher's Hill, and wagons could not bring up food in time from such a distant place.

Nevertheless the men gleaned. They searched the fields for any corn that might be left, and ate it roasted or parched. Along the slopes of the mountains they found nuts already ripening, and these were prizes indeed.

Among the gleaners were Harry Kenton, the staunch young Presbyterian, Dalton, and the South Carolinians, St. Clair and Langdon. St. Clair alone was impeccable of uniform, absolutely trim, and Langdon alone deserved his nickname of Happy.

"Don't be discouraged, boys," he said as he pulled from the stalk an ear of corn that the hoofs of the Northern cavalry had failed to trample under. "Now this is a fine ear, a splendid ear, and if you boys search well you may be able to find others like it. All things come to him who looks long enough. Remember how Nebuchadnezzar ate grass, and he must have had to do some hunting too, because I understand grass didn't grow very freely in that part of the world, and then remember also that we are not down to grass yet. Corn, nuts and maybe a stray pumpkin or two. 'Tis a repast fit for the gods, noble sirs."

"I can go without, part of the time," said Harry, "but it hurts me to have to hunt through a big field for a nubbin of corn and then feel happy when I've got the wretched, dirty, insignificant little thing. My father often has a hundred acres of corn in a single field, producing fifty bushels to the acre."

"And my father," said Dalton, "has a single field of fifty acres that produces fifteen hundred bushels of wheat, but it's been a long time since I've seen a shock of wheat."

"Console yourself with the knowledge," said Harry, "that it's too late in the year for wheat to be in the stack."

"Or anywhere else, either, so far as we're concerned."

"Don't murmur," said Happy. "Mourners seldom find anything, but optimists find, often. Didn't I tell you so? Here's another ear."

Harry had approached the edge of the field and he saw something red gleaming through a fringe of woods beyond. The experienced eye of youth told him at once what it was, and he called to his comrades.

"Come on, boys," he said. "There's a little orchard beyond the wood. I know there is because I caught a glimpse of a red apple hanging from a tree. I suppose the skirt of forest kept the Yankee raiders from seeing it."

They followed with a shout of joy.

"Treasure trove!" exclaimed Happy.

"Who's an optimist now?" asked Harry.

"All of us are," said St. Clair.

They passed through the wood and entered a small orchard of not more than half an acre. But it was filled with apple trees loaded with red apples, big juicy fellows, just ripened by the October sun. A little beyond the orchard in a clearing was a small log house, obviously that of the owner of the orchard, and also obviously deserted. No smoke rose from the chimneys, and windows and doors were nailed up. The proprietor no doubt had gone with his family to some town and the apples would have rotted on the ground had the young officers not found them.

"There must be bushels and bushels here," said St. Clair. "We'll fill up our sacks first and then call the other men."

They had brought sacks with them for the corn, but the few ears they had found took up but little space.

"I'll climb the trees, and shake 'em down," said Harry. He was up a tree in an instant, all his boyhood coming back to him, and, as he shook with his whole strength, the red apples, held now by twigs nearly dead, rained down. They passed from tree to tree and soon their sacks were filled.

"Now for the colonels," said St. Clair, "and on our way we'll tell the others."

Bending under the weight of the sacks, they took their course toward a snug cove in the first slope of the Massanuttons, hailing friends on the way and sending them with swift steps toward the welcome orchard. They passed within the shadow of a grove, and then entered a small open space, where two men sat on neighbouring stumps, with an empty box between them. Upon the box reposed a board of chessmen and at intervals the two intent players spoke.

"If you expect to capture my remaining knight, Hector, you'll have to hurry. We march tomorrow."

"I can't be hurried, Leonidas. This is an intellectual game, and if it's played properly it demands time. If I don't take your remaining knight before tomorrow I'll take him a month from now, after this campaign is over."

"I have my doubts, Hector; I've heard you boast before."

"I never boast, Leonidas. At times I make statements and prophecies, but I trust that I'm too modest a man ever to boast."

"Then advance your battle line, Hector, and see what you can do. It's your move."

The two gray heads bent so low over the narrow board that they almost touched. For a little space the campaign, the war, and all their hardships floated away from them, their minds absorbed thoroughly in the difficult game which had come in the dim past out of the East. They did not see anything around them nor did they hear Harry as he approached them with the heavy sack of apples upon his back.

Harry's affection for both of the colonels was strong and as he looked at them he realized more than ever their utter unworldliness. He, although a youth, saw that they belonged to a passing era, but in their very unworldliness lay their attraction. He knew that whatever the fortunes of the war, they would, if they lived, prove good citizens after its close. All rancour—no, not rancour, because they felt none—rather all hostility would be buried on the battlefield, and the friend whom they would be most anxious to see and welcome was John Carrington, the great Northern artilleryman, who had done their cause so much damage.

He opened his sack and let the red waterfall of apples pour down at their feet. Startled by the noise, they looked up, despite a critical situation on the board. Then they looked down again at the scarlet heap upon the grass, and, powerful though the attractions of chess were, they were very hungry men, and the shining little pyramid held their gaze.

"Apples! apples, Harry!" said Colonel Talbot. "Many apples, magnificent, red and ripe! Is it real?"

"No, Leonidas, it can't be real," said Lieutenant Colonel Hector St. Hilaire. "It can't be possible in a country that Sheridan swept as bare as the palm of my hand. It's only an idle dream, Leonidas. I was deceived by it myself, for a moment, but we will not yield any longer to such weakness. Come, we will return to our game, where every move has now become vital."

"But it isn't a dream, sir! It's real!" exclaimed Harry joyfully. "We found an abandoned orchard, and it was just filled with 'em. Help yourselves!"

The colonels put away their chessmen, remembering well where every one had stood, and fell on with the appetites of boys. Other officers, and then soldiers who were made welcome, joined them. Harry and Dalton, after having eaten their share, were walking along the slope of the mountain, when they heard the sound of a shot. It seemed to come from a dense thicket, and, as no Northern skirmishers could be near, their curiosity caused them to rush forward. When they entered the thicket they heard Langdon's voice raised in a shout of triumph.

"I got him! I got him!" he cried. Then they heard a heavy sliding sound, as of something being dragged, and the young South Carolinian appeared, pulling after him by its hind legs a fine hog which he had shot through the head.

"It was fair game," he cried, as he saw his friends. "Piggy here was masterless, roaming around the woods feeding on nuts until he was fat and juicy! My, how good he will taste! At first I thought he was a bear, but bear or hog he was bound to fall to my pistol!"

Langdon had indeed found a prize, and he had robbed no farmer to obtain it. Harry and Dalton stood by for a half minute and gloated with him. Then they helped him drag the hog into the cove, where the colonels sat. A half dozen experts quickly dressed the animal, and the Invincibles had a feast such as they had not tasted in a long time.

"Didn't I tell you," said Happy as he gazed contentedly into the coals over which the hog had been roasted in sections, "that those who look hard generally discover, that is, 'seek and ye shall find.' It's the optimists who arrive. Your pessimist quits before he comes to the apple trees, or before he reaches the thicket that conceals the fine fat pig. As for me, I'm always an optimist, twenty-four carats fine, and therefore I'm the superior of you fellows."

"You're happier than we are because you don't feel any sense of responsibility," said Dalton. "I'd rather be unhappy than have an empty head."

"Oh, it's just jealous you are, George Dalton. Born with a sour disposition you can't bear to see me shedding joy and light about me."

Dalton laughed.

"It's true, Happy," he said. "You do help, and for that reason we tolerate you, not because of your prowess in battle."

"Has anybody seen that fellow Slade again?" asked St. Clair.

"I'm thankful to say no," replied Harry. "He came out of the South-west promising big things, and he certainly does have great skill in the forest, but our officers don't like his looks. Nor did I. If there was ever a thorough villain I'm sure he's one. I've heard that he's drawn off and is operating with a band of guerrillas in the mountains, robbing and murdering, I suppose."

"And they say that a big ruffian from the Kentucky mountains with another band has joined him," said Happy.

"What's his name?" asked Harry with sudden interest.

"Skelly, I think, Bill Skelly."

"Why, I know that fellow! He comes from the hills back of our town of Pendleton, and he claimed to be on the Union side. He and his band fired upon me at the very opening of the war."

"If you are not careful he'll be firing upon you again. He may have started out as a Union man, but he's shifting around now, I fancy, to suit his own plundering and robbing forces. We'll hear of their operations later, and it won't be a pretty story."

They talked of many things, and after a while Harry and St. Clair were sent with a message to the crest of Three Top Mountain, where the Confederate signal station was located, and from which the Union officers had taken the dispatch about the coming of Longstreet with a strong force. Both were fully aware of the great movement contemplated by Early and their minds now went back to march and battle.

The climb up the mountain was pleasant to such muscles and sinews as theirs, and they stopped at intervals to look over the valley, now a great desolation, until nature should come again with her healing touch. Harry smothered a sigh as he recalled their early and wonderful victories there, and the tremendous marches with the invincible Stonewall. Old Jack, as he sat somewhere with Washington and Cromwell and all the group of the mighty, must feel sad when he looked down upon this, his beloved valley, now trodden into a ruin by the heel of the invader.

He resolutely put down the choking in his throat, and would not let St. Clair see his emotion. They reached the signal station, which at that hour was in charge of a young officer named Mortimer, but little older than themselves. They delivered to him their message and stood by, while he talked with flags to another station on the opposite mountain. Harry watched curiously although he could read none of the signals.

"This is our only newspaper and I can't read it," he said when Mortimer had finished. "What's the news?"

"There's a lot of it, and it's heavy with importance," replied Mortimer.

"Tell us a bit of it, can't you?"

"Sheridan has left his army and gone north. That's one bit."

"What?"

"It's so. We know absolutely, and we've signalled it to General Early. But we don't know why he has gone."

"That is important."

"It surely is, and he's taken his cavalry with him. Our men have seen the troops riding northward. Since Sheridan went away, the Union commander, whoever he is, has been strengthening his right, fearing an attack there, since he learned of our reappearance in the valley."

"Therefore General Early will attack on the left?"

"Correct. You can see now the value of signal stations like ours. We can look down upon the enemy and see his movements. Then we know what to do."

"And what have they on their left?" asked Harry. "Do you know that, too?"

"Of course. General Crook with two divisions is there. He has Cedar Creek in front of him, and on his own left the north fork of the Shenandoah. He's considerably in front of the main Union force, and they haven't posted much of a picket line."

"I suppose they're relying upon the natural strength of the ground."

"That's it, I take it, but we may give them a surprise."

Harry and Dalton used their glasses and far to the north they saw dim figures, not larger than toys. At first view they appeared to be stationary, but, as the eyes became used to the distance, Harry knew they were moving. Apparently they were infantry going toward the Union right, where danger was feared, and he felt a grim satisfaction in knowing that the real danger lay on their left. But could Early with his small numbers, with the habit now of defeat, make any impression upon the large Union armies flushed with victories?

Harry wondered if Dick was among those moving troops, but his second thought told him it was not likely. They had learned from spies that the Winchester regiment was mounted, and in all probability it was part of the cavalry that had gone north with Sheridan. But he thought again how strange it was that the two should have been face to face at the Second Manassas, and then after a wide separation, involving so many great battles and marches, should come here into the Valley of Virginia, face to face once more.

Mortimer and his assistants presently began to manipulate the flags again, and Confederate signalmen, on a far peak, replied. Harry and St. Clair watched them with all the curiosity that a mystery inspires.

"Can we ask again," said Harry, when they had finished, "what you fellows were saying?"

Mortimer laughed.

"It was a quick dialogue," he replied, "but it was intended for the Yankees down in the valley, who, we learn, have deciphered some of our signals. I said to Strother on the other peak: 'Six thousand?' He replied: 'No, eight thousand!' I said: 'In centre or on their right flank?' He replied: 'On their right flank.' I said: 'Two thousand fresh horses?' He replied: 'Nearer twenty-five hundred.' I said: 'Five hundred fresh beeves from the other side of the Blue Ridge.' He replied: 'Great news, we need 'em!' I wish it was true, but it will set our Yankee friends to thinking."

"I see. Your talk was meant to fool the Yankees."

"Yes, and we need to fool 'em as much as we can. It's a daring venture that we're entering upon, but it's great luck for us to have Sheridan away. It looks like a good omen to me."

"And to me, too. We used to say that Old Jack was an army corps, and he was, two of them for that matter. Then Sheridan is worth at least ten thousand men to the Yankees. Good-by, we'd like to see more of your work with the flags, but down below they need Captain St. Clair, who is a terrible fighter. We can't hope to beat the Yankees with St. Clair away."

Mortimer smiled, waved them farewell, and, a few minutes later, was at work once more with the flags. Meanwhile, Harry and St. Clair were descending the mountain, pausing now and then to survey the valley with their glasses, where they could yet mark the movements of the Northern troops. When they reached the cove they found that the board and the chess men were put away, and the two colonels were inspecting the Invincibles to see that the last detail was done, while Early made ready for his desperate venture.

Harry and his comrades were fully conscious that it was a forlorn hope. They had been driven out of the valley once by superior numbers and equipment, directed by a leader of great skill and energy, but now they had come back to risk everything in a daring venture. The Union forces, of course, knew of their presence in the old lines about Fisher's Hill—Shepard alone was sufficient to warn them of it—but they could scarcely expect an attack by a foe of small numbers, already defeated several times.

Harry's thought of Shepard set him to surmising. The spy no longer presented himself to his mind as a foe to be hated. Rather, he was an official enemy whom he liked. He even remembered with a smile their long duel when Lee was retreating from Gettysburg, and particularly their adventure in the river. Would that duel between them be renewed? Intuition told him that Shepard was in the valley, and if Sheridan was worth ten thousand men the spy was worth at least a thousand.

The Invincibles were ready to the last man, and it did not require any great counting to reach the last. Yet the two colonels, as they rode before their scanty numbers, held themselves as proudly as ever, and the hearts of their young officers, in spite of all the odds, began to beat high with hope. The advance was to be made after dark, and their pulses were leaping as the twilight came, and then the night.

The march of the Southern army to deal its lightning stroke was prepared well, and, fortunately for it, a heavy fog came up late in the night from the rivers and creeks of the valley to cover its movements and hide the advancing columns from its foe. When Harry felt the damp touch of the vapour on his face his hopes rose yet higher. He knew that weather, fog, rain, snow and flooding rivers played a great part in the fortunes of war. Might not the kindly fog, encircling them with its protection, be a good omen?

"Chance favours us," he said to St. Clair and Langdon, as the fog grew thicker and thicker, almost veiling their faces from one another.

"I told you that the optimists usually had their way," said Happy. "We persisted and found that orchard of apples. We persisted and found that fat porker. Now, I have been wishing for this fog, and I kept on wishing for it until it came."

Harry laughed.

"You do make the best of things, Happy," he said.

The fog thickened yet more, but the Invincibles made their sure way through it, the different portions of the army marching in perfect coordination. Gordon led three divisions of infantry, supported by a brigade of cavalry across the Shenandoah River and marched east of Fisher's Hill. Then he went along the slope of the Massanuttons, recrossed the river, and silently came in behind the left flank of the Union force under Crook.

Early himself, with two divisions of infantry and all the artillery, marched straight toward Cedar Creek, where he would await the sound of firing to tell him that Gordon had completed his great circling movement. Then he would push forward with all his might, and he and Gordon appearing suddenly out of the fog and dark would strike sledge hammer blows from different sides at the surprised Union army. It was a conception worthy of Old Jack himself, although there was less strength with which to deal the blows.

The Invincibles were with Early, and they arrived in position before Cedar Creek long before Gordon could complete his wide flanking movement. Both artillery and infantry were up, and there was nothing for them to do but wait. The officers dismounted and naturally those who led the Invincibles kept close together. The wait was long. Midnight came, and then the hours after it passed one by one.

It was late in the year, the eighteenth of October, and the night was chill. The heavy fog which hung low made it chillier. Harry as he stood by his horse felt it cold and damp on his face, but it was a true friend for all that. Whether Happy wishing for the fog had made it come or not they could have found no better aid.

He could not see far, but out of the vapours came the sound of men moving, because they were restless and could not help it. He heard too the murmur of voices, and now and then the clank of a cannon, as it was advanced a little. More time passed. It was the hour when it would be nearly dawn on a clear day, and thousands of hearts leaped as the sound of shots came from a distant point out of the fog.

CHAPTER 11

Cedar Creek

The Winchester Regiment and the rest of the cavalry returned to the Union army, and, on the memorable night of the eighteenth of October, they were north of Cedar Creek with the Eighth Corps, most of the men being then comfortably asleep in tents. A courier had brought word to General Wright that all was quiet in front, and the same word was sent to Sheridan, who, returning, had come as far as Winchester where he slept that night, expecting to rejoin his command the next day.

But there were men of lower rank than Wright and Sheridan who were uneasy, and particularly so Sergeant Daniel Whitley, veteran of the plains, and of Indian ambush and battle. None of the Winchester officers had sought sleep either in the tents or elsewhere, and, in the night, Dick stood beside the suspicious sergeant and peered into the fog.

"I don't like it," said the veteran. "Fogs ain't to be taken lightly. I wish this one hadn't come at this time. I'm generally scared of most of the things I can't see."

"But what have we to be afraid of?" asked Dick. "We're here in strong force, and the enemy is too weak to attack."

"The Johnnies are never too weak to attack. Rec'lect, too, that this is their country, and they know every inch of it. I wish Mr. Shepard was here."

"I think he was detailed for some scout duty off toward the Blue Ridge"

"I don't know who sent him, but I make bold to say, Mr. Mason, that he could do a lot more good out there in the fog on the other side of Cedar Creek, a-spyin' and a-spyin', a-lookin' and a-lookin', a-listenin' and a-listenin'."

"And perhaps he would neither see nor hear anything"

"Maybe, sir, but if I may make bold again, I think you're wrong. Why, I just fairly smell danger."

"It's the fog and your fear of it, sergeant."

"No, sir; it's not that. It's my five senses working all together and telling me the truth."

"But the pickets have brought in no word."

"In this fog, pickets can't see more'n a few yards beyond their beats. What time is it, Mr. Mason?"

"A little past one in the morning, sergeant."

"Enough of the night left yet for a lot of mischief. I'm glad, sir, if I may make bold once more, that the Winchester men stay out of the tents and keep awake."

Warner joined them, and reported that fresh messengers from the front had given renewed assurances of quiet. Absolutely nothing was stirring along Cedar Creek, but Sergeant Daniel Whitley was still dissatisfied.

"It's always where nothin' is stirrin' that most is doin', sir," he said to Dick.

"You're epigrammatic, sergeant."

"I'm what, sir? I was never called that before."

"It doesn't depreciate you. It's a flattering adjective, but you've set my own nerves to tingling and I don't feel like sleeping."

"It never hurts, sir, to watch in war, even when nothing happens. I remember once when we were in a blizzard west of the Missouri, only a hundred of us. It was in the country of the Northern Cheyennes, an' no greater fighters ever lived than them red demons. We got into a kind of dip, surrounded by trees, an' managed to build a fire. We was so busy tryin' to keep from freezin' to death that we never gave a thought to Indians, that is 'ceptin' one, the guide, Jim Palmer, who knowed them Cheyennes, an' who kept dodgin' about in the blizzard, facin' the icy blast an' the whirlin' snow, an' always lookin' an' listenin'. I owe my life to him, an' so does every other one of the hundred. Shore enough the Cheyennes come, ridin' right on the edge of the blizzard, an' in all that terrible storm they tried to rush us. But we'd been warned by Palmer an' we beat 'em off at last, though a lot of good men bit the snow. I say again, sir, that you can't ever be too careful in war. Do everything you can think of, and then think of some more. I wish Mr. Shepard would come!"

They continued to walk back and forth, in front of the lines, and, at times, they were accompanied by Colonel Winchester or Warner or Pennington. The colonel fully shared the sergeant's anxieties. The fact that most of the Union army was asleep in the tents alarmed him, and the great fog added to his uneasiness. It came now in heavy drifts like clouds sweeping down the valley, and he did not know what was in the heart of it. The pickets had been sent far forward, but the vast moving column of heavy whitish vapour hid everything from their eyes, too, save a circle of a few yards about them.

Toward morning Dick, the colonel and the sergeant stood together, trying to pierce the veil of vapour in front of them. The colonel did not hesitate to speak his thought to the two.

"I wish that General Sheridan was here," he said.

"But he's at Winchester," said Dick. "He'll join us at noon."

"I wish he was here now, and I wish, too, that this fog would lift, and the day would come. Hark, what was that?"

"It was a rifle shot, sir," said the sergeant.

"And there are more," exclaimed Dick. "Listen!"

There was a sudden crackle of firing, and in front of them pink dots appeared through the fog.

"Here comes the Southern army!" said Sergeant Whitley.

Out of the fog rose a tremendous swelling cry from thousands of throats, fierce, long-drawn, and full of menace. It was the rebel yell, and from another point above the rising thunder of cannon and rifles came the same yell in reply, like a signal. The surprise was complete. Gordon had hurled himself upon the Union flank and at the same moment Early, according to his plan, drove with all his might at the centre.

Dick was horrified, and, for a moment or two, the blood was ice in his veins.

"Back!" cried Colonel Winchester to him and the sergeant, and then after shouting, "Up men! Up!" he blew long and loud upon his whistle. All of his men were on their feet in an instant, and they were first to return the Southern fire, but it had little effect upon the torrent that was now pouring down upon them. Other troops, so rudely aroused from sleep, rushed from their tents, still dazed, and firing wildly in the fog.

Again that terrible yell arose, more distinct than ever with menace and triumph, and so great was the rush of the men in gray that they swept everything before them, their rifles and cannon raking the Union camp with a withering fire. The Winchesters, despite their quickness to form in proper order, were driven back with the others, and the whole corps, assailed with frightful force on the flank also, was compelled continually to give ground, and to leave long rows of dead and wounded.

"Keep close to me!" shouted Colonel Winchester to his young officers, and then he added to the sergeant, who stood beside him: "Whitley, you were right!"

"I'm sorry to say I was, sir," replied the sergeant. "It was a great ambush, and it's succeeding so far."

"But we must hold them! We must find some way to hold them!" cried the colonel.

He said more, but it was lost in the tremendous uproar of the firing and the shouting. All the officers were dismounted—their horses already had been taken by the enemy—and now, waving their swords, they walked up and down in front of the lines, seeking to encourage their own troops. Despite the surprise and the attack from two sides, the men in blue sustained their courage and made a stubborn fight. Nevertheless the attack in both front and flank was fatal. Again and again they sought to hold a position, but always they were driven from it, leaving behind more dead and wounded and more prisoners.

Dick's heart sank. It was bitter to see a defeat, after so many victories. Perhaps the fortunes of the South had not passed the zenith after all! If Sheridan were defeated and driven from the valley, and Lee's flank left protected, Grant might sit forever before him at Petersburg and not be able to force his trenches. All these thoughts and fears swept before him, vague, disconnected, and swift.

But he saw that Warner, Pennington and the colonel were still unhurt, and that the Winchesters, despite their exposed position, had not suffered as much loss as some of the other regiments. General Wright in the absence of Sheridan retained his head, and formed a strong core of resistance which, although it could not yet hold the ground, might give promise of doing so, if help arrived.

Dawn came, driving the fog away, and casting a red glow over the field of battle. The ground where the Union troops had slept the night before was now left far behind, and the Southern army, full of fire and the swell of victory, was pushing on with undiminished energy, its whole front blazing with the rapid discharge of cannon and rifles.

The terrible retreat lasted a long time, and the whole Union army was driven back a full five miles before it could make a permanent stand. Then, far in the morning, the regiments reformed, held their ground, and Dick, for the first time, took a long free breath.

"We've been defeated but not destroyed," he said.

"No, we haven't," said a voice beside him, "but the fact that the Johnnies were so hungry has saved us a lot."

It was Shepard, who seemed to have risen from the ground.

"I've got back from places farther north," he said. "Chance kept me away from here last night."

"What do you mean about the Southern hunger helping us?" asked Dick.

"I've been on the flank, and I saw that when they drove us out of our camps the temptation was too great for many of their men. They scattered, seizing our good food and devouring it. It was impossible for their officers to restrain them. They've suffered losses too, and they can drive us no farther."

Then Shepard spoke briefly with Colonel Winchester, and disappeared again. The fire had now died somewhat and the banks of smoke were rising, enabling Dick to see the field with a degree of clearness. Union batteries and regiments were in line, but behind them a mass of fugitives, who had not yet recovered from the surprise and who thought the defeat complete, were pouring along the turnpike toward Winchester. When Dick saw their numbers his fears were renewed. He believed that if the Southern army could gather up all its forces and attack once more it would win another success.

But while he looked at the long line of fire in front of them a sudden roar of cheering rose from the Union ranks. It became a shout, tremendous and thrilling. Dick turned in excitement and he was about to ask what it meant, when he distinguished a name thundered again and again:

"Sheridan! Sheridan! Sheridan!"

Then before them galloped their own Little Phil, seeming to bring strength, courage and victory with him. His hat was thrown back, his face flushed, and his eyes sparkling. Everywhere the men rallied to his call and the shouts: "Sheridan! Sheridan!" rolled up and down. The fugitives too came pouring back to swell the line of battle. Dick caught the enthusiasm at once, and felt his own pulses leaping. He and Pennington and Warner joined in the shouts: "Sheridan! Sheridan!" and snatching off their caps waved them with all their vigour.

It was an amazing transformation. A beaten and dispirited army, holding on from a sense of duty, suddenly became alive with zeal, and asked only to be led against the enemy by the general they trusted. One man alone had worked the miracle and as his enemies had truly said his presence was worth ten thousand men.

His coming had been dramatic. He had spent the night quietly at Winchester, but, early in the morning, he had heard the sounds of firing which steadily grew louder. Apprehensive, he rode at once toward the distant field, and, before he had gone two miles, he met the first stragglers, bringing wild tales that the army had been routed, and that the Southerners were hot on their heels. Sheridan rode rapidly now. He met thicker streams of fugitives, but turned them back toward the enemy, and when he finally came upon the field itself he brought with him all the retreating regiments.

Dick never beheld a more thrilling and inspiring sight than that which occurred when Sheridan galloped among them, swinging his hat in his hand.

"What troops are these?" he had asked.

"The Sixth Corps!" hundreds of voices shouted in reply.

"We are all right! We'll win!" cried Sheridan.

And then, as he galloped along the line he added:

"Never mind, boys, we'll whip 'em yet! We'll whip 'em yet! We'll sleep in their quarters tonight!"

The roar of cheering swept up and down the line again, and Sheridan and his officers began to prepare the restored army for a new battle. All the time the Union numbers swelled, and, as the Southern army was hesitating, Sheridan was able to post his divisions as he pleased.

The Winchester regiment was drawn up towards the flank. All the officers were still on foot, but they stood a little in front, ready to lead their men into the new battle. It was now about noon, and there was a pause in the combat, enabling the smoke to lift yet higher, and disclosing the whole field. Sheridan was still riding up and down the lines, cool, determined and resolved to turn defeat into victory. Wherever he went he spoke words of encouragement to his troops, but all the time his eye, which was the eye of a true general, swept the field. He put the gallant young Custer with his cavalry on the right, Crook and Merritt with their horse on the left, while the infantry were massed in the centre. The Winchester men were sent to the right.

The doubts in the ranks of the South helped Sheridan. Early after his victory in the morning was surprised to see the Union army gather itself together again and show such a formidable front. Neither he nor his lieutenants could understand the sudden reversal, and the pause, which at first had been meant merely to give the troops opportunity for fresh breath, grew into a long delay. Here and there, skirmishers were firing, feeling out one another, but the masses of the army paid no attention to those scattered shots.

The Winchester men were elated. Colonel Winchester and the young officers knew that delay worked steadily for them. All the defeated troops of the morning were coming back into line, and now they were anxious to retrieve their disaster. Dick, through his glasses, saw that the Confederates so far from continuing the advance were now fortifying behind stone fences and also were spreading across the valley to keep from being flanked on either side by the cavalry. But he saw too that their ranks were scanty. If they spread far enough to protect their flanks they would become dangerously thin in the centre. He handed his glasses to the sergeant, and asked him to take a look.

"Their surprise," said Whitley, "has spent its force. Their army is not big enough. Our general has seen it, and it's why he delays so long. Time works for us, because we can gather together much greater numbers than they have."

The delay lasted far into the afternoon. The smoke and dust settled, and the October sun gleamed on cannon and bayonets. Dick's watch showed that it was nearly four o'clock.

"We attack today surely," said Pennington, who was growing nervous with impatience.

"Don't you worry, young man," said Warner. "The two armies are here in line facing each other and as it would be too much trouble to arrange it all again tomorrow the battle will be fought today. The whole program will be carried out on time."

"I think," said Dick, "that the attack is very near, and that it's we who are going to make it. Here is General Sheridan himself."

The general rode along the line just before the Winchesters and nodded to them approvingly. He came so close that Dick saw the contraction of his face, and his eager burning look, as if the great moment had arrived. Suddenly, he raised his hand and the buglers blew the fierce notes of the charge.

"Now we go!" cried Pennington in uncontrollable excitement, and the whole right wing seemed to lift itself up bodily and rush forward. The men, eager to avenge the losses of the morning, began to shout, and their cheers mingled with the mighty tread of the charge, the thunder of the cannon and the rapid firing of thousands of rifles. They knew, too, that Sheridan's own eye was upon them, and it encouraged them to a supreme effort.

Infantry and cavalry swept on together in an overwhelming mass. Cannon and rifles sent a bitter hail upon them, but nothing could stop their rush. Dick felt all his pulses beating heavily and he saw a sea of fire before him, but his excitement was so intense that he forgot about danger.

The centre also swung into the charge and then the left. All the divisions of the army, as arranged by Sheridan, moved in perfect time.

The soldiers advanced like veterans going from one victory to another, instead of rallying from a defeat. The war had not witnessed another instance of such a quick and powerful recovery.

Dick knew, as their charge gathered force at every step, that they were going to certain triumph. The thinness of the Southern lines had already told him that they could not withstand the impact of Sheridan. A moment later the crash came and the whole Union force rushed to victory. Early's army, exhausted by its efforts of the morning, was overwhelmed. It was swept from the stone fences and driven back in defeat, while the men in blue, growing more eager as they saw success achieved, pressed harder and harder.

No need for bugle and command to urge them on now. The Southern army could not withstand anywhere such ardour and such weight. Position after position was lost, then there was no time to take a new stand, and the defeat became a rout. Early's army which had come forward so gallantly in the morning was compelled to flee in disorder in the afternoon. The brave Ramseur, fighting desperately, fell mortally wounded, Kershaw could save but a few men, Evans held a ford a little while, but he too was soon hurled from it. The Invincibles were driven on with the rest, cannon and wagons were lost, and all but the core of Early's force ceased to exist.

The sun set upon the Union army in the camps that it had lost in the fog of the morning. It had been driven five miles but had come back again. It had recovered all its own guns, and had taken twenty-four belonging to the South. It was the most complete victory that had yet been won by either side in the war, and it had been snatched from the very jaws of defeat and humiliation. Small wonder that there was great rejoicing in the ranks of northern youth! Despite their immense exertions and the commands of their officers they could not yet lie down and sleep or rest. Now and then a tremendous cheer for Little Phil who had saved them arose. Huge bonfires sprang up in the night, where they were burning the captured Confederate ambulances and wagons, because they did not have the horses with which to take them away.

Long after the battle was over, Dick's heart beat hard with exertion and excitement. But he shared too in the joy. He would not have been human, and he would not have been young if he had not. Warner and Pennington and he had collected four more small wounds among them, but they were so slight that they had not noticed them in the storm and fury of the battle. Colonel Winchester had not been touched.

When Dick was at last able to sit still, he joined his comrades about one of the fires, where they were serving supper to the victors. Shepard had just galloped back from a long ride after the enemy to say that they had been scattered to the winds, and that another surprise was not possible, because there were no longer enough Southern soldiers in the valley to make an army.

"They made a great effort," said Colonel Winchester. "We must give them credit for what they achieved against numbers and resources. They organized and carried out their surprise in a wonderful manner, and perhaps they would be the victors tonight if we didn't have such a general as Sheridan."

"It was a great sight," said Warner, "when he appeared, galloping before our line, calling upon us to renew our courage and beat the enemy."

"One man can influence an army. I've found out that," said Dick.

They rose and saluted as General Sheridan walked past with some of the higher officers. He returned the salutes, congratulated them on their courage and went on. After a long while the exhausted victors fell asleep.

* * * * * * * *

That night a band of men, a hundred perhaps, entered the woods along the slopes of the Massanuttons. They were the remains of the Invincibles. Throughout those fatal hours they had fought with all the courage and tenacity for which they had been famous so long and so justly. In the heat and confusion of the combat they had been separated from the other portions of Early's army, and, the Northern cavalry driving in between, they had been compelled to take refuge in the forest, under cover of darkness. They might have surrendered with honour, but not one among them thought of such a thing. They had been forced to leave their dead behind them, and of those who had withdrawn about a third were wounded. But, their hurts bandaged by their comrades, they limped on with the rest.

The two colonels were at the head of the sombre little column. It had seemed to Harry Kenton as they left the field that each of them had suddenly grown at least ten years older, but now as they passed within the deep shadows they became erect again and their faces grew more youthful. It was a marvellous transformation, but Harry read their secret. All the rest of the Invincibles were lads, or but little more, and they two middle-aged men felt that they were responsible for them. In the face of defeat and irretrievable disaster they recovered their courage, and refused to abandon hope.

"A dark sunset, Hector," said Colonel Talbot, "but a bright dawn will come, even yet."

"Who can doubt it, Leonidas? We won a glorious victory over odds in the morning, but when a million Yankees appeared on the field in the afternoon it was too much."

"That's always the trouble, Hector. We are never able to finish our victories, because so many of the enemy always come up before the work is done."

"It's a great pity, Leonidas, that we didn't count the Yankees before the war was started."

"It's too late now. Don't call up a sore subject, Hector. We've got to take care of these lads of ours, and try to get them across the mountain somehow to Lee. It's useless to seek Early and we couldn't reach him if we tried. He's done for."

"Alas! It's true, Leonidas! We're through with the valley for this autumn at least, and, since the organization of the army here is broken up, there is nothing for us to do but go to Lee. Harry, is this a high mountain?"

"Not so very high, sir," replied Harry Kenton, who was just behind him, "but I don't think we can cross it tonight."

"Maybe we don't want to do so," said Colonel Talbot. "You boys have food in your knapsacks, taken from the Union camps, which we held for a few short and glorious hours. At least we have brought off those valuable trophies, and, when we have climbed higher up the mountain side, we will sup and rest."

The colonel held himself very erect, and spoke in a firm proud tone. He would inspire a high spirit into the hearts of these boys of his, and in doing so he inspired a great deal of it into his own. He looked back at his column, which still limped bravely after him. It was too dark for him to see the faces of the lads, but he knew that none of them expressed despair.

"That's the way, my brave fellows," he said. "I know we'll find a warm and comfortable cove higher up. We'll sleep there, and tomorrow we'll start toward Lee. When we join him we'll whip Grant, come back here and rout Sheridan and then go on and take Washington."

"Where I mean yet, sir, to sleep in the White House with my boots on," said the irrepressible Happy.

"You are a youth frivolous of speech, Thomas Langdon," said Colonel Leonidas Talbot gravely, "but I have always known that beneath this superficiality of manner was a brave and honest heart. I'm glad to see that your courage is so high."

"Thank you, sir," said Happy sincerely.

Half way up the mountain they found the dip they wished, sheltered by cedars and pines. Here they rested and ate, and from their covert saw many lights burning in the valley. But they knew they were the lights of the victorious foe, and they would not look that way often.

The October winds were cold, and they had lost their blankets, but the dry leaves lay in heaps, and they raked them up for beds. The lads, worn to the bone, fell asleep, and, after a while, only the two colonels remained awake.

"I do not feel sleepy at all, Hector," said Colonel Leonidas Talbot.

"I could not possibly sleep, Leonidas," said Lieutenant Colonel St. Hilaire.

"Then shall we?"

"Why not?"

Colonel Talbot produced from under his coat a small board, and Lieutenant Colonel St. Hilaire took from under his own coat a small box.

They put the board upon a broad stone, arranged the chessmen, as they were at the latest interruption, and, as the moonlight came through the dwarfed pines and cedars, the two gray heads bent over the game.

CHAPTER 12

In the Cove

General Sheridan permitted the Winchester men to rest a long time, or rather he ordered them to do so. No regiment had distinguished itself more at Cedar Creek or in the previous battles, and it was best for it to lie by a while, and recover its physical strength—strength of the spirit it had never lost. It also gave a needed chance to the sixteen slight wounds accumulated by Dick, Pennington and Warner to heal perfectly.

"Unless something further happens," said Warner, regretfully, "I won't have a single honourable scar to take back with me and show in Vermont."

"I'll have one slight, though honourable, scar, but I won't be able to show it," said Pennington, also with regret.

"I trust that it's in front, Frank," said Dick.

"It is, all right. Don't worry about that. But what about you, Dick?"

"I had hopes of a place on my left arm just above the elbow. A bullet, travelling at the rate of a million miles a minute, broke the skin there and took a thin flake of flesh with it, but I'm so terribly healthy it's healed up without leaving a trace."

"There's no hope for us," said Warner, sighing. "We can never point to the proof of our warlike deeds. You didn't find your cousin among the prisoners?"

"No, nor was he among their fallen whom we buried. Nor any of his friends either. I'm quite sure that he escaped. My intuition tells me so."

"It's not your intuition at all," said Warner reprovingly. "It's a reasonable opinion, formed in your mind by antecedent conditions. You call it intuition, because you don't take the trouble to discover the circumstances that led to its production. It's only lazy minds that fall back upon second sight, mind-reading and such things."

"Isn't he the big-word man?" said Pennington admiringly. "I tell you what, George, General Early is still alive somewhere, and we're going to send you to talk him to death. They say he's a splendid swearer, one of the greatest that ever lived, but he won't be able to get out a single cuss, with you standing before him, and spouting the whole unabridged dictionary to him."

"At least when I talk I say something," replied Warner sternly. "It seems strange to me, Frank Pennington, that your life on the plains, where conditions, for the present at least, are hard, has permitted you to have so much frivolity in your nature."

"It's not frivolity, George. It's a gay and bright spirit, in the rays of which you may bask without price. It will do you good."

"Do you know what's to be our next duty?"

"No, I don't, and I'm not going to bother about it. I'll leave that directly to Colonel Winchester, and indirectly to General Sheridan. When you rest, put your mind at rest. Concentration on whatever you are doing is the secret of continued success."

They were lying on blankets near the foot of the mountain, and the time was late October. The days were growing cold and the nights colder, but a fine big fire was blazing before them, and they rejoiced in the warmth and brightness, shed from the flames and the heaps of glowing coals.

"I'll venture the prediction," said Pennington, "that our next march is not against an army, but against guerrillas. They say that up there in the Alleghenies Slade and Skelly are doing a lot of harm. They may have to be hunted out and the Winchester men have the best reputation in the army for that sort of work. We earned it by our work against these very fellows in Tennessee."

"For which most of the credit is due to Sergeant Whitley," said Dick. "He's a grand trailer, and he can lead us with certainty, when other regiments can't find the way."

Dick gazed westward beyond the dim blue line of the Alleghenies, and he knew that he would feel no surprise if Pennington's prediction should come true. The nest of difficult mountains was a good shelter for outlaws, and the Winchesters, with the sergeant picking up the trail, were the very men to hunt them.

He knew too that, unless the task was begun soon, it would prove a supreme test of endurance, and there would be dangers in plenty. Snow would be falling before long on the mountains, and they would become a frozen wilderness, almost as wild and savage as they were before the white man came.

But it seemed for a while that the intuition of both Dick and Pennington had failed. They spent many days in the valley trying to catch the evasive Mosby and his men, although they had little success. Mosby's rangers knowing the country thoroughly made many daring raids, although they could not become a serious menace.

When they returned through Winchester from the last of these expeditions the Winchester men were wrapped in heavy army cloaks, for the wind from the mountains could now cut through uniforms alone. Dick, glancing toward the Alleghenies, saw a ribbon of white above their blue line.

"Look, fellows! The first snow!" he said.

"I see," said Warner. "It snows on the just and the unjust, the unjust being Slade and Skelly, who are surely up there."

"Just before we went out," sad Pennington, "the news of some fresh and special atrocity of theirs came in. I'm thinking the time is near when we'll be sent after them."

"We'll need snow shoes," said Warner, shivering as he looked. "I can see that the snow is increasing. Which way is the wind blowing, Dick?"

"Toward us."

"Then we're likely to get a little of that snow. The clouds will blow off the mountains and sprinkle us with flakes in the valley."

"I like winter in peace, but not in war," said Pennington. "It makes campaigning hard. It's no fun marching at night in a driving storm of snow or hail."

"But what we can't help we must stand," said Warner with resignation.

Both predictions, the one about the snow and the other concerning the duty that would be assigned to them, quickly came to pass. Before sunset the blue line of the Alleghenies was lost wholly in mist and vapour. Then great flakes began to fall on the camp, and the young officers were glad to find refuge in their tents.

It was not a heavy snow fall where they were, but it blew down at intervals all through the night, and the next morning it lay upon the ground to the depth of an inch or so. Then the second part of the prophecy was justified. Colonel Winchester himself aroused all his staff and heads of companies.

"A fine crisp winter morning for us to take a ride," he said cheerfully. "General Sheridan has become vexed beyond endurance over the doings of Slade and Skelly, and he has chosen his best band of guerrilla-hunters to seek 'em out in their lairs and annihilate 'em."

"I knew it," groaned Pennington in an undertone to Dick. "I was as certain of it as if I had read the order already." But aloud he said as he saluted: "We're glad we're chosen for the honour, sir. I speak for Mr. Mason, Mr. Warner and myself."

"I'm glad you're thankful," laughed the colonel. "A grateful and resolute heart always prepares one for hardships, and we'll have plenty of them over there in the high mountains, where the snow lies deep. But we have new horses, furnished especially for this expedition, and Sergeant Whitley and Mr. Shepard will guide us. The sergeant can hear or see anything within a quarter of a mile of him, and Mr. Shepard, being a native of the valley, knows also all the mountains that close it in."

The young lieutenants were sincerely glad the sergeant and Shepard were to go along, as with them they felt comparatively safe from ambush, a danger to be dreaded where Slade and Skelly were concerned.

"We agreed that General Sheridan was worth ten thousand men," said Warner, "and I believe that the battle of Cedar Creek proved it. Now if Sheridan is worth ten thousand, the sergeant and Shepard are certainly worth a thousand each. It's a simple algebraic problem which I could demonstrate to you by the liberal use of x and y, but in your case it's not necessary. You must accept my word for it."

"We'll do it! We'll do it! say no more!" exclaimed Pennington hastily.

It was a splendid column of men that rode out from the Union camp and General Sheridan himself saw them off. Colonel Winchester at their head was a man of fine face and figure, and he had never looked more martial. The hardships of war had left no mark upon him. His face was tanned a deep red by the winds of summer and winter, and although a year or two over forty he seemed to be several years less. Behind him came Dick, Pennington and Warner, hardy and well knit, who had passed through the most terrible of all schools, three and a half years of incessant war, and who although youths were nevertheless stronger and more resourceful than most men.

Near them rode the sergeant, happy in his capacity as scout and guide, and welcoming the responsibility that he knew would be his, as soon as they reached the mountains, looming so near and white. He felt as if he were back upon the plains, leading a troop in a great blizzard, and guarding it with eye and ear and all his five senses against Sioux or Cheyenne ambush. He was not a mere trainer of a squad of men, he was, in a real sense, a leader of an army.

Shepard, the spy, also felt a great uplift of the spirits. He was a man of high ideals, whose real nature the people about him were just beginning to learn. He did not like his trade of a spy, but being aware that he was peculiarly fitted for it intense patriotism had caused him to accept its duties. Now he felt that most of his work in such a capacity was over. He could freely ride with the other men and fight openly as they did. But if emergency demanded that he renew his secret service he would do so instantly and without hesitation.

Colonel Winchester looked back with pride at his column. Like most of the regiments at that period of the war it was small, three hundred sinewy well-mounted young men, who had endured every kind of hardship and who could endure the like again. All of them were wrapped in heavy overcoats over their uniforms, and they rode the best of horses, animals that Colonel Winchester had been allowed to choose.

The colonel felt so good that he took out his little silver whistle, and blew upon it a mellow hunting call. The column broke into a trot and the snow flew behind the beating hoofs in a long white trail. Spontaneously the men burst into a cheer, and the cold wind blowing past them merely whipped their blood into high exaltation.

But as they rode across the valley Dick could not help feeling some depression over its ruined and desolate appearance, worse now in winter than in summer. No friendly smoke rose from any chimney, there were no horses nor cattle in the fields, the rails of the fences had gone long since to make fires for the soldiers and the roads rutted deep by the rains had been untouched. Silence and loneliness were supreme everywhere.

He was glad when they left it all behind, and entered the mountains through a pass fairly broad and sufficient for horsemen. He did not feel so much oppression here. It was natural for mountains to be lonely and silent also, particularly in winter, and his spirits rose again as they rode between the white ridges.

At the entrance to the pass a mountaineer named Reed met them. It was he who had brought the news of the latest exploit by Slade and Skelly, but he had returned quickly to warn some friends of his in the foothills and was back again in time to meet the soldiers. He was a long thin man of middle age, riding a large black mule. An immense gray shawl was pinned about his shoulders, and woollen leggings came high over his trousers. As he talked much he chewed tobacco vigorously. But Dick saw at once that like many of the mountaineers he was a shrewd man, and, despite lack of education, was able to look, see and judge.

Reed glanced over the column, showed his teeth, yellowed by the constant use of tobacco, and the glint of a smile appeared in his eyes.

"Look like good men. I couldn't hev picked 'em better myself, colonel," he said, with the easy familiarity of the hills.

"They've been in many battles, and they've never failed," said the colonel with some pride.

"You'll hev to do somethin' more than fight up thar on the high ridges," said the mountaineer, showing his yellow teeth again. "You'll hev to look out fur traps, snares an' ambushes. Slade an' Skelly ain't soldiers that come out an' fight fa'r an' squar' in the open. No, sirree, they're rattlesnakes, a pair uv 'em an' full uv p'ison. We've got to find our rattlesnakes an' ketch 'em. Ef we don't, they'll be stingin' jest the same after you've gone."

"That's just the way I look at it, Mr. Reed. Sergeant Whitley here is a specialist in rattlesnakes. He used to hunt down and kill the big bloated ones on the plains, and even the snow won't keep him from tracing 'em to their dens here in the mountains."

Reed, after the custom of his kind, looked the sergeant up and down with a frank stare.

"'Pears to be a good man," he said, "hefty in build an' quick in the eye. Glad to know you, Mr. Whitley. You an' me may take part in a shootin' bee together an' this old long-barrelled firearm uv mine kin give a good account uv herself."

He patted his rifle affectionately, a weapon of ancient type, with a long slender barrel of blue steel, and a heavy carved stock. It was just such a rifle as the frontiersmen used. Dick's mind, in an instant, travelled back into the wilderness and he was once more with the great hunters and scouts who fought for the fair land of Kain-tuck-ee. His imagination was so vivid that it required only a touch to stir it into life, and the aspect of the mountains, wild and lonely and clothed in snow, heightened the illusion.

"I s'pose from what you tell us that you'll have the chance to use it, Mr. Reed," said the sergeant.

"I reckon so," replied the mountaineer emphatically. "'Bout five miles up this pass you'll come to a cove in which Jim Johnson's house stood. Some uv them gorillers attacked it, three nights ago. Jim held 'em off with his double-barrelled shotgun, 'til his wife an' children could git out the back way. Then he skedaddled hisself. They plundered the house uv everythin' wuth carryin' off an' then they burned it plum' to the groun'. Jim an' his people near froze to death on the mounting, but they got at last to the cabin uv some uv their kin, whar they are now. Then they've carried off all the hosses an' cattle they kin find in the valleys an' besides robbin' everybody they've shot some good men. Thar is shorely a good dose uv lead comin' to every feller in that band."

The mountaineer's face for a moment contracted violently. Dick saw that he was fairly burning for revenge. Among his people the code of an eye for an eye and a tooth for a tooth still prevailed, unquestioned, and there would be no pity for the guerrilla who might come under the muzzle of his rifle. But his feelings were shown only for the moment. In another instant, he was a stoic like the Indians whom he had displaced. After a little silence he added: "That man Slade, who is the brains uv the outfit, is plum' devil. So fur ez his doin's in these mountings are concerned he ain't human at all. He hez no mercy fur nuthin' at no time."

His words found an echo in Dick's own mind. He remembered how venomously Slade had hunted for his own life in the Southern marshes, and chance, since then, had brought them into opposition more than once. Just as Harry had felt that there was a long contest between Shepard and himself, Dick felt that Slade and he were now to be pitted in a long and mortal combat. But Shepard was a patriot, while Slade was a demon, if ever a man was. If he were to have a particular enemy he was willing that it should be Slade, as he could see in him no redeeming quality that would cause him to stay his hand, if his own chance came.

"Have you any idea where the guerrillas are camped now?" asked Colonel Winchester.

"When we last heard uv 'em they wuz in Burton's Cove," replied the mountaineer, "though uv course they may hev moved sence then. Still, the snow may hev held 'em. It's a-layin' right deep on the mountings, an' even the gorillers ain't so anxious to plough thar way through it."

"How long will it take us to reach Burton's Cove?"

"It's jest ez the weather sez, colonel. Ef the snow holds off we might make it tomorrow afore dark, but ef the snow makes up its mind to come tumblin' down ag'in, it's the day after that, fur shore."

"At any rate, another fall of snow is no harder for us than it is for them," said the colonel, who showed the spirit of a true leader. "Now, Mr. Reed, do you think we can find anybody on this road who will tell us where the band has gone?"

"It ain't much uv a road an' thar ain't many people to ride on it in the best uv times, so I reckon our chance uv meetin' a traveller who knows much is jest about ez good as our chance uv findin' a peck uv gold in the next snowdrift."

"Which means there's no chance at all."

"I reckon that's 'bout the size uv it. But, colonel, we don't hev to look to the road fur the word."

"What do you mean?"

"We'll turn our eyes upward, to the mounting heights. Some uv us who are jest bound to save the Union are settin' up on top uv high ridges, whar that p'ison band can't go, waitin' to tell us whar *we* ought to go. They've got some home-made flags, an' they'll wave 'em to me."

"Mr. Reed, you're a man of foresight and perception."

"Foresight? I know what that is. It's the opposite uv hindsight, but I ain't made the acquaintance uv perception."

"Perception is what you see after you think, and I know that you're a man who thinks."

"Thank you, colonel, but I reckon that in sech a war ez this a man hez jest got to set right plum' down, an' think sometimes. It's naterally forced upon him. Them that starts a war mebbe don't do much thinkin', but them that fights it hev to do a power uv it."

"Your logic is sound, Mr. Reed."

"I hev a pow'ful good eye, colonel, an' I think I see a man on top uv that high ridge to the right. But my eye ain't ez good ez your glasses, an' would you min' takin' a look through 'em? Foller a line from that little bunch of cedars to the crest."

"Yes, it's a man. I can see him quite plainly. He has a big, gray shawl like your own, wrapped around his shoulders. Perhaps he's one of your friends."

"I reckon so, but sence he ain't makin' no signs he ain't got nuthin' to tell. It wuz agreed that them that didn't know nuthin' wuz to keep it to theirselves while we rode on until we come to them that did. It saves time. Now he's gone, ain't he, colonel?"

"Yes, something has come in between."

"It's the first thin edge uv the mist. Them's clouds out thar in the northwest, floatin' over the mountings. I'm sorry, colonel, but more snow is comin'. The signs is too plain. Look through that gap an' see what big brown clouds are sailin' up! They're just chock full uv millions uv millions uv tons uv snow!"

"You know your own country and its winter ways, Mr. Reed. How long will it be before the snow comes?"

"Lend me your glasses a minute, colonel."

He examined the clouds a long time through the powerful lenses, and when he handed them back he replied:

"Them clouds are movin' up in a hurry, colonel. They hev saw us here ridin' into the mountings, an' they want to pour their snow down on us afore we git whar we want to go."

Colonel Winchester looked anxious.

"I don't like it," he said. "It doesn't suit cavalry to be plunging around in snowdrifts."

"You're right, colonel. Deep snow is shorely hard on hosses. It looks ez ef we'd be holed up. B'ars an' catamounts, how them clouds are a-trottin' 'cross the sky! Here come the fust flakes an' they look ez big ez feathers!"

The colonel's anxiety deepened, turning rapidly to alarm.

"You spoke of our being holed up, Mr. Reed, what did you mean by it?" he asked.

"Shet in by the snow. But I know a place, colonel, that we kin reach, an' whar we kin stay ef the snow gits too deep fur us. These mountings are full uv little valleys an' coves. They say the Alleghenies run more than a thousand miles one way an' mebbe three hundred or so another. I reckon that when the Lord made 'em, an' looked at His job, he wondered how He wuz goin' to hev people live in sech a mass uv mountings. Then He took His fingers an' pressed 'em down into the ground lots an' lots uv times, an' He made all sorts of purty valleys an' ravines through which the rivers an' creeks an' branches could run, an' snug little coves in which men could build thar cabins an' be shel-tered by the big cliffs above an' the forest hangin' on 'em. I reckon that He favoured us up here, 'cause the mountings jest suit me. Nuthin' on earth could drive me out uv 'em."

He looked up at the lofty ridges hidden now and then by the whirling snow, and his eyes glistened. It was a stern and wild scene, but he knew that it made the snug cove and the log cabins all the snugger. The flakes were increasing now, and an evil wind was driving them hard in the men's faces. The wind, as it came through the gorges, had many voices, too, howling and shrieking in wrath. The young troopers were devoutly grateful for the heavy overcoats and gloves with which a thoughtful general had provided them.

But there was one man in the regiment to whom wind and snow brought a certain pleasure. It took Sergeant Whitley back to earlier days. He was riding once more with his command over the great plains, and the foe they sought was a Cheyenne or Sioux band. Here, they needed him and his wilderness lore, and he felt that a full use for them all would come.

The mountaineer now led them on rapidly, but the snow was in-creasing with equal rapidity. Fortunately, the road through the pass was level enough to provide good footing for the horses, and they proceeded without fear of falls. Soon the entire column turned into a white procession. Men and horses alike were covered with snow, but, after their first chill, the hardy young riders began to like it. They sang one of their marching songs, and the colonel made no effort to restrain them, knowing that it was raising their spirits.

"It's all rather picturesque," said Warner, when the song was over, "but it'll be a good thing when Reed leads us into one of those heavenly coves that he talks so much about. I think this snow is going to be about forty feet deep, and it will be hard for a column of three hundred men to proceed by means of tunnels."

The mountaineer riding by the side of Colonel Winchester was looking eagerly, whenever a break in the clouds occurred. At length, he asked him for the glasses again and, after looking intently, said:

"Jest between the edges uv two clouds I caught a glimpse uv a man, an' he wuz wavin' a flag, which wuz a sheet from his own bed. It would be Jake Hening, 'cause that wuz his place, an' he told me to go straight on to the cove, ez they wuz now expectin' us thar!"

"Who is expecting us?"

"Friends uv ours. People 'roun' here in the mountings who want to see you make hash uv them gorillers. I reckon they're fixin' things to keep you warm. We oughter see another man an' his sheet afore long. Thar would be no trouble 'bout it, ef this snow wuzn't so thick."

As they advanced farther into the mountains the noise of the wind increased. Confined in the gorges it roared in anger to get out, and then whistled and shrieked as it blew along the slopes. The snow did not cease to fall. The road had long since been covered up, but Reed led them on with sure eye and instinct.

An hour later he was able to detect another figure on the crest of a ridge, this time to their left, and he observed the waving of the signal with great satisfaction.

"It's all right," he said to Colonel Winchester. "They're waitin' for us in the cove, not many uv 'em, uv course, but they'll help."

"Have we much more riding?" asked the colonel. "I don't think the men are suffering, but our horses can't stand it much longer."

"Not more'n an hour."

They passed soon between high cliffs, and faced a fierce wind which almost blinded them for the time, but, when they emerged they found better shelter and, presently, Reed led them off the main road, then through another narrow gorge and into the cove. They had passed around a curving wall of the mountain and, as it burst upon them suddenly, the spectacle was all the more pleasant.

Before them, like a sunken garden, lay a space of twenty or thirty acres, hemmed in by the high mountains, which seemed fairly to overhang its level spaces. A small creek flowed down from a ravine on one side, and dashed out of a ravine on the other. Splendid oaks, elms and maples grew in parts of the valley, and there was an orchard and a garden, but the greater part of it was cleared, and so well protected by the lofty mountains that most of the snow seemed to blow over it. In the snuggest corner of the cove stood a stout double log cabin and, in the open space around, great fires were roaring and sending up lofty flames, a welcome sight to the stiff and cold horsemen. Fully twenty mountaineers, long and lank like Reed, were gathered around them, and were feeding them constantly.

"What's this I see?" exclaimed Warner. "A little section of heaven?"

"Not heaven, perhaps," said Dick, "but the next door to it."

"This wuz Dick Snyder's home an' place, colonel," said Reed. "On account uv the gorillers he found it convenient to light out with his folks three or four days ago, but he's come back hisself, an' he's here to he'p welcome you. Thar's room in the house, an' the stable, which you can't see 'cause uv the trees, fur all the officers, an' they're buildin' lean-tos here to protect the soldiers an' the hosses. A lot uv the fellers hev brought forage down on thar own hosses fur yourn."

"Mr. Reed," said the colonel, gratefully, "you and your men are true friends. But there's no danger of an ambush here?"

"Nary a chance, colonel. We've got watchers on the mountings, men that hev lived here all thar lives, an' them gorillers hev about ez much chance to steal up on us ez the snowflakes hev to live in the fires thar."

"That being so, we'll all alight and prepare for the night."

When Dick sprang from his horse he staggered at first, not realizing how much the cold had affected him, but a little vigorous flexing of the muscles restored the circulation, and, when an orderly had taken their mounts, his comrades and he went to one of the fires, where they spread out their hands and basked in the glow.

They had brought food on extra horses, and expert cooks were at work at once. Colonel Winchester knew that if his men had plenty to eat and good shelter they would be better fitted for the fierce work before them, and he spared nothing. Bacon and ham were soon frying on the coals and the pots of coffee were bubbling.

The horses were put behind the high trees which formed a kind of windrow, and there they ate their forage, and raised their heads now and then to neigh in content. Around the fires the hardy youths were jesting with one another, and were dragging up logs, on which they could sit before the fires, while they ate their food and drank their coffee. Far over their heads the wind was screaming among the ridges, but they did not heed it nor did they pay any attention to the flakes falling around them. The sheltered cove caused such a rebound after the long cold ride that they were boys again, although veterans of a hundred battles large and small.

Dick shared the exaltation of the rest, and had words of praise for the mountaineer who had guided them to so sheltered a haven. He had no doubt that his famous ancestor, Paul Cotter, and the great Henry Ware had often found refuge in such cosy nooks as this, and it pleased him to think that he was following in their steps. But he was surrounded by comrades and the great fires shed warmth and light throughout the whole basin.

"It's a good log house," said Warner, who had been investigating, "and as it's two stories, with two rooms on each floor, a lot of us can sleep there. The stable and the corn crib will hold many more, but, as for me, I think I'll sleep against one of these lean-tos the mountaineers are throwing up. With that behind me, a big fire before me, two heavy blankets around me, and dead leaves under me, I ought to fare well. It will at least have better air than those sod houses in which some of the best families of Nebraska live, Frank Pennington."

"Never mind about the sod houses," rejoined Pennington, cheerfully. "They're mighty good places in a blizzard. But I think I'll stay outside too, if Colonel Winchester will let us."

The colonel soon disposed his force. The younger officers were to sleep before a fire as they wished, although about half way between midnight and morning they were to join the watch, which he intended to be strong and vigilant. Meanwhile they ate supper and their spirits were so high that they almost made a festival of it. The aroma of the ham and bacon, broiled in the winter open, would have made a jaded epicure hungry. They had sardines and oysters, in tins, and plenty of coffee, with army biscuits which were not hard to them. Some of them wanted to sing, but the colonel would not allow it in the cove, although they could chatter as much as they pleased around the fires.

"We don't need to sing," said Dick. "The wind is doing it for us. Just listen to it, will you?"

All the mountain winds were blowing that night, coming from every direction, and then circling swiftly in vast whirlwinds, while the ridges and peaks and gorges made them sing their songs in many keys. Now it was a shriek, then a whistle, and then a deep full tone like an organ. Blended, it had a majestic effect which was not lost on the young soldiers.

"I've heard it in the Green Mountains," said Warner, "but not under such conditions as we have here. I'm glad I have so much company. I think it would give me the creeps to be in the cove alone, with that storm howling over my head."

"Not to mention Slade and Skelly hunting through the snowdrifts for you," said Pennington. "They'd take a good long look for you, George, knowing what a tremendous fellow you are, and then Dick and I would be compelled to take the trouble and danger of rescuing you."

"I hold you to that," said Warner. "You do hereby promise and solemnly pledge yourselves in case of my capture by Slade, Skelly or anybody else, to come at once through any hardship and danger to my rescue."

"We do," they said together, and they meant it.

Their situation was uncommon, and their pleasure in it deepened. The snow still fell, but the lean-tos, built with so much skill by soldiers and mountaineers, protected them, and the fires before them sank to great beds of gleaming coals that gave out a grateful warmth. Far overhead the wind still shrieked and howled, as if in anger because it could not get at them in the deep cleft. But for Dick all these shrieks and howls were transformed into a soothing song by his feeling of comfort, even of luxury. The cove was full of warmth and light and he basked in it.

Pennington and Warner fell asleep, but Dick lay a while in a happy, dreaming state. He felt as he looked up at the cloudy sky and driving snow that, after all, there was something wild in every man that no amount of civilization could drive out. An ordinary bed and an ordinary roof would be just as warm and better sheltered, but they seldom gave him the same sense of physical pleasure that he felt as he lay there with the storm driving by.

His dreamy state deepened, and with it the wilderness effect which the little valley, the high mountains around it and the raging winter made. His mind travelled far back once more and he easily imagined himself his great ancestor, Paul Cotter, sleeping in the woods with his comrades and hidden from Indian attack. While the feeling was still strong upon him he too fell asleep, and he did not awaken until it was time for him to take the watch with Pennington and Warner.

It was then about two o'clock in the morning, and the snow had ceased to fall, but it lay deep in all places not sheltered, while the wind had heaped it up many feet in all the gorges and ravines of the mountains. Dick thought he had never beheld a more majestic world. All the clouds were gone and hosts of stars glittered in a sky of brilliant blue. On every side of them rose the lofty peaks and ridges, clothed in gleaming white, the forests themselves a vast, white tracery. The air was cold but pure and stimulating. The wind had ceased to blow, but from far points came the faint swish of sliding snow.

Dick folded his blankets, laid them away carefully, put on his heavy overcoat and gloves, and was ready. Colonel Winchester maintained a heavy watch, knowing its need, fully fifty men, rifle on shoulder and pistol at belt, patrolling all the ways by which a foe could come.

Dick and his comrades were with a picket at the farther end of the valley, where the creek made its exit, rushing through a narrow and winding gorge. There was a level space on either side of the creek, but it was too narrow for horsemen, and, clogged as it was with snow, it looked dangerous now for those on foot too. Nevertheless, the picket kept a close watch. Dick and his friends were aware that guerrillas knew much of the craft and lore of the wilderness, else they could never have maintained themselves, and they did not cease for an instant to watch the watery pass.

They were joined very soon by Shepard, upon whose high boots snow was clinging to the very tops, and he said when Dick looked at him inquiringly:

"I see that you're an observer, Mr. Mason. Yes, I've been out on the mountainside. Colonel Winchester suggested it, and I was glad to do as he wished. It was difficult work in the snow, but Mr. Reed, our guide, was with me part of the time, and we climbed pretty high."

"Did you see anything?"

"No footsteps. That was impossible, because of the falling snow, but I think our friends, the enemy, are abroad in the mountains. The heavy snow may have kept them from coming much nearer to us than they are now."

"What makes you think so?"

Shepard smiled.

"We heard sounds, odd sounds," he replied.

"Were they made by a whistle?" Dick asked eagerly. Shepard smiled again.

"It was natural for you to ask that question, Mr. Mason," he replied, "but it was not a whistle. It was a deeper note, and it carried much farther, many times farther. Mr. Reed explained it to me. Somebody with powerful lungs was blowing on a cow's horn."

"I've heard 'em. They use 'em in the hills back of us at home. The sound will carry a tremendous distance on a still night like this. Do you think it was intended as a signal?"

"It's impossible to say, but I think so. I think, too, that the bands—

there were two of them, one replying to the other—belong to the Slade and Skelly outfit. Skelly has lived all his life in the mountains and Slade is learning 'em fast."

"Then it behoves us to be watchful, and yet more watchful."

"It does. Maybe they're attempting an ambush, with which they might succeed against an ordinary troop, but not against such a troop as this, led by such a man as Colonel Winchester. Hark, did you hear that noise?"

All of them listened. It sounded at first like the cow's horn, but they concluded that it was the rumble, made by sliding snow, which would be sending avalanches down the slopes all through the night.

"Are you going out again, Mr. Shepard?" Dick asked.

"I think not, sir. Colonel Winchester wants me to stay here, and, even if the enemy should come, we'll be ready for him."

They did not speak again for a while and they heard several times the noise of the sliding snow. Then they heard a note, low and deep, which they were sure was that of the cow's horn, or its echo. It was multiplied and repeated, however, so much by the gorges that it was impossible to tell from what point of the compass it came.

But it struck upon Dick's ears like a signal of alarm, and he and all the others of the picket stiffened to attention.

CHAPTER 13

Dick's Great Exploit

It was a singular and weird sound, the blowing of the great cow's horn on the mountain, and then the distant reply from another horn as great. It was both significant and sinister, such an extraordinary note that, despite Dick's experience and courage, his hair lifted a little. He was compelled to look back at the camp and the coals of the fire yet glowing to reassure himself that everything was normal and real.

"I wish there wasn't so much snow," said Shepard, "then the sergeant, Mr. Reed and myself could scout all over the country around here, mountains or no mountains."

They were joined at that moment by Reed, the long mountaineer, who had also been listening to the big horns.

"That means them gorillers, shore," he said. "We've got some p'ison people uv our own, an' when the gorillers come in here they j'ined 'em, and knowin' ev'ry inch uv the country, they kin guide the gorillers wherever they please."

"You agree then with Mr. Shepard that these signals are made by Slade and Skelly's men?" asked Dick.

"Shorely," replied the mountaineer, "an' I think they're up to some sort uv trick. It pesters me too, 'cause I can't guess it nohow. I done told the colonel that we'd better look out."

Colonel Winchester joined them as he was speaking, and listened to the double signal which was repeated later. But it did not come again, although they waited some time. Instead they heard, as they had heard all through the night, the occasional swish of the soft snow sliding down the slopes. But Dick saw that the colonel was uneasy, and that his apprehensions were shared both by Shepard and the mountaineer.

"Do you know how many men these brigands have?" Colonel Winchester asked of Reed.

"I reckon thar are five hundred uv them gorillers," replied the mountaineer. "Some uv our people spied on 'em in Burton's Cove an' counted 'bout that number."

Colonel Winchester glanced at his sleeping camp.

"I have three hundred," he said, "but they're the very flower of our youth. In the open they could take care of a thousand guerrillas and have something to spare. Still in here—"

He stopped short, but the shrewd mountaineer read his meaning.

"In the mountings it ain't sech plain sailin'," he said, "an' you've got to watch fur tricks. I reckon that when it comes to fightin' here, it's somethin' like the old Injun days."

"I can't see how they can get at us here," said Colonel Winchester, more to himself than to the others. "A dozen men could hold the exit by the creek, and fifty could hold the entrance."

Despite his words, his uneasiness continued and he sent for the sergeant, upon whose knowledge and instincts he relied greatly in such a situation. The sergeant, who had been watching at the other end of the valley, came quickly and, when the colonel looked at him with eyes of inquiry, he said promptly:

"Yes, sir; I think there's mischief a-foot. I can't rightly make out where it's going to be started, but I can hear it, smell it an' feel it. It's like waitin' in a dip on the prairies for a rush by the wild Sioux or Cheyenne horsemen. The signs seem to come through the air."

Dick's oppression increased. A mysterious danger was the worst of all, and his nerves were on edge. Think as he might, he could not conceive how or where the attack would be made. The only sound in the valley was the occasional stamp of the horses in the woods and behind the windrows. The soldiers themselves made no noise. The steps of the sentinels were softened in the snow, and the fires, having sunk to beds of coals, gave forth no crackling sounds.

He stared down the gap, and then up at the white world of walls circling them about. The sky seemed to have become a more dazzling blue than ever, and the great stars with the hosts of their smaller brethren around them gleamed and quivered. The stamp of a horse came again, and then a loud shrill neigh, a piercing sound and full of menace in the still night.

"What was that?" exclaimed the sergeant in alarm. "A horse does not neigh at such a time without good reason!"

And then the storm broke loose in the valley. There was a series of short, fierce shouts. Torches were suddenly waved in the air. Many horses neighed in the wildest terror and, all of them breaking through the forest and windrows, poured in a confused and frightened stream toward the entrance of the valley.

Then the experience of the sergeant in wild Indian warfare was worth more than gold and diamonds. He knew at once what was occurring and he shouted:

"It's a stampede! There have been traitors here, and they've driven the horses with fire!"

"And maybe some of them have managed to slip down the mountain side!" said Shepard.

It was well for them all that they were men of decision and supreme courage. The terrible tumult in the valley was increasing. The horses, a stampeded mass, were driving directly for the entrance. Only one thing could stop them and that the guards then did. They snatched many burning brands from the nearest fire and waved them furiously in the face of the frightened herd, which turned and ran back the other way, only to be confronted by other waving brands that filled them with terror. Then the horses, instinctively following some leader, turned again and ran back to their old places among the trees and behind the windrows, where they stood, quivering with terror.

A crackling of rifles had begun before the horses were driven back, and bullets pattered in the valley. Dark figures appeared crouched against the slopes, and jets of fire ran like a red ribbon upon the white of the snow.

"The gorillers!" cried Reed. "They've crep' over the ridges, spite uv all our watchin'."

Colonel Winchester did not lose his head for an instant, nor did any of his young soldiers, who had been trained to think as well as obey. Without waiting for orders they had already won an important victory by turning the horses back with fire, and the colonel, with the help of his officers, formed them rapidly to meet the attack. The house, the stable and the corn crib were filled with sharpshooters and others lay down among the trees or behind any shelter they could find. A number were detailed rapidly to tether the horses, and make them secure against a second fright. Warner was sent to the men guarding the entrance, Pennington to those at the exit, while Dick was kept with the colonel, who crouched, after his arrangements were made, in a little clump of trees near the centre of the valley.

Colonel Winchester was willing enough to risk his life but knowing that it was of the highest importance now to preserve it he did not take any risks through false pride. Besides Dick he kept Reed, Shepard and the sergeant with him.

The ring of fire on the slopes had been increasing fast, and the assailants found much shelter there among the dwarf pines and cedars. Bullets were pattering all over the valley. Several of the Winchesters had been slain in the early firing, and they lay where they had fallen. Others were wounded, but they bound up their own hurts and used their rifles, whenever they could pick out a figure on the slopes.

"You spoke of traitors, Mr. Reed," said the colonel. "Did you know well all the men who came to help in the preparations for us?"

"All but two," replied the mountaineer. "One was named Leonard and the other Bosley. They come from the other side uv the mounting with some uv the boys an' we thought they wuz all right, but I reckon they must be the traitors, an' I reckon too they must hev helped some uv the gorillers into the camp. I ain't seed a sign uv either sence them hosses wuz headed back. I guess we wuz took in, an' I'm pow'ful sorry, colonel."

"You're not to blame, Mr. Reed. It's not always possible to guard against treachery, but since we've defeated their attempt to stampede our horses we'll defeat all other efforts of theirs."

"Colonel, would you mind lendin' me them glasses uv yourn fur a look? The night's so bright I guess I kin use 'em nigh ez well ez in the day."

"Certainly you can have them, Mr. Reed. Here they are."

The mountaineer took a long look through them, and when he handed them back he uttered a clucking sound, significant of satisfaction.

"I 'lowed it was him, when I saw him crawlin' behind that bush," he said, "an' now I know."

"Who is who?" said Dick.

"It's that feller Bosley what came with the rest uv the boys. I know that gray comfort what's tied 'roun' his neck, an' the 'coonskin cap what's on his head. He jest crawled behind that little twisted pine up thar, an' took a pot shot at some uv us down here."

"I wish I could reach him," said Shepard.

"Ef you could I wouldn't let you," said the mountaineer grimly.

"Why?"

"'Cause he's my meat. He come here with my people, an' played a trick on us, a trick that might hev wiped out all uv Colonel Winchester's men. No man kin do that with me an git away. He's piled up a pow'ful big score an' I'm goin' to settle it myself."

"How?"

"See this rifle uv mine? I reckon it ain't got all the fancy tricks that some uv the new repeatin' breech-loadin' rifles hev. It's jest a cap an' ball rifle, but it's got a long, straight barrel an' a delicate trigger, an' it sends a bullet wherever you p'int it. It's killed squirrels, an' rabbits, an' wil' turkeys an' catamounts, an' b'ars, an' now I reckon it's goin' to hunt higher game."

The man was talking very quietly, but when Dick caught the light in his eye he knew that he meant every word. It was a cold, implacable look, and the face of the mountaineer was like that of an avenging fate.

"I loaded it with uncommon care," he continued, looking affectionately at his rifle, and then looking up again, "an' now that the colonel's glasses hev showed the way I kin see that feller peepin' from roun' his bush, tryin' to git another shot, mebbe at me an' mebbe at you. It's a long carry, but I'm shore to hit. I had a chance at him then, but I 'low to wait a little!"

"Why do you wait?" asked Dick curiously.

"I'm givin' him time to say his prayers."

"Why, he doesn't know that you're going to shoot at him, and he wouldn't pray, even if he did."

"Mebbe not, but I was raised right, an' I know my duty. I ain't goin' to send no man to kingdom without givin' him *time* to pray. Ef he won't use it the blame is his'n, but that ain't no reason why I oughtn't to give him the *time*."

"How long?"

"Wa'al, I reckon 'bout three minutes is 'nough fur a right good prayer. Thar, he's shot ag'in, but I don't know whar his bullet went. He's usin' up his prayin' time fast."

Reed never altered his quiet, assured tone. He reminded Dick of Warner, talking about his algebra, and the lad was impressed so much by his manner that he believed he was going to do as he said. He began unconsciously to count the seconds.

"Time's up," said Reed at length, "an' that traitor is pokin' his head 'roun' fur another shot."

He raised suddenly his long-barrelled rifle, took a quick aim, and pulled the trigger. A stream of fire poured from the muzzle, the figure of a man leaped from the bush and then rolled down the snowy slope.

"I give him plenty uv time," said Reed as he reloaded. "Now I reckon I'll look fur that other feller, Leonard. I'll know him when I see him, an' this old cap-an'-ball rifle uv mine knows too how to talk to traitors."

Dick left presently with a message to a captain who was in command of the force detached to hold the entrance to the valley. He ran part of the way in the shelter of the trees and crept the rest, reaching the captain in safety. Warner was there also, and the fire upon them from the slopes was hot.

"There has been no attempt to force the gate-way here," said Warner. "Since they failed with the horses they wouldn't dare try it. Besides, our sharpshooters are doing execution. Those in the upper story of the house have an especially good chance. Look at the black dots in the snow high up on the slopes. Those are dead guerrillas. There, two men fell! Perhaps if they had known the kind of regiment it was they were coming after they wouldn't have been in such a hurry to attack us."

He spoke with pride, but Dick felt some chagrin.

"That's true," he said, "though I don't like our regiment to be besieged here by a lot of guerrillas. It's an ignominy. It's not enough for us to hold our own against 'em, because they're the people we came to get, and we ought to get 'em."

"I dare say the colonel thinks as you do and he's already planning how to do it. This is a smart little battle, as it is. Those sharpshooters of ours in the houses are certainly making it warm for the enemy!"

The firing was now very fast, and, as long as the brilliancy of the night remained unobscured, much of it was deadly, but a great amount of smoke gathered, and, as it rose, it formed a cloud. The showers of bullets then decreased in volume and a comparative lull came. But the men of Slade and Skelly could yet be seen on the crests and slopes, and there was no indication that they would draw off.

Dick made his way back to Colonel Winchester, who was still in the clump of trees, a central point, from which he could direct the defence. The colonel, as Dick clearly saw, felt chagrin. While they had prevented the stampede of the horses, and were holding off Slade and Skelly, the roles which he had intended for the forces to play were reversed. They had come forth to destroy the guerrillas, and now they had to fight hard to keep the guerrillas from destroying them. Despite their shelter, about fifteen of the Winchester men had been slain, and perhaps twenty-five wounded, a loss over which the colonel grieved. Doubtless as many of the guerrillas had fallen or had been hurt, but that was a poor consolation.

It was obvious too that Slade and Skelly were handling their forces with much skill, utilizing for shelter every bush and dwarfed tree on the slopes, and never exposing themselves, except for a moment or two. Had there not been so many sharpshooters among the Winchester men they might have escaped almost without any damage, but for some of the deadly riflemen in the valley a single glimpse was enough. Nevertheless Colonel Winchester's dissatisfaction remained. He felt that a force such as his, which had come forth to do so much, should do it, and he ransacked his brain for a plan.

"Mr. Reed," he said to the mountaineer, who had remained with him. "do you think we could send a detachment through the pass down the stream and take them in the rear? That is, this force might climb the slopes behind them, and attack from above?"

The mountaineer chewed his tobacco thoughtfully, looked up at the ridges, and then at the gorge down which they could hear the waters of the little creek rushing.

"It's a big risk," he replied, "but I 'low it kin be done, though you'll hev to pick your men, colonel. You let me be guide and be shore to send the sergeant, 'cause he's a full fo'-hoss team all by hisself. An' Mr. Shepard ought to go along too. All the others ought to be youngsters, an' spose you let Mr. Mason here lead 'em."

Colonel Winchester did not resent at all these suggestions, which he knew to be excellent, and, while at first, for personal reasons of his own, he hesitated about sending Dick on so perilous an errand, he knew that he was better fitted for it than any other young officer in his command, and so he chose him. The plan, too, appealed to him strongly. He had taken lessons from the grand tactics of Lee and Jackson. Lee would keep up a great demonstration in front, while Jackson, circling in silence, would strike a tremendous and deadly blow on the flank. The longer he thought about it the more he was pleased with it. If the flanking force could cut through the gorge the prospect of success was good, and fortunately the night had turned darker, the snow clouds reappearing.

The colonel picked one hundred and fifty of his best men, with Shepard, Reed and Whitley to guide, and Dick to lead them. Warner and Pennington protested when they were not allowed to go, but the colonel quieted them with the assurance that they would soon have plenty of dangerous work to do in the valley. To Dick he said gravely:

"Before now you've nearly always been a staff officer and messenger, and this is the most important command you've ever held. I know you'll acquit yourself well, but trust a lot to your guides."

"I will, sir," said Dick earnestly. He felt the full weight of his responsibility, but his courage rose to meet it. It was the largest task yet confided to him, and he was resolved to make it a success. He noticed also that fortune, as if determined to help the brave, was already giving him aid. More stars were withdrawing into the void, and the clouds were increasing. The night had grown much darker, and a few flakes of snow wandered lazily down, messengers of the multitude that might follow.

The increasing dusk did not diminish the activity of the brigands on the slopes. It was obvious that they had an unlimited supply of ammunition, as they sent an unbroken stream of bullets into the valley, and pink dots ran like ribbons around its entire snowy rim. But in the valley itself all the fires had been put out, and it was fairly dark there, enabling Dick's command to gather unseen by the enemy.

"Now, Dick," said Colonel Winchester, "I trust you. Go, and may luck go with you."

He led his men away, the three guides by his side, and they used every particle of cover they could find, in order that the movement might remain invisible until the last possible moment. They hugged the fringe of forest, and when they reached the gorge he felt sure they were still unseen, although it was only the easy part of their task that had yet been done. But the lazy flakes had increased in number, and the canopy of cloud was still being drawn across the heavens. He gave the word to his men to be as silent as possible, not to let any weapon rattle or fall, and then they entered the gorge in two files separated by the creek, the narrow ledges affording room for only one man on either side.

Dick kept his outward calm, but the great pulses in his throat and temples were beating hard. Reed was just ahead of him, and on the other side of the creek the sergeant led, with Shepard following. Large flakes of snow fell on his face and melted there, but they were welcome messengers, telling him that the cloak for the movement would not only remain, but would increase in extent.

After the first curve the stream took a sharp descent, but the land on either side widened a little, permitting two to walk abreast. The valley and the slopes encircling it were now entirely shut out from their view, but they heard the crackling of the rifles in greater volume than ever. Colonel Winchester, true to Lee and Jackson's plan of grand tactics, had opened an extremely heavy fire on the enemy, as soon as his flanking column had disappeared in the gorge.

"I 'low the signs are good," whispered Reed. "Them that lay an ambush sometimes git laid in an ambush theirselves. I felt pow'ful bad at bein' held in a trap here in my own mountings by them gorillers, but mebbe we'll do some trap-layin' uv our own."

"I feel sure of it," said Dick. "Look! the stream ahead of us is lined with bushes which will afford concealment for our march, and the slopes beyond are covered with scrub forest."

"Like ez not the gorillers come that way, an' when we circle about we kin foller in thar tracks."

Dick felt that fortune was showering her favours upon him. The last star was now gone, and the entire sky was veiled. The big flakes of snow were falling fast enough to help their concealment, but not fast enough to impede their movements. A mile down the gorge and they halted, still unseen by the enemy, due doubtless to the heavy firing in the valley which was engrossing all the attention of the guerrillas. They could hear it very distinctly where they were, and they were quite sure that it would not permit Slade and Skelly to detach any part of their force for purposes of observation. So Dick gave orders for his men to turn and begin the ascent of the slope, under shelter of the scrub forest of cedars. They were to go in a column four abreast, carefully treading in the tracks of one another, in order that they might not start a slide of snow.

Dick's pulses beat hard, until they reached the shelter of the cedars, but no lurking guerrilla or posted sentinel saw them and they drew into the forest in silence and unobserved. Here they paused a few minutes and listened to the heavy rifle fire in the valley.

"It looks like a success, sir," said Shepard. "If we catch 'em between two fires victory is surely ours."

"Besides beatin' 'em, thar's one thing I hope fur," said Reed. "Ef that traitor Leonard hasn't fell already I'm prayin' that I git a look at him. My old cap-an'-ball rifle here is jest ez true ez ever."

The mountaineer's eyes glittered again, and Dick did not feel that Leonard's fate was in any doubt. But there was little time for talk, as the column began the march again and pressed on under cover of the cedars until they came without interruption and triumphantly to the very crest of the slope. The firing was still distinctly audible here, and the other half of the army was undoubtedly keeping the guerrillas busy.

On the summit Dick gave his men another brief breathing spell, and then they began their advance toward the battle. He threw in advance the best of the sharpshooters and scouts, including Whitley, Shepard and Reed, and then followed swiftly with the others. Half the distance and a man behind a tree saw them, shouted, fired and ran toward the guerrillas.

Dick, knowing that concealment was no longer possible, cried to his men to rush forward at full speed. A light, scattering fire met them. Two or three were wounded but none fell, and the entire column swept on at as much speed as the deep snow would allow, sending in shot after shot from their own rifles at the guerrillas clustered along the crests and slopes. The light was sufficient for them to take aim, and as they were sharpshooters the fire was accurate and deadly.

Their shout of victory rose and swelled, and the mountain gave it back in many echoes. Dick, feeling his responsibility, managed to keep cool, but he continually shouted to his men to press on, knowing how full advantage should be taken of a surprise. But they needed no urging. Aflame with fire and zeal they charged upon the guerrillas, pulling the trigger as fast as they could slip in the cartridges, and Slade and Skelly, despite all their cunning and quickness, were unable to make a stand against them.

A great shout came up from the valley. The moment Colonel Winchester heard the fire on the flank he knew that his plan, executed with skill by one of his lieutenants, was a success, and, gathering up his own force, he crept up the slopes, his men sending their fire into the guerrillas, who were already breaking.

Dick's troop was doing great damage. The guerrillas in their rovings and robberies had never before faced such a fire and they fell fast, the deep snow making flight difficult. Reed, who was at Dick's side, suddenly uttered a cry.

"I see him! I see him!" he shouted.

The long-barrelled cap-and-ball rifle leaped to his shoulder, and when the stream of fire gushed from the muzzle, Leonard, the mountaineer, fell in the snow and would never betray anybody else. Most of the guerrillas were now fleeing in panic, and Dick heard the shrill, piercing notes of Slade's whistle as he tried to draw his men off in order. For a moment or two he forgot his duties as a leader as, pistol in hand, he looked for the little man under the enormous slouch hat. Once more the feeling seized him that it was a long duel between Slade and himself that must end in the death of one or the other, and he meant to end it now. Despite the fierce notes of the whistle, coming from one point and then another, he did not see him. He caught a glimpse of the gigantic form of Skelly, but he too was soon gone, and then when he felt the restraining hand of Shepard upon his arm he came out of his rage.

"Look there!" cried Shepard.

About a score of the guerrillas had been cut off from their comrades and were driven toward the valley, where they remained on its edge, crouched down, and firing. The deep snow in which they knelt was quivering. Dick shouted to his men to draw back. Then the huge bank of snow gave way and slid down the slope, carrying the guerrillas, and gathering volume and force as it went. A terrified shouting came from the thick of it, as the avalanche hurled itself into the valley, where the bruised and broken guerrillas were taken prisoners without resistance.

Dick, after one glance at their fate, continued the pursuit of the main band down the other slope. He knew that they were robbers and murderers, and he felt little scruple. His sharpshooters fairly mowed them down as they fled in terror, but all who threw up their hands or signified otherwise that they wished to surrender were spared.

Still bearing in mind that it was their duty not merely to scatter but to destroy, he urged on the pursuit continually, and Shepard and the sergeant aided him. They gave Slade and Skelly no time to reform their men, driving them from every clump of trees, when they attempted it, and continually reducing their numbers.

The rout was complete, and Dick's heart beat high with triumph, because he knew that his force had been the striking arm. They were nearly at the foot of the far side of the mountain, when he saw Slade among the bushes. He shouted to him to surrender, but the outlaw, suddenly aiming a pistol, fired pointblank at the young lieutenant's face. Dick felt the bullet grazing his head, and he raised his own pistol to fire, but Slade was gone, and, although they trailed him a long distance in the snow, they did not find him.

CHAPTER 14

The Mountain Sharpshooter

Colonel Winchester's own mellow whistle finally recalled his men, as he did not wish them to become scattered among the mountains in pursuit of detached guerrillas. Although the escape of both Slade and Skelly was a great disappointment the victory nevertheless was complete. The two leaders could not rally the brigand force again, because it had ceased to exist. Nearly half, caught between the jaws of the Union vice, had fallen, and most of the others were taken. Perhaps not more than fifty had got away, and they would be lucky if they were not captured by the mountaineers.

Dick's head was bound up hastily but skilfully by Sergeant Whitley and Shepard. Slade's bullet had merely cut under the hair a little, and the bandage stopped the flow of blood. The sting, too, left, or in his triumph he did not notice it. His elation, in truth, was great, as he had succeeded in carrying out the hardest part of a difficult and delicate operation.

As he led his men back toward the valley, their prisoners driven before them, he felt no weariness from his great exertions, and both his head and his feet were light. At the rim of the valley Colonel Winchester met him, shook his hand with great heartiness, and congratulated him on his success, and Warner and Pennington, who were wholly without envy, added their own praise.

"I think it will be Captain Mason before long," said Warner. "Lots of boys under twenty are captains and some are colonels. Your right to promotion is a mathematical certainty, and I can demonstrate it with numerous formulae from the little algebra which even now is in the inside pocket of my tunic."

"Don't draw the algebra!" exclaimed Pennington. "We take your word for it, of course."

"I shouldn't want to be a captain," said Dick sincerely, "unless you fellows became captains too."

Further talk was interrupted by the necessity for care in making the steep descent into the valley, where the fires were blazing anew from the fresh wood which the young soldiers in their triumph had thrown upon the coals. Nor did Colonel Winchester and his senior officers make any effort to restrain them, knowing that a little exultation was good for youth, after deeds well done.

It was still snowing lazily, but the flames from a dozen big fires filled the valley with light and warmth and illuminated the sullen faces of the captives. They were a sinister lot, arrayed in faded Union or Confederate uniforms, the refuse of highland and lowland, gathered together for robbery and murder, under the protecting shadow of war. Their hair was long and unkempt, their faces unshaven and dirty, and they watched their captors with the restless, evasive eyes of guilt. They were herded in the centre of the valley, and Colonel Winchester did not hesitate to bind the arms of the most evil looking.

"What are you going to do with us?" asked one bold, black-browed villain.

"I'm going to take you to General Sheridan," replied the colonel. "I'm glad I don't have the responsibility of deciding your fate, but I think it very likely that he'll hang some of you, and that all of you richly deserve it."

The man muttered savage oaths under his breath and the colonel added: "Meanwhile you'll be surrounded by at least fifty guards with rifles of the latest style, rifles that they can shoot very fast, and they are instructed to use them if you make the slightest sign of an attempt to escape. I warn you that they will obey with eagerness."

The man ceased his mutterings and he and the other captives cowered by the fire, as if their blood had suddenly grown so thin that they must almost touch the coals to secure warmth. Then Colonel Winchester ordered the cooks to prepare food and coffee again for his troopers, who had done so well, while a surgeon, with amateur but competent assistants, attended to the hurt.

While they ate and drank and basked in the heat, the mountaineer, Reed, came again to Colonel Winchester. Dick, who was standing by, observed his air of deep satisfaction, and he wondered again at the curious mixture of mountain character, its strong religious strain, mingled with its merciless hatred of a foe. He knew that much of Reed's great content came from his slaying of the two traitors, but he did not feel that he had a right, at such a time, to question the man's motives and actions.

"Colonel," said Reed, "it's lucky that my men brought along plenty of axes, an' that your men ez well ez mine know how to use 'em."

"Why so, Mr. Reed?"

"'Cause it's growin' warmer."

"But that doesn't hurt us. We're certainly not asking for more cold."

"It will hurt us, ef we don't take some shelter ag'in it. It's snowin' now, colonel, an' ef it gits a little warmer it'll turn to rain, an' it kin rain pow'ful hard in these mountings."

"Thank you for calling my attention to it, Mr. Reed. I can't afford to have the troops soaked by winter rains. Not knowing what we had to expect in the mountains I fortunately ordered about twenty of my own men to bring axes at their saddlebows. We'll put 'em all at work."

In a few minutes thirty good axmen were cutting down trees, saplings and bushes, and more than a hundred others were strengthening the lean-tos, thatching roofs, and making rude but serviceable floors. Dick, owing to his slight wound, but much against his wish, was ordered into the house, where he spread his blankets near a window, although he could not yet sleep, all the heat of the battle and pursuit not yet having left him. His nerves still tingling with excitement, he stood at the window and looked out.

He saw the great fire blazing and many persons passing and repassing before the red glow. He saw the captives crouching together, and the red gleam on the bayonets of the men who guarded them. He saw Warner and Pendleton go into one of the lean-tos, and he saw Colonel Winchester, accompanied by Shepard and the sergeant, go down the valley toward the exit.

After a while the prisoners moved to the lean-tos, and then everybody took shelter. The crackle of the big fires changed to a hiss, and more smoke arose from them. The reason was obvious. The big flakes of snow had ceased to fall, and big drops of rain were falling in their place. Reed had been a true prophet, and he had not given his warning too soon.

The rain increased. Dick heard it driving on the window panes and beating on the roof. All the fires in the valley were out now, and rising mists and vapours hid nearly everything. The faint, sliding sound of more snow-falls precipitated by the rain came to his ears. He realized suddenly how fine a thing it was to be inside four walls, and with it came a great feeling of comfort. It was the same feeling that he had known often in childhood, when he lay in his bed and heard the storm beat against the house.

There were others in the room—the floor was almost covered with them—but all of them were asleep already, and Dick, wrapping himself in his blanket, joined them, the last thing that he remembered being the swish of the rain against the glass. He slept heavily and was not awakened until nearly noon, when he saw through the window a world entirely changed. The rain had melted only a portion of the snow, and when it ceased after sunrise the day had turned much colder, freezing every thing hard and tight. The surface of valley, slopes and ridges was covered with a thick armour of ice, smooth as glass, and giving back the rays of a brilliant sun in colours as vivid and varied as those of a rainbow. Every tree and bush, to the last little twig, was sheathed also in silver, and along the slopes the forests of dwarfed cedar and pines were a vast field of delicate and complex tracery.

It was a glittering and beautiful world, but cold and merciless. Dick saw at once that the whole force, captors and captured, was shut in for the time. It was impossible for horses to advance over a field of ice, and it was too difficult even for men to be considered seriously. There was nothing to do but remain in the valley until circumstances allowed them to move, and reflection told him they would not lose much by it. They had done the errand on which they were sent, and there was little work left in the great valley itself.

The big fires had been lighted again, the cove furnishing wood enough for many days, and within its limited area they brought back glow and cheeriness. Dick went outside and found all the men in high spirits. They expected to be held there until a thaw came, but there would be no difficulty, except to obtain forage for the horses, which they must dig from under the snow, or which some of the surest footed mountaineers must bring over the ridge. He heard that Colonel Winchester was already making arrangements with Reed, and he was too light-hearted to bother himself any more about it.

Warner and Pennington saluted him with bows as a coming captain, and declared that he looked extremely interesting with a white bandage around his head.

"It's merely to prevent bleeding," said Dick. "The bullet didn't really hurt me, and it won't leave a scar under the hair."

"Then since you're not even an invalid," said Pennington, "come on and take your bath. The boys have broken the ice for a long distance on the creek and all of us early risers have gone there for a plunge, and a short swim. It'll do you a world of good, Dick, but don't stay in too long."

"Not over a half hour," said Warner.

"O, a quarter of an hour will be long enough," said Pennington, "but I'd advise you to rub yourself down thoroughly, Dick."

"I'll do just as you did," laughed Dick.

"And what's that?"

"I'll go to the edge of the creek, look at it, and shiver when I see how cold its waters are. Then I'll kneel down on the bank, bathe my face, and come away."

"You've estimated him correctly, Dick," said Warner, "but you don't have to shiver as much as Frank did."

The cold bath, although it was confined to the face only, made his blood leap and sparkle. He was not a coming captain but a boy again, and he began to think about pleasant ways of passing the time while the ice held them. After his breakfast he joined Colonel Winchester, who debated the question further with a group of officers. But there was only one conclusion to which they could come, and that had presented itself already to Dick's mind, namely, to wait as patiently as they could for a thaw, while Shepard, the sergeant and two or three others made their way on foot into the Shenandoah valley to inform Sheridan of what had transpired.

The messengers departed as soon as the conference closed, and the little army was left to pass the time as it chose in the cove. But time did not weigh heavily upon the young troops. As it grew colder and colder they added to the walls and roofs of their improvised shelters. There was scarcely a man among them who had not been bred to the axe, and the forest in the valley rang continually with their skilful strokes. Then the logs were notched and in a day or two rude but real cabins were raised, in which they slept, dry and warm.

The fires outside were never permitted to die down, the flames always leaped up from great beds of coals, and warmth and the comforts that follow were diffused everywhere. The lads, when they were not working on the houses, mended their saddles and bridles or their clothes, and when they had nothing else to do they sang war songs or the sentimental ballads of home. It was a fine place for singing—Warner described the acoustics of the valley as perfect—and the ridges and gorges gave back the greatest series of echoes any of them had ever heard.

"If this place didn't have a name already," said Pennington, "I'd call it Echo Cove, and the echoes are flattering, too. Whenever George sings his voice always comes back in highly improved tones, something that we can stand very well."

"My voice may not be as mellow as Mario's," said Warner calmly, "but my technique is perfect. Music is chiefly an affair of mathematics, as everybody knows, or at least it is eighty per cent, the rest being voice, a mere gift of birth. So, as I am unassailable in mathematics, I'm a much better singer than the common and vulgar lot who merely have voice."

"That being the case," said Pennington, "you should sing for yourself only and admire your own wonderful technique."

"I never sing unless I'm asked to do so," said Warner, with his old invincible calm, "and then the competent few who have made an exhaustive study of this most complex science appreciate my achievement. As I said, I should consider it a mark of cheapness if I pleased the low, vulgar and common herd."

"With that iron face and satisfied mind of yours you ought to go far, George," said Pennington.

"Everything is arranged already. I will go far," said Warner in even tones.

"I wonder what's happening outside in the big valley," said Dick.

"Whatever it is it's happening without us," said Warner. "But I fancy that General Sheridan will be more uneasy about us than we are about him. We know what we have done, that our task is finished, but for all he knows we may have been trapped and destroyed."

"But Shepard or the sergeant will get through to him."

"Not for three or four days anyhow. Not even men on foot can travel fast on a glassy sheet of ice. Every time I look at it on the mountain it seems to grow smoother. If I were standing on top of that ridge and were to slip I'd come like a catapult clear into the camp."

"Nothing could tempt me to go up there now," said Dick.

"Maybe not, nor me either, but as I live somebody is on top of that ridge now."

Dick's eyes followed his pointing finger, saw a black dot on the utmost summit, and then he snatched up his glasses.

"It's Slade, his very self!" he exclaimed in excitement. "I'd know that hat anywhere. Now, how under the sun did he come there!"

"It's more important to know why he has come," said Warner, using his own glasses. "I see him clearly and there is no doubt that it's the same robber, traitor and assassin who, unfortunately, escaped when we shot his horde to pieces."

"He has a rifle with him, and as sure as we live he's sitting down on the ice, and picking out a target here in the valley."

"A risky business for Slade. Shooting upward we can take better aim at him than he can at us."

There was a great stir in the valley, as others saw the figure on the mountain and read Slade's intentions. Fifty men sprang to their feet and seized their rifles. But the guerrilla moved swiftly along the knife-edge of the ridge, obviously sure of his footing, and before any of them could fire, dropped down behind a little group of cedars. Every stem and bough was cased in a sheath of silver mail, but they hid him well. Dick, with his glasses, could not discern a single outline of the man behind the glittering tracery.

But as they looked, a head of red appeared suddenly in the silver, smoke floated away, and a bullet knocked up the ice near them. They scattered in lively fashion, and from shelter watched the silver bush. A second bullet came from its foliage and wounded slightly a man who was carrying wood to one of the fires. But the annoying sharpshooter remained invisible.

"He's lying down on the ice like a Sioux or Cheyenne in a gully," said Pennington.

"Maybe he has a gully in the ice," said Dick, "and he can crouch here and shoot at us all day, almost in perfect safety."

But Colonel Winchester appeared and ordered a score of the men, with the heaviest rifles, to shoot away the entire clump of cedars. They did it with a method and a regard for mathematics that filled Warner's soul with delight, firing in turn and planting their bullets in a line along the front of the clump, cutting down everything like a mower with a scythe.

Dick with the glasses saw the ice fly into the air in a silver spray as bush after bush fell. Presently they were all cut away by that stream of heavy bullets, but no human being was disclosed.

"He's just gone over the other side of the ridge," said Warner in disgust, "and is waiting there until we finish. We couldn't shoot through a mountain, even if we had one of our biggest cannon here. He'll find another clump of bushes soon and be potting us from it."

"But we can shoot that away too," said Dick hopefully.

"We can't shoot down all the forests on the mountain. He must have heavy hobnails, or, like the mountaineers, he has drawn thick yarn socks over his boots, else he couldn't scoot about on the ice the way he does."

"Ah, there goes his rifle, behind the clump of bushes to the right of the one that we shot away!"

A second man was wounded by the bullet, and then an extraordinary siege ensued, a siege of three hundred men by a single sharpshooter on top of a mountain as smooth as glass. Whenever they shot his refuge away he moved to another, and, while they were shooting at it he had nothing to do but drop down a few feet on the far side of the ridge and remain in entire safety until he chose another ambush.

"I suppose this was visited upon us because we were puffed up with pride over our exploits," said Pennington, "but it's an awful jolt to us to have the whole Winchester regiment penned up here and driven to hiding by a single brigand."

"It's not a jolt," said Warner, "it's a tragedy. Unless we get him we can never live it down. We may win another Gettysburg all by ourselves, but history and also the voice of legend and ironic song will tell first of the time when Slade, the outlaw, held us all in the cove at the muzzle of his rifle."

Colonel Winchester, although he did not show it, raged the most of them all. The great taunt would be for him rather than his young officers and troopers, and the blood burned in his veins as he watched the operations of the sharpshooter on the ridges. One of his men had been killed, three had been wounded, and all of them were compelled to seek shelter for their lives as none knew where Slade's bullet would strike next. In his perplexity he called in Reed, the mountaineer, who fortunately was in camp, and he suggested that they send out a group of men through the entrance, who might stalk him from the far side in the same way that they had crushed his band.

"But how are they to climb on the smooth ice?" asked the colonel.

"Wrap the feet uv the men in blankets, an' let 'em use their bayonets for a grip in the ice," replied the mountaineer, "an' ef you don't mind, colonel, I'd like to go along with the party. Mebbe I'd git a shot at that big hat uv Slade's."

The idea appealed to the colonel, especially as none other offered, and Warner, to his great delight, received command of the party detailed for the difficult and dangerous duty. Several of the coarsest and heaviest blankets were cut up, and the feet of the men were wrapped in them in such manner that they would not slip on the ice, although retaining full freedom of movement. They tried their "snow shoes" behind the house, where they were sheltered from Slade's bullets, and found that they could make good speed over the ice.

"Now be careful, Warner," said Colonel Winchester. "Remember that your party also may present a fair target to him, and we don't wish to lose another man."

"I'll use every precaution possible, sir," replied Warner, "and I thank you for giving me this responsibility."

Then keeping to the shelter of trees he led his men out through the pass, and the soul of Warner, despite his calm exterior, was aflame. Dick had achieved his great task with success, and, in the lesser one, he wished to do as well. It was not jealousy of his comrade, but emulation, and also a desire to meet his own exacting standards. As he disappeared with his picked sharpshooters and turned the shoulder of the mountain his blood was still hot, but his Vermont head was as cool as the ice upon which he trod.

Warner heard the distant reports of Slade's rifle, and also the crackle of the firing in reply. He knew the colonel would keep Slade so busy that he was not likely to notice the flank movement, and he pressed forward with all the energy of himself and his men. The heavy cloth around their shoes gave them a secure foothold until they reached the steeper slopes, and there, in accordance with Reed's suggestion, they used their bayonets as alpenstocks.

A third of the way up the slope, and they reached one of the clumps of cedars, into which they crawled. Although a glittering network of silver it was a cold covert, but they lay on the ice there and watched for Slade's next shot. They heard it a minute later, and then saw him behind a pine about five hundred yards away. After sending his bullet into the valley he had withdrawn a little and was slipping another cartridge into the fine breech-loading rifle that he carried, the most modern and highly improved weapon then used, as Warner could clearly see.

"Would you let me take a look at him through your glasses?" asked Reed.

"Certainly," replied Warner, handing them to him.

"Jest as I thought," said Reed, as he took a long look. "He's done gone plum' mad with the wish to kill. It strikes them evil-minded critters that way sometimes, an' he's had so much luck shootin' down at us, an' keepin' a whole little army besieged that it's mounted to his head. Ef he had his way he'd jest wipe us all out."

"A sanguinary and savage mind," said Warner. "It's the spirit of the rattlesnake or the cobra, and we must exterminate him. He's moving further along the ridge, and he's exactly between us and that clump of cedars, higher up and about three hundred yards away. If we could make those cedars we would bring him within range. It's a pretty steep climb, but I want to try it."

"We kin do it shore by stabbin' our bayonets into the ice and hangin' on to 'em ez we edge up," said Reed optimistically. "The clump itself will help hide us, an' Slade ain't likely to look this way. Ez I told you he hez gone plum' mad with the blood fever, an' he ain't got eyes for anythin' except the soldiers in the valley what he wants to shoot."

"Poison, nothing but poison," said Warner. "We must remove him as speedily as possible for the sake of the universe. Come on! I mean to lead."

He emerged from the clump and took his way toward the second cluster, digging a heavy hunting knife into the ice whenever he felt that he was about to slip. Reed was just behind him, breathing hard from the climb, and then came the whole detachment. Warner felt a momentary shiver lest the guerrilla see them. If he caught them on the steep ice between the two cedar clumps he could decimate them with ease.

But fortune was kind and they breathed mighty sighs of relief as they drew into the second network of silver, where they lay close watching for Slade, who had fired three times into the valley while they were on the way.

He had gone farther down the ridge, but they saw him partially as he kneeled for another shot. If he moved again in the same direction after firing they would not be able to reach him, and Warner, Reed agreeing with him, decided that they must make the attempt to remove him now or never. It was a hard target, not much of Slade's body showing, but the entire party took aim and fired together at the leader's word.

Slade threw up his arms, fell back on their side of the mountain and then slid down the slippery slope. Warner watched him with a kind of horrified fascination as he shot over the clear ice. His body struck a small pine presently and shattered it, the broken pieces of the icy sheath flying in the air like crystals. After a momentary pause from the resistance Slade went on, slid over a shelf, and disappeared in a deep drift.

"He's out o' business," said Reed. "I reckon we'd better go down thar, an' see ef he's all broke to pieces."

They climbed down slowly and painfully, reaching the drift, but to their amazement Slade was not there. They found his rifle and spots of blood, but the outlaw was gone, a thin red trail that led down a rift showing the way he went.

"We hit our b'ar an' took the bite out uv him," said Reed philosophically, "but we ain't got his hide to show. Still he's all broke up, jest the same, 'cause he didn't even think to take his gun, an' this red trail shows that we won't be bothered by him ag'in fur a long time."

Warner would have preferred the annihilation or capture of Slade, whom he truly called a rattlesnake or cobra, but he was satisfied, nevertheless. He had destroyed the guerrilla's power to harm for a long time, at least, and not a man of his had been hurt. He was sure to receive Colonel Winchester's words of approval, and he felt the swell of pride, but did not show it by word or manner.

Carrying the rifle, as the visible proof of victory, they returned to the cove, and received from Colonel Winchester the words for which they were grateful. Further proof was the failure of Slade to return and the lifting of the terrible weight which a single man had put upon them. They could now go about in the open, as they pleased, the big fires were built up again, and cheerfulness returned.

The mountaineers brought in more food the next day, and the following night Reed and another mountaineer crossed the ridge and were lucky enough to shoot a fat bear in a ravine. They dressed it there, and, between them, managed to bring the body back to the camp. A day later they secured another, and there was a great feast of fresh meat.

That night the weather rapidly turned warmer and all knew the big thaw was at hand. A long heavy rain that lasted almost until daylight hastened it and great floods roared down the slopes. Tons and tons of melting snow also slid into the valley, and the creek became a booming torrent. They were more thankful than ever for their huts and lean-tos, and all except the sentinels clung closely to their shelter.

Throughout the day the mountains were veiled in vapours from the rain and the melting snow, and, after another night, the troop saddled and departed, the horses treading ankle deep in mud, but their riders eager to get away.

"We overstayed our time," said Dick, looking back, "but it was a good cove for us. Our presence there tempted the enemy to battle, and we destroyed him. Then we had shelter and a home when the great storm came."

"A good cove, truly," said Pennington, "and we sha'n't forget it."

When they reached the main pass they found it also deep in mud and melting snow, and their progress was slow and painful. But before noon they met Shepard and the sergeant returning with news that they had carried an account of the victory to General Sheridan, but that nothing had happened in the main valley save a few raids by Mosby. Shepard, who acted as spokesman, was too tactful to say much, but he indicated very clearly that the commander-in-chief was highly pleased with the destruction of the Slade and Skelly band, the maraudings of which had become a great annoyance and danger. Dick was eager to hear more, and, when the opportunity presented itself, he questioned the sergeant privately.

"What do we hear from Petersburg?" he asked. "Is the deadlock there broken?"

"Not yet, sir," replied the sergeant. "The winter being so very severe the troops are not able to do much. General Lee still holds his lines."

"I suppose that General Grant doesn't care to risk another Cold Harbor, but what has been done here in the Valley of Virginia should enable him to turn Lee's flank in the spring."

"I take it that you're right, sir. General Lee is a hard nut to crack, as we all know, but his army is wearing away. In the spring the shell of the nut will be so thin that we'll smash it."

The column, after its exploit, reported to Sheridan at Winchester, the little city around which and through which the war rolled for four long years, and where two great commanders, one of the gray and the other of the blue, had their headquarters at times. But Colonel Winchester and his young staff officers rode through streets that were faced by closed shutters and windows. Nowhere was the hostility to the Northern troops more bitter and intense than in Winchester, the beloved city of the great Stonewall which had seen with its own eyes so many of his triumphs.

Dick and his comrades had learned long since not to speak to the women and girls for fear of their sharp tongues, and in his heart he could not blame them. Youth did not keep him from having a philosophical and discerning mind, and he knew that in the strongest of people the emotions often triumph over logic and reason. Warner's little algebra was all right, when the question was algebraic, but sentiment and passion had a great deal to do with the affairs of the world, and, where they were concerned, the book was of no value at all.

Dick's new rank of captain was conferred upon him by General Sheridan himself, and it was accompanied by a compliment which though true made him blush in his modesty. A few days later Warner received the same rank for his achievement in driving away Slade, and it was conferred upon Pennington too for general excellence. The three were supremely happy and longed for more enemies to conquer, but a long period of comparative idleness ensued. The winter continued of unexampled severity, and they spent most of the time in camp, although they did not waste it. Several books of mathematics came from the North to Warner and he spent many happy evenings in their study. Dick got hold of a German grammar and exercise book, and, several others joining him, they made a little class, which though it met irregularly, learned much. Pennington was a wonder among the horses. When the veterinarians were at a loss they sent for him and he rarely failed of a cure. He modestly ascribed his merit to his father who taught him everything about horses on the great plains, where a man's horse was so often the sole barrier between him and death.

Thus the winter went on, and they longed eagerly for spring, the breaking up of the great cold, and the last campaign.

CHAPTER 15

Back With Grant

Despite the inevitable hostility of the people their stay at Winchester was pleasant and fruitful. All three of the new young captains experienced a mental growth, and their outlook upon the enemy was tempered greatly. They had been through so many battles and they had measured their strength and courage against the foe so often that all hatred and malice had departed. North and South, knowing too little of each other before the war, had now learned mutual respect upon the field of combat. And Dick, Warner and Pennington, feeling certain that the end was at hand, could understand the loss and sorrow of the South, and sympathize with the fallen. Their generous young hearts did not exult over a foe whom they expected soon to conquer.

Late in January of the fateful year 1865 Dick was walking through the streets of Winchester one cold day. The wind from the mountains had a fierce edge, and, as he bent his head to protect his face from it, he did not see a stout, heavily built man of middle age coming toward him, and did not stop until the stranger, standing squarely in his way, hailed him.

"Does the fact that you've become a captain keep you from seeing anything in your path, Mr. Mason?" asked the man in a deep bass, but wholly good-natured voice.

Dick looked up in surprise, because the tones were familiar. He saw a ruddy face, with keen, twinkling eyes and a massive chin, a face in which shrewdness and a humorous view of the world were combined. He hesitated a moment, then he remembered and held out his hand.

"It's Mr. Watson, the contractor," he said.

"So it is, lad," said John Watson, grasping the outstretched hand and shaking it heartily. "Don't mind my calling you lad, even if you are a captain. All things are comparative, and to me, a much older man, you're just a lad. I've heard of your deed in the mountains, in fact, I keep track of all of you, even of General Sheridan himself. It's my business to know men and what they do."

"I hope you're still making money," said Dick, smiling.

"I am. That's part of a merchant's duty. If he doesn't make money he oughtn't to be a merchant. Oh, I know that a lot of you soldiers look down upon us traders and contractors."

"I don't and I never did, Mr. Watson."

"I know it, Captain Mason, because you're a lad of intelligence. The first time I saw you I noticed that the reasoning quality was strong in you, and that was why I made you an offer to enter my employ after the war. That offer is still open and will remain open at all times."

"I thank you very much, Mr. Watson, but I can't accept it, as I have other ambitions."

"I was sure you wouldn't take it, but I like to feel it's always waiting for you. It's well to look ahead. This war, vast and terrible as it has been, will be over before the year is. Two or three million men who have done nothing but fighting for four years will be out of employment. Vast numbers of them will not know which way to turn. They will be wholly unfit, until they have trained themselves anew, for the pursuits of peace. Captains, majors, colonels and, yes, generals, will be besieging me for jobs, as zealously as they're now besieging Lee's army in the trenches before Petersburg, and with as much cause. When the war is over the soldier will not be of so much value, and the man of peace will regain his own. I hope you've thought of these things, Captain Mason."

"I've thought of them many times, Mr. Watson, and I've thought of them oftener than ever this winter. My comrades and I have agreed that as soon as the last battle is fought we'll plunge at once into the task of rebuilding our country. We amount to little, of course, in such a multitude, but one can do only what one can."

"That's so, but if a million feel like you and push all together, they can roll mountains away."

"You're not a man to come to Winchester for nothing. You've been doing business with the army?"

"I've been shoeing, clothing and bedding you. I deliver within two weeks thirty thousand pairs of shoes, thirty thousand uniforms, and sixty thousand blankets. They are all honest goods and the price is not too high, although I make the solid and substantial profit to which I am entitled. You soldiers on the battle line don't win a war alone. We who feed and clothe you achieve at least half. I regret again, Captain

405

Mason, that you can't join me later. Mine's a noble calling. It's a great thing to be a merchant prince, and it's we, as much as any other class of people, who spread civilization over the earth."

"I know it," said Dick earnestly. "I'm not blind to the great arts of peace. Now, here come my closest friends, Captain Warner and Captain Pennington, who have understanding. I want you to meet them."

Dick's hearty introduction was enough to recommend the contractor to his comrades, but Warner already knew him well by reputation.

"I've heard of you often from some of our officers, Mr. Watson," he said. "You deliver good goods and you're a New Englander, like myself. Ten years from now you'll be an extremely rich man, a millionaire, twenty years from now you'll be several times a millionaire. About that time I'll become president of Harvard, and we'll need money—a great university always needs money—and I'll come to you for a donation of one hundred thousand dollars to Harvard, and you'll give it to me promptly."

John Watson looked at him fixedly, and slowly a look of great admiration spread over his face.

"Of course you're a New Englander," he said. "It was not necessary for you to say so. I could have told it by looking at you and hearing you talk. But from what state do you come?"

"Vermont."

"I might have known that, too, and I'm glad and proud to meet you, Captain Warner. I'm glad and proud to know a young man who looks ahead twenty years. Nothing can keep you from being president of Harvard, and that hundred thousand dollars is as good as given. Your hand again!"

The hands of the two New Englanders met a second time in the touch of kinship and understanding. Theirs was the clan feeling, and they had supreme confidence in each other. Neither doubted that the promise would be fulfilled, and fulfilled it was and fourfold more.

"You New Englanders certainly stand together," said Dick.

"Not more than you Kentuckians," replied the contractor. "I was in Kentucky several times before the war, and you seemed to be one big family there."

"But in the war we've not been one big family," said Dick, somewhat sadly. "I suppose that no state has been more terribly divided than Kentucky. Nowhere has kin fought more fiercely against kin."

"But you'll come together again after the war," said Watson cheerfully. "That great bond of kinship will prove more powerful than anything else."

"I hope so," said Dick earnestly.

They had the contractor to dinner with them, and he opened new worlds of interest and endeavour for all of them. He was a mighty captain of industry, a term that came into much use later, and mentally they followed him as he led the way into fields of immense industrial achievement. They were fascinated as he talked with truthful eloquence of what the country could become, the vast network of railroads to be built, the limitless fields of wheat and corn to be grown, the mines of the richest mineral continent to be opened, and a trade to be acquired, that would spread all over the world. They forgot the war while he talked, and their souls were filled and stirred with the romance of peace.

"I leave for Washington tonight," said the contractor, when the dinner was finished. "My work here is done. Our next meeting will be in Richmond."

All three of the young men took it as prophetic and when John Watson started north they waved him a friendly farewell. Another long wait followed, while the iron winter, one of the fiercest in the memory of man, still gripped both North and South. But late in February there was a great bustle, portending movement. Supplies were gathered, horses were examined critically, men looked to their arms and ammunition, and the talk was all of high anticipation. An electric thrill ran through the men. They had tasted deep of victory since the previous summer, and they were eager to ride to new triumphs.

"It's to be an affair of cavalry altogether," said Warner, who obtained the first definite news. "We're to go toward Staunton, where Early and his remnants have been hanging out, and clean 'em up. Although it's to be done by cavalry alone, as I told you, it'll be the finest cavalry you ever saw."

And when Sheridan gathered his horsemen for the march Warner's words came true. Ten thousand Union men, all hardy troopers now, were in the saddle, and the great Sheridan led them. The eyes of Little Phil glinted as he looked upon his matchless command, bold youths who had learned in the long hard training of war itself, to be the equals of Stuart's own famous riders. And the eyes of Sheridan glinted again when they passed over the Winchesters, the peerless regiment, the bravest of the brave, with the colonel and the three youthful captains in their proper places.

The weather was extremely cold, but they were prepared for it, and when they swung up the valley, and forty thousand hoofs beat on the hard road, giving back a sound like thunder, their pulses leaped, and they took with delight deep draughts of the keen frosty air.

While they carried food for the entire march, the rest of their equipment was light, four cannon, ammunition wagons, some ambulances and pontoon boats. Dick thought they would make fast time, but fortune for awhile was against them. The very morning the great column started the weather rapidly turned warmer, and then a heavy rain began to fall. The hard road upon which the forty thousand hoofs had beat their marching song turned to mud, and forty thousand hoofs made a new sound, as they sank deep in it, and were then pulled out again.

"If it keeps us from going fast," said the philosophical sergeant, "it'll keep them that we're goin' after from gettin' away. We're as good mud horses as they are."

"Do you think we'll go through to Staunton?" asked Dick of Warner.

"I've heard that we will, and that we'll go on and take Lynchburg too. Then we're to curve about and in North Carolina join Sherman who has smashed the Confederacy in the west."

"I don't like the North Carolina part," said Dick. "I hope we'll go to Grant and march with him on Richmond, because that's where the death blow will be dealt, if it's dealt at all."

"And that it will be dealt we don't doubt, neither you, nor I nor any of us."

"Yes, that's so."

While mud and rain could impede the progress of the great column they could not stop it. Neither could they dampen the spirits of the young troopers who rode knee to knee, and who looked forward to new victories. Through the floods of rain the ten thousand, scouts and skirmishers on their flanks, swept southward, and they encountered no foe. A few Southern horsemen would watch them at a great distance and then ride sadly away. There was nothing in the valley that could oppose Sheridan.

Dick's leggings, and his overcoat with an extremely high collar, kept him dry and warm and he was too seasoned to mind the flying mud which thousands of hoofs sent up, and which soon covered them. The swift movement and the expectation of achieving something were exhilarating in spite of every hardship and obstacle.

That night they reached the village of Woodstock, and the next day they crossed the north fork of the Shenandoah, already swollen by the heavy rains. The engineers rapidly and dexterously made a bridge of the pontoon boats, and the ten thousand thundered over in safety.

The next night they were at a little place called Lacy's Springs, sixty miles from Winchester, a wonderful march for two days, considering the heavy rains and deep mud, and they had not yet encountered an enemy. How different it would have been in Stonewall Jackson's time! Then, not a mile of the road would have been safe for them. It was ample proof of the extremities to which the Confederacy was reduced. Lee, at Petersburg, could not reinforce Early, and Early, at Staunton, could not reinforce Lee!

They intended to move on the next day, and they heard that night that Rosser, a brave Confederate general, had gathered a small Confederate force and was hastening forward to burn all the bridges over the middle fork of the Shenandoah, in order that he might impede Sheridan's progress. Then it was the call of the trumpet and boots and saddles early in the morning in order that they might beat Rosser to the bridges.

"I hope for their own sake that they won't try to fight us," said Dick.

"I'm with you on that," said Pennington. "They can't be more than a few hundreds, and it would take thousands, even with a river to help, to stop an army like ours."

It was not raining now and the roads growing dryer thundered with the hoofs of ten thousand horses. The Winchesters had an honoured place in the van, and, as they approached the middle fork of the Shenandoah, the three young captains raised themselves in their saddles to see if the bridge yet stood. It was there, but on the other side of the stream a small body of cavalrymen in gray were galloping forward, and some had already dismounted for the attempt to destroy it. The arrival of the two forces was almost simultaneous, but the Union army, overwhelming in numbers, exulting in victory, swept forward to the call of the trumpets.

"They're not more than five or six hundred over there," said Warner, "too few to put up a fight against us. I feel sorry for 'em, and wish they'd go away."

The Southerners nevertheless were sweeping the narrow bridge with a heavy rifle fire, and Sheridan drew back his men for a few minutes. Then followed a series of mighty splashes, as two West Virginia regiments sent their horses into the river, swam it, and, as they emerged dripping on the farther shore, charged the little Confederate force in flank, compelling it to retreat so swiftly that it left behind prisoners and its wagons.

It was all over in a few minutes, and the whole army, crossing the river, moved steadily on toward Staunton, where Early had been in camp, and where Sheridan hoped to find him. The little victory did not bring Dick any joy. He knew that the Confederacy could now make no stand in the Valley of Virginia, and it was like beating down those who were already beaten. He sincerely hoped that Early would not await them at Staunton or anywhere else, but would take his futile forces out of the valley and join Lee.

The heavy rains began again. Winter was breaking up and its transition into spring was accompanied by floods. The last snow on the mountains melted and rushed down in torrents. The roads, already ruined by war, became vast ruts of mud, but Sheridan was never daunted by physical obstacles. The great army of cavalry, scarcely slacking speed, pressed forward continually, and Dick knew that Early did not have the shadow of a chance to withstand such an army.

The next day they entered Staunton, another of the neat little Virginia cities devoted solidly and passionately to the Southern cause. Here, they were faced again by blind doors and windows, but Early and his force were gone. Shepard brought news that he had prepared for a stand at Waynesborough, although he had only two thousand men.

"Our general will attack him at once," said Warner, when he heard of it. "He sweeps like a hurricane."

"He is surely the general for us at such a time," said Pennington, who began to feel himself a military authority.

"It's humane, at least," said Dick. "The quicker it's over the smaller the toll of ruin and death."

Nor had they judged Sheridan wrongly. His men advanced with speed, hunting Early, and they found him fortified with his scanty forces on a ridge near the little town of Waynesborough. The daring young leader, Custer, and Colonel Winchester, riding forward, found his flank exposed, and it was enough for Sheridan. He formed his plan with rapidity and executed it with precision. The Custer and Winchester men were dismounted and assailed the exposed flank at once, while the remainder of the army made a direct and violent charge in front.

It seemed to Dick that Early was swept away in an instant, and the attack was so swift and overwhelming that there was but little loss of life on either side. Four fifths of the Southern men and their cannon were captured, while Early, several of his generals and a few hundred soldiers escaped to the woods. His army, however, had ceased to exist, and Sheridan and his muddy victors rode on to the ancient town of Charlottesville, which, having no forces to defend it, the mayor and the leading citizens surrendered.

Dick, Warner and Pennington walked through the silent halls of the University of Virginia, the South's most famous institution of learning, founded by Thomas Jefferson, one of the republic's greatest men.

"I hope they will re-open it next year," said Warner generously, "and that it will grow and grow, until it becomes a rival of Harvard. We want to defeat the South, but not to destroy it. Since it is to be a part of the Union again, and loyal forever I hope and believe, we want it strong and prosperous."

"I'm with you in that," said Dick, "and I feel it with particular strength while I am here. There have been many great Virginians and I hope there'll be many more."

They also visited Monticello, the famous colonial mansion which the great Jefferson had built, and in which he had lived and planned for the republic. They trod there with light steps, feeling that his spirit was still present. Virginia was the greatest of the border states, but it seemed to Dick that here he was in the very heart of the South. Virginia was the greatest of the Southern fighting states too, and it had furnished most of the great Southern leaders, at least two of her sons ranking among the foremost military geniuses of modern times. For nearly four years they had barred the way to every Northern advance, and had won great victories over numbers, but Dick was sure as he stood on a portico at Monticello, in the very heart of valiant Virginia, that the fate of the South was sealed.

They did not stay long at Charlottesville and Monticello, but a portion of the army, including the Winchester men, went on, tearing up the railroad, while another column demolished a canal used for military purposes. Then the two forces united at a town called New Market, but they could go no farther. The heavy rains and the melting snows had swollen the rivers enormously, all the bridges before them were destroyed, and their own pontoons proved inadequate in face of the great rushing streams. Then they turned back.

Dick and his comrades were secretly glad. The rising of the waters had prevented them from going into North Carolina and joining Sherman. Hence, they deduced that so active a man as Sheridan would march for a junction with Grant, and that was where they wanted to go. They did not believe that the Confederacy was to be finished in North Carolina, but at Richmond. They knew that Lee's army yet stood between Grant and the Southern capital, and, there, would be the heart of great affairs.

Spring was now opening and Sheridan's army marched eastward. Men and horses were covered with mud, but they still had the flush of victories won, and the incentive of others expected. They were even yet worn by hard marching and some fighting, but it was a healthy leanness, making their muscles as tough as whipcord, while their eyes were keen like those of hawks.

Dick did not rejoice now in the work they were doing, although he saw its need. Theirs was a task of destruction. For a distance of more than fifty miles they ruined a canal important to the Confederacy. Boats, locks, everything went, and they also made cuts by which the swollen James poured into the canal, flooding it and thrusting it out of its banks. They met no resistance save a few distant shots, and Sheridan rejoiced over his plan to join the Army of the Potomac, although he had not yet been able to send word of it to Grant.

But the omens remained propitious. They saw now that there were no walls in the rear of the Confederacy and they had little to do but march. The heavy rains followed them, roads disappeared, and it seemed to the young captains that they lived in eternal showers of mud. Horses and riders alike were caked with it, and they ceased to make any effort to clean themselves.

"This is not a white army," said Warner, looking down a long column, "it's brown, although it would be hard to name the shade of brown."

"It's not always brown," said Pennington. "Lots of the Virginia mud is a rich, ripe red. Bet you anything that before tomorrow night we will have turned to some hue of scarlet."

"We won't take the wager," said Dick, "because you bet on a certainty."

That afternoon the scouts surprised a telegraph station on the railroad, and found in it a dispatch from General Early. To the great amazement of Sheridan, Early was not far away. He had only two hundred men, but with them the grim old fighter prepared to attack the Union army. Sheridan himself felt a certain pity for his desperate opponent, but he promptly sent Custer in search of him. The young cavalryman quickly found him and scattered or captured the entire band.

Early escaped from the fight with a lone orderly as his comrade, and the next day the general who had lost all through no fault of his own, rode into Richmond with his single companion, and from him Jefferson Davis, President of the Confederacy, heard the full tale of Southern disaster in the Valley of Virginia.

Meanwhile Sheridan and his victorious army rode on to a place called White House, where they found plenty of stores, and where they halted for a long rest, and also to secure new mounts, if they could. Their horses were worn out completely by the great campaign and were wholly unfit for further service. But it was hard to obtain fresh ones and the delay was longer than the general had intended. Nevertheless his troops profited by it. They had not realized until they stopped how near they too had come to utter exhaustion, and for several days they were in a kind of physical torpor while their strength came back gradually.

"I think I've removed the last trace of the Virginia mud from my clothes and myself," said Warner on the morning of the second day, "but I've had to work hard to do it, as time seemed to have made it almost a part of my being."

"I've spent most of my time learning to walk again, and getting the bows out of my legs," said Dick. "I've been a-horse so long that I felt like a sailor coming ashore from a three years' cruise."

"Agreed with me pretty well, all except the mud, since I was born on horseback," said Pennington. "But I don't like to ride in a brown plaster suit of armour. What do you think is ahead, boys?"

"Junction with General Grant," said Dick. "They say, also, that General Sherman, after completing his great work in Georgia and North Carolina, is coming to join them too. It will be a great meeting, that of the three successful generals who have destroyed the Confederacy, because there's nothing of it left now but Lee's army, and that they say is mighty small."

It was in reality a triumphant march that they began after they left White House, refreshed, remounted and ready for new conquests. They soon came into touch with the Army of the Potomac, and the great meeting between Grant, Sherman and Sheridan took place, Sherman having come north especially for the purpose. Then Sheridan's force became attached to the Army of the Potomac, and his cavalry columns advanced into the marshes about Petersburg. All fear that they would be sent to cooperate with Sherman passed, and Dick knew that the Winchester men would be in the final struggle with Lee, a struggle the success of which he felt assured.

April was not far away. The fierce winter was broken up completely, but the spring rains were uncommonly heavy and much of the low country about Petersburg was flooded, making it difficult for cavalry and impossible for infantry. Nevertheless the army of Grant, with Sheridan now as a striking arm, began to close in on the beleaguered men in gray. Lee had held the trenches before Petersburg many months, keeping at bay a resolute and powerful army, led by an able and tenacious general, but it was evident now that he could not continue to hold them. Sheridan's victorious force on his flank made it impossible.

The Winchester men were in a skirmish or two, but for a few days most of their work was manoeuvring, that is, they were continually riding in search of better positions. At times, the rain still poured, but the three young captains were so full of expectancy that they scarcely noticed it. Dick often heard the trumpets singing across the marshes, and now and then he saw the Confederate skirmishers and the roofs of Petersburg. He beheld too with his own eyes the circle of steel closing about the last hope of the Confederacy, and he felt every day, with increasing strength, that the end was near.

But the outside world did not realize that the great war was to close so suddenly. It had raged with the utmost violence for four years and it seemed the normal condition in America. Huge battles had been fought, and they had ended in nothing. Three years before, McClellan had been nearer to Richmond than Grant now was, and yet he had been driven away. Lee and Jackson had won brilliant victories or had held the Union numbers to a draw, and to those looking from far away the end seemed as distant as ever. At that very moment, they were saying in Europe that the Confederacy was invincible, and that it was stronger than it had been a year or two years earlier.

Dick, all unconscious of distant opinion, watched the tightening of the steel belt, and helped in the task. He and his comrades never doubted. They knew that Sherman had crushed the Southeast, and that Thomas, that stern old Rock of Chickamauga, had annihilated the Southern army of Hood at Nashville. Dick was glad that the triumph there had gone to Thomas, whom he always held in the greatest respect and admiration.

He often saw Grant in those days, a silent, resolute man, thinner than of old and stooped a little with care and responsibility. Dick, like the others, felt with all the power of conviction that Grant would never go back, and Shepard, who had entered Petersburg twice at the imminent risk of his life, assured him that Lee's force was wearing away. There was left only a fraction of the great Army of Northern Virginia that had fought so brilliantly at Chancellorsville, Gettysburg, the Wilderness and on many another battlefield.

"Only we who are here and who can see with our own eyes know what is about to happen," said the spy. "Even our own Northern states, so long deluded by false hopes, can't yet believe, but we know."

"Did you hear anything of the Invincibles when you were in Petersburg?" asked Dick.

"I heard of them, and I also saw them, although they did not know I was near. I suppose Harry Kenton could scarcely have contained himself had he known it was my sister who filched that map from the Curtis house in Richmond and that it was to me she gave it."

"But he was all right? He escaped unhurt from the Valley?"

"Yes, or if he took a hurt it was but a slight one, from which he soon recovered. He and his comrades, Dalton, St. Clair and Langdon, and the two Colonels, Talbot and St. Hilaire, are back with Lee, and they've organized another regiment called the Invincibles, which Talbot and St. Hilaire lead, although your cousin and Dalton are on Lee's staff again."

"I suppose we'll come face to face again, and this time at the very last," said Dick. "I hope they'll be reasonable about it, and won't insist on fighting until they're all killed. Have you heard anything of those two robbers and murderers, Slade and Skelly?"

"Not a thing. But I didn't expect it. They'd never leave the mountains. Instead they'll go farther into 'em."

That night many messengers rode with dispatches, and the lines of the Northern army were tightened. Dick saw all the signs that portended a great movement, signs with which he had long since grown familiar. The big batteries were pushed forward, and heavy masses of infantry were moved closer to the Confederate trenches. He felt quite sure that the final grapple was at hand.

CHAPTER 16

The Closing Days

Within the Southern lines and just beyond the range of the Northern guns, two men sat playing chess. They were elderly, gray and thin, but never had the faces of the two colonels been more defiant. With the Confederacy crumbling about them it was characteristic of both that they should show no despair, if in truth they felt it. Their confidence in Lee was sublime. He could still move mountains, although he had no tools with which to move them, and the younger officers, mere boys many of them, would come back to them again and again for encouragement. Spies had brought word that Grant, after nine months of waiting, and with Sheridan and a huge cavalry force on his flank, was about to make his great attack. But the dauntless souls of Colonel Leonidas Talbot and Lieutenant Colonel Hector St. Hilaire remained unmoved.

"I'm glad the rains are apparently about to cease, Hector," said Colonel Talbot. "When the ground grows firmer it will give General Lee a chance to make one of his great circling swoops, and rout the Yankee army."

"So it will, Leonidas. We've been waiting for it a long time, but the chance is here at last. We've had enough of the trenches. It's a monotonous life at best. Ah, I take your pawn, the one for which I've been lying in ambush more than a month."

"But that pawn dies in a good cause, Hector. When he fell, he uncovered the path to your remaining knight, as a dozen more moves will show you. What is it, Harry?"

Harry Kenton, thin, but hardy and strong, saluted.

"We have news, sir," he replied, "that the portion of the Union army under General Sheridan is moving. I bring you a dispatch from General Lee to march and meet them. Other regiments, of course, will go with you."

They put away the chessmen and with St. Clair and Langdon marshalled the troops in line of battle. Harry felt a sinking of the heart when he saw how thin their ranks were, but the valiant colonels made no complaint. Then he went back to General Lee, whose manner was calm in face of the storm that was so obviously impending. The information had come that Grant and the bulk of his army were marching to the attack on the White Oak road, and, if he broke through there, nothing could save the Army of Northern Virginia.

Harry, after taking the dispatch to the Invincibles, carried orders to another regiment, while Dalton was engaged on similar errands. It was obvious to him that Lee was gathering his men for a great effort, and his heart sank. There was not much to gather. Throughout all that long autumn and winter the Army of Northern Virginia had disintegrated steadily. Nobody came to take the place of the slain, the wounded and the sick. All the regiments were skeletons. Many of them could not muster a hundred men apiece.

But Harry saw no sign of discouragement on the face of the chief whom he respected and admired so much. Lee was thinner and his hair was whiter, but his figure was as erect and vigorous as ever, and his face retained its ruddy colour. Yet he knew the odds against him. Grant outside his works mustered a hundred thousand trained fighters, not raw levies, and the seasoned Army of the Potomac, that had persisted alike through victory and defeat, and proof now against any adversity, saw its prize almost in its hand. And the worn veterans whom the Southern leader could marshal against Grant were not one third his numbers.

The orderly who usually brought Lee's horse was missing on another errand, and Harry himself was proud to bring Traveler. The general was absorbed in deep thought, and he did not notice until he was in the saddle who held the bridle.

"Ah, it is you, Lieutenant Kenton!" he said. "You are always where you are needed. You have been a good soldier."

Harry flushed deeply with pleasure at such a compliment from such a source.

"I've tried to do my best, sir," he replied modestly.

"No one can do any more. You and Mr. Dalton keep close to me. We must go and deal with those people, once more."

His calm, steady tones brought Harry's courage back. To the young hero-worshiper Lee himself was at least fifty thousand men, and even with his scanty numbers he would pluck victory from the very heart of defeat.

There could no longer be any possible doubt that Grant was about to attack, and Lee made his dispositions rapidly. While he led the bulk of his army in person to battle, Longstreet was left to face the army north of the James, while Gordon at the head of Ewell's old corps stood in front of Petersburg. Then Lee turned away to the right with less than twenty thousand men to meet Grant, and fortified himself along the White Oak Road. Here he waited for the Union general, who had not yet brought up his masses, but Harry and Dalton felt quite sure that despite the disparity of numbers Lee was the one who would attack. It had been so all through the war, and they knew that in the offensive lay the best defensive. The event soon proved that they read their general's mind aright.

It was the last day of March when Lee suddenly gave the order for his gaunt veterans to advance, and they obeyed without faltering. The rains had ceased, a bright sun was shining, and the Southern trumpets sang the charge as bravely as at the Second Manassas or Chancellorsville. They had only two thousand cavalry on their flank, under Fitz Lee, but the veteran infantry advanced with steadiness and precision. Colonel Leonidas Talbot and Lieutenant Colonel Hector St. Hilaire were on foot now, having lost their horses long since, but, waving their small swords, they walked dauntlessly at the head of their little regiment, St. Clair and Langdon, a bit farther back, showing equal courage.

The speed of the Southern charge increased and they were met at first by only a scattering fire. The Northern generals, not expecting Lee to move out of his works, were surprised. Before they could take the proper precautions Lee was upon them and once more the rebel yell that had swelled in victory on so many fields rang out in triumph. The front lines of the men in blue were driven in, then whole brigades were thrown back, and Harry felt a wild thrill of delight when he beheld success where success had not seemed possible.

He saw near him the Invincibles charging home, and the two colonels still waving their swords as they led them, and he saw also the worn faces of the veterans about him suffused once more with the fire of battle. He watched with glowing eyes as the fierce charge drove the Northern masses back farther and farther.

But the Union leaders, though taken by surprise, did not permit themselves and their troops to fall into a panic. They had come too far and had fought too many battles to lose the prize at the very last moment. Their own trumpets sounded on a long line, calling back the regiments and brigades. Although the South had gained much ground Harry saw that the resistance was hardening rapidly. Grant and Sheridan were pouring in their masses. Heavy columns of infantry gathered in their front, and Sheridan's numerous and powerful cavalry began to cut away their flanks. The Southern advance became slow and then ceased entirely.

Harry felt again that dreadful sinking of the heart. Leadership, valour and sacrifice were of no avail, when they were faced by leadership, valour and sacrifice also added to overwhelming numbers.

The battle was long and fierce, the men in gray throwing away their lives freely in charge after charge, but they were gradually borne back. Lee showed all his old skill and generalship, marshalling his men with coolness and precision, but Grant and Sheridan would not be denied. They too were cool and skilful, and when night came the Southern army was driven back at all points, although it had displayed a valour never surpassed in any of the great battles of the war. But Lee's face had not yet shown any signs of despair, when he gathered his men again in his old works.

It was to Harry, however, one of the gloomiest nights that he had ever known. As a staff officer, he knew the desperate position of the Southern force, and his heart was very heavy within him. He saw across the swamps and fields the innumerable Northern campfires, and he heard the Northern bugles calling to one another in the dusk. But as the night advanced and he had duties to do his courage rose once more. Since their great commander-in-chief was steady and calm he would try to be so too.

The opposing sentinels were very close to one another in the dark and as usual they often talked. Harry, as he went on one errand or another, heard them sometimes, but he never interfered, knowing that nothing was to be gained by stopping them. Deep in the night, when he was passing through a small wood very close to the Union lines, a figure rose up before him. It was so dark that he did not know the man at first, but at the second look he recognized him.

"Shepard!" he exclaimed. "You here!"

"Yes, Mr. Kenton," replied the spy, "it's Shepard, and you will not try to harm me. Why should you at such a moment? I am within the Confederate lines for the last time."

"So, you mean to give up your trade?"

"It's going to give me up. Chance has made you and me antagonists, Mr. Kenton, but our own little war, as well as the great war in which we both fight, is about over. I will not come within the Southern lines again because there is no need for me to do so. In a few days there will be no Southern lines. Don't think that I'm trying to exult over you, but remember what I told you four years ago in

Montgomery. The South has made a great and wonderful fight, but it was never possible for her to win."

"We are not beaten yet, Mr. Shepard."

"No, but you will be. I suppose you'll fight to the last, but the end is sure as the rising of tomorrow's sun. We have generals now who can't be driven back."

Harry was silent because he had no answer to make, and Shepard resumed: "I'm willing to tell you, Mr. Kenton, that your cousin, Mr. Mason, a captain now, is here with General Sheridan, and that he went through today's battle uninjured."

"I'm glad at any rate that Dick is now a captain."

"He has earned the rank. He is my good friend, as I hope you will be after the war."

"I see no reason why we shouldn't. You've served the North in your own way and I've served the South in mine. I want to say to you, Mr. Shepard, that if in our long personal struggle I held any malice against you it's all gone now, and I hope that you hold none against me."

"I never felt any. Good-by!"

"Good-by!"

Shepard was gone so quickly and with so little noise that he seemed to vanish in the air, and Harry turned back to his work, resolved not to believe the man's assertion that the war was over. He slept a little, and so did Dalton, but both were awake, when a red dawn came alive with the crash of cannon and rifles.

Shepard had spoken truly, when he said that the North now had generals who would not be driven back. Nor would they cease to attack. As soon as the light was sufficient, Grant and Sheridan began to press Lee with all their might. Pickett, who had led the great charge at Gettysburg, and Johnson, who held a place called Five Forks, were assailed fiercely by overpowering numbers, and, despite a long and desperate resistance, their command was cut in pieces and the fragments scattered, leaving Lee's right flank uncovered.

The day, like the one before it, ended in defeat and confusion, and, at the next dawn, Grant, silent, tenacious, came anew to the attack, his dense columns now assailing the front before Petersburg, and carrying the trenches that had held them so long. The thin Confederate lines there fought in vain to hold them, but the Union brigades, exultant and cheering, burst through everything, flung aside those of their foes whom they did not overthrow, and advanced toward the city. Here fell the famous Lieutenant General A. P. Hill, a man of frail body and valiant soul, beloved of Lee and the whole army.

The next noon came, sombre to Harry beyond all description. The youngest officer knew that while General Lee was still in Petersburg he could no longer hold it, and that they were nearly surrounded by the victorious and powerful Union host. The break in the lines had been made just after sunrise, and had been widened in the later hours of the morning. Now there was a momentary lull in the firing, but the lifting clouds of smoke enabled them to see vast masses of men in blue advancing and already in the suburbs of the town.

Lee's headquarters were about a mile and a half west of Petersburg, where he stood on a lawn and watched the progress of the combat. Nearly opposite him was a tall observatory that the Union men had erected, and from its summit the Northern generals also were watching. Harry and Dalton stood near Lee, awaiting with others his call, and every detail he saw that day always remained impressed upon Harry Kenton's mind.

He intently watched his general. Feeling that the Southern army was so near destruction he thought that the face of Lee would show agitation. But it was not so. His calm and grave demeanour was unchanged. He was in full uniform of fine gray, and had even buckled to his belt his dress sword which he seldom carried. It was told of him that he said that morning if he were compelled to surrender he would do so in his best. But he had not yet given up hope.

Harry turned his eyes away from Lee to the enemy. Without the aid of glasses now, he saw the great columns in blue advancing, preceded by a tremendous fire of artillery that filled the air with bursting shells. The infantry themselves were advancing with the bayonet, the sunlight gleaming on the polished metal. As far as he could see the ring of fire and steel extended. One heavy column was advancing toward the very lawn on which they stood.

"Looks as if they were going to trample us under foot," said Dalton.

"Yes, but the general may still find a way out of it," said Harry.

"They are still coming," said Dalton.

The shells were bursting about them and bullets too soon began to strike upon the lawn. A battery that sought to drive back the advancing column was exposed to such a heavy fire that it was compelled to limber up and retreat. The officers urged Lee to withdraw and at length, mounting Traveler, he rode back slowly and deliberately to his inner line. Harry often wondered what his feelings were on that day, but whatever they were his face expressed nothing. When he stopped in his new position he said to one of his staff, but without raising his voice: "This is a bad business, colonel."

Harry heard him say a little later to another officer:

"Well, colonel, it has happened as I told them it would at Richmond. The line has stretched until it has broken."

But the general and his staff were not permitted to remain long at their second stop. The Union columns never ceased to press the shattered Southern army. Their great artillery, served with the rapidity and accuracy that had marked it all through the war, poured showers of shell and grape and canister upon the thin ranks in gray, and the rifles were close enough to add their own stream of missiles to the irresistible fire.

Harry was in great fear for his general. It seemed as if the Northern gunners had recognized him and his staff. Perhaps they knew his famous war horse, Traveler, as he rode slowly away, but in any event, the shells began to strike on all sides of the little group. One burst just behind Lee. Another killed the horse of an officer close to him, and the bursting fragments inflicted slight wounds upon members of the staff. Lee, for the first time, showed emotion. Looking back over his shoulder his eyes blazed, and his cheeks flushed. Harry knew that he wished to turn and order a charge, but there was nothing with which to charge, and, withdrawing his gaze from the threatening artillery, he rode steadily on.

The general's destination now was an earthwork in the suburbs of the city, manned by a reserve force, small but ardent and defiant. It welcomed Lee and his staff with resounding cheers, and Harry's heart sprang up again. Here, at least, was confidence, and as they rode behind them the guns replied fiercely to the advancing Northern batteries, checking them for a little while, and giving the retreating troops a chance to rest.

Now came a lull in the fighting, but Harry knew well that it was only a lull. Presently Grant and Sheridan would press harder than ever. They were fully aware of the condition of the Southern army, its smallness and exhaustion, and they would never cease to hurl upon it their columns of cavalry and infantry, and to rake it with the numerous batteries of great guns, served so well. Once more his heart sank low, as he thought of what the next night might bring forth. He knew that General Lee had sent in the morning a messenger to the capital with the statement that Petersburg could be held no longer and that he would retreat in the night.

Every effort was made to gather the remaining portion of the Southern army into one strong, cohesive body. Longstreet, at the order of Lee, left his position north of the James River, while Gordon took charge of the lines to the east of Petersburg. It was when they gathered for this last stand that Harry realized fully how many of the great Confederate officers were gone. It was here that he first heard of the death of A. P. Hill, of whom he had seen so much at Gettysburg. And he choked as he thought of Stonewall Jackson, Jeb Stuart, Turner Ashby and all the long roll of the illustrious fallen, who were heroes to him.

The Northern infantry and cavalry did not charge now, but the cannon continued their work. Battery after battery poured its fire upon the earthworks, although the men there, sheltered by the trenches, did not suffer so much for the present.

Harry found time to look up his friends, and discovered the Invincibles in a single trench, about sixty of them left, but all showing a cheerfulness, extraordinary in such a situation. It was characteristic of both Colonel Talbot and Lieutenant Colonel St. Hilaire that they should present a bolder front, the more desperate their case. Nor were the younger officers less assured. Captain Arthur St. Clair was carefully dusting from his clothing dirt that had been thrown there by bursting shells, and Lieutenant Thomas Langdon was contemplating with satisfaction the track of a bullet that had gone through his left sleeve without touching the arm.

"The sight of you is welcome, Harry," said Colonel Leonidas Talbot in even tones. "It is pleasant to know at such a time that one's friend is alive, because the possibilities are always against it. Still, Harry, I've always felt that you bear a charmed life, and so do St. Clair and Langdon. Tell me, is it true that we evacuate Petersburg tonight?"

"It's no secret, sir. The orders have been issued and we do."

"If we must go, we must, and it's no time for repining. Well, the town has been defended long and valiantly against overwhelming numbers. If we lose it, we lose with glory. It can never be said of the South that we were not as brave and tenacious as any people that ever lived."

"The Northern armies that fight us will be the first to give us that credit, sir."

"That is true. Soldiers who have tested the mettle of one another on innumerable desperate fields do not bear malice and are always ready to acknowledge the merits of the foe. Ah, see how closely that shell burst to us! And another! And a third! And a fourth! Hector, you read the message, do you not?"

"Certainly, Leonidas, it's as plain as print to you and me. John Carrington—good old John! honest old John!—is now in command of that group of batteries on the right. He has been in charge of guns elsewhere, and has been suddenly shifted to this point. The great increase in volume and accuracy of fire proves it."

"Right, Hector! He's as surely there as we are here. The voice of those cannon is the voice of John Carrington. Well, if we're to be crushed I prefer for good old John to do it."

"But we're not crushed, Leonidas. We'll go out of Petersburg to-night, beating off every attack of the enemy, and then if we can't hold Richmond we'll march into North Carolina, gather together all the remaining forces of the Confederacy, and, directed by the incomparable genius of our great commander, we'll yet win the victory."

"Right, Hector! Right! Pardon me my moment of depression, but it was only a moment, remember, and it will not occur again. The loss of a capital—even if it should come to that—does not necessarily mean the loss of a cause. Among the hills and mountains of North Carolina we can hold out forever."

Harry was cheered by them, but he did not fully share their hopes and beliefs.

"Aren't they two of the greatest men you've ever known?" whispered St. Clair to him.

"If honesty and grandeur of soul make greatness they surely are," replied Harry feelingly.

He returned now to his general's side, and watched the great bombardment. Scores of guns in a vast half circle were raining shells upon the slender Confederate lines. The blaze was continuous on a long front, and huge clouds of smoke gathered above. Harry believed that the entire Union army would move forward and attack their works, but the charge did not come. Evidently Grant remembered Cold Harbor, and, feeling that his enemy was in his grasp, he refrained from useless sacrifices.

Another terrible night, lighted up by the flash of cannon and thundering with the crash of the batteries came, and Lee, collecting his army of less than twenty thousand men, moved out of Petersburg. It tore Harry's heart to leave the city, where they had held Grant at bay so long, but he knew the necessity. They could not live another day under that concentrated and awful fire. They might stay and surrender or retreat and fight again, and valiant souls would surely choose the latter.

The march began just after twilight turned to night, and the darkness and clouds of skirmishers hid it from the enemy. They crossed the Appomattox, and then advanced on the Hickory road on the north side of the river. General Lee stood on foot, but with the bridle of Traveler in his hand and his staff about him, at the entrance to the road, and watched the troops as they marched past.

His composure and steadiness seemed to Harry as great as ever, and his voice never broke, as he spoke now and then to the marching men. Nor was the spirit of the men crushed. Again and again they cheered as they saw the strong figure of the gray commander who had led them so often to victory. Nor were they shaken by the booming of the cannon behind them, nor by the tremendous crashes that marked the explosions of the magazines in Petersburg.

When the last soldier had passed, General Lee and his staff mounted their horses and followed the army in the dusk and gloom. Behind them lofty fires shed a glaring light over fallen Petersburg.

CHAPTER 17

Appomattox

The morning after Lee's retreat the Winchester regiment rode into Petersburg and looked curiously at the smouldering fires and what was left of the town. They had been before it so long it seemed almost incredible to Dick Mason that they were in it now. But the Southern leader and his army were not yet taken. They were gone, and they still existed as a fighting power.

"We have Petersburg at last," he said, "but it's only a scorched and empty shell."

"We've more than that," said Warner.

"What do you mean?"

"We've Richmond, too. The capital of the Confederacy, inviolate for four years, has fallen, and our troops have entered it. Jefferson Davis, his government and its garrison have fled, burning the army buildings and stores as they went. A part of the city was burned also, but our troops helped to put out the fires and saved the rest. Dick, do you realize it? Do you understand that we have captured the city over which we have fought for four years, and which has cost more than a half million lives?"

Dick was silent, because he had no answer to make. Neither he nor Warner nor Pennington could yet comprehend it fully. They had talked often of the end of the war, they had looked forward to the great event, they had hoped for the taking of Richmond, but now that it was taken it scarcely seemed real.

"Tell it over, George," he said, "was it Richmond you were speaking of, and did you say that it was taken?"

"Yes, Dick, and it's the truth. Of course it doesn't look like it to you or to me or to Frank, but it's a fact. Today or tomorrow we may go there and see it with our own eyes, and then if we don't believe the sight we can read an account of it in the newspapers."

It was a process of saturation, but in the next hour or two they believed it and understood it fully. On the following day they rode into the desolate and partly burned capital, now garrisoned heavily by the North, and looked with curiosity at the little city for which such torrents of blood had been shed. But as at Winchester and Petersburg, they gazed upon blind doors and windows. Nor did they expect anything else. It was only natural, and they refrained carefully from any outward show of exultation.

Richmond was to hold them only a few hours, as Grant and Sheridan continued hot on the trail of Lee. They knew that he was marching along the Appomattox, intending to concentrate at Amelia Court House, and they were resolved that he should not escape. Sheridan's cavalry, with the Winchester regiment in the van, advanced swiftly and began to press hard upon the retreating army. The firing was almost continuous. Many prisoners and five guns were taken, but at the crossing of a creek near nightfall the men in gray, still resolute, turned and beat off their assailants for the time.

The pursuit was resumed before the next daylight, and both Grant and Sheridan pressed it with the utmost severity. In the next few days Dick felt both pity and sympathy for the little army that was defending itself so valiantly against extermination or capture. It was almost like the chase of a fox now, and the hounds were always growing in number and power.

The Northern cavalry spread out and formed a great net. The Southern communications were cut off, their scouts were taken, and all the provision trains intended for Lee were captured. The prisoners reported that the Southern army was starving, and the condition of their own bodies proved the truth of their words. As Dick looked upon these ragged and famished men his feeling of pity increased, and he sincerely hoped that the hour of Lee's surrender would be hastened.

During these days and most of the nights too Dick lived in the saddle. Once more he and his comrades were clothed in the Virginia mud, and all the time the Winchester regiment brought in prisoners or wagons. They knew now that Lee was seeking to turn toward the South and effect a junction with Johnston in North Carolina, but Dick, his thoughts being his own, did not see how it was possible. When the Confederacy began to fall it fell fast. It was only after they passed through Richmond that he saw how frail the structure had become, and how its supporting timbers had been shot away. It was great cause of wonder to him that Lee should still be able to hold out, and to fight off cavalry raids, as he was doing.

And the Army of Northern Virginia, although but a fragment, was dangerous. In these its last hours, reduced almost to starvation and pitiful in numbers, it fought with a courage and tenacity worthy of its greatest days. It gave to Lee a devotion that would have melted a heart of stone. Whenever he commanded, it turned fiercely upon its remorseless pursuers, and compelled them to give ground for a time. But when it sought to march on again the cavalry of Sheridan and the infantry of Grant followed closely once more, continually cutting off the fringe of the dwindling army.

Dick saw Lee himself on a hill near Sailor's Creek, as Sheridan pressed forward against him. The gray leader had turned. The troops of Ewell and Anderson were gathered at the edge of a forest, and other infantry masses stood near. Lee on Traveler sat just in front of them, and was surveying the enemy through his glasses. Dick used his own glasses, and he looked long, and with the most intense curiosity, mingled with admiration, at the Lion of the South, whom they were about to bring to the ground. The sun was just setting, and Lee was defined sharply against the red blaze. Dick saw his features, his gray hair, and he could imagine the defiant blaze of his eyes. It was an unforgettable picture, the one drawn there by circumstances at the closing of an era.

Then he took notice of a figure, also on horseback, not far behind Lee, a youthful figure, the face thin and worn, none other than his cousin, Harry Kenton. Dick's heart took a glad leap. Harry still rode with his chief, and Dick's belief that he would survive the war was almost justified.

Then followed a scattering fire to which sunset and following darkness put an end, and once more the Southern leader retreated, with Sheridan and his cavalry forever at his heels, giving him no rest, keeping food from reaching him, and capturing more of his men. The wounded lion turned again, and, in a fierce attack drove back Sheridan and his men, but, when the battle closed, and Lee resumed his march, Sheridan was at his heels as before, seeking to pull him down, and refusing to be driven off.

Grant also dispatched Custer in a cavalry raid far around Lee, and the daring young leader not only seized the last wagon train that could possibly reach the Confederate commander, but also captured twenty-five of his guns that had been sent on ahead. Dick knew now that the end, protracted as it had been by desperate courage, was almost at hand, and that not even a miracle could prevent it.

The column with which he rode was almost continually in sight of the Army of Northern Virginia, and the field guns never ceased to pour shot and shell upon it. The sight was tragic to the last degree, as the worn men in gray retreated sullenly along the muddy roads, in rags, blackened with mire, stained with wounds, their horses falling dead of exhaustion, while the pursuing artillery cut down their ranks. Then the news of Custer's exploit came to Grant and Sheridan, and the circle of steel, now complete, closed in on the doomed army.

It was the seventh of April when the Winchester men rested their weary horses, not far from the headquarters of General Grant, and also gave their own aching bones and muscles a chance to recover their strength. Dick, after his food and coffee, watched the general, who was walking back and forth before his tent.

"He looks expectant," said Dick.

"He has the right to look so," said Warner. "He may have news of earth-shaking importance."

"What do you mean?"

"I know that he sent a messenger to Lee this morning, asking him to surrender in order to stop the further effusion of blood."

"I wish Lee would accept. The end is inevitable."

"Remember that they don't see with our eyes."

"I know it, George, but the war ought to stop. The Confederacy is gone forever."

"We shall see what we shall see."

They didn't see, but they heard, which was the same thing. To the polite request of Grant, Lee sent the polite reply that his means of resistance were not yet exhausted, and the Union leader took another hitch in the steel girdle. The second morning afterward, Lee made a desperate effort to break through at Appomattox Court House, but crushing numbers drove him back, and when the short fierce combat ceased, the Army of Northern Virginia had fired its last shot.

The Winchester men had borne a gallant part in the struggle, and presently when the smoke cleared away Dick uttered a shout.

"What is it?" exclaimed Colonel Winchester.

"A white flag! A white flag!" cried Dick in excitement. "See it waving over the Southern lines."

"Yes, I see it!" shouted the colonel, Warner and Pennington all together. Then they stood breathless, and Dick uttered the words:

"The end!"

"Yes," said Colonel Winchester, more to himself than to the others. "The end! The end at last!"

Thousands now beheld the flag, and, after the first shouts and cheers, a deep intense silence followed. The soldiers felt the immensity of the event, but as at the taking of Richmond, they could not comprehend it all at once. It yet seemed incredible that the enemy, who for four terrible years had held them at bay, was about to lay down his arms. But it was true. The messenger, bearing the flag, was now coming toward the Union lines.

The herald was received within the Northern ranks, bearing a request that hostilities be suspended in order that the commanders might have time to talk over terms of surrender, and, at the same time, General Grant, who was seven or eight miles from Appomattox Court House in a pine wood, received a note of a similar tenor, the nature of which he disclosed to his staff amid much cheering. The Union chief at once wrote to General Lee:

Your note of this date is but at this moment (11:50 A.M.) received, in consequence of my having passed from the Richmond and Lynchburg road to the Farmville and Lynchburg road. I am at this writing about four miles west of Walker's Church, and will push forward to the front for the purpose of meeting you. Notice sent to me on this road where you wish the interview to take place will meet me.

It was a characteristic and modest letter, and yet the heart under the plain blue blouse must have beat with elation at the knowledge that he had brought, what was then the greatest war of modern times, to a successful conclusion. The dispatch was given to Colonel Babcock of his staff, who was instructed to ride in haste to Lee and arrange the interview. The general and his staff followed, but missing the way, narrowly escaped capture by Confederate troops, who did not yet know of the proposal to suspend hostilities. But they at last reached Sheridan about a half mile west of Appomattox Court House.

Dick and his comrades meanwhile spent a momentous morning. It would have been impossible for him afterward to have described his own feelings, they were such an extraordinary compound of relief, elation, pity and sympathy. The two armies faced each other, and, for the first time, in absolute peace. The men in blue were already slipping food and tobacco to their brethren in gray whom they had fought so long and so hard, and at many points along the lines they were talking freely with one another. The officers made no effort to restrain them, all alike feeling sure that the bayonets would now be rusting.

The Winchester men were dismounted, their horses being tethered in a grove, and Dick with the colonel, Warner and Pennington were at the front, eagerly watching the ragged little army that faced them. He saw soon a small band of soldiers, at the head of whom stood two elderly men in patched but neat uniforms, their figures very erect, and their faces bearing no trace of depression. Close by them were two tall youths whom Dick recognized at once as St. Clair and Langdon. He waved his hand to them repeatedly, and, at last, caught the eye of St. Clair, who at once waved back and then called Langdon's attention. Langdon not only waved also, but walked forward, as if to meet him, bringing St. Clair with him, and Dick, responding at once, advanced with Warner and Pennington.

They shook hands under the boughs of an old oak, and were unaffectedly glad to see one another, although the three youths in blue felt awkwardness at first, being on the triumphant side, and fearing lest some act or word of theirs might betray exultation over a conquered foe. But St. Clair, precise, smiling, and trim in his attire, put them at ease.

"General Lee will be here presently," he said, "and you, as well as we, know that the war is over. You are the victors and our cause is lost."

"But you have lost with honour," said Dick, won by his manner. "The odds were greatly against you. It's wonderful to me that you were able to fight so long and with so much success."

"It was a matter of mathematics, Captain St. Clair," said Warner. "The numbers, the big guns and the resources were on our side, If we held on we were bound to win, as anyone could demonstrate. It's certainly no fault of yours to have been defeated by mathematics, a science that governs the world."

St. Clair and Langdon smiled, and Langdon said lightly:

"It would perhaps be more just to say, Mr. Warner, that we have not been beaten, but that we've worn ourselves out, fighting. Besides, the spring is here, a lot of us are homesick, and it's time to put in the crops."

"I think that's a good way to leave it," said Dick. "Do you know where my cousin, Harry Kenton, is?"

"I saw him this morning," replied St. Clair, "and I can assure you that he's taken no harm. He's riding ahead of the commander-in-chief, and he should be here soon."

A trumpet sounded and they separated, returning respectively to their own lines. Standing on a low hill, Dick saw Harry Kenton and Dalton dismount and then stand on one side, as if in expectancy. Dick knew for whom they were waiting, and his own heart beat hard. A great hum and murmur arose, when the gray figure of an elderly man riding the famous war horse, Traveler, appeared.

It was Lee, and in this moment, when his heart must have bled, his bearing was proud and high. He was worn somewhat, and he had lost strength from the great privations and anxieties of the retreat, but he held himself erect. He was clothed in a fine new uniform, and he wore buckled at his side a splendid new sword, recently sent to him as a present.

Near by stood a farm house belonging to Wilmer McLean, but, Grant not yet having come, the Southern commander-in-chief dismounted, and, as the air was close and hot, he remained a little while under the shade of an apple tree, the famous apple tree of Appomattox, around which truth and legend have played so much.

Dick was fully conscious of everything now. He realized the greatness of the moment, and he would not miss any detail of any movement on the part of the principals. It was nearly three o'clock in the afternoon when Grant and his staff rode up, the Union leader still wearing his plain blue blouse, no sword at his side, his shoulder straps alone signifying his rank.

The two generals who had faced each other with such resolution in that terrible conflict shook hands, and Dick saw them talking pleasantly as if they were chance acquaintances who had just met once more. Presently they went into the McLean house, several of General Grant's staff accompanying him, but Lee taking with him only Colonel Thomas Marshall.

Before the day was over Dick learned all that had occurred inside that unpretentious but celebrated farm house. The two great commanders, at first did not allude to the civil war, but spoke of the old war in Mexico, where Lee, the elder, had been General Winfield Scott's chief of staff, and the head of his engineer corps, with Grant, the younger, as a lieutenant and quartermaster. It never entered the wildest dreams of either then that they should lead the armies of a divided nation engaged in mortal combat. Now they had only pleasant recollections of each other, and they talked of the old days, of Contreras, Molino del Rey, and other battles in the Valley of Mexico.

They sat down at a plain table, and then came in the straightforward manner characteristic of both to the great business in hand. Colonel Marshall supplied the paper for the historic documents now about to be written and signed.

General Grant, humane, and never greater or more humane than in the hour of victory, made the terms easy. All the officers of the Army of Northern Virginia were to give their parole not to take up arms against the United States, until properly exchanged, and the company or regimental commanders were to sign a like parole for their men. The artillery, other arms and public property were to be turned over to the Union army, although the officers were permitted to retain their side arms and their own horses and baggage. Then officers and men alike could go to their homes.

It was truly the supreme moment of Grant's greatness, of a humanity and greatness of soul the value of which to his nation can never be overestimated. Surrenders in Europe at the end of a civil war had always been followed by confiscations, executions and a reign of terror for the beaten. Here the man who had compelled the surrender merely told the defeated to go to their homes. Lee looked at the terms and said:

"Many of the artillerymen and cavalrymen in our army own their horses, will the provisions allowing the officers to retain their horses apply to them also?"

"No, it will not as it is written," replied Grant, "but as I think this will be the last battle of the war, and as I suppose most of the men in the ranks are small farmers who without their horses would find it difficult to put in their crops, the country having been swept of everything movable, and as the United States does not want them, I will instruct the officers who are to receive the paroles of your troops to let every man who claims to own a horse or mule take the animal to his home."

"It will have a pleasant effect," said Lee, and then he wrote a formal letter accepting the capitulations. The two generals, rising, bowed to each other, but as Lee turned away he said that his men had eaten no food for several days, except parched corn, and he would have to ask that rations, and forage for their horses, be given to them.

"Certainly, general," replied Grant. "For how many men do you need them?"

"About twenty-five thousand," was Lee's reply.

Then General Grant requested him to send his own officers to Appomattox Station for the food and forage. Lee thanked him. They bowed to each other again, and the Southern leader who no longer had an army, but who retained always the love and veneration of the South, left the McLean house. Thus and in this simple fashion—the small detached fighting elsewhere did not count—did the great civil war in America, which had cost six or seven hundred thousand lives, and the temporary ruin of one section, come to an end.

Dick saw Lee come out of the house, mount Traveler and, followed by Colonel Marshall, ride back toward his own men who already had divined the occurrences in the house. The army saluted him with undivided affection, the troops crowding around him, cheering him, and, whenever they had a chance, shaking his hand. The demonstration became so great that Lee was moved deeply and showed it. The water rose in his eyes and his voice trembled as he said, though with pride:

"My lads, we have fought through the war together. I have done the best I could for you. My heart is too full to say more."

He could not be induced to speak further, although the great demonstration continued, but rode in silence to his headquarters in a wood, where he entered his tent and sat alone, no one ever knowing what his thoughts were in that hour.

Twenty-six thousand men who were left of the Army of Northern Virginia surrendered the next day, and the blue and the gray fraternized. The Union soldiers did not wait for the rations ordered by Grant, but gave of their own to the starved men who were so lately their foes.

Dick and his friends hastened at once to find Harry Kenton and his comrades, and presently they saw them all sitting together on a log, thin and pale, but with no abatement of pride. Harry rose nevertheless, and received his cousin joyfully.

"Dick," he said as their hands met, "the war is over, and over forever. But you and I were never enemies."

"That's so, Harry," said Dick Mason, "and the thing for us to do now is to go back to Kentucky, and begin life where we left it off."

"But you don't start this minute," said Warner. "There is a small matter of business to be transacted first. We know all of you, but just the same we've brought our visiting cards with us."

"I don't understand," said Harry.

"We'll show you. Frank Pennington, remove that large protuberance from beneath your blouse. Behold it! A small ham, my friends, and it's for you. That's Frank's card. And here I take from my own blouse the half of a cheese, which I beg you to accept with my compliments. Dick, you rascal, what's that you have under your arm?"

"It's a jar of prime bacon that I've brought along for the party, George."

"I thought so. We're going to have the pleasure of dining with our friends here. We've heard, Captain Kenton, that you people haven't eaten anything for a month."

"It's not that bad," laughed Harry. "We had parched corn yesterday."

"Well, parched corn is none too filling, and we're going to prepare the banquet at once. A certain Sergeant Whitley will arrive presently with a basket of food, such as you rebels haven't tasted since you raided our wagon trains at the Second Manassas, and with him will come one William Shepard, whom you have met often, Mr. Kenton."

"Yes," said Harry, "we've met often and under varying circumstances, but we're going to be friends now."

434

"Will you tell me, Captain St. Clair," said Dick, "what has become of the two colonels of your regiment, which I believe you call the Invincibles?"

St. Clair led them silently to a little wood, and there, sitting on logs, Colonel Leonidas Talbot and Lieutenant Colonel Hector St. Hilaire were bent intently over the chess board that lay between them.

"Now that the war is over we'll have a chance to finish our game, eh, Hector?" said Colonel Talbot.

"A just observation, Leonidas. It's a difficult task to pursue a game to a perfect conclusion amid the distractions of war, but soon I shall checkmate you in the brilliant fashion in which General Lee always snares and destroys his enemy."

"But General Lee has yielded, Hector."

"Pshaw, Leonidas! General Lee would never yield to anybody. He has merely quit!"

"Ahem!" said Harry loudly, and, as the colonels glanced up, they saw the little group looking down at them.

"Our friends, the enemy, have come to pay you their respects," said Harry.

The two colonels rose and bowed profoundly.

"And to invite you to a banquet that is now being prepared not far from here," continued Harry. "It's very tempting, ham, cheese, and other solids, surrounded by many delicacies."

The two colonels looked at each other, and then nodded approval.

"You are to be the personal guests of our army," said Dick, "and we act as the proxies of General Grant."

"I shall always speak most highly of General Grant," said Colonel Leonidas Talbot. "His conduct has been marked by the greatest humanity, and is a credit to our common country, which has been reunited so suddenly."

"But reunited with our consent, Leonidas," said Lieutenant Colonel St. Hilaire. "Don't forget that I, for one, am tired of this war, and so is our whole army. It was a perfect waste of life to prolong it, and with the North re-annexed, the Union will soon be stronger and more prosperous than ever."

"Well spoken, Hector! Well spoken. It is perhaps better that North and South should remain together. I thought otherwise for four years, but now I seem to have another point of view. Come, lads, we shall dine with these good Yankee boys and we'll make them drink toasts of their own excellent coffee to the health and safety of our common country."

The group returned to a little hollow, in which Sergeant Whitley and Shepard had built a fire, and where they were already frying strips of bacon and slices of ham over the coals. Shepard and Harry shook hands.

"I may as well tell you now, Mr. Kenton," said Shepard, "that Miss Henrietta Carden, whom you met in Richmond, is my sister, and that it was she who hid in the court at the Curtis house and took the map. Then it was I who gave you the blow."

"It was done in war," said Harry, "and I have no right to complain. It was clever and I hope that I shall be able to give your sister my compliments some day. Now, if you don't mind, I'll take a strip of that wonderful bacon. It is bacon, isn't it? It's so long since I've seen any that I'm not sure of its identity, but whatever it is its odour is enticing."

"Bacon it surely is, Mr. Kenton. Here are three pieces that I broiled myself and a broad slice of bread for them. Go ahead, there's plenty more. And see this dark brown liquid foaming in this stout tin pot! Smell it! Isn't it wonderful! Well, that's coffee! You've heard of coffee, and maybe you remember it."

"I do remember tasting it some years ago and finding it good. I'd like to try it again. Yes, thank you. It's fine."

"Here's another cup, and try the ham also."

Harry tried it, not once but several times. Langdon sat on the ground before the fire, and his delight was unalloyed and unashamed.

"We have raided a Yankee wagon train again," he said, "and the looting is splendid. Arthur, I thought yesterday that I should never eat again. Food and I were such strangers that I believed we should never know each other, any more, or if knowing, we could never assimilate. And yet we seem to get on good terms at once."

While they talked a tall thin youth of clear dark complexion, carrying a long bundle under his arm, approached the fire and Lieutenant Colonel St. Hilaire welcomed him with joy.

"Julien! Julien de Langeais, my young relative!" he cried. "And you are indeed alive! I thought you lost!"

"I'm very much alive, sir," said young De Langeais, "but I'm starved."

"Then this is the place to come," said Dick, putting before him food, which he strove to eat slowly, although the effort at restraint was manifestly great. Lieutenant Colonel St. Hilaire introduced him to the Union men, and then asked him what was the long black bag that he carried under his arm.

"That, sir," replied De Langeais, smiling pathetically, "is my violin. I've no further use for my rifle and sword, but now that peace is coming I may be able to earn my bread with the fiddle."

"And so you will! You'll become one of the world's great musicians. And as soon as we've finished with General Grant's hospitality, which will be some time yet, you shall play for us."

De Langeais looked affectionately at the black bag.

"You're very good to me, sir," he said, "to encourage me at such a time, and, if you and the others care for me to play, I'll do my best."

"Paganini himself could do no more, but, for the present, we must pay due attention to the hospitality of General Grant. He would not like it, if it should come to his ears that we did not show due appreciation, and since, in the course of events, and in order to prevent the mutual destruction of the sections, it became necessary for General Lee to arrange with someone to stop this suicidal war, I am glad the man was General Grant, a leader whose heart does him infinite credit."

"General Grant is a very great man, and he has never proved it more fully than today," said Dick, who sat near the colonels—his first inclination had been to smile, but he restrained it.

"Truly spoken, young sir," said Colonel Leonidas Talbot. "General Lee and General Grant together could hold this continent against the world, and, now that we have quit killing one another, America is safe in their hands. Harry, do you think I've eaten too much? I wouldn't go beyond the exploits of a gentleman, but this food has a wonderful savour, and I can't say that I have dined before in months."

"Not at all, sir, you have just fairly begun. As Lieutenant Colonel St. Hilaire pointed out, General Grant would be displeased if we didn't fully appreciate his hospitality and prove it by our deeds. Here are some sardines, sir. You haven't tasted 'em yet, but you'll find 'em wonderfully fine."

Colonel Leonidas Talbot took the sardines, and then he and Lieutenant Colonel St. Hilaire rose suddenly and simultaneously to their feet, a look of wonder and joy spreading over their faces.

"Is it really he?" exclaimed Colonel Talbot.

"It's he and none other," said Lieutenant Colonel St. Hilaire.

A tall, powerfully built, gray-haired man was coming toward them, his hands extended. Colonel Talbot and Lieutenant Colonel St. Hilaire stepped forward, and each grasped a hand.

"Good old John!"

"Why, John, it's worth a victory to shake your hand again!"

"Leonidas, I've been inquiring, an hour or two, for you and Hector."

"John Carrington, you've fulfilled your promise and more. We always said at West Point that you'd become the greatest artilleryman in the world, and in this war you've proved it on fifty battle fields. We've

437

often watched your work from the other side, and we've always admired the accuracy with which you sent the shells flying about us. It was wonderful, John, wonderful, and it did more than anything else to save the North from complete defeat!"

A smile passed over John Carrington's strong face, and he patted his old comrade on the shoulder.

"It's good to know, Leonidas, that neither you nor Hector has been killed," he said, "and that we can dine together again."

"Truly, truly, John! Sit down! It's the hospitality of your own general that you share when you join us. General Lee would never make terms with men like McClellan, Burnside and Hooker. No, sir, he preferred to defeat them, much as it cost our Union in blood and treasure, but with a man of genius like General Grant he could agree. Really great souls always recognize one another. Is it not so, John?"

"Beyond a doubt, Leonidas. We fully admit the greatness and lofty character of General Lee, as you admit the greatness and humanity of General Grant. One nation is proud to have produced two such men."

"I agree with you, John. All of us agree with you. The soldiers of General Lee's army who are here today will never dispute what you say. Now fall on, and join us at this board which, though rustic, is indeed a most luxurious and festive one. As I remember at West Point, you were a first-class trencherman."

"And I am yet," said John Carrington, as he took his share. They were joined a little later by a gallant young Southern colonel, Philip Sherburne, who had led in many a cavalry attack, and then the equally gallant Northern colonel, Alan Hertford, came also, and as everybody was introduced to everybody else the good feeling grew. At last the hunger that had been increasing so long was satisfied, and as they leaned back, Lieutenant Colonel St. Hilaire turned to Julien de Langeais:

"Julien," he said, "take out your violin. There is no more fitting time than this to play. Julien, John, is a young relative of mine from Louisiana who has a gift. He is a great musician who is going to become much greater. Perhaps it was wrong to let a lad of his genius enter this war, but at any rate he has survived it, and now he will show us what he can do."

De Langeais, after modest deprecations, took out his violin and played. Upon his sensitive soul the war had made such a deep impression that his spirit spoke through his instrument. He had never before played so well. His strings sang of the march, the camp, of victory and defeat, and defeat and victory, and as he played he became absorbed in his music. The people around him, although they were rapidly increasing in numbers, were not visible to him. Yet he played upon their hearts. There was not one among them who did no dream dreams as he listened. At last his bow turned ever young, *Home Sweet Home.*

'Mid pleasures and palaces though we may roam,
Be it ever so humble, there's no place like home.
An exile from home, splendour dazzles in vain,
Oh! give me my lowly, thatched cottage again.

Into the song he poured all his skill and all his heart, and as he played he saw the house in which he was born on the far Louisiana plantation. And those who listened saw also, in spirit, the homes which many of them had not seen in fact for four years. Stern souls were softened, and water rose to eyes which had looked fearlessly and so often upon the charging bayonets of the foe.

He stopped suddenly and put away his violin. There was a hush, and then a long roll of applause, not loud, but very deep.

"I hear Pendleton calling," said Harry to Dick.

"So do I," said Dick. "I wonder what they're doing there. Have you heard from your father?"

"Not for several months. I think he's in North Carolina with Johnston, and I mean to go home that way. I've a good horse, and he'll carry me through the mountains. I think I'll find father there. An hour or two ago, Dick, I felt like a man and I was a man, but since De Langeais played I've become a boy again, and I'm longing for Pendleton, and its green hills, and the little river in which we used to swim."

"So am I, Harry, and it's likely that I'll go with you. The war is over and I can get leave at once. I want to see my mother."

They stayed together until night came over Appomattox and its famous apple tree, and a few days later Harry Kenton was ready to start on horseback for Kentucky. But he was far from being alone. The two colonels, St. Clair, Langdon, Dick, De Langeais, Colonel Winchester and Sergeant Whitley were to ride with him. Warner was to go north and Pennington west as soon as they were mustered out. Dick wrung their hands.

"Good-by, George! Good-by, Frank! Old comrades!" he said. "But remember that we are to see a good deal of one another all through our lives!"

"Which I can reduce to a mathematical problem and demonstrate by means of my little algebra here," said Warner, fumbling for his book to hide his emotion.

"I may come through Kentucky to see you and Harry," said Pennington, "when I start back to Nebraska."

sure to come," said Dick with enthusiasm, "and remember that
latch string is hanging out on both doors."

Then, carrying their arms, and well equipped with ammunition,
food and blankets, the little party rode away. They knew that the
mountains were still extremely unsettled, much infested by guerrillas,
but they believed themselves strong enough to deal with any difficulty,
and, as the April country was fair and green, their hearts, despite everything, were light.

CHAPTER 18

The Final Reckoning

They rode a long time through a war-torn country, and the days bound the young men together so closely that, at times, it seemed to them they had fought on the same side all through the war. Sergeant Whitley was usually their guide and he was an expert to bargain for food and forage. He exhibited then all the qualities that afterward raised him so high in the commercial world.

Although they were saddened often by the spectacle of the ruin the long war had made, they kept their spirits, on the whole, wonderfully well. The two colonels, excellent horsemen, were an unfailing source of cheerfulness. When they alluded to the war they remembered only the great victories the South had won, and invariably they spoke of its end as a compromise. They also began to talk of Charleston, toward which their hearts now turned, and a certain handsome Madame Delaunay whom Harry Kenton remembered well.

As they left Virginia and entered North Carolina they heard that the Confederate troops everywhere were surrendering. The war, which had been so terrible and sanguinary only two or three months before, ended absolutely with the South's complete exhaustion. Already the troops were going home by the scores of thousands. They saw men who had just taken off their uniforms guiding the ploughs in the furrows. Smoke rose once more from the chimneys of the abandoned homes, and the boys who had faced the cannon's mouth were rebuilding rail fences. The odour of grass and newly turned earth was poignant and pleasant. The two colonels expanded.

"Though my years have been devoted to military pursuits, Hector," said Colonel Leonidas Talbot, "the agricultural life is noble, and many of the hardy virtues of the South are due to the fact that we are chiefly a rural population."

441

"Truly spoken, Leonidas, but for four years agriculture has not had much chance with us, and perhaps agriculture is not all. It was the mechanical genius of the North that kept us from taking New York and Boston."

"Which reminds me, Happy," said St. Clair to Langdon, "that, after all, you didn't sleep in the White House at Washington with your boots on."

"I changed my mind," replied Happy easily. "I didn't want to hurt anybody's feelings."

Soon they entered the mountains, and they met many Confederate soldiers returning to their homes. Harry always sought from them news of his father, and he learned at last that he was somewhere in the western part of the state. Then he heard, a day or two later, that a band of guerrillas to the south of them were plundering and sometimes murdering. They believed from what details they could gather that it was Slade and Skelly with a new force, and they thought it advisable to turn much farther toward the west.

"The longest way 'round is sometimes the shortest way through," said Sergeant Whitley, and the others agreed with him. They came into a country settled then but little. The mountains were clothed in deep forest, now in the full glory of early spring, and the log cabins were few. Usually they slept, the nights through, in the forest, and they helped out their food supply with game. The sergeant shot two deer, and they secured wild turkeys and quantities of smaller game.

Although they heard that the guerrillas were moving farther west, which necessitated the continuation of their own course in that direction, they seemed to have entered another world. Where they were, at least, there was nothing but peace, the peace of the wilderness which made a strong appeal to all of them. In the evenings by their campfire in the forest De Langeais would often play for them on his violin, and the great trees about them seemed to rustle with approval, as a haunting melody came back in echoes from the valleys.

They had been riding a week through a wilderness almost unbroken when, just before sunset, they heard a distant singing sound, singularly like that of De Langeais' violin.

"It is a violin," said De Langeais, "but it's not mine. The sound comes from a point at the head of the cove before us."

They rode into the little valley and the song of the violin grew louder. It was somebody vigorously playing *Old Dan Tucker*, and as the woods opened they saw a stout log cabin, a brook and some fields. The musician, a stalwart young man, sat in the doorway of the house.

A handsome young woman was cooking outside, and a little child was playing happily on the grass.

"I'll ride forward and speak to them," said Harry Kenton. "That man and I are old friends."

The violin ceased, as the thud of hoofs drew near, but Harry, springing from his horse, held out his hand to the man and said:

"How are you, Dick Jones? I see that the prophecy has come true!"

The man stared at him a moment or two in astonishment, and then grasped his hand.

"It's Mr. Kenton!" he cried, "an' them's your friends behind you. 'Light, strangers, 'light! Yes, Mr. Kenton, it's come true. I've been back home a week, an' not a scratch on me, though I've fit into nigh onto a thousand battles. I reckon my wife, that's Mandy there, wished so hard fur me to come back that the Lord let her have her way. But 'light, strangers! 'Light an' hev supper!"

"We will," said Harry, "but we're not going to crowd you out of your house. We've plenty of food with us, and we're accustomed to sleeping out of doors."

Nevertheless the hospitality of Dick Jones and his wife, Mandy, was unbounded. It was arranged that the two colonels should sleep inside, while the others took to the grass with their blankets. Liberal contributions were made to the common larder by the travellers, and they had an abundant supper, after which the men sat outside, the colonels smoking good old North Carolina weed, and Mrs. Jones knitting in the dusk.

"Don't you and your family get lonesome here sometimes, Mr. Jones?" asked Harry.

"Never," replied the mountaineer. "You see I've had enough o' noise an' multitudes. More than once I've seen two hundred thousand men fightin', and I've heard the cannon roarin', days without stoppin'. I still git to dreamin' at night 'bout all them battles, an' when I awake, an' set up sudden like an' hear nothin' outside but the tricklin' o' the branch an' the wind in the leaves, I'm thankful that them four years are over, an' nobody is shootin' at nobody else. An' it's hard now an' then to b'lieve that they're really an' truly over."

"But how about Mrs. Jones?"

"She an' the baby stayed here four whole years without me, but we've got neighbours, though you can't see 'em fur the trees. Jest over the ridge lives her mother, an' down Jones' Creek, into which the branch runs, lives her married sister, an' my own father ain't more'n four miles away. The settlements are right thick 'roun' here, an' we hev good times."

Mrs. Jones nodded her emphatic assent.

"Which way do you-all 'low to be goin' tomorrow?" asked Jones.

"We think we'd better keep to the west," replied Colonel Talbot. "We've heard of a guerrilla band under two men, Slade and Skelly, who are making trouble to the southward."

"I've heard of 'em too," said Jones, "an' I reckon they're 'bout the meanest scum the war hez throwed up. The troops will be after 'em afore long, an' will clean 'em out, but I guess they'll do a lot o' damage afore then. You gen'lemen will be wise to stick to your plan, an' keep on toward the west."

They departed the next morning, taking with them the memory of a very pleasant meeting, and once more pursued their way through the wilderness. Harry, despite inquiries at every possible place, heard nothing more of his father, and concluded that, after the surrender, he must have gone at once to Kentucky, expecting his son to come there by another way.

But the reports of Slade and Skelly were so numerous and so sinister that they made a complete change of plan. The colonels, St. Clair and Langdon, would not try to go direct to South Carolina, but the whole party would cling together, ride to Kentucky, and then those who lived farther south could return home chiefly by rail. It seemed, on the whole, much the wiser way, and, curving back a little to the north, they entered by and by the high mountains on the line between Virginia and Kentucky. Other returning soldiers had joined them and their party now numbered thirty brave, well-armed men.

They entered Kentucky at a point near the old Wilderness Road, and, from a lofty crest, looked down upon a sea of ridges, heavy with green forest, and narrow valleys between, in which sparkled brooks or little rivers. The hearts of Harry and Dick beat high. They were going home. What awaited them at Pendleton? Neither had heard from the town or anybody in it for a long time. Anticipation was not unmingled with anxiety.

Two days later they entered a valley, and when they stopped at noon for their usual rest Harry Kenton rode some distance up a creek, thinking that he might rouse a deer out of the underbrush. Although the country looked extremely wild and particularly suited to game, he found none, but unwilling to give up he continued the hunt, riding much farther than he was aware.

He was just thinking of the return, when he heard a rustling in a thicket to his right, and paused, thinking that it might be the deer he wanted. Instead, a gigantic figure with thick black hair and beard rose up in the bush. Harry uttered a startled exclamation. It was Skelly, and beside him stood a little man with an evil face, hidden partly by an enormous flap-brimmed hat. Both carried rifles, and before Harry could take his own weapon from his shoulder Skelly fired. Harry's horse threw up his head in alarm, and the bullet, instead of hitting the rider, took the poor animal in the brain.

As the horse fell, Harry sprang instinctively and alighted upon his feet, although he staggered. Then Slade pulled trigger, and a searing, burning pain shot through his left shoulder. Dizzy and weak he raised his rifle, nevertheless, and fired at the hairy face of the big man. He saw the huge figure topple and fall; he heard another shot, and again felt the thrill of pain, this time in the head, heard a shrill whistle repeated over and over, and did not remember anything definite until some time afterward.

When his head became clear once more Harry believed that he had wandered a long distance from that brief but fierce combat, but he did not know in what direction his steps had taken him. Nearly all his strength was gone, and his head ached fearfully. He had dropped his rifle, but where he did not know nor care. He sat down on the ground with his back against a tree, and put his right hand to his head. The wound there had quit bleeding, clogged up with its own blood. He was experienced enough to know that it was merely a flesh wound, and that any possible scar would be hidden by his hair.

But the wound in his left shoulder was more serious. The bullet had gone entirely through, for which he was glad, but the hurt was still bleeding. He made shift to bandage it with strips torn from his underclothing, and, after a long rest, he undertook to walk back to the camp. He was not sure of the way, and after two or three hundred yards he grew dizzy and sat down again. Then he shouted for help, but his voice sounded so weak that he gave it up.

He was never sure, but he thought another period of unconsciousness followed, because when he aroused himself the sun seemed to be much farther down in the west. His head was still aching, though not quite so badly as before, and he made a new effort to walk. He did not know where he was going, but he must go somewhere. If he remained there in the wilderness, and his comrades could not find him, he would die of weakness and starvation. He shuddered. It would be the very irony of fate that one who had gone through Chancellorsville, Gettysburg and all the great battles in the East should be slain on his way home by a roving guerrilla.

He rested again and summoned all his strength and courage, and he was able to go several hundred yards farther. As he advanced the forest seemed to thin and he was quite sure that he saw through it a valley and open fields. The effect upon him was that of a great stimulant, and he found increased strength. He tottered on, but stopped soon and leaned against a tree. He dimly saw the valley, the fields, and a distant roof, and then came something that gave him new strength. It was a man's voice singing, a voice clear, powerful and wonderfully mellow:

They bore him away when the day had fled,
And the storm was rolling high,
And they laid him down in his lonely bed
By the light of an angry sky. The
lightning flashed and the wild sea lashed
The shore with its foaming wave,
And the thunder passed on the rushing blast
As it howled o'er the rover's grave.

He knew that voice. He had heard it years ago, a century it seemed. It was the voice of a friend, the voice of Sam Jarvis, the singer of the mountains. He rushed forward, but overtaxing his strength, fell. He pulled himself up by a bush and stood, trembling with weakness and anxiety. Still came the voice, but the song had changed:

Soft o'er the fountain, lingering falls the Southern moon,
Far o'er the mountain breaks the day too soon,
In thy dark eyes' splendour, where the warm light loves to dwell,
Weary looks yet tender speak their fond farewell,
Nita! Juanita!
Ask thy soul if we should part,
Nita! Juanita!
Lean thou on my heart!

It was an old song of pathos and longing, but Harry remembered well that mellow, golden voice. If he could reach Sam Jarvis he would secure help, and there was the happy valley in which he lived. As he steadied himself anew fresh strength and courage poured into his veins, and leaving the fringe of forest he entered a field, at the far end of which Jarvis was ploughing.

The singer was happy. He drove a stout bay horse, and as he walked along in the furrow he watched the rich black earth turn up before the ploughshare. He hated no man, and no man hated him. The war had never invaded his valley, and he sang from the sheer pleasure of living. The world about him was green and growing, and the season was good. His nephew, Ike Simmons, was ploughing in another field, and whenever he chose he could see the smoke rising from the chimney of the strong log house in which he lived.

Harry thought at first that he would go down the end of the long field to Jarvis, but the ploughed land pulled at his feet, and made him very weak again. So he walked straight across it, though he staggered, and approached the house, the doors of which stood wide open.

He was not thinking very clearly now, but he knew that rest and help were at hand. He opened the gate that led to the little lawn, went up the walk and, scarcely conscious of what he was doing, stood in the doorway, and stared into the dim interior. As his eyes grew used to the dusk the figure of an old, old woman, lean and wrinkled, past a hundred, suddenly rose from a chair, stood erect, and regarded him with startled, burning eyes.

"Ah, it's the governor, the great governor, Henry Ware!" she exclaimed. "Didn't I say to you long ago: 'You will come again, and you will be thin and pale and in rags, and you will fall at the door.' I see you coming with these two eyes of mine!"

As she spoke, the young man in the tattered Southern uniform, stained with the blood of two wounds, reeled and fell unconscious in the doorway.

When Harry came back to the world he was lying in a very comfortable bed, and all the pain had gone from his head. A comfortable, motherly woman, whom he recognized as Mrs. Simmons, was sitting beside him, and Colonel Leonidas Talbot, looking very tall, very spare and very precise, was standing at a window.

"Good morning, Mrs. Simmons," said Harry in a clear, full voice.

She uttered an exclamation of joy, and Colonel Talbot turned from the window.

"So you've come back to us, Harry," he said. "We knew that it was only a matter of time, although you did lose a lot of blood from that wound in the shoulder."

"I never intended to stay away, sir."

"But you remained in the shadowy world three days."

"That long, sir?"

"Yes, Harry, three days, and a great deal of water has flowed under the bridge in those three days."

"What do you mean, colonel?"

"There was a military operation of a very sharp and decisive character. When you fell in the doorway here, Mrs. Simmons, who happened to be in the kitchen, ran at once for her brother, Mr. Jarvis, a most excellent and intelligent man. You were past telling anybody anything just then, but he followed your trail, and met some of us, led by Sergeant Whitley, who were also trailing you."

"And Slade and Skelly, what of them?"

"They'll never plunder or murder more. We divined much that had happened. You were ambushed, were you not?"

"Yes, Slade and Skelly fired upon me from the bushes. I shot back and saw Skelly fall."

"You shot straight and true. We found him there in the bushes, where your bullet had cut short his murderous life. Then we organized, pursued and surrounded the others. They were desperate criminals, who knew the rope awaited them, and all of them died with their boots on. Slade made a daring attempt to escape, but the sergeant shot him through the head at long range, and a worse villain never fell."

"And our people, colonel, where are all of them?"

"Most of the soldiers have gone on, but the members of our own immediate group are scattered about the valley, engaged chiefly in agricultural or other homely pursuits, while they await your recovery, and incidentally earn their bread. Sergeant Whitley, Captain St. Clair and Captain Mason are putting a new roof on the barn, and, as I inspected it myself, I can certify that they are performing the task in a most workmanlike manner. Captain Thomas Langdon is ploughing in the far field, by the side of that stalwart youth, Isaac Simmons, and each is striving in a spirit of great friendliness to surpass the other. My associate and second in command, Lieutenant Colonel Hector St. Hilaire, has gone down the creek fishing, a pursuit in which he has had much success, contributing greatly to the larder of our hostess, Mrs. Simmons."

"And where is Sam Jarvis?" The colonel raised the window.

"Listen!" he said:

Up from the valley floated the far mellow notes:

I'm dreaming now of Hallie, sweet Hallie,
For the thought of her is one that never dies.
She's sleeping in the valley
And the mocking bird is singing where she lies.
Listen to the mocking bird singing o'er her grave,
Listen to the mocking bird, where the weeping willows wave.

"The words of the song are sad," said Colonel Talbot, "but sad music does not necessarily make one feel sad. On the contrary we are all very cheerful here, and Mr. Jarvis is the happiest man I have ever known. I think it's because his nature is so kindly. A heart of gold, pure gold, that extraordinary old woman, Aunt Suse, insists that you are great-grandfather, the famous governor of Kentucky."

"I was here before in the first year of the war, colonel, and she foretold that I would return just as I did. How do you account for that, sir?"

"I don't try to account for it. A great deal of energy is wasted in trying to account for the unknowable. I shall take it as it is."

"What has become of Colonel Winchester, sir?"

"He rode yesterday to a tiny hamlet about twenty miles away. We had heard from a mountaineer that an officer returning from the war was there, and since we old soldiers like to foregather, we decided to have him come and join our party. They are due here, and unless my eyes deceive me—and I know they don't—they're at the bead of the valley now, riding toward this house."

Harry detected a peculiar note in Colonel Talbot's voice, and his mind leaped at once to a conclusion.

"That officer is my father!" he exclaimed.

"According to all the descriptions, it is he, and now you can sit up and welcome him."

The meeting between father and son was not demonstrative, but both felt deep emotion.

"Fortune has been kind to us, Harry, to bring us both safely out of the long war," said Colonel Kenton.

"Kinder than we had a right to hope," said Harry.

The entire group rode together to Pendleton, and Dick was welcomed like one risen from the dead by his mother, who told him a few weeks later that he was to have a step-father, the brave colonel, Arthur Winchester.

"He's the very man I'd have picked for you, mother," said Dick.

The little town of Pendleton was unharmed by the war, and, since bitter feeling had never been aroused in it, the reunion of North and South began there at once. In an incredibly short period everything went on as before.

The two colonels and their younger comrades remained a while as the guests of Colonel Kenton and his son, and then they started for the farther south where St. Clair and Langdon were to begin the careers in which they achieved importance.

Harry and Dick in Pendleton entered upon their own life work, which they were destined to do so well, but often, in their dreams and for many years, they rode again with Stonewall in the Valley, charged with Pickett at Gettysburg, stood with the Rock of Chickamauga, or advanced with Grant to the thunder of the guns through the shades of the Wilderness.

LEONAUR

ALSO FROM LEONAUR

AVAILABLE IN SOFTCOVER OR HARDCOVER WITH DUST JACKET

TROS OF SAMOTHRACE 1: WOLVES OF THE TIBER *by Talbot Mundy*—When his ship is taken and his crew slaughtered Tros of Samothrace is captured by Imperial Rome.

TROS OF SAMOTHRACE 2: DRAGONS OF THE NORTH *by Talbot Mundy*—Tros of Samothrace burns for vengeance and has declared himself the implacable enemy of Rome.

TROS OF SAMOTHRACE 3: SERPENT OF THE WAVES *by Talbot Mundy*—Tros, his allies and the forces of Rome have drawn apart to prepare for the conflict to come.

TROS OF SAMOTHRACE 4: CITY OF THE EAGLES *by Talbot Mundy*—As Tros of Samothrace continues in his attempts to confound Caesar's plans for the invasion of Britain, he journeys to the Eternal City to seek the aid of its great leaders—and Caesar's opponents—Cato, Pompey and the Vestal Virgins themselves!

TROS OF SAMOTHRACE 5: CLEOPATRA *by Talbot Mundy*—Cleopatra—Queen of Egypt—is a formidable character ever ready to play the game of intrigue, betrayal and shifting loyalties to suit her own objectives. Blood will surely be spilt and once again Tros finds himself inexorably caught up in monumental events that threaten his life and those he loves.

TROS OF SAMOTHRACE 6: THE PURPLE PIRATE *by Talbot Mundy*—The epic saga of the ancient world—Tros of Samothrace—draws to a conclusion in this sixth—and final—volume. Julius Caesar has been assassinated and Queen Cleopatra of Egypt finds herself in a perilous position and desperate for allies to secure her power.

THE ILLUSTRATED & COMPLETE BRIGADIER GERARD *by Sir Arthur Conan Doyle*—These are the adventures of Conan Doyle's incomparable French hero-the finest swordsman in the Light Cavalry-Etienne Gerard. Arranged for the first time in historical chronological order, his many enthusiasts can now properly appreciate his colourful career as he fights, loves and blunders his way through the Napoleonic epoch-from his earliest adventure as a young blade determined to reach his lady love despite the unwelcome attention of her fathers bull-through many campaigns and special missions-to the bloody field of Waterloo, the downfall of his beloved Emperor and beyond. This is the complete collection of these classic stories. What makes this edition exceptional is the inclusion of nearly 140 illustrations-mostly by the famed military artist William Barnes Wollen-which accurately portray the spirit of the stories and the uniforms and scenes of the events they portray.

CPSIA information can be obtained at www.ICGtesting.com
Printed in the USA
LVOW122020070613

337466LV00001B/119/P

9 781846 776137